WEABONS

THE KING & SLATER SERIES BOOK ONE

MATT ROGERS

Join the Reader's Group and get a free 200-page book by Matt Rogers!

Sign up for a free copy of '**HARD IMPACT**'.

Experience King's most dangerous mission — action-packed insanity in the heart of the Amazon Rainforest.

No spam guaranteed.

Just click here.

BOOKS BY MATT ROGERS

THE JASON KING SERIES

Isolated (Book 1)

Imprisoned (Book 2)

Reloaded (Book 3)

Betrayed (Book 4)

Corrupted (Book 5)

Hunted (Book 6)

THE JASON KING FILES

Cartel (Book 1)

Warrior (Book 2)

Savages (Book 3)

THE WILL SLATER SERIES

Wolf (Book 1)

Lion (Book 2)

Bear (Book 3)

Lynx (Book 4)

Bull (Book 5)

Hawk (Book 6)

THE KING & SLATER SERIES

Weapons (Book 1)

BLACK FORCE SHORTS

1

Manhattan
New York City

Gianni wasn't comfortable.

Granted, he hadn't been comfortable since childhood — that was the nature of his profession — but certain levels of discomfort were cause for alarm.

This was one of them.

He was in the Meatpacking District late at night, and he was a man who ordinarily had little reason to be in the Meatpacking District late at night. He wasn't accustomed to opulence. His world was not the world of trendy chic establishments and indoor marketplaces and overpriced designer clothing and cocktails and laughter and fun.

No, his world was a little more straightforward than that.

He dealt in fear, and intimidation, and he considered himself a master in the art of the prolonged silence that followed a threat. He was a low-level Italian street thug, and despite his reputation he didn't resort to violence often. Those who relied on physical force too often were desperate to set an example. Those types were the poker players that went all-in with regularity.

Eventually the violence became the same, and people figured you out.

No-one would ever figure Gianni out, because he was almost never aggressive.

He kept the anger locked deep inside, and he rarely ever tapped into it. He let people imagine what he could do to them. He was six foot five and built like a truck, with slabs of muscle hanging off his frame in all the right places. He had a barrel chest and burly forearms and thick meaty fingers. He looked like he could crush a saucepan with his grip strength alone, and he probably could. He'd never tried it.

He was the guy who showed up at your establishment to demand a protection fee. If you asked what he'd be protecting you from, he'd walk away silently, and that night a car would drive by and throw rocks through all your shopfront windows. The next day, he'd return and ask for a slightly higher protection fee for the inconvenience.

Rinse and repeat.

The oldest trick in the book, but he'd succeeded at it for nearly a decade.

Time flies when you're having fun.

He and his ragtag group of miscreant buddies pulled the same scam on half the small businesses in Hell's Kitchen. If a cop came sniffing around, Gianni paid them off or slipped photos of their wife and kids under the front doorstep. Whichever made them cave first. And they always caved. Gianni had become something of an expert at manipulation, but he'd never evolved from petty extortion. He knew his limits. He wasn't a mob boss. He didn't have the book smarts. He wasn't good with numbers. He knew if he tried, he'd get ripped off a thousand different ways without even realising.

No, Gianni liked control over his life. He stuck to the same highly profitable actions that had consistently put a few bucks in his bank account ever since he was big enough to scare people. Which, in his case, had been from the age of fifteen.

Now he was twenty-five, with his hair buzzed short and thin stubble dotting his jawline. He was sitting in the driver's seat of a rented box truck on Washington Street, only a few hundred feet from the Hudson River. There were bars and restaurants ahead, and bars and restaurants behind, but this little stretch of the sidewalk was dark, and all the shops were closed for the night.

He'd picked this space strategically.

To intimidate.

If any drunk patrons stumbled out of the upmarket establishments and sauntered toward the truck, he'd get out and stare daggers into their soul until they turned right around and went back the way they came. He'd been hired for the job for those tactics alone. He wasn't the type to get involved in gang warfare. If that was the case — given his brashness and refusal to back down from anything — he would have ended up riddled with lead a long time ago.

He picked his fights.

And he picked his jobs.

'Why'd you fuckin' do it?' he muttered in the freezing cabin. 'Why'd you say yes this time?'

He'd been offered jobs before.

He'd turned them all down.

Not this time.

Because the offer had come from the Whelans.

And you don't say no to the Whelans.

Gianni rubbed his cold hands together and exhaled a cloud. He glanced around with nervous anticipation and waited for the payload to show up.

2

The payload in question arrived on the dark, deserted bank of the Hudson River.

The crates were brought in by boat and dumped overboard a hundred feet from shore, along with a cluster of five small men in wetsuits wearing fins on their feet. The divers pushed the crates — all of them equipped with a flotation lining — to shore.

Gianni's men were dotted along the riverbank to watch for onlookers.

The crates arrived amidst trash and gravel and muddy silt in a shadowy corner at the base of Pier 54. The divers stripped off their wetsuits and buried them under the loose gravel. Underneath they wore civilian garments — faded jeans and simple long-sleeved shirts. They were all the same build and ethnicity — short, slim Asian men with cold beady eyes and pale skin.

Gianni's men studied them. The divers were professionals — probably from the triad, probably recruited by the Whelans to ensure the job went off without a hitch, but

Gianni and his posse were strangers to this world, so they didn't assume anything.

The men on shore ranged from early twenties to late forties. There were eight of them in total. They were all big and well-built and intimidating like Gianni — he only recruited a certain type. Together they ran nearly every protection racket in Hell's Kitchen, and they'd started expanding into new territories with their ever-growing bankroll.

Maybe that was why their boss had been willing to give this new job a go.

It was the era of trying new things.

But although they collectively outweighed the five divers by close to a thousand pounds, they weren't exactly bristling with confidence.

There were four crates in total, each the size of a large refrigerator. They were sealed tight in some sort of water-proof material — like cling wrap, only stronger. The eight men fanned out on the shoreline, and two took each crate by the thick metal handles on either side. They each heaved, and with pumping muscles and glistening veins, managed to inch the crates off the ground.

It was laborious, back-breaking work.

Under cover of darkness they carried the crates into the mouth of an alleyway. The shadows swallowed them whole. On the other side they found a box truck.

On cue, Gianni climbed down out of the cabin and greeted them with a silent nod. He opened the rear doors and helped each pair heave their respective crate over the lip, adding his size and strength to each movement.

In seconds, the truck was loaded.

Gianni wordlessly jerked a thumb into the dark hollow space in the back of the truck. It beckoned like a gaping maw. All eight of his men leapt up into the hold. The last man to enter reached out with both hands and snatched hold of the rear doors. He was about to pull them closed when he took a final glance at the alleyway, wondering if the five divers had followed them out of sheer curiosity.

But, as he suspected, they were true professionals.

There was no sign of them.

They'd melted into the night as if they'd never existed at all.

The two parties hadn't even exchanged a word with each other.

The eighth man swung the doors shut.

Gianni pulled at the exterior handles one by one, checking the truck was sealed. Then he turned on his heel to get back in the driver's seat.

There was a young couple staring at him from the other side of the street.

Staring at the truck.

They were stereotypes of the Meatpacking District — in their twenties, affluent, loaded with alcohol. The guy was dressed expensively to hide his soft body, and the woman was wearing a dress so tight that Gianni could picture her naked from across the road. He liked what he saw. She was curvaceous in all the right places.

He banged a fist hard on the back of the truck. The doors sprang open.

Gianni said, 'Two witnesses.'

His men let out a collective sigh.

Two of them got out of the truck to lend a helping hand, and the other six stayed put.

Trailing Gianni, the pair crossed the street to where the young couple stood frozen.

3

*S*hould have kept walking, Gianni thought. *You could have avoided this.*

He snatched two handfuls of the guy's shirt before either of the rich yuppies knew what hit them. He shoved the guy into the alley, hard. The kid tripped over his own feet and went down in a heap, landing in a puddle of ankle-deep water.

Gianni followed him into the shadows.

The girl opened her mouth to scream — Gianni had spent so much time in the business of intimidation that he could almost time their reactions to the millisecond. So he turned on his heel before she could make a sound and grabbed her by the throat, cutting her off mid-outcry.

Gianni flashed a dark look at his men, who were standing there like fish out of water.

He said, 'Never hit a woman before?'

They shrugged.

'Thought you'd take care of that,' one of them said.

'You think that matters right now?' Gianni said. 'You

know what's in those crates. You think we can afford to have either of them make a fuckin' sound?'

The woman sobbed. He was digging his fat fingers into her throat hard enough to bruise the skin. Tears turned her mascara to black treacle. It ran down her face as she gasped for air.

'Sorry, boss,' the second guy said.

Gianni noted the dull yellow streetlights nearby. They were still in the lip of the alleyway. If anyone saw him squeezing a young woman by the throat, they'd start a riot.

So he said, 'Watch and learn,' to his hired help.

Then he threw her into the shadows after her boyfriend.

The young guy was getting to his feet when she hurtled into him. They both went back down to the ground.

The girl tried to scream again.

Don't you learn? Gianni thought.

He kicked her in the stomach, putting all his weight into it, sapping every ounce of breath from her lungs. He figured it didn't matter if he broke a couple of her ribs.

The end result would be the same.

'What'd you see?' Gianni muttered, bearing down on them in the darkness.

'Please,' the guy gasped. He had a Jersey accent. 'We didn't see nuthin'.'

'Ohh—' the girl said.

But she said it softly.

Quietly.

Music to Gianni's ears.

He kicked her again, then kicked the guy in the face.

It was hard to see in the dark, but he *heard* the blood spray.

'Did I say you could speak?' Gianni said. 'You saw the truck.'

'Please,' the guy said.

It was only a single syllable, but it came out jumbled and garbled. The young guy's mouth was filled with blood, and he was probably missing a few teeth.

Gianni felt good. There was liquid power surging through his veins. His penchant for avoiding violence had finally bubbled up inside him, and now it was all coming out.

He shied away from it during standard business hours.

But this was a special job, and it had special rules.

He *lived* for this shit, but any more of a beating and it would become extraneous. He wasn't here to fuck around. They'd seen the truck, and the stakes were high. He'd never taken a job for a crime family before. He couldn't risk it going belly up.

He pulled a switchblade from his belt.

Best to keep it quiet.

He couldn't risk a couple of gunshots in the Meatpacking District.

He reached down in the dark and snatched a handful of the girl's hair. He yanked her off the alley floor, suspending her from her scalp. She almost cried out, but thought better of it.

'Good girl,' Gianni said.

He pressed the knife to her bruised throat, and another surge of *something* ran through him. He was going to kill her in front of her boyfriend, then finish him off too. There was something sick about that, but he loved it. He loved all of it.

He bared his teeth and threw a glance over his shoulder to make sure his hired help were watching. That way, they could learn from him. They could understand the ruthlessness it took to get ahead in their game. They could see the reality of the path they'd all chosen.

But they weren't there.

The mouth of the alleyway was empty.

Gianni felt strangely naked. If they'd bitched out and retreated to the truck, he would never forgive them. He might kill the both of them, to set an example for the rest of his men. He couldn't fathom their incompetence. He'd given them an order — *Watch and learn* — and they'd disobeyed it.

They weren't watching.

They weren't learning.

They were nowhere to be seen.

The surge of invigoration turned to a surge of rage. Gianni dropped the sobbing girl back into the puddle and grappled with indecision.

Then he said, 'I have a guy with a gun on you. If either of you move or make a sound, he'll shoot you in the legs. Then I'll come back and make it real painful. So don't move. And don't make a sound.'

They didn't confirm or deny his request.

But he knew they would obey.

They lay on their sides on the damp alleyway floor and moaned and sobbed and dribbled blood into the fetid water.

Gianni strode hard for the mouth of the alleyway. He tried to contain his anger, but it was futile. His breath came in ragged gasps.

'Where are you?' he whispered under his breath. 'Where are you, you cheap—'

He reached the sidewalk, and weak light spilled over him.

He looked left.

Nothing.

He looked right.

Both his men were sprawled out on the concrete, deep in

the throes of unconsciousness. One of them was violently twitching. The other had a face like a crimson mask. They were broken and bloody and dishevelled. They each looked like they'd been living on the streets for days. They'd been roughed up beyond comprehension.

A cold chill ran down the back of Gianni's neck.

Now he felt naked.

He turned back to the truck, but there was no sign of movement. The rest of his men were loyal. They were inside the hold, doing what they'd been told.

Gianni needed them here with him.

He was ashamed to admit he panicked. He figured it didn't matter what happened to the two witnesses in the alley if he didn't make it out of here alive. And there was foul play afoot. Whether it be a rival gang, or an old enemy come back to haunt him, or some new problem... it didn't matter.

What mattered was his own safety.

He took off at a sprint for the truck.

But he only made it a few steps.

A hand seized him by the back of the collar and hauled him off his feet.

4

He wasn't used to being on the back foot.

Not at all.

Not in the slightest.

He landed on his rear and shot straight back up, overwhelmed by adrenaline. He thought he could take on an entire army with this much juice in his veins. He'd dropped the switchblade when the mystery assailant had jerked him by the collar, but he didn't care in the slightest. He sprang up and turned around with his fists raised and his teeth clenched.

He was a big guy, and no-one *ever* threw him around.

When he laid eyes on his attacker, he bristled with confidence.

The guy was roughly six feet tall, African-American, sporting a powerful build. He had the frame of an Olympic athlete. He was wearing jeans and an expensive sweater, but underneath the clothes his musculature rippled. He had a sharp handsome face and a shaved head and a strong jawline. And his eyes were ice.

But Gianni was five inches taller, and probably fifty pounds heavier, and *angry.*

And the guy didn't have a gun or a knife.

Big mistake, you fuckin' punk.

Gianni swung a fist with reckless abandon. He hit fast, and he hit hard. He had crisp technique from a lifetime of boxing in old school NYC gyms. And he'd never been pumped full of this much adrenaline in his life. He figured he could take the assailant's head off with a single right hook. He sure wanted to. If he found even a moment's advantage in the coming brawl, he'd drop elbows down on the guy's face until his head was mashed to a pulp. And he'd savour every second of it.

But the hook missed.

Gianni got real worried.

He never missed.

The fist hit nothing but empty air, because the assailant simply wasn't there anymore. The guy was inches away from the swing, still close to the action, but it didn't matter whether you missed by an inch or a mile.

A miss was a miss.

Gianni stumbled one step forward, off-balance from overcommitting to the punch, and he thought, *Oh, fuck.*

The guy crushed Gianni's nose to pieces with a single well-placed elbow.

Gianni had never felt pain like that.

He'd been hit clean in the past, but it was usually a glancing blow off the side of his head, or a sucker punch from behind that put his lights out. The ones you didn't see coming were the worst. Back in the day, he'd had his fair share of street fights. You didn't grow up and thrive in a world like this without getting your hands dirty. As his reputation had grown, the violence steadily faded away, until he could intimidate based on his presence alone.

So, he had to admit, he was rusty in the fight department.

He could dish out a beating, but beatings didn't require the act of pushing through adversity, pushing through pain and discomfort. He hadn't acclimatised. He figured, if anyone in his path ever got physical, he'd wipe the floor with them without a problem.

And now his nose was completely shattered and his vision was gone and his brain was screaming, *What the hell is this?*

He landed on his rear on the sidewalk and sat there, stunned into submission. For some reason, he didn't even consider getting to his feet. His nose was pure molten agony, and frankly he wasn't in the mood to do anything else but sit motionless and feel awfully sorry for himself.

He almost let out a moan of pain, but common sense caught it at the last second.

He couldn't show weakness.

If he made it out of this alive, he'd have a reputation to salvage.

His vision came back piece by piece. The pain had been so intense, so all-encompassing, that it had shut down the rest of his senses as his body grappled with what had occurred. He could already feel the broken bones swimming around in his septum. He could feel his nostrils closing, the skin swelling, turning purple.

The assailant loomed over him.

Gianni lifted his gaze to look the man in the eyes. He wanted to see the face of the guy who had bested him.

The man crouched down and stared hard at Gianni, like a lion observing its prey.

He said, 'You'd better hope those two kids you dragged into that alleyway are alive.'

'They are,' Gianni mumbled.

'I'm about to go and check.'

'You do that.'

'I hope you're telling the truth.'

'And what would happen if they're not?'

'That wouldn't bode well for you.'

'I have six men in that truck across the street.'

'I don't see them.'

'They're there. Trust me.'

'Let them come, then.'

Something about the sincerity with which the assailant spoke sent a shiver down Gianni's spine.

Gianni said, 'Did the Whelans send you? Is that what this is about?'

Silence.

Gianni said, 'I knew I shouldn't have trusted those pricks. Serves me right for taking a job like this. Fuck...'

The assailant said, 'Did you say the Whelans? The Whelan family?'

'Yes.'

'They didn't send me. I've had a run-in with them before, though. A long time ago. Right here in this city.'

'What?'

The assailant squatted in front of Gianni, so they could see eye-to-eye. He had a withering intensity about him. There was a seriousness in his eyes that Gianni couldn't decipher.

There was a strange sensation in Gianni's chest.

Anxiety.

He hadn't been scared like this for as long as he could

remember. It was like the assailant was a different breed. Another species. Faster, stronger...

...better.

The dark-skinned man said, 'Remember when the Whelans ran this city? They had control of everything. The unions, the docks, racketeering, extortion, murder. They were doing all of it. And they sure as shit weren't recruiting second-rate gangsters like you to do their dirty work.'

Gianni brushed off the insult, simply because he wasn't prepared to take another elbow to the face for his troubles. He said, 'I remember.'

'What happened to them, then?'

'Rumour on the street is that a mystery man beat the shit out of the whole family. All the top dogs. That sort of thing could get you locked up in a dungeon and tortured for the rest of your life. So we didn't stop talking about it. Because he vanished right afterwards. No-one heard from him again.'

Gianni knew where this was headed.

The assailant said, '*I* destroyed the Whelans. That's who you're dealing with now. I've got some free time on my hands, so I guess you could count this as my official return. That's the message I want you to pass up the chain of command. Got it?'

'Yeah, okay,' Gianni mumbled. 'Whatever you say. Who the fuck are you anyway?'

'Will Slater.'

5

S later regarded the pathetic shell of a man at his feet.
The guy was a thug, through and through. He was big and beefy, at least five inches taller than Slater, but all that mass hadn't achieved a thing when he'd tried to put up a fight.

Over his shoulder, Slater could hear two soft sets of whimpers from the alleyway. So the young couple were alive. He'd seen the thugs manhandle them into the shadows from across the street. He'd been tailing the box truck for a couple of hours when it had all kicked off. He hadn't planned to intervene here, in the hustle and bustle of the Meatpacking District. He would have preferred somewhere quieter.

But it was late, and he didn't have a choice anymore.

Those kids would have died had he not stepped in.

Now he contemplated what to do with the thug. He was sure the guy was a big shot in certain places. Probably ran a union operation, swindling hundreds of small businesses out of "protection" fees. But those skills didn't exactly translate to fighting.

It took something special to intimidate Will Slater.

Slater bent down and said, 'Stick your right leg out straight.'

The thug said, 'What?'

Slater said, 'What's your name?'

'Gianni.'

'Gianni, I'm only going to ask you one more time, and then I'm going to punch you in your broken nose. And trust me, that hurts.'

Gianni had been seated cross-legged on the concrete, but now he extended his right leg, as Slater requested. Slater lined up his aim, then stomped down on the outside of the guy's knee. It wasn't a traditional stomp. It was a strike honed over years and years of practice. Slater considered himself the master of generating force over a short distance, and he probably ruptured every ligament and tendon in Gianni's knee with the sole of his boot.

Gianni stifled a scream.

Slater said, 'Now I know you're not going anywhere.'

He strode over to the unconscious bodies of Gianni's two bodyguards, and dragged them by their collars into the alleyway. They were waking up, stirring from their slumbers, so Slater hit each of them one more time behind the ear and dropped them in a heap behind one of the dumpsters.

Then he went to check on the young couple.

They were in a state. The guy was bent over clutching his face, and the woman was curled up in the foetal position holding her mid-section. Pain creased both their faces. Slater whispered reassurances, trying not to bring them any more stress, and helped them to their feet.

They took their sweet time, both hurting, both shocked, both traumatised.

Slater said, 'I took care of the problem.'

'Thank you,' the guy said. 'Who are—'

'Don't bother. Just go to the nearest hospital and tell them you were mugged. You didn't get a good look at your attacker. You have no information for them.'

'But I know what he looks like,' the woman said.

'The cops won't do anything. He pays the cops. Leave the punishment to me.'

'Okay...'

'And besides, however you remember him looking ... he doesn't look like that anymore.'

With that, Slater sent them on their way, ushering them to the other end of the alleyway. They disappeared into the darkness, strangely silent. Slater had seen it all before. They were deep in their own heads. Victims reacted differently in each situation. Some panicked, some handled it well, and some went quiet.

Slater forgot about them.

He went back out into the street.

Gianni had passed out from the pain. He was lying on his back, mouth agape, nose swollen, leg straightened.

More importantly, there were a group of five rowdy partygoers stumbling down the sidewalk toward them. They were all inebriated, arms around each others shoulders. Three guys and two girls.

Slater instantly transformed his demeanour.

He laughed hard, and snatched Gianni by the collar, and hauled him into the mouth of the alleyway.

At the same time, he yelled, 'He's had a few! I'll handle this.'

Someone shouted back, 'Happens to the best of us.'

Slater shoved Gianni into a dark corner amidst trash bags and dumpsters and fetid puddles, and crouched over the unconscious man. The party of five stumbled past, firing barbs and harsh laughter in Slater's direction. He gave them a short wave, as if to say, *Look at the shit I have to deal with.*

Then they were gone, heading on their merry way.

Gianni came to a couple of minutes later. He stirred, and groaned, and reached for his leg.

Slater batted his hands away and said, 'Where are your friends?'

'What?' the thug mumbled.

He was barely lucid.

'Thought you had six friends coming.'

'They'll be out of that truck any moment.'

'Don't you think they would have tried it already?'

Silence.

Slater said, 'Probably not the smartest idea to make them wait in the back of the box truck.'

Silence.

Slater said, 'There's a latch on the outside. Didn't take much effort to drop it on my way across the street.'

Gianni sighed. 'What exactly do you want out of this?'

'I want to know what's in those crates.'

'You'll have to go and see for yourself.'

'Wrong answer.'

'Break my other leg. I don't care.'

'Okay,' Slater said, and did exactly that.

He stomped down again, and this time Gianni screamed.

But there was no one around to hear.

Slater threw a glance at the box truck. He had a sneaking suspicion that the six men would soon be free.

He said, 'You're lucky I didn't kill you for what you did to those kids, but this'll do. I'm hanging around the city for a while, so I can keep tabs on you from afar. I'd wager that I tore both your ACLs, but a couple of MRIs will tell you everything you need to know. You'll be in a wheelchair for a couple of months, then you'll have to learn how to walk again. Consider that punishment enough. Okay?'

Gianni had a subtle smile on his face as he listened to Slater speak. His pale face gleamed in the lowlight.

'What?' Slater said.

'You're real confident for someone that's about to get their head kicked in.'

'By who?'

'There's more than one way out of that truck. Have a look.'

Slater threw a glance over his shoulder, and sure enough Gianni was right. Four men were already out. They were big brutes with sleek black pistols in their hands, and they'd wormed their way through a front compartment and shimmied over the driver and passenger seats. Two more were spilling their way out onto the asphalt.

They were disoriented, frustrated that they'd been made to look like fools.

They couldn't see Slater and Gianni in the lee of the alleyway.

Yet.

Slater said under his breath, 'If you make a sound, I'll kill you.'

'Do you even have a gun?'

Slater withdrew a compact Beretta M9 from an appendix holster under his shirt and pressed the barrel to Gianni's forehead.

'Bet you're wondering why I didn't use that earlier.'

Gianni shrugged. 'I don't understand anything you do.'

'Use a gun from the get-go, and it's impersonal. Which is why you didn't shoot those two kids right away. You wanted them to suffer, for reasons I'll never know. But you can understand why I want you to suffer.'

Gianni said, 'They'll find you eventually.'

'Probably.'

'Are you a good shot?'

'I'd like to think so.'

'It's six on one.'

Slater smiled and said, 'Well, it's a good thing I brought a friend, then.'

Gianni went quiet.

He knew Slater wasn't bluffing.

They watched the six men fan out across the street.

Three went to the opposite sidewalk, and three came close to Slater and Gianni's position. But they hadn't narrowed down the source of their troubles. They were looking everywhere at once, keeping their guns low, keenly aware they were in the public arena. It was late — technically the early morning — but there were still drunk socialites trickling out of various establishments. The six men had to keep their weapons inside their jackets to avoid starting a panic. There was no-one in sight right now, but that could change.

One man spotted bloodstains on the sidewalk, where Slater had beat down the two bodyguards.

The other pair walked right into the mouth of the alleyway.

Slater held his breath.

Then a large silhouette materialised out of the gloom on the opposite side of the road.

A man, maybe six foot three, maybe two hundred and twenty pounds. Larger than Slater, with the same rock-solid build. Like a battering ram in human form. He'd stepped out from underneath an awning, emerging out of a nook that ran between two shopfronts.

Slater watched Jason King walk right up to the trio across the road.

They regarded King warily.

After all, he wasn't armed, and they'd never seen him before. They didn't immediately identify him as a hostile. They were more concerned about where their boss had run off to. They didn't yet suspect foul play.

They should have.

King launched an uppercut underneath the chin of the first guy, crumpling him where he stood. On the way down King stripped the unconscious man of his weapon and used it to pistol whip the second guy in the face. Breaking a nose, or a jaw, or an eye socket. Hard to tell exactly what. He followed that up with a brazen charge, like an angry bull, ploughing straight through the chest of the third man. He connected with a dropped shoulder and took the guy off his feet before he even had a chance to fire his weapon, let alone aim it. As the guy spilled to the ground King stomped down on his wrist, shattering the delicate bones, and the gun spilled from his palm.

King scooped up all three pistols, and melted back into the shadows.

It was a shocking hurricane of violence, enacted over four or five seconds in total, and an observer would have seen nothing but a flash of carnage, followed swiftly by the messy aftermath. The three men on Slater's side of the street saw nothing at all. From the darkness, King watched them twirl around in confusion, their eyes going everywhere and nowhere at the same time. They weren't tactical. They weren't measured. They weren't composed.

They would be easy work.

One of them — both the bravest and the dumbest — peeled off from the pack and sprinted across the deserted street. He reached his friends and crouched by their moaning forms like a protective guard dog. With eyes like saucers, he raised his weapon and swept it in a tight arc over the shadows. He covered every alleyway, every hole in the wall, every corner. But he didn't linger his aim on anything in particular.

He didn't see King standing there, biding his time, probing for the first opportunity to strike.

He didn't see it coming.

He was tall and beefy and had a cold gaze, but King could see the fear in his eyes. Even in the lowlight. Finally, the guy became unnerved by the silence and threw a glance over his shoulder, checking to see if his two buddies had followed his lead.

They were still across the street, frozen.

Unsure what to do.

Unsure what the hell was happening to them.

The guy turned back to his three beaten co-workers, and King was standing right there in front of his face.

He nearly gasped in surprise.

But King kicked him square in the face before he had a chance to move.

The guy went limp almost immediately, even though he wasn't unconscious. He sprawled out on the dirty sidewalk, then thought better of leaving himself unprotected, so he rolled onto his knees and pressed his forehead to the ground and covered his ears with his hands.

The classic turtle shell.

An age-old display of submission.

The fastest way to say, *Please, sir, no more. I'm in pain. I don't know how bad I'm hurt. I yield.*

King kicked him in the head again, this time behind the ear, helping him along the path to unconsciousness.

The guy joined his three buddies in defeat.

King stood over the four of them and gave himself the once-over. He wasn't hurt. Far from it. He was good as new. Which he damn well expected to be, given what he put himself through on a daily basis to fashion himself into a human weapon.

He looked up, and noticed the last two wise guys staring at him across the street.

They had guns in their hands.

King didn't.

But he didn't react.

One of them raised his pistol with a shaking hand. 'Stay right there, you fuckin' scum.'

King sighed. 'I wouldn't do that if I were you.'

'Get on the ground.'

'No.'

'I won't warn you again.'

'I know that.'

'Then do what I say. The game's over. Get on the fuckin' ground and stay there.'

Silence.

King didn't budge.

He said, 'What happens now?'

'Where's our boss?'

'In that alleyway behind you.'

'You think we're that stupid? You expect us to turn around?'

'You might want to.'

'And why's that?'

'Because that's the reason you won't warn me again. You won't be able to.'

Something in his voice told them the truth. Not that it would do them any good. They seemed to put two and two together. They finally figured that there must be a second assailant.

By the time one of them threw a look over his shoulder, Will Slater was already on them.

S later figured Gianni wasn't going anywhere with two destroyed knees, so he took the gun away from his head as King beat down the three men across the street.

Then one of the trio on Slater's side ran over to check on his comrades.

A noble act, but carried out with misplaced judgment.

Slater watched the dark silhouette emerge once again from the shadows and smash a boot into the young thug's face. The guy crumpled, and King kicked him again, and he went still.

Then the oldest scenario of all played out before him.

The Mexican standoff.

King stayed right where he was, yet his weapon didn't materialise. What the remaining pair didn't know was that King *was* armed. He had a trick up his sleeve.

He had Slater.

A brief conversation played out, but Slater didn't hear it. He looked down at Gianni and saw the big goon had passed out from the pain again, so he focused all his attention on the pair standing on the sidewalk. They had their backs turned.

He crept up behind them, holding his Beretta at the ready.

If it came to it, he would fire a shot.

But he preferred not to.

He thought he heard the words, 'You won't be able to,' float across the street.

He figured that was his cue.

He smashed the butt of the Beretta into the back of the bigger guy's head, who pitched forward on wobbly legs. He was the one with his gun pointing at the floor, but that had been a tactical decision from the get-go. If Slater took out the other guy when he had a loaded barrel pointed in King's direction, there was the risk of an impulsive jerk of the trigger as his lights went out. Slater didn't want to take the chance. So when he thundered the Beretta into the back of the first guy's head, the second whirled around on the spot, and his aim swung with it.

Slater head-butted him in the nose the moment the gun barrel wandered into empty space.

Both assailants went down on their knees, and Slater figured he'd wasted enough time. What ordinarily would have been a pair of body kicks ended up slamming home against a pair of foreheads. Bad move to take a knee in front of a seasoned Muay Thai practitioner.

Their brains rattled around in their skulls like bowling pins and they went right to sleep.

Slater eyed off King across the street. 'You hurt?'

'No. You?'

'Not a scratch.'

'What's the final count?'

'Eight. Plus the boss.'

'Where's the boss?'

Slater jerked a thumb over his shoulder.

'Did he tell you what's in the crates?' King said.

'Not yet. He will.'

'We can't linger. Get the keys.'

'What if it turns out to be something real bad? I'd want to know that now. When I've got the opportunity to kill him.'

'How badly did you hurt him?'

'I broke both his legs.'

'Then he's not going anywhere in a hurry, is he?'

'If it's real bad, I want to make him pay before the cops scoop him up.'

'The cops won't be able to make anything stick if we take the truck. So he'll be back out on the street before long. We take the goods, we peek inside, and we come back if we need to. How's that sound?'

'That works.'

'Get the keys,' King repeated.

Slater hustled back into the alleyway. Gianni was awake again, hunched in a ball in a dark alcove, surrounded by trash. He looked deathly pale in the lowlight. Slater crouched over him and said, 'You'd better tell me what's in the crates. I'll give you five seconds.'

'Go fuck yourself.'

Slater didn't have time for games. There were injured and semi-conscious wise guys scattered all over the street, and this was the Meatpacking District. There'd be a patrol car cruising by intermittently, and it wouldn't take long to piece together what had happened. He and King didn't want to be anywhere near the scene when that went down. And there'd be more witnesses before long, spilling out from the clubs like clockwork. The last survivors, stumbling home inebriated.

Slater slapped Gianni in the face, then fished around in his inside jacket pockets until he came away with a set of keys.

He got up and said, 'You were going to kill those two kids, weren't you?'

Gianni didn't respond.

Slater said, 'I should kill you right now.'

Gianni said nothing.

Slater said, 'I'll be honest — I'm not in a killing mood. You're too dumb for your own good. I'm going to track you down in a few months. It should take you about that long to recover. If you're still in the same business, you're dead. Are we on the same page?'

Gianni stared up at this strange man that had stripped him of everything.

Slater thought, *The Whelans will probably kill you anyway, for butchering this job.*

That gave him some peace of mind.

He walked away from the pathetic thug.

He and King clambered up into the box truck and Slater fired it to life. They pulled away from the sidewalk and trundled down the empty street. Sure enough, within a hundred feet they passed a couple of bars that had turned the main lights on. Civilians were sauntering out into the cold night, frustrated to leave the warmth and the drinks behind. Soon enough, they'd get the shock of their lives. They'd find eight mobsters in various states of disrepair. Some conscious, some not. They'd find blood and broken bones.

They'd either run, or call the cops.

Slater didn't mind either way.

Neither did King.

Gianni and his crew were in a world of trouble, no matter what happened to them. They'd be arrested, or vilified by their own employers if they managed to escape scot-free. Neither option seemed appealing.

But what do I know? Slater thought. *I'm not a gangster.*

He turned at the next T-junction and the box truck vanished.

Dawn broke over New York City, and under the soft glow of the dark blue light, four big Italian men with swollen faces and puffy eyes and purple noses and jaws carried an even larger Italian man into the lobby of an impressive residential building on the Upper East Side.

The night receptionist looked the other way. He knew who the men were, and who they associated with. He'd been paid to keep his mouth shut, no matter what tomfoolery he witnessed.

And he'd be damn sure he stayed true to his word, or he'd find himself at the bottom of the Hudson for his troubles.

The four big thugs hauled Gianni into the elevator and hit the button for the ninth floor. There was no-one around at five-thirty in the morning. The nine-to-fivers had a couple more hours sleep to manage. But the night owls roamed, and the man they were paying a visit to would be awake.

The Whelans were professionals, after all.

Gianni moaned and protested and opened and closed his eyes with dizzying frequency.

'Hospital,' he muttered. 'Get me to a fuckin' hospital.'

They gave him another pain pill to shut him up. They'd loaded him with enough OxyContin to sedate a horse, but Gianni was a tough son-of-a-bitch, and they'd never disobeyed the man directly. They were also in pain themselves, so overall they weren't exactly the calmest bunch of small-timers in the world. They were none too happy about drugging their boss and bringing him to meet the man who was most likely to punish him for fucking up the job.

The request had come down the chain of command and ended up at their feet, as soon as they'd let the Whelans know they'd lost the package.

Despite the oxycodone coursing through his system, Gianni became lucid as soon as the elevator arrived on the ninth floor.

He recognised the walls.

He started to squirm.

Then he groaned, because trying to resist had aggravated his broken legs. The pain would be unbearable. All four wise guys winced, but one of them clamped a hand over Gianni's mouth, so he didn't wake the other residents.

The Whelans lived comfortably amidst civilisation, because what was the point of having all that money if they became social outcasts in the process.

They carried Gianni to a nondescript black wooden door and knocked softly.

It opened a couple of seconds later.

Tommy Whelan stood there in his trademark wool suit.

He was furious.

'Get inside,' he said.

Gianni sure looked like a sight for sore eyes then. He

went pale and started thrashing, but when the four thugs carried him over the threshold he quietened right down. He probably realised there was no use resisting once he was inside. It was futile now. He was in Tommy Whelan's den. Granted, looking around, none of the thugs thought the Upper East Side apartment compared to the magnificent penthouse the Whelans used to reside in. But after an incident involving the very man who'd ambushed them tonight, they'd figured it would prove more discreet to spread out across the district instead of condensing into one single location.

Hence the downgrade.

The four thugs dumped Gianni onto an expensive leather couch, and stood at attention as Tommy Whelan followed them. The ceiling stretched out far above their heads. The space echoed. They could hear the soles of Whelan's shoes scuffing against the marble floor. Everything was white. The sun came up over the horizon as they stood there, and they squinted against the glare.

Tommy Whelan said, 'Go wait on the balcony, and close the door behind you. I need to have a private chat with your boss.'

They went right away. They didn't protest. They didn't even give their employer a second look.

Self-preservation was more important than loyalty. No matter what Gianni had done for them.

There was no goodwill in this game.

Silence descended over the room, and Whelan thought he heard Gianni sob. Whoever had assaulted them must have done a number on them. Gianni wasn't the type to complain about anything.

Not even a pair of shattered knees.

The old Gianni would have sucked it up and barely let it

register on his face, no matter how bad it affected him, no matter how likely it was to kill him.

Now, he was demoralised.

And Whelan started to get uncomfortable. Because he'd felt the same sensation, about a year earlier. That total, utter defeat at the hands of another man. There were rumours floating around that it had been a single guy.

It stirred a sinister déjà vu in his chest.

Gianni fought back the pain. Through clenched teeth he muttered, 'The guy said his name was Will Slater. He said he had history with your family.'

Whelan didn't react.

Inside, he screamed.

Whelan said, 'You sure?'

'Positive.'

'Describe him.'

'Big black guy. Well, not that big. Shorter than me. Maybe six feet tall. But built like a pro sprinter. And I ... I couldn't touch him. He ran right through me. No-one's ever done that to me.'

Me neither, Whelan thought.

He recalled his own run-in with Slater — the incident that had left six of his family in the hospital with life-threatening injuries and derailed their family's trajectory to the top of the underworld.

He missed that penthouse...

Whelan bowed his head, because he now knew what he needed to do.

Regarding Gianni's pathetic form sprawled out on the couch, he said, 'You know what must happen, right?'

'What?' Gianni said. 'You want me to track him down for you?'

Whelan managed a harsh laugh. 'What are you going to

do with two mangled legs? You'll be in a wheelchair for months.'

'I can heal up fast. I promise.'

'And what are you going to do in the meantime?'

'What?'

'I know you, Gianni. We've been keeping a close eye on you for a long time. You think this job offer was the first we'd heard of you? Your reputation precedes you. You were hired for your effectiveness and your ability to get the job done without fail.'

'I'm sorry.'

'But you know what else I know about you? You talk.'

'I won't say nothin'.'

'But you will. You'll run to your friends all across the city — all the small-timers — and tell them that the guy who fucked up the Whelans also fucked you up. Rumours will spread like a virus. Soon, everyone will know what happened to us. We cannot afford that risk to our reputation.'

On the couch, Gianni stiffened. But there was nothing he could do. He was unarmed, and his face had swollen like a pumpkin, and he couldn't get to his feet if his life depended on it.

Whelan withdrew a Glock 23 equipped with a Silencerco Osprey 40 Silencer from the rear of his waistband. He held it in his palm. He said, 'I guess it doesn't make a difference what I tell you anymore, does it?'

'Come on, Tommy...'

Whelan leant forward. 'We were paid tens of millions to ensure those crates were delivered to the townhouse on time. I won't tell you who funded the job. You wouldn't believe it if I did. But it was vital that they reached their destination. Now my entire organisation is at risk, and my reputation is on the line too.'

'Tommy, please—'

Whelan shot him through the forehead.

The Glock coughed in the apartment, and still made a considerable sound, but the neighbours would think he was watching a movie at an obnoxiously loud volume. Plus, the apartments were expensive, so the walls were thick and sound-absorbent.

Whelan flashed a glance at the balcony.

The four beat-up thugs were watching with solemn expressions.

That would change soon.

Soon, they would panic, and their stomachs would drop, and their veins would turn to ice.

Tommy Whelan advanced toward the balcony.

If he left Gianni's men alive, they'd spread the same rumours.

As he opened the glass door and shot each of them once in the face, he made a mental note to have his men clean the rest of Gianni's crew off the street later that day.

10

S later pulled the box truck to a halt beside an electronic security interface in front of a vast metal gate.

He reached down and swiped a keycard across the scanner. A sharp *beep* sounded, and the gate rumbled off the ground.

Slater drove into an underground parking garage.

Beside him, King muttered, 'Home sweet home.'

'We can't leave it here for long,' Slater said.

'We'll take the crates upstairs if we need to. Then I'll torch the truck.'

'I can do it, if you need.'

'You were tracking them all day yesterday. I slept in. I've had more rest.'

Slater shrugged. 'Fair enough. I *am* running on fumes.'

'We both are.'

'When's the last time you knocked some heads together?'

King sighed. 'Not since ... you know.'

That was the only way to describe it.

Their recent history defied belief. Slater recalled the madness in New Zealand, the incident that had reunited them after a long spell apart. Before that, they shared a long and equally turbulent history. They were brothers in arms, united in their mutual penchant for chaos, both cut from the same cloth. Together they'd contributed to the foundations of Black Force, a secret division of the U.S. government that honed and forged solo warriors with inhuman reflexes. They were genetic specimens, and they'd sacrificed most of their lives and their own personal comforts for their country. And now the division that had formed their separate identities was dead, and after a period of mutual exile they were back together.

They'd tried to stay apart, but normal civilisation didn't suit them.

Their minds didn't stop running.

Their morality never wavered.

They couldn't sit back and let their talents go to waste as the world fell apart around them.

So here they were — unemployed vigilantes, cast out from the system that had built them, both with more money than they knew what to do with.

Hence the building they'd driven the truck underneath.

They'd agreed to unite two months ago, and they'd been busy ever since. After discovering they were no longer wanted by the U.S. government, they'd been free to move back into the country that had forged them. Slater was worth four hundred million dollars after a detour through the bank accounts of a Macau triad, so it hadn't taken much of an effort to snatch up two penthouse suites in one of New York's most expensive residential buildings on the Upper East Side. The luxury apartments had cost fifteen million dollars apiece, and they resided side by side on the top floor with a sprawling view of Central Park and enough amenities to keep them both in obscene comfort for the rest of their lives.

But comfort had never been part of their agenda.

So after a brief acclimatisation period to get used to their new surroundings, they'd figured it was time to get back out there and put their skills to work.

They'd put out the feelers and started sniffing leads, and it had all culminated in the assault on Gianni and his men.

Now, Slater parked in a dark corner of the garage. The space was quiet and desolate and empty. There was no-one in sight. He spotted the same handful of luxury supercars dotted around the garage — Ferraris and Lamborghinis and the odd McLaren or two. But they weren't in use. Some of the supercars had lain dormant for months, purchased by residents with no idea how to splurge their cash. They had chauffeurs to pick them up, and rarely drove their own vehicles. This section of the building was reserved for those on the top five levels, where apartments didn't fall under the low eight figures.

So there was privacy, and anonymity.

It worked well for King and Slater.

They piled out of the truck and Slater skirted round back. He lifted the latches out of their holsters and swung the doors outward. Then he and King set to work dragging the crates out of the hold, one by one. They lowered them to the concrete, arms and legs straining. Each crate had to weigh north of four hundred pounds. They could deadlift that weight on their own, but there was a difference between lifting a barbell with perfect form and manhandling an object the size of a refrigerator out of an enclosed space.

With the four crates out of the truck, Slater slammed the doors closed.

They stood with their hands on their hips, panting for breath, and stared down at the payload.

King scrutinised the keyholes on each crate and said, 'How are we going to do this? They look like they're designed to be impenetrable.'

Slater said, 'They came off the river. I saw Gianni's men collect them. There was no other handover. I was keeping a close eye on how it went down. They didn't even interact with the divers who brought the crates in. So the keys are here. They were supposed to go straight to their destination. There was no need to hide the keys.'

King bent down and ran a calloused palm along the side of the closest crate. There was a *snap* as he found a loose piece of reinforced plastic and ripped it off the lining. It exposed a small nook carved into the side of the box. Inside rested a small silver key.

'Well, what do you know,' he said.

He took it out and unlocked the crate.

Slater stepped forward and lifted the lid.

They looked inside.

'Oh,' King said.

'Where the hell were these going?' Slater pondered.

They settled into an uneasy silence.

11

W eapons.
Lots of weapons.
Serious firepower.

Enough to start a civil war on the streets of New York City.

On top there were brand new Heckler & Koch HK417 rifles. They were variants of the base model, with 20 inch barrels, telescopic sights and detachable bipods. Putting one in the hands of a trained marksman with an agenda would result in unimaginable destruction. Then there were dozens of spare magazines neatly slotted into cutouts in a layer of foam. All .308 Winchester cartridges.

Slater lifted the assault rifles out and found dozens of claymore mines underneath, also carefully slotted into foam. They were the miniature variant designed for use by U.S. Special Forces — MM-1 Minimores. Slater was intimately familiar with them, as was King. They'd taken many on Black Force operations in the past. The mines were lightweight — easy to carry, hard for an enemy to spot, yet they packed practically the same punch as the larger M18A1 clay-more mine.

You could use them to set up an impenetrable fortress anywhere in New York. It told Slater this was a defensive operation.

Someone was anticipating a siege.

If only they knew who...

'Is that it?' King said. 'I was expecting something... more.'

Slater said, 'There's another layer.'

He lifted out the MM-1 Minimores.

And, of course, it wasn't only guns and mines.

The most valuable cargo was always unassuming.

At the bottom of the crate lay nondescript black boxes, and their exteriors were entirely featureless. There were nine of them arranged in a three by three grid, and Slater used his limited knowledge of computers to liken them to CPUs. He figured there was enough processing power in those boxes to do something incredibly sinister.

And the mystery around them made it so much worse.

King said, 'You're the computer guy. What are we looking at?'

'I'm afraid this is above my pay grade.'

'What do we do with them?'

'Would be great if we still had our government contacts, wouldn't it?'

'That's not our world anymore.'

'No,' Slater said, forlorn. 'It isn't.'

King glanced at him. 'You don't sound thrilled. Do you want it to be?'

'I don't know what I want. You ever feel like an imposter living this life?'

'This is our first independent job. We're just getting started. There's always going to be growing pains.'

'You like where we live? What we do?'

'What's not to like?'

'You ever feel empty inside? Like something's missing?'

King stared around the empty garage. Their words were echoing off the walls. 'You really want to have that conversation here?'

'Is there a better place to have it?'

'Are you still thinking about New Zealand?'

'Considering I almost went under the knife and got my brain altered by a lunatic, I'd say it's hard to stop thinking about it.'

King said, 'I remember you were worried the world's passing us by. Technology's advancing, and our type is becoming obsolete. The old-fashioned type. The type who knock heads together.'

He gestured to the black boxes.

'That's what you think this is,' King continued. 'More horrors. More things we know nothing about. You're overwhelmed. You're out of your depth. Right?'

'Yeah,' Slater admitted.

'They didn't change your brain,' King said. 'Back in New Zealand, they didn't achieve anything. I stopped them. We stopped them.'

'They almost did.'

King shrugged.

Slater said, 'They *could* have. That's the point. If you hadn't intervened, I would have been a mental slave. Programmed to do the bidding of my master. That's where society is headed. Genetic alterations. There's going to be a fundamental shift, if it hasn't already happened yet.'

'No use getting caught up on hypotheticals.'

Silence.

King said, 'It didn't *happen*.'

'Something *will* happen. Eventually. And we'll be powerless to stop it.'

'We destroy these boxes,' King said. 'Whatever they are. If they're out of the picture, then it doesn't matter what their purpose is. That's all we can focus on. Like I said, no use concentrating on anything else.'

'Yeah,' Slater said, dejected.

King grabbed the back of his shirt and hauled him to his feet like a disobedient child.

Slater said, 'You'd better get your fucking hands off me.'

'Pull yourself together. We didn't set up this life to back out when the going gets tough.'

Slater said, 'Help me get these upstairs. Then we'll torch the truck, and the boxes along with them. That's one plan we foiled, at least.'

King said, 'Are you frustrated that this isn't official? Because it means we know nothing about what we're trying to prevent.'

'I guess. There's usually briefings, and after-action reports, and investigations. All on the down-low, obviously, because of what we used to do. But I hate not knowing. What did we prevent? We'll never know.'

'This is the way it's going to work moving forward,' King said. 'We don't have a choice. We have no resources. No contacts. We're cut off from that world. We're on our own.'

Slater shrugged. 'Better than doing it solo, I guess.'

'Exactly.'

King offered out an open palm, and Slater slapped it. King thumped him hard on the back. 'You're okay, soldier. We're okay.'

'Strange new world,' Slater muttered under his breath.

'Let's get these upstairs.'

They bent down, hauled the first crate off the ground, and shuffled toward the private elevator.

12

Half an hour later, Slater sat alone in his penthouse and looked out at Central Park.

Watching the sun rise from the height of luxury.

There was a lidless blender filled with green juice in his hand.

Not a tumbler filled with whiskey.

At least that much had changed.

He hadn't touched alcohol since he and King had reunited in Budapest. It wasn't conducive to an optimal state of being, and he figured with his early thirties behind him there was nowhere to go but downward. The decline of old age was inevitable, not to mention the accumulative wear and tear on his body. He and King were no longer young hungry lions with something to prove.

But that gave him some reassurance, at least.

Beware of an old man in a profession where men usually die young.

In truth, he wasn't old. He was thirty-five. In some sports, that would be considered his athletic prime. But this was not a sport. It was a game that was all but guaranteed to kill him sooner or later, so he figured he'd do his best to slow that decline, and that meant not drinking himself into a coma every time he needed to destress.

He watched the orange glow spill over Central Park and shine into his apartment through the floor-to-ceiling windows.

This was the American dream.

Worth millions — hundreds of millions, to be exact. Living in the most desirable location in the country. Financially free. Physically unstoppable. Mentally ... alright, all things considered. He'd had enough life experience to give ten Navy SEALs PTSD, but somehow he'd managed to keep the demons from consuming him. They weren't the problem.

So why was it that he felt so terrible?

He hadn't been the same since New Zealand. There, his view on the enemy had shifted forever. He always thought he'd be up against the same level of competition, and his enemies hadn't changed in a decade. Terrorists, mercenaries, rogue agents, common criminals, organised crime. Scum was the same in all shapes and forms.

But not this time.

This time he'd run into Ali Hawk, a techno-terrorist who specialised in neuroscience. The reclusive venture capitalist billionaire had recruited the world's best brain surgeons to fundamentally alter the human mind, and he'd succeeded at it. He'd captured Slater with plans to put electrodes deep in his head, killing his ability to make decisions on his own. Effectively controlling him. It wasn't science fiction. It was real. It was binary. It was, above all, actually possible.

And Slater had been on the operating table when Jason King had burst in and saved his life.

Another few minutes, and he never would have been the same.

Now he shivered and got out of the armchair. If he sat there for too long, he'd fall asleep.

He didn't want to dream.

Not yet.

He knew what to do. It was best to physically exhaust himself before he crashed. He'd sleep through the day after warring all night, then set to work correcting his sleep pattern the following morning.

But first ... a workout.

He moved past the four crates and went into his private gymnasium. He'd fitted it with every piece of fitness equipment under the sun — it hadn't even made the slightest dent in his fortune, and what he could do with some iron and a few state-of-the-art cardio machines was unparalleled.

He always approached the Versa Climber with a slight reluctance, but he'd managed to overpower his distaste for exercise a long time ago. It was a total body cardio machine that he'd found the most effective for keeping his body fat down and his cardiovascular health in top condition. In his line of work, he had to focus on every facet of fitness and capability — from every effective form of martial arts (boxing, kickboxing, wrestling, jiu-jitsu), to endurance, to strength, to power — so he didn't have time to waste messing around with suboptimal exercises.

The Versa Climber was simply the fastest way to burn calories on a stationary machine.

He gripped the handles, slotted each foot into the grooves and pre-selected a workout that burned eight hundred calories. Then he fought tooth and nail to improve on his previous best time. Within minutes, his arms and legs were on fire, and his heart thudded in his chest, and stitches creased his ribs, but he didn't let up.

He never let up.

It wasn't in his DNA.

When he finally reached the 800-calorie mark and dropped off the machine into a puddle of sweat, he looked up at the display screen and realised he'd beaten his best time by over two minutes. Perspiration fell off him in rivulets, and his muscular chest heaved. He clambered to his feet and set to work wrapping his hands in athletic tape. He slipped MMA gloves over the top of the tape, and put in a trio of five-minute rounds on the heavy bag. He drilled combinations non-stop until his muscles were spent, throwing earth-shattering left and right hooks into the leather.

When it was over, he cut the athletic tape off, then spent twenty minutes in the infrared sauna he'd constructed up the back of the gymnasium. He sweated non-stop the entire time, bathed in the red glow. Thoroughly cleansed, he stumbled to the shower, where he used a jet of ice-cold water to stop the flow of perspiration and bring his heart rate back down to a reasonable level.

When he turned the water off, he stood there naked in the marble bathroom and took a deep breath, in and out.

He emptied his mind.

It worked.

Physical exertion had always been his cure. It could silence the most terrifying demons, and if his solution to the chaos in his own head made him healthier and stronger and better and faster at the same time, then that was a sacrifice he was willing to make each and every day. Discomfort no longer played on his mind.

He lived in discomfort.

He walked naked to the bedroom and climbed under the covers, pressing himself into the memory foam. He kept the blackout blinds up for a few minutes to admire the view. It hadn't grown old yet. He didn't know if it ever would.

He was the one unlikely to grow old.

He drifted into an uneasy sleep, exhausted from the last twenty-four hours.

13

J ason King suffered his own turmoil as he drove the box truck through bustling New York City streets under a dawn sky.

He knew Slater had his own issues to work through.

After long and uninterrupted conversations over many nights, he'd realised their differences.

You see, Slater hadn't been in a committed relationship for over a decade. He was the womanising type, treating sexual conquests with the same intensity that he approached the rest of his life with. King had dabbled in the same patterns early in his career, but the reason he'd pulled himself away from Black Force was to settle down with the woman he loved.

On the tropical island of Koh Tao, two men had forced their way into his villa when he wasn't home and shot her in the head.

He'd closed that chapter of his life, and delivered vengeance on everyone involved, but the emptiness would never leave him.

He gripped the wheel and let the dark cloud encase him. He had to let it in. Keeping it at bay would drive him mad. When he was alone, he let it wash over him. Then he forced the evil away when he had to communicate with others.

But he was the solitary type, so spending most of his waking hours dwelling on the cruelness of the world wasn't healthy.

Why did she have to pay for my mistakes?

Why wasn't it me instead?

He knew the answer. It seemed like everyone on the planet had tried to kill him at some point in his life, but he'd mowed them down each and every time. He had the capacity to defend himself, and Klara didn't. He'd dragged her into his world, so she'd been forced to pay the consequences.

He sighed and bowed his head to the wheel.

He wasn't watching where he was going.

He figured if the box truck drifted off-course at top speed and slammed into a wall, he wouldn't care...

Then he snapped himself out of it and refocused on the road.

The black boxes were in the back of the truck. There were thirty-six in total — nine per box. But King had kept one in the passenger seat, and it was sitting there now, tantalising in its mystery.

He figured he'd keep one in the back of his closet.

In case there was ever an opportunity to find out what they were.

The sun rose in all its glory, revealing a cool and bright New York day. King drove the box truck out of the city limits, heading over the Brooklyn Bridge, moving south.

On the way, he kept an eye out for any strange looks from passers-by. Gianni might have half the city's underworld on the payroll. King had one of the Heckler & Koch rifles from the crates lying on the centre console, and he was more than ready to use it.

When he reached Flatlands, with its urban industrial sprawl, he found an empty lot wedged between two abandoned buildings and drove in like he had all the business in the world being there. There wasn't a soul in sight. He found an open shed covered in rust, with old broken tools and plastic bottles converted into bongs and heroin needles strewn all over the floor, and drove the box truck in. The building itself was surrounded by nothing but gravel — there was no fire hazard if he torched the truck in here.

And he figured if a vagrant caught him in the act, there'd be little risk of them alerting the authorities.

No, the truck would be unrecognisable by the time anyone came across it.

King got out and withdrew the lone black box from the passenger seat. He tucked it into a canvas carry-bag, taking care not to damage it in the process, then shut the doors. He fetched three cans of gasoline from the back and poured them over every surface of the truck. Then he slipped the bag over one shoulder, pulled a lighter out of his pocket, and set the whole thing aflame.

He walked away fast, letting it burn, and the flames consumed the vehicle.

The boxes in the back, probably priceless, burned too.

He hailed a cab several blocks away from the scene and gently lowered the carry bag to the rear seats alongside him.

He gave the cab driver his address on the Upper East Side.

'You're a long way from home,' the guy noted, glancing in the rear view mirror to get a better look at King.

He knew the building.

King said, 'Had business out this way.'

'What kind of business?'

King looked over his shoulder and saw smoke billowing from between two abandoned buildings.

There was no-one on the sidewalks.

No witnesses.

It would burn bright for half an hour before anyone came across it.

It would be a shell.

King turned back around and pressed five $100 bills into the driver's palm.

'The kind of business that would be better left undisclosed.'

'Of course, sir,' the taxi driver said. 'I've been in Manhattan all morning.'

King smiled. 'Yes, you have.'

14

S later came awake from a knock at the front door.

He'd never been a deep sleeper — a byproduct of a life spent sleeping deep behind enemy lines, in places he had no business being, expecting an ambush.

So he woke up in a flurry and vaulted out of bed.

He might have employed more caution, but he recognised the knock.

It was almost midday, according to the digital clock on his bedside table. He slipped into underwear, a pair of athletic shorts, and a skin-tight compression shirt in his walk-in wardrobe, and went to answer the door.

He opened it to find Jason King staring at him.

'I was sleeping,' Slater said. 'I needed the rest.'

'I thought I'd drop by.'

'Job done?'

King gestured to the carry bag hanging off his shoulder. 'I figured we should keep one.'

Silence.

King said, 'I wanted to see how you'd react.'

'You know I don't want any part of that.'

'I didn't take you for the superstitious type.'

'Yeah, well...'

'You're paranoid. There's no room for paranoia in this world.'

Slater glanced over King's shoulder. 'You want to come inside? Best we have this conversation in private.'

'Sure.'

King stepped in, and Slater sensed the tension bristling in the air. They didn't disagree often. When they did, it sometimes led to reckless behaviour. He remembered the last time they'd fought — on a rural track in Hungary, when King's emotions had reached boiling point. Slater had dodged a punch, taken him down, and locked in the choke. King tapped.

They hadn't laid a hand on each other since.

But they both knew full well that whoever got the upper hand could end the other's life in seconds.

That was the reality of their world.

Most of it was restraint.

Because the truth was, if they wanted to murder every one of Gianni's thugs on the street last night, they could have.

But that wasn't who they were.

They retaliated viciously when their lives were threatened, but when they were on the offensive they employed restraint.

King brushed past and swept into the living room. Slater followed.

King placed the black box gently on the floor next to the four open crates, and turned around. He didn't seem impressed by the view, or the luxury surroundings.

No wonder — his penthouse suite was virtually identical, and the view was the same.

Slater said, 'I don't like this.'

'I told you — you don't like it because you're superstitious. If you were in the right mindset, you'd want to keep it.'

'What do we do with it?'

'I'll leave it in my closet.'

'I wouldn't do that.'

'Why not?'

Slater stared at King like he was an idiot. 'You're sleep deprived.'

'What am I missing?'

'How hard do you think it is to put a tracker in each of them?'

'Oh. Right.'

'Use your head.'

'Destroy it, then?'

'Probably our best bet. Which is what I've been saying all along. Which is what I thought you did.'

King stared at the walls, then the floor, then the view.

Then back to Slater.

He said, 'You think they're tracking it right now?'

'Only one way to know for sure.'

'Want my opinion?' King said.

Slater said, 'Will I care?'

The atmosphere bristled again.

King said, 'I'm not from the nineteenth century like you think I am.'

'Did I say that?'

'You're implying I have no idea what I'm talking about when it comes to technology.'

'Oh,' Slater said. 'Didn't know I was making it so obvious.'

The sarcasm leached through his tone.

King said, 'They won't be tracking the boxes themselves.

Why would they put a tracker in it? They'd put it some-where easily accessible. Somewhere that doesn't require taking apart a priceless piece of technology to retrieve it. They'd put it in the crates, or the truck.'

'Or nowhere at all,' Slater said. 'Maybe they got brazen and figured they'd reach their destination without a problem.'

'Maybe,' King said.

Silence.

A long, drawn-out silence.

Slater said, 'That was a good point.'

'Thank you.'

'I still don't like this.'

'I can tell.'

'You keep it. If anything comes from it, you'll be the one who gets murdered in the middle of the night.'

King said, 'I'm flattered.'

But he picked the box up with a wry smile and carried it by its thin handle to the front door.

'You going back to sleep?' he said.

Slater said, 'I'll try to.'

King paused by the door. 'You still having dreams?'

'Don't you?'

'Sometimes. Not often.'

'Then I guess one of us got lucky, huh?'

King said, 'Look, Will... if you want out, then get out. This can't be helping your headspace. I'm doing this because I want to, and because it's the only thing that makes me forget about Klara. The stress and the intensity and the violence... it suppresses my issues. But if that's what triggers *your* issues, then maybe this path isn't what you need.'

'I appreciate the armchair psychology,' Slater said, 'but I'll be fine.'

'You sure?'

Slater waved a hand around the apartment. 'You think I have any reason to complain? Look at where we are. Look at what we do. We help people. And we have our health.'

'Our physical health, maybe,' King said. Then he reached out and tapped a single finger against the side of Slater's head. 'This is what I'm worried about.'

'I'll be fine. I'll attack it like I attack all my other problems. I'll sort myself out.'

'Is it because of what we do?' King said. 'Or is it because of what happened in New Zealand?'

'I'm not sure.'

'You'll figure it out.'

'I hope so.'

King shifted the black box in his grip and nodded down to it. 'I'll take care of this. Sorry I interrupted your sleep. I should have waited.'

'I appreciate you running it by me.'

'What happens now?' King said. 'We got no answers. Do we go back for Gianni?'

'I have a gut feeling that he's already been taken care of.'

'What do you mean?'

Slater pointed at the black box. 'Those were incredibly important, and they were being delivered on behalf of the Whelans.'

'Who?'

'A crime family here in New York. I've had a run-in with them in the past.'

'Of course you have. Is that where we go next?'

Slater shrugged. 'I caught them by surprise last time. From what I hear, they went to ground. They don't flaunt their riches in public anymore. They're spread out — tactical. I don't think it'll be as easy to assault them as last time.'

'But now there's two of us.'

Slater sighed. 'Maybe. Then what? We take down all organised crime in the city? Not much chance of that happening.'

'One step at a time. We haven't been vigilantes for long. We need to build momentum.'

'So we start smaller than the Whelans.'

'We just did.'

Slater paused. 'Time to take things to the next level?'

'I think so.'

'Sleep first,' Slater said. 'Then we'll discuss going after the Whelans.'

'Sounds good to me.'

King closed the door behind him, and Slater padded back to bed and returned to his slumber. The blackout blinds were down, and it didn't take him long to drift off.

But the whole time he dreamt about guns and knives and fists and blood and bullets.

And it didn't excite him like it used to.

15

King unlocked the door to his own penthouse, and slipped inside.

It was a mirror image of Slater's. The same furniture, arranged in the same positions, with slight variations in colour and size. But neither of them had any interest in interior design, so they'd hired a firm to fit out the properties on an equally extravagant budget.

Design was not their specialty, so they outsourced it.

As they outsourced nearly everything in their life.

So they could concentrate every waking moment on doing what they do best.

Fighting.

King's muscles throbbed from throwing maximum output strikes against Gianni's thugs. They hadn't landed a blow, but that didn't matter. Slamming home an elbow with the power he could generate disrupted the muscle fascia, and made his bones ache, and rattled his central nervous system. He felt a thousand pound weight on his shoulders. Thankfully, he'd learnt to deal with it. He'd seen it all before. He placed the box on the floor near the entranceway, ensured all three of the security locks on his front door were firmly in place, and sauntered through to the open plan living area.

He was tired, too.

He had to admit it.

He crossed to the Eames chair in the corner and stretched out on it, folding his hands behind his head. He exhaled all the turbulence of the previous night. There was uncertainty, sure, but there'd always been uncertainty. He didn't know what they'd be doing in twenty-four hours time. He'd never had this much freedom. The military was structured, and his post-military career had been whimsical, floating from one confrontation to the next. This was different. This was a focused ploy to target the worst scum in New York City.

It was like they were running their own covert division, in a way.

Without the manpower.

So they were stumbling around in the dark.

King closed his eyes and thought long and hard about that. When he opened them, something glinted out the window.

His heart rate spiked and his adrenaline flared. He threw himself off the chair, overturning it in the process, and landed on his stomach. He pressed himself to the cool ground and scrambled in a crab crawl for the kitchen island a couple of dozen feet away. When he made it to the giant bulletproof husk and threw himself behind it, he opened and closed his mouth in an attempt to control his breathing.

There's a shooter out there.

You were in his sights.

He was ready to kill. If someone came through the door right now, he'd rip them apart with his bare hands. He was sure of it. His chest heaved, rising and falling, and the back part of his brain took over. It snarled, *Fight. Kill. Win.*

Then he slowed his breathing down.

And he peered over the countertop.

And he realised it was the sun, reflecting off the floor-to-ceiling windows in a certain way.

He closed his eyes and slid back down onto his rear. He touched the back of his neck to the kitchen island. It came away sticky. Wet with perspiration.

He clambered to his feet, looked all around, and shook his head.

'Fuck,' he said to himself. 'Maybe you've got your own problems to work through.'

He stumbled to the bedroom and fell asleep, drenched in sweat.

16

A phone rang in the kitchen.

Slater's phone.

He rubbed his eyes and groaned in protest. He reached over and stabbed a button on the bedside table, and the blinds lifted.

It was dark.

He rubbed his eyes again, and shook away the tendrils of deep, all-encompassing sleep.

For the first time in months, he hadn't dreamed at all.

He didn't know what that meant.

He'd slept sound.

He threw the covers off and looked down at himself. He'd slept in the same clothes — the athletic shorts, and the compression shirt. He climbed out of bed and headed straight for the phone. It was a slim black smartphone, brand new, top of the line. He could afford it.

The screen said, No Caller ID.

He swiped a finger across the touch screen, and lifted it to his ear.

He didn't say a word.

A male voice said, 'Don't hang up.'

'I probably should if that's what you're leading with,' Slater said.

'Give me one minute to explain myself.'

Slater cast a paranoid glance through the giant windows. The New York City skyline sparkled around the dark abyss of Central Park.

He said, 'I shouldn't.'

'But you will. Because you're curious.'

It sounded like the guy was deliberately trying to disguise his voice.

Slater said, 'Alright. One minute.'

'Promise you will give me the full minute.'

'Okay.'

The man slipped back into his regular tone and said, 'It's Russell Williams.'

He didn't even have to say the name.

Slater recognised the voice immediately.

He said, 'Holy shit.'

There was dead silence.

Russell Williams was one of Slater's old government handlers, and the two hadn't exactly parted ways amicably. In Macau, nearly two years ago, Slater had rescued a nine-year-old girl named Shien from a sadistic underground sex trafficking ring. Aware that she couldn't be a part of his turbulent life, he'd handed her over to Williams with the reassurance that he'd find a suitable foster home for her so she could have some semblance of a normal childhood.

Instead, Williams had inducted Shien into the Lynx program against her will — a clandestine U.S. government operation that raised young girls and shaped them into barbaric assassins. These women were taught to seduce and deceive, and were used to slaughter dictators and corrupt businessmen that regularly hired prostitutes and models to parade around in their entourage. Slater had met a fully grown graduate of the Lynx program — a woman named Ruby Nazarian — and she'd been one of the most alluring and vicious people he'd ever met.

Slater had righted the wrongs, and destroyed the program, and eventually Ruby had seen the light and confronted her old handler for what he'd done to her.

For brainwashing her, and stripping her of her free will, and butchering her childhood.

That was the last time Slater had seen Williams — alone with Ruby in the North Maine Woods, with a knife blade pressed under his chin.

He figured there was a ninety-nine percent chance she'd slashed his throat.

Now, Slater said, 'You've got some fucking nerve calling me.'

'I know. But I'm doing it anyway.'

'Why?'

'I need my minute first.'

'You're already halfway through it. The clock's ticking.'

'Come on, Will.'

'Oh, you're going to act like that with me? That's the route you want to go down? You're hard done by, are you? You want me to give you a break?'

'I won't try to apologise for what I did to Shien, because there aren't words that would suffice.'

'You're damn right.'

'I've changed.'

'Like a crack addict changes, right? For about two days, and then they fall right back into the same routine.'

'I'm serious.'

'I don't care.'

'I'd be willing to show you if you'd give me the opportunity.'

'Don't think so.'

'But I can't right now. There are more important issues at hand.'

'Shut the fuck up, Williams. Nice talking to you.'

'*Wait.*'

He practically screamed the word, and Slater realised he'd never heard desperation like that come from the ordinarily stoic government handler.

So he hesitated with his finger hovering over the END CALL button.

'Your one minute starts now,' Slater said. 'Make it count.'

'I'm back with the government,' Williams said.

Of course you are, Slater thought. *Corruption never dies.*

'But it's not what you think,' Williams continued.

'Uh-huh.'

'I've genuinely changed. Ruby spoke to me for a long time in those woods, and it tore me up inside. I realised everything I'd done. I saw it all in a new light. I thought of the family I'd taken her away from. She could tell she'd broken me, and she left me there to kill myself, because she could see I was about to do it. And I almost did. I picked up the gun she'd left me and put it in my mouth and pulled the trigger, but nothing happened. Then I passed out from the fear, and when I woke up I stumbled back to my superiors and pleaded with them to let me clean up the mess.'

'And they did?'

'Reluctantly. I'd fucked up the Lynx program about as badly as you can fuck up anything. But I laid it all out for them, and told them where I'd gone wrong, and how I thought things could change.'

'And?'

'And now I'm paving the way toward sweeping change in the secret world. With a focus on ethics.'

'Not much chance of that happening.'

'It's an uphill battle. But we're being taken seriously. And that's all I care about at this point.'

'Who's "we?"'

'Myself and a few key players. We've formed a union of sorts. We're enacting change.'

'What the hell do you want from me, then?'

'I need to speak to you and King in person.'

'Why?'

'I can't tell you over the phone.'

'You just shared all that information with me.'

'This line is encrypted with the best tech money can buy, but that's not enough. Not when I tell you what I need you for.'

'I'm not going to meet with you. I don't want to see your face.'

'Will, I told you—'

'You think that makes a difference? Saying you're all of a sudden a decent person? You wouldn't have changed one iota if I hadn't interfered. Don't tell me you would have.'

'I'm not pretending I'm a good person,' Williams said. 'I'm not. But I'm trying to become better. Isn't that all anyone can ask? I'm doing the best I can to turn my life around.'

'I still think you're a disgusting piece of shit.'

'And I want you to think that. Because you can be damn sure I deserve every morsel of hate. But all I need to do is convince you that I'm respectable enough to meet with. You will be safe. There will be no ambush—'

Slater scoffed.

'What?' Williams said.

'You didn't need to tell me that.'

'Tell you what?'

'That there won't be an ambush.'

'Ah—'

'And if there is one, then all I can say is good luck. Especially if you want King to come along, too.'

'He has to.'

'I've told him about you.'

'I assume that was a pleasant conversation.'

'He might punch your nose into the back of your skull when he sees you.'

'I sincerely hope not.'

'Where do you want to meet?'

17

King was two hours into a non-stop flow-rolling jiu-jitsu session at a revered New York City BJJ gym when his phone rang from the corner of the mats.

Dressed in his traditional *gi,* he transitioned into full mount by swinging his left leg over his rolling partner's stomach. The guy squirmed, and King tightened the position, wrapping around his torso like a boa constrictor. The guy was a second degree black belt, but he rolled over all the same in a last-ditch attempt to escape the position before the inevitable occurred.

He didn't get the chance.

King slipped an arm around the guy's throat, and it took barely any effort whatsoever. To a bystander, their sparring would seem like the stuff of magicians, like anacondas that had mastered the ability to mirror the movements of the human body. It was the result of painstaking discipline and relentless dedication to the craft, but it meant that if King encountered anyone in combat without a jiu-jitsu base, he could take them down and strangle the life out of them before they had the opportunity to throw a single punch. They wouldn't know what had hit them.

One instant they'd be pumped full of adrenaline, ready for the fight of their lives, and the next they would be on the ground with a two hundred and twenty pound deadweight on top of them and an arm like a tree trunk crushing the air out of their windpipe. They'd see nothing but darkness.

A smooth transition to the great beyond.

You only had to squeeze for ten or fifteen seconds past the point of unconsciousness to cause irreversible damage.

With someone of King's size and strength, it was more like five seconds.

The second degree black belt tapped out, and King rolled off the guy with the sort of satisfaction you could only earn by pushing yourself to an extreme limit over and over and over again until you earned your reward.

There was no feeling like it on earth.

Which was probably why he'd come out of retirement. He could chalk it up to Klara's death, but deep down he was the same warrior he'd always been.

Nothing else sufficed.

He heard his phone shrilling, and he knew it could only mean one thing. He'd set it to silent for anyone but a single individual. Which meant it was important.

He crossed the mats, his *gi* damp with perspiration, and lifted the phone to his ear.

'What is it?' he said.

Slater said, 'I got a phone call.'

'Good for you. Moving on up in the world. What's it like to be a socialite?'

'I'm serious.'

Usually Slater was the wisecracking one, so King stiffened. 'What's wrong?'

'Remember everything I told you about the Lynx program?'

'For the most part.'

'Russell Williams called.'

'Your old handler?'

'The one and only.'

'He's alive?'

'Apparently so.'

'I thought you were sure he was dead.'

'That's what I suspected. Ruby Nazarian wanted to kill him. I could see it in her eyes. She must have had a change of heart.'

'Why do you think that? I assume he's blackmailing you.'

'No. Quite the contrary.'

'The way you spoke about him ... he's got some nerve making the call if it wasn't hostile in nature.'

'That's exactly what I told him.'

'Then what did he say?'

'He wants to meet.'

'With you?'

'With both of us.'

'He knows about me?'

'He *was* a Black Force handler once upon a time. That shouldn't come as a surprise.'

'What does he want?'

'I don't know.'

'Then that's that.'

'I want to do it.'

King sat down on the bench running along the far wall, and watched the black belts struggle and writhe and fight for position on the mats. He said, 'Why would you give him the time of day?'

'Because I believe what he told me.'

King let the silence drag out.

Slater said, 'Ruby spared him, and he says it changed him. He gave me some spiel about how he's guiding the secret world in a new, ethical direction. I'm not sure if I buy that, but he *did* seem different.'

'Probably because he killed Ruby before she could kill him, and now he wants to clean up the loose ends.'

'He's a pen pusher. He's never done a hard day's work in his life — I mean, in comparison to what we used to do. And she had a knife to his throat when I saw them. He didn't do a thing.'

'There are other alternatives,' King said. 'Alternatives that are more likely than her letting him go.'

'Such as?'

'Did you leave any guards alive in the woods that could have rescued him?'

'No.'

'Are you absolutely certain?'

A pause.

Then, 'No.'

'That might be something to consider before you show up out of goodwill.'

'I think I'm going to do it.'

'Why?'

'Many reasons. I need closure on that chapter of my life, I'm not sure what the hell we're doing acting like vigilantes, and I guess I need to shake things up and see what happens.'

'That was our first night taking matters into our own hands,' King snarled. 'And you're getting cold feet already?'

'Come with me. If you do, then I stand at least half a chance.'

'If this goes wrong, I'll never forgive you.'

'Won't matter,' Slater said. 'We'll both be dead.'

King stewed restlessly on the bench. He bowed his head. He said, 'I'm only doing this because I can tell you're torn up inside and you desperately need something new. Any other reason, and it'd be a firm *no*.'

'And because you owe me,' Slater said. 'Because we owe each other. Forever.'

'That, too.'

It was true. They'd pulled each other out of hell too many times to count. King remembered an abandoned gold mine on the Kamchatka Peninsula, many years ago. If Slater hadn't dropped everything and put his life on the line, King wouldn't be sitting here today.

King said, 'I hope your judgment is right.'

'I'm telling you it is.'

'What makes you so sure?'

'A hunch.'

'Great,' King said, and hung up.

18

S   later had the instructions.

But despite his talk with King, he wasn't sure whether he was going to follow them or not. He'd convinced King to come along, but the final decision rested on his shoulders.

He sat in the darkness of his penthouse, hunched over in an armchair, cradling a drink.

This time, it was a tumbler.

This time, there was whiskey in it.

He had to admit it felt good. Better than good. Like sweet nectar, and he knew how badly he'd struggled to suppress the urge to drink. The truth was, in the midst of the most successful years of his career, he'd been a raging alcoholic with a drug dependency. He could go cold turkey on a whim, and always sobered up when an operation arose, but in the downtime he'd tested the limits of his tolerance with each passing day.

Now, it was threatening to come roaring back.

He'd never experienced turmoil like this.

He drained the warm liquid, and it burned its way down

his throat, and he picked up the phone and dialled a number Williams had given him.

It went straight to a burner phone.

Williams said, 'Getting cold feet?'

'I don't know yet. I'm weighing the consequences.'

'I need this, Slater. The government needs this. Trust me when I tell you how important it is.'

'I suggested a public place. Why the need for a car?'

'I can't meet you in a public place. I'll be there in the town car. It'll pull up, you two will get in, and we'll talk. That way I know it's secure, and we can constantly stay on the move. Look — bring guns if you want. We won't search you. Arm yourself to the teeth if it makes you feel better. But please don't no-show.'

'Okay,' Slater said. 'One hour?'

'One hour.'

'We'll be there.'

Slater ended the call and tossed the phone at the sofa cushions on the other side of the room. He ran a hand across his bare scalp, and reached instinctively for the tumbler. When he touched the glass, he remembered it was empty.

He glanced longingly at the full decanter sitting on the bar shelf.

The amber liquid glowed in the ambient light.

He got up to refill his glass.

There was a knock at the door.

He grumbled and went to open it. King stood there, his brown hair damp from a recent shower, his clothes fresh. He wore denim jeans, a plain T-shirt and an expensive leather jacket. All the garments clung to his frame like they'd been tailored to the inch, but Slater knew the man had the optimal physique for any style of clothing.

He knew, because he had the same build.

He ushered King inside, unaware that he was still clutching the empty glass.

King looked down at it on the way past. 'Calming the nerves?'

Slater followed his gaze, and noticed it resting there between his fingers. 'Oh. Forgot I was still holding that.'

'Don't overdo it,' King muttered.

'You drink, too,' Slater said.

He poured a splash more into the tumbler.

King eyed him warily as he sat down on the sofa across from the armchair. 'Not like you.'

Slater lowered himself into the armchair. 'You have in the past.'

'Occasionally. Then I got it under control. That was years ago.'

'I've been sober for months.'

'Which is why this worries me.'

'Don't know if you were aware, but things are tense right now.'

'I'm about to accompany you to meet a man who, if he had any sense, would try to kill us. I *know* things are tense.'

'There we go,' Slater said.

He tipped the rim of the tumbler in King's direction and took a sip.

'What if we need to be on our A-game for this?' King said.

'Then I'll be on my A-game. I'll compartmentalise. As I've always done.'

'You can fight drunk?'

Slater smirked. 'If you'd seen me consume substances in the past, you'd know I can do almost anything drunk.'

King glanced uncomfortably to the side.

Slater said, 'Relax. I'm not even tipsy. If my substance issues had any positive benefit, it was that they gave me a tolerance to be reckoned with.'

'How long until this goes down?' King said.

'An hour, I'm told.'

'And he's picking us up out the front?'

'That's what he said.'

'You gave him our address?'

'I told him we live in the fourth building over,' Slater said.

King nodded. 'Glad to hear you're still somewhat sensible.'

Slater nodded back. Then he put the empty tumbler down, and didn't touch it again.

'Restraint,' King said. 'I'm impressed.'

'I can take care of myself. I was doing it for years before you came around. You don't need to babysit me.'

'Mental health isn't that straightforward. You might not be the same person you used to be.'

'You think?'

'I don't know for sure. You're hard to read.'

'And what about you?'

'What about me?'

'Do you think you're the same?'

King looked away. 'I don't want to talk about what happened with Klara right now.'

'Why not? You had no problem mentioning my rampant alcoholism.'

'That's different.'

'Is it?'

King stared at him with pure fury in his eyes. 'Yes.'

Slater figured the whiskey had affected him more than

he thought. His social awareness had dulled, and he'd touched a nerve he ordinarily would have skirted around.

He said, 'I'm sorry. It is different. You're right.'

But now King was deep in his own head. Slater could see it.

He couldn't tell what the man was thinking, but he had a rough idea.

Finally, unprompted, King said, 'I killed the ones who did it. But it doesn't change a thing. Now there's an emptiness. I thought revenge like that would feel... I don't know...'

'Better,' Slater said.

King nodded.

Slater figured it was best to let him grapple with it in silence. They sat there, surrounded by the height of luxury — two broken men who had the whole world in the palm of their hands but no appreciation for it. Probably because they understood how quickly it could all be stripped away. They'd spent their careers dealing with the worst human atrocities under the sun, and those memories would always fester in their head when they put their feet up and relaxed.

So relaxing would never come.

It would tear them both apart, individually.

It almost had in the past.

Some time later, Slater checked his watch as night truly fell across the city. Dusk gave way to darkness, and he nodded once to King.

Wordlessly, they rose to their feet and went to the door. They caught the elevator down to the garage and used the building's private rear exit for residents who preferred to leave anonymously. It dumped them out into a tidy alleyway, and they walked to the fourth building on the left of their own. They loitered around in the shadows until a valet hurried out through a rear door. They let him bustle past.

King dashed forward and caught the door before it clicked closed. They moved through staff corridors with their chins held high and their shoulders back, exuding confidence. Pretending they belonged. A couple of staff gave them peculiar looks, but they didn't return them.

They just kept moving forward.

They reached the lobby and rounded the front desk, passing a bewildered receptionist who couldn't remember letting them in.

Slater turned to her and flashed his trademark smile and said, 'All fixed back there, ma'am. Thanks for the hospitality. We'll be on our way.'

She smiled back, and nodded.

Confused, but also slightly infatuated by their charm, which cancelled out any suspicion.

They made it through the revolving door and stepped out onto the sidewalk as a black town car with tinted windows slid to a stop in front of the building.

19

Together, they wasted no time.

Slater had a Beretta M9 in an appendix holster, and King had a Glock 23. Slater reached for the door handle as casually as he could, and at the last millisecond, when the door was halfway open, he wrenched the Beretta out in one explosive movement and slammed himself down in the seat next to Russell Williams. He pushed the barrel to the man's head, and as soon as he had effectively taken him hostage he swept his gaze over the interior.

It was a miniature limousine, with the seats forming a U shape in the back. There was a man behind the wheel, and an unassuming pasty man in a charcoal suit opposite Williams. Neither the unknown man nor the driver made a move to react. There was no violent opposition. Just quiet acceptance.

Like, *If this is the way it's going to go, then so be it.*

Slater said, 'We're good. All clear.'

Still outside the car, King said, 'Great.'

Slater put the Beretta back in its holster.

Beside him, Williams exhaled sharply. He'd been scared. Terrified, even. He knew Slater was a wild card, which meant he *was* desperate. Slater scrutinised the man. It seemed he'd aged ten years since Slater had last seen him. The close-cropped hair had always been flecked with grey, but now it was silver all over, and receding. Williams' slate grey eyes were a little less refined, a little more unfocused. His appearance was somewhat dishevelled. He'd been wearing a tie at some point throughout the day, but he'd ripped it off before arriving here.

His suit was creased, and too big.

Williams had lost weight.

Slater said, 'Move over. I brought a friend.'

Williams shifted across to the seats running along the side, and Slater scooted across to let King in.

The town car peeled away.

Slater said, 'This had better be good.'

'It's not,' Williams said. 'Not for me. Not for you. Not for anyone.'

'How the hell did they let you back into the government after Lynx imploded?' Slater said.

Williams narrowed his eyes, as if to say, *Really?*

King nudged Slater in the side.

Slater said, 'Right. They funded it in the first place.'

'It was my idea, but they gave me full approval.'

'And now you magically recognise the error of your ways?'

'I told you I have. It's up to you whether you believe it.'

'I don't — not yet, at least.'

Williams said, 'Your friend's talkative.'

An attempt to inject some camaraderie back into the atmosphere. An attempt to kill the tension.

King used his massive frame to lean across Slater and

shove Williams against the town car's window by wrapping a hand around his throat.

King said, 'You got something to say, little man?'

Williams gasped for breath and shook his head.

The other guy — the pasty one — looked tense. But he didn't move to interfere.

King let go.

Williams gasped for breath, and Slater gently elbowed King back into his seat. 'That's enough.'

'What the fuck was that for?' Williams gasped.

King said, 'I think kids deserved a childhood, that's all.'

'Look, I understand that you're both—'

'Speak,' Slater snarled. 'You wanted us here. Now you have us.'

'Okay, okay, okay.'

King jabbed a thumb in the direction of the unknown man. 'Who's this guy?'

'Turner,' Williams said. 'He's my aide.'

'Why's he here?'

'Because he has a near-photographic memory and I need every detail of this goddamn thing correct when I tell you. And I trust him.'

'Turner,' Slater said, nodding at the man.

The guy nodded back.

He didn't say a word.

The driver said, 'Boss.'

Softly.

Barely audible.

Slater heard it.

King heard it.

Williams didn't.

The town car coasted to a stop at a giant intersection somewhere in Manhattan. Neither King nor Slater had been paying attention to the direction they'd been travelling, so they weren't sure exactly where they were. They'd been focused on sweeping for anything suspicious. Now, they both stiffened as they heard the driver speak.

Williams pressed on, oblivious. He said, 'Look, there's some serious shit happening in the government right now behind closed doors, and I think I've opened a can of worms. I think—'

'Boss,' the driver said, louder.

Williams looked up. 'What?'

'Might have a problem.'

'What do you mean — might have a problem?'

'Car behind us isn't acting right.'

Several things happened at once. The atmosphere tightened up, tension constricting the air. Slater spun around in his seat, but he saw nothing except headlights. King burst off his seat and slumped down beside Williams. He wrapped an arm over the man's shoulder, withdrew his Glock, and pressed it to Williams' ear.

'If you're trying to disguise this little traffic stop as a spontaneous ambush, it's not going to work.'

Williams gasped and went pale as the barrel skewered its way into his ear canal. He said, 'This isn't an ambush. I don't know what this is.'

King said, 'You're a bad actor.'

Slater wasn't looking at them anymore. He wasn't even paying attention to the conversation. He was looking in every direction at once, hyper-alert, hyper-reactionary, ready to fight for his goddamn life at the slightest provocation.

Maybe it was all a false alarm.

Maybe not.

The driver said, 'Boss,' again without turning around.

'What?!' Williams barked, white as a ghost.

King kept the barrel pressed into the side of his head.

The driver said, 'Dead ahead. A car ran the red light. Big long sedan. Coming right for us.'

'Fuck,' Williams said.

Slater wasn't sure whether he believed it.

The timing was awfully convenient for Williams.

He hadn't told them a thing yet.

Then Turner reached into his jacket lining and came out with a switchblade, and he lunged.

Not at Slater.

Not at King.

At Russell Williams.

20

The driver muttered a sharp, 'What the fuck,' as Turner dove across the cabin.

Slater intercepted him, crash-tackling him into the opposite seats. The impact knocked his head *hard* against Turner's shoulder. Under the suit, the man was all skin and bone, which almost made things worse. Slater felt a sharp *crack* in his skull and his neck pitched violently to one side, and he thought that it was all going to come to an end. A simple mishap, an unintended collision, and his entire fifteen-year career crashing into the dirt...

But it didn't end there, because Turner was jumpy and overly nervous. He clearly had some sort of combat training, because he threw an elbow at close range, and he put his entire body into it, twisting at the waist and opening his mouth in a wide snarl as he overcompensated. If it connected it might have done real damage, but things were unfolding too fast, and it sailed on harmlessly by.

Slater punched Turner in the nose, head-butted him in the mouth, scythed an elbow up into his chin, and finally separated himself from the seats and kicked him in the chest hard enough to break his sternum.

The aide slumped to the seats, broken and bloody, and Slater stripped the switchblade from his hand and stabbed him in the throat.

Then he bounced back, breathing hard, and assessed the situation.

'Jesus Christ,' Williams said. 'What did you do?'

Slater held up the knife. 'You didn't see this?'

Williams blinked hard. 'He had that on him?'

The silence said everything.

King took the gun barrel away from Williams' ear, turned to Slater, and said, 'Well, we need to keep him alive.'

'No shit.'

Then the driver said, 'Boss! Car's stopped in front of us.'

'We're boxed in?' Williams said, pale and in shock but still able to process information.

Turner's body bled profusely over the seats in front of them.

'Think so,' the driver said. 'What the fuck is going on back there?'

'Can you go around?' King said.

'Not anymore.'

'Why not?'

'You see this shit?'

Slater peered through the open partition. There was a sedan with tinted windows parked horizontally across two lanes of traffic. Horns were blaring, and drivers were gesticulating, but it wasn't going anywhere.

Something bumped them from behind.

Hard.

Slater twisted in his seat and saw the bright headlights behind them buried in their rear bumper. The impact nudged them forward into the car in front, trapping them tight.

'Do we get out?' King said.

'Uh...'

'Slater!'

'I'm *thinking*.'

King tightened his grip on his Glock, and Slater brandished the Beretta at the ready.

Both of them exchanged a tense, measured glance.

Syncing their decision-making skills. It was the subtle, subconscious connection that those who had seen war together shared. All the quibbling, and politics, and disagreements, and trivial matters — it all fell to the wayside, replaced by intense focus.

They entered that mode now.

King said, 'Williams.'

'Yes?'

'You scared?'

'I thought this would happen.'

'I need you to explain, briefly, and succinctly, exactly why you called us here. Because you might not get another opportunity.'

Williams said, 'There is an active operation within the U.S. government to destabilise our economy and bring about—'

He abruptly stopped talking when bullets smashed into the window right next to his head. The glass was bulletproof, and all three of them knew it, but Williams recoiled all the same. Even Slater and King flinched involuntarily, but Williams almost dove to the floor of the town car out of fright.

Growing irate, King said, 'Keep talking!'

'Look, all I know is that people are being paid off left,

right and centre, and I can't tell you who's doing it because I don't know. But what I can tell you is that within the next couple of weeks, two separate events are being planned, and when I stumbled across—'

As Williams spoke, Slater saw the lane beside them clear up — the sedan at the front had backed up a few feet to allow the cars through. They sped off one by one, desperate to flee the war zone. And it left the town car wide open for—

'Down!' Slater roared. 'Get the fuck down!'

Too late.

Williams wouldn't shut up, because King was sponging information out of him as fast as humanly possible, so he didn't notice the oncoming tank on wheels. It was a big 4x4 with a jacked-up suspension and a massive bull bar. It had its lights on high beam to blind and disorient. King saw it coming and dove for a seatbelt and wrapped the strap around his upper body in one fluid movement. Slater did the same, but at the last second he reached for Williams.

He didn't make it.

21

He got his fingers around Williams' suit jacket when the truck hit them in the side, and the violent lurch practically concussed all three of them.

Thankfully, King and Slater had spent a lifetime learning how to absorb impacts, often in live situations. So they cradled up and prevented themselves getting whiplash as the car screamed in protest and went up on its side, and all the windows groaned and bent and shattered, like grenades popping one after the other, and the sheer force of everything unfolding at once nearly hurled them out of the vehicle through the jagged window frames.

Slater felt Williams spin away, wrenched out from between his fingers, then he had to close his eyes — there was glass everywhere, whipping around the space like it was a centrifuge, and there was blood and heat and deafening sound and pain.

The town car came to rest on its roof, and Slater didn't even stop to *consider* that he was too injured to continue. He figured he was bleeding, and bruised, and perhaps had a couple of broken bones, but he wasn't paralysed, so he let go of the seatbelt and dropped away from the seats and shimmied out of the car.

Turned out that King had the exact same idea.

In seconds, they were both free from a wreckage that should have killed them.

The power of adrenaline, and training, and compartmentalisation.

They looked at each other for maybe half a second in total, then figured out where they were.

They were still in the intersection — now closer to the middle. Traffic was trying to disperse, but it was typical New York chaos. There was gridlock, and that led to horns blaring in a grotesque cacophony, and people screaming, and civilians abandoning their cars. And there were gunmen in between the vehicles — dark mysterious shapes, brandishing rifles. At least five or six of them.

Everywhere.

Anyone else would have caved.

Anyone else would have surrendered on the spot — outnumbered, outgunned, injured, stranded in the open.

Slater had the Beretta in his hand in a heartbeat, and he shot the first enemy silhouette he saw through the gap in the guy's combat helmet. The bulky figure had his visor flipped up, because it was dark, and the bullet *thwacked* home between his eyes and snapped his head back and he dropped out of sight between two small hatchbacks.

Slater said, 'Split up. I'll get a rifle and give you cover — you try and get Williams out of there.'

'Yeah,' King muttered.

Slater sprinted for the row of cars where he'd seen the first dead enemy drop.

He was a different person. There were *no* thoughts running through his head. His life was forward movement, and he felt the same supreme concentration falling over him. Because if he died, then he died, but until that happened he would fight until the last breath.

Because what the hell else was there to do?

So he ran through the most dangerous stretch of open pavement — his vision blurring, the shapes around him threatening to materialise as armed men wanting to rip his head off.

But they didn't.

The wild rollercoaster ride was over and he made it to the cover that the banked-up traffic provided. He ducked low, out of the line of sight, and a volley of shots cracked through the air above his head.

He dropped to his stomach, shocked by the proximity of the bullets, and crab crawled the last few yards to the dead mercenary. The guy was big and decked out in combat gear, and the rifle lay across his chest.

Slater scrutinised it.

And his heart skipped a beat.

It was a Heckler & Koch HK417 with a 20 inch barrel, a telescopic sight and a detachable bipod.

Identical in make, model, shape and size to the guns they'd taken out of the crates.

No time to think. No time to comprehend what was happening. No time to speculate on how it all connected. It *was* all connected — he knew that much — but anything past that emptied from his mind. It wasn't necessary to the situation at hand, and he'd trained his body and mind to focus only on what was important.

So he snatched the HK417 off the body and worked at lowering his heart rate. If he was shaky and panicked and terrified — as *anyone* would be in the middle of a war zone — he wouldn't be able to make use of the telescopic sight the way he knew he could.

He stayed low, and figured out his next move.

22

King spotted the armour-clad silhouettes sweeping across the rows of traffic, like a nightmarish vision come to life, then ducked behind the overturned town car.

He was still obscenely vulnerable, but Slater had already made his mad dash for cover, and King wasn't about to follow suit. They'd have their guns trained on that path, anticipating their targets making a run for it.

But no-one did, and an uneasy silence played out.

Well, not a *true* silence, as the sounds of civilian panic were still resonating through the city streets, but King had long ago learned to tune that out. The screams and the horns and the general uproar were like an eerie choir floating up to the heavens, but he didn't think about that. He thought about anything that could make a difference to his general wellbeing — like bullets.

But there were none, apart from the initial shot that Slater had fired at the start of the carnage.

And that proved their adversaries were efficient.

They were also brazen as hell, allowing this to unfold on the streets of New York. If it was anyone who had a stake in public wellbeing, they would have saved it for a more secluded location.

This was someone who didn't give a *shit*.

Someone who needed Russell Williams dead yesterday.

King dropped into a crouch amidst shards of glass and peered inside the destroyed interior of the town car. He saw the driver slumped upside down in his seat, suspended by the belt. The man's face was a bloody mask, and his skull looked dented.

Dead as nails.

He was beyond saving.

King turned his attention to the main compartment, and saw Williams lying there in a bloody heap.

He was semi-conscious.

Barely lucid.

But at least he was alive.

'Williams,' King barked. 'Get out here, now.'

'The glass...' Williams moaned.

He was cut bad, bleeding from several deep gashes, pouring the stuff out. And, to make matters worse, he was surrounded by a sea of shattered glass fragments whichever way he turned. Getting out of the town car would be a painful and laborious process. But it needed to happen, and it needed to happen *fast* if he wanted a chance of making it out of this alive.

'You're going to get cut,' King said. 'That's inevitable. Please get the fuck out of the car.'

Williams' head lolled around on his shoulders like it weighed a hundred pounds. The man lifted his glassy eyes to meet King's gaze and said, 'It's...'

'What?'

'It's the Chinese.'

King stared at him.

Then a shower of bullets riddled the town car from the other side. Most ricocheted off the armoured chassis, sounding like deafening *thwack-thwack-thwack*s in King's eardrums, but a couple made it through the window frames. One of them bounced harmlessly off the dented and twisted roof, but the other blew Russell Williams' neck apart in a shower of gore and blood and bone. He managed a final, desperate moan as he looked down at his own anatomy.

Then he died.

King punched the side of the car.

Purely out of rage.

He might as well have shattered all five of his knuckles. He didn't feel a thing. Not physically, at least. Mentally, he was overwhelmed with helplessness. The fact that Williams was dead highlighted his poor positioning, and his overall lack of strategy for what would come next, and...

And a million other things.

He was in serious, serious danger.

He adjusted his grip on the Glock and calmed his shaking wrists. Then he peeked over the top of the town car and saw the dark silhouettes fanning out tactically across the traffic, spreading out.

He had no idea what to do.

He ducked below the line of sight, and rode out a few bullets passing over his head.

He peeked again.

This time, one of the silhouettes turned and fired on his comrades.

King smirked.

He'd seen the same thing in Russia — a long, long time ago.

Will Slater, wearing a combat helmet to disguise his identity, unloading rounds into the other hostiles.

23

S later wasn't exactly comfortable.

There was blood all over the inside of his visor, having pooled out of the bullet wound in the head of the man he'd killed. But that was a small price to pay for the mass hysteria and confusion he created when he spun around and fired two shots into the nearest man, three into the second closest, and four into the third closest. A tiered firing system, constructed in his own head to make up for the increasing distance and therefore the increasing likelihood he'd miss with a couple of shots.

But he didn't, so he killed three of the hostiles in a bloody fury, and the others ducked for cover as they realised how rapidly the tables had turned.

Slater had been crouching there amidst the traffic, and realised the solution was in front of him the whole time. He'd twisted and turned and pulled until the armoured helmet slid off the corpse, and shoved it on his own head. The dead man's leather jacket had come next, covering his civilian attire. There was no time to unclip and steal the Kevlar vest the guy was wearing, but that didn't matter. He looked like the rest of the hostiles at first glance, and that was all he needed.

He'd snuck down the line of cars and slipped between two pick-up trucks, heading behind enemy lines as they searched for him near the front of the queue. Then he'd sprung to his feet in an instant, well away from his last known location, and flashed a thumbs-up sign as if he'd been searching below the cars in his sector.

No-one had reacted.

No-one had shot him for his troubles.

Which was all that mattered.

Thirty seconds later, he killed three of them in a single flurry.

Now, King sprinted out from behind the wreckage of the town car and made a beeline for Slater's position. Slater was surprised King had figured it out so quickly. Then he remembered a gold mine on the Kamchatka Peninsula in the Russian Far East, where he'd used the exact same tactic to slaughter a group of mercenaries holding King hostage.

And he smiled to himself.

They knew each other better than they knew themselves.

King leapfrogged the hood of a stationary car and slid to a halt alongside Slater. 'How many more?'

'Three, I think. Get down.'

They both ducked, and Slater said, 'Next aisle there's a rifle. I killed a guy right nearby. You need it?'

King shook his head. 'Three left, you said?'

'I think.'

'I'll take one, you take two.'

'Right.'

And that was that. They sprinted in different directions,

now on the offensive, and there was a world of difference when Jason King and Will Slater stopped playing defence.

It was over in seconds.

Slater had the superior firepower, so he went straight for the two hostiles clustered close together a couple of rows away. He checked to make sure they were still taking cover, then leapt over the hood of a low sedan. Then he vaulted into the rear tray of an abandoned pick-up truck, fully exposing himself to the field of fire, and waited for the pair to take the bait.

They came up first, because they felt safer as a pair. The lone guy King had been tasked with taking care of stayed down, somewhere to the left. Slater kept his peripheral vision open, but he trusted his intuition. There was a certain flow to combat that only a veteran could get the hang of. When you spent enough time in situations that would kill almost anyone else, you got used to the chaos, and you learned to thrive in it.

When the two enemies materialised, one by one, Slater worked his aim left to right. He stayed tactical, and kept his shots measured. He hit the first guy in the throat with three rounds, and when he spiralled away Slater turned to his comrade and shot him through the crook of his elbow. The second guy had his chin tucked to his chest, so it was the last remaining option that was most likely to incapacitate.

It worked.

The bullet blew out the back of his elbow and his arm swung loosely away from the rifle. Not separated from his body, but close to it. There was no hope of the guy managing to hold the Heckler & Koch rifle in his other hand and squeeze off shots that were anywhere near accurate. So Slater paused to make sure his own aim was steady, and took his sweet time, which in his world was less than a second.

Then he finished it with a shot through the neck.

He looked instantly for the last man, and spotted him.

To his credit, the final enemy had heard his comrades under fire and decided to leap up and join the firefight. He came up with his HK417 raised, and Slater took a beat longer than usual to get his own aim focused. He felt a sharp pang of terror, and thought, *Did I screw this up?*

Then Jason King launched over the hood of the car right next to the guy and thundered a boot into his chest, smashing him into the vehicle behind, probably damaging internal organs, and when the guy went down in a crumpled heap King planted the Glock's barrel against the back of his neck and pulled the trigger.

In the sudden quiet, King looked all around at the carnage they'd unleashed, then to Slater in the bed of the pick-up.

'Run,' he said.

24

They immediately split up.

Slater shed the leather jacket and leapt out of the tray, keenly aware of the possibility of long-distance shooters, and he tucked his collar up over his features, feeling intensely vulnerable.

Thankfully, when chaos erupts on civilian streets — particularly fully automatic gunfire — no-one looks for the source of the commotion. They cower away, they cover their eyes, they run in the opposite direction. So it's awfully confusing when the gunfire dies down and the authorities ask what they saw. Because they didn't see a thing. They weren't looking. They were trying to survive.

Slater used that to his advantage, and in seconds he was enmeshed in the waves of civilians teeming away from the disaster zone. He hunched his shoulders and let fear spread across his face and tried to minimise his target area, and suddenly no-one knew the difference between a trained killer and a scared bystander. He ended up running along-side a thirty-something woman clutching a child, and they made brief eye contact.

The woman moaned, 'What's happening?'

'It's going to be okay,' Slater said, but he made sure his voice wavered.

He didn't want her remembering anything out of the ordinary afterward.

If he appeared too calm, it'd stand out. She'd remember later.

He peeled away and ran down a laneway between two buildings, passing a couple of hole-in-the-wall cafés closed for the evening. Then he came out on another street — less chaotic, but still sporting signs of stress from the nearby incident. The traffic hadn't come to a standstill yet — it was too far from the initial contact point — but there were traumatised pedestrians everywhere, weaving between cars with no concern for their safety. In their minds, the moving traffic was the least of their concerns.

They'd seen a war break out in their city.

The world as they knew it was coming to an end.

Slater weaved this way and that, zigzagging left and right. He orientated himself, realised he was in Lower Manhattan, and charted a course for the Upper East Side.

He was sore, and he'd suffered an adrenaline dump, and fatigue was already setting in. The after-effects of the crash were beginning to present themselves. His left arm hurt like hell, and there was blood running down his chest, and he realised his neck was cut. There was blood on the top of his head, too, and the left side of his face was numb and puffy. All these symptoms rolled over him like a tidal wave, and he steadied himself against a parked car.

Then someone slammed into him from behind.

He skewered his legs into the ground and twisted on the spot, ready to break his own knuckles with a staggering punch to the face, but it wasn't a hostile. It was a scared teenager, probably sixteen or seventeen, with no colour in his face and terror in his eyes. He mumbled an apology and tried to weave around, but Slater gripped him by the shoulders.

'Kid,' he said. 'Danger's over. Breathe. You're going to live.'

The kid breathed.

Slater could see some semblance of colour return to his face. Right now he wasn't playing the part of a civilian blending in, but he was worried the teenager might sprint into oncoming traffic in his panic.

'Walk fast, but pay attention,' Slater said. 'Get yourself home, and stay there until you're calmer. Then go to the authorities and tell them what happened. Got it?'

'Yeah,' the kid said, gulping back air. 'Okay. Thanks.'

'Go.'

They walked in opposite directions. The exchange meant nothing in the grand scheme of things, and Slater had technically compromised his position, but then again, it could mean everything.

That was the way the world worked.

He might have saved a life.

He crossed the street and went straight into another darkened laneway. No-one saw him. Everyone was focused on whatever the hell had happened a couple of streets over. Closing his mouth tight and holding his breath, Slater bent down and heaped dirty water off the alley floor into his palms. He splashed it over the top of his head, and scrubbed until the blood was gone. He still had a couple of scratches on his neck, and the knocks to the head had been severe enough to discombobulate him, and his muscles and bones hurt like hell, but outwardly he was presentable.

He stepped back out onto the street and walked hard.

It took him thirty minutes to stride back to his building on the Upper East Side. He kept his head down and his demeanour a little tighter, a little more aggravated. He didn't want to be bothered — he needed to get home and regroup without interference. He passed a group of millennials hunched over their phones, whispering quiet concerns to each other. Immediately, Slater knew that rumours of an incident had already hit the news cycle.

Right now, the perimeter would be secured, and the bodies would be counted, and sweeps would be made. But there was no-one alive to interrogate, and he and King had disappeared from the scene in seconds. There would be mass hysteria and confusion, and for the next few weeks the incident would be played to death on national television. Speculation would be made, theories would be posited, and talking heads would bicker back and forth about who had died, and why, and where the culprits had gone.

Like clockwork, everyone would move on.

Tragedy would strike, then be swept away as soon as it grew stale.

Slater powered into his lobby and nodded to Victor, one of the night staff.

'Hey, Will,' the guy said. 'You okay?'

Slater paused. 'Yeah. Why?'

'There's some weird stuff coming out on the news. Something happened in Lower Manhattan.'

Slater raised an eyebrow. 'Something like...?'

'Reports of shots fired. That's about all I know.'

'Goddamn. Crazy times we live in. I didn't see anything. On that note — have you seen Jason?'

Victor shook his head. 'I haven't seen him yet. You expecting him?'

'Thought he'd be here by now.'

'I hope he's safe.'

'Me too, Victor,' Slater said. 'Me too.'

25

K ing stepped into the lobby, breathless, and took in the scene.

The sweeping reception was empty, save for a familiar face behind the main desk. Victor was tapping away at his computer, hunched over the keyboard, and there were beads of sweat on his forehead. The Hispanic man barely fit into his suit — he'd bought it a couple of years and a few dozen pounds ago and hadn't made the effort to get a new once since. But they were all the regular sights, and nothing seemed out of the ordinary, aside from the strange amount of perspiration on the concierge's brow.

Slater was nowhere to be found.

King approached the main desk and said, 'Hey, Victor.'

Victor looked up. He was pale. He was doing his best to disguise it, but King could tell.

'Oh, hi, Jason,' he said. 'How are you?'

'Can't complain.'

'That's good,' Victor said. 'Have a great night.'

King paused, and decided to loiter. Victor squirmed uncomfortably in place. They were incredibly subtle gestures, but King picked up on each and every one of them. He was still hyper-alert after the shootout, and although the cocktail of stress chemicals had faded away, he was still attuned to anything unusual.

'Everything okay, Victor?' King said.

'Fine, sir. Just ... some personal problems. I'll be okay.'

'You sure?'

'Yes, sir.'

'You've never called me sir.'

'Sorry, Jason. Got a bit of bad news. Family matters.'

'Want to talk about it?'

'No, thank you.'

'Right. Well, I hope everything's okay.'

'Yes. Thank you.'

King nodded and tapped a palm on the hard shiny surface of the counter, wondering what else he could say.

But there was nothing.

And he figured, *Shit happens.* Loved ones die. Terminal diagnoses are made. Life goes on. It wasn't right to be inherently suspicious about everything. Victor was acting jittery as hell, but what could it have to do with anything that had happened earlier that night? Unless news of the slaughter was already doing the rounds.

Maybe that was it.

Chaos on the streets of New York.

Victor, worried that gunmen would stream through the revolving doors and riddle him with bullets where he sat.

King said, 'It's okay, Victor. You're safe here.'

The man looked up. 'What?'

'You're safe.'

'Okay.'

King shrugged, at a conversational dead end, and moved past the reception desk. 'Have a good night, buddy.'

'You too.'

King stepped into the private elevator for the upper floors, swiped his keycard, and punched in his floor number. The doors whisked closed, and he shrugged off a feeling of discontent. It had been a long night. The crash had smashed him to and fro, bruising and bloodying him under the shirt.

He needed the isolation and protection of his apartment, to unwind and take stock of his injuries, and figure out their next move.

The elevator shot upward.

As soon as the elevator doors closed on Jason King, Victor hyperventilated in the lobby.

He *hated* this. He'd never been put in a position like this in his life. Every morsel of fear in his body was thrumming inside his head, making conversation impossible. He'd been told to act normal. He couldn't do it. It was the simplest request in the world, and he still couldn't do it.

He wondered if they would kill him too, at the end of this, for his abysmal failure.

Because maybe now King knew.

Victor wiped sweat off his brow, straightened his creased suit, and tried to control his breathing.

And thank God he did.

Because ten minutes later Will Slater stepped into the lobby, suspecting nothing awry.

He rehearsed the lines in his head.

I haven't seen King yet.

Then he said, 'Hey, Will. You okay?'

27

King immediately knew something was up.

The elevator doors opened, and he stepped out quietly and looked around.

He and Slater had their own private corridor running from one front door to the other. It was architecturally superb, with an angled ceiling and one-off art pieces adorning the walls, and imported Egyptian rugs, and a muted minimalistic colour scheme. They'd modelled their own penthouse suites after the building's style. Whoever had developed the structure had meticulous attention to detail.

But it wasn't right.

There was a different vibe. He couldn't pinpoint it, but even with a raging headache and an aching body, even deep in the throes of an adrenaline crash, he could sense someone had been here that hadn't belonged. Call it intuition, call it a subconscious eye for detail. Call it whatever you want. But as he crept toward his front door, he listened to the insulated silence and knew nothing was at it seemed.

Victor had been hiding something.

King knew it instantly.

Everyone can be bought.

He reached his door, and laid a hand flat on it, then knocked three times. He kept it subdued, as if he was embarrassed to be disturbing the owner.

Like he was staff.

He took the Glock out of his jacket, and pressed the barrel to the peephole, and prayed that whoever was on the other side was that stupid.

He counted to three, and pulled the trigger.

There was a dull explosion of fragments as he shattered the thin membrane of glass. Someone on the other side of the door let out a primal grunt. It was uncontrollable — they'd been hit by a hollow point bullet, and it must have blown out the back in an explosion of blood and muscle and tissue. King figured he'd hit them in the shoulder.

He slammed his other palm down on the handle and shouldered the door inward.

He hit someone on the other side.

The guy was smart, but King was overwhelming him with offence. Most people, after taking a hollow point round to the shoulder, fell to the floor in unimaginable pain. This man had thrown himself at the door in a last-ditch attempt to stop King forcing his way in.

But King was two hundred and twenty pounds of fast-twitch muscle fibres, and he was angry as hell.

So he floored the guy with a single shove, using the door as a battering ram, and he aimed the Glock through the narrow sliver of space and put another hollow point round through the man's head. He took in crucial details — the guy was big, muscular, wearing combat attire, and had a balaclava over his face.

All King needed to see to understand his life was on the line.

Then he reached out and gripped the handle and pulled the door closed again, and he waited with bated breath and his heart in his ears.

Sure enough, dull reverberations sounded on the other side of the door — thudding impacts, but without the accompanying roar of unsuppressed gunfire. The penthouse suites were fully soundproofed, and both King and Slater's front doors were bulletproof. They valued their privacy, and it helped them sleep at night if they knew they were sleeping in a fortress in the sky.

But that hadn't stopped the building's staff from betraying them.

King decided to wait. He held the Glock at the ready, one hand underneath his wrist, the other fixed on the door.

He had endless patience.

It turned out that the enemy didn't.

They must have thought he'd ran away, which proved their lack of experience in live combat situations. You could simulate the real thing all day long, but it wasn't the real thing. Maybe in theory they'd told themselves they could wait it out, but now they were stuck staring at their comrade's corpse in the entranceway, wondering how to proceed.

So, before long, someone came and hurled the door open.

King put one in his forehead.

28

The balaclava exploded, and the guy collapsed before he could even get a shot off.

King stayed right where he was.

No-one else materialised. King looked past the two bodies, to the luxuries of his penthouse and the sweeping view of Central Park at night. Nothing looked out of place. It wasn't a robbery. It was too calculated for that.

Icy awareness trickled up the back of his neck. He knew there were more. But they weren't showing themselves. He'd bought a ticket to a waiting game, and he couldn't stay out here in the corridor for long with the knowledge that Victor had betrayed him. It wouldn't be difficult to send reinforcements up in the private elevator by overriding the security protocol.

No, King had to go inside.

Like a warped haunted house walkthrough.

Danger at every corner.

With his heart rate spiking he stepped over the threshold and gently pushed the door shut with a boot. It got quiet. Real quiet. The penthouse was soundproof, and there wasn't a peep from the bustling New York streets below.

There wasn't the din of traffic, or the ambient murmur of pedestrians, or even the soft whispering of the elevators moving up and down in their shafts.

There was nothing at all.

And he couldn't hear anything important — especially not the subtleties of a trained hostile trying their best to wait in silence. Gunshots in an enclosed space were ruinous for your hearing — he was surprised his eardrums were still somewhat intact after a lifetime of neglecting his senses.

So with a high-pitched whining in his head, and a pounding ache behind his eyes, and the overall fatigue pressing down on his body, he moved forward.

Into the unknown.

There was a slight reaction to his left. He twisted that way and had the Glock trained on the corner of the wall before he'd even registered what he'd heard. He spotted the toe of a combat boot sliding back out of sight — there was a man there, lying in wait, and he'd begun a reckless charge before realising King was too close. Then he'd retreated.

King lowered his aim and shot the guy in the foot.

The hollow-point round exploded, and blood sprayed, and an involuntary wince sounded.

King froze, plagued by indecision.

Push forward? Throw yourself into the open?

This might be the best chance you'll get to capitalise.

But he waited, and thank God he did, because a guy in a balaclava with an automatic rifle — some sort of carbine — reared around the right-hand corner. They'd been waiting there, one on each side, for him to come barrelling in. When he hadn't, they'd been forced to improvise.

King almost jumped out of his skin, but he controlled

his instinctive responses and pivoted in that direction, smoothly lining up his aim.

He fired.

The bullet struck the throat, and went right through.

There was too much unfolding at once. King hadn't been keeping track of the number of rounds left in the clip. That thought distracted him as the guy went down, and prevented him from doing what he should have done *immediately,* which was to pivot back in the other direction.

So when the guy on the left-hand side charged, King didn't adjust his aim in time.

The guy barrelled out into the hallway, operating on pure adrenaline. It must have been coursing through his veins, because his combat boot was a downright mess. A few of his toes no longer existed, and the hollow-point round had speared a jagged hole in the top of the boot. But he charged all the same, and swung his identical carbine around to put a few rounds through the top of King's head.

King saw this, and panicked, and lunged forward himself, and they met at close-range like a clash of titans.

Skin met steel and flesh met bone, and no-one got shot in the chaos.

The carbine fell from the man's grip, and King raised his Glock to plant the barrel against the guy's forehead, but a meaty forearm cracked him in the mouth and he tasted warm blood and felt his head rattle on his shoulders like a bowling ball. He tried to readjust his aim but his equilibrium was all off.

The Glock was no longer in his hand.

He didn't know where it was.

He was dizzy.

Nausea rose up in his chest.

The guy in the balaclava ducked down, wrapped his

arms around King's mid-section, locked his fingers together behind the small of his back...

King knew exactly how to take a man to the ground. He knew all about wrestling technique, and single-legs and double-legs and proper leverage and technique.

He wasn't used to being on the receiving end.

The guy in the balaclava picked him up — all two hundred and twenty pounds of him — and lifted him high and slammed him down.

King felt dizzying vertigo, followed by the *crunch* of the back of his head against the ground.

Now there was an angry hostile on top of him, straddling him, raining down punches.

If one got through, it'd knock his brain into Neverland.

King pressed his forearms to each side of his head, adopting a defensive posture, and protected himself as best he could.

And terror rippled through him as knuckles crashed down against his face.

29

S later gave himself a rudimentary medical examination in the elevator.

He figured he'd be okay. His headache was a little worse than usual. He was a seasoned veteran of knocks to the brain, but the way his skull had been smashed to one side in the car wreck unnerved him. He had a deep ache running down each side of his neck, and a dull throbbing in the temples. His ribs hurt when he inhaled, but they weren't broken. There were cuts and gashes on his arms and face, but they were superficial. Overall, his condition would have put nearly anyone in the hospital for a few days, but to someone like Slater it was nothing out of the ordinary.

He needed a drink.

And he needed to rest.

Then he needed to figure out what the hell he and King had got themselves into.

The elevator reached his floor and the doors whispered open. He made straight for his place, but before he went in he stopped and glanced at King's closed door a few dozen feet further down. It was closed, but he could only see a sliver of it from this angle. He paused for a second, and listened out for anything awry, but the corridor was dead silent. Besides, his ears were ringing from the skirmish earlier.

He unlocked his door, and picked up something on the edge of his hearing.

Like the muted grunts and impacts of a fistfight.

But it was barely above a whisper, and he chalked it up to his own imagination and stepped into his penthouse.

He stood inside the threshold and let the door swing shut. The sudden isolation, coupled with the luxury, threw him off. He wasn't used to this. Most of his prior combat experience took place in harrowing, desolate locations across the globe. He usually had no resources to rely on, no comrades to operate with, and no backup to call in. He had to fight, and bleed, and win. Then the real battle started. Because he had to extract himself from hostile territory, often relying on ration packs and water purification tablets to survive.

Now he stood in a fifteen million dollar penthouse and tasted clean air, and he had cold water in the tap and healthy food in the fridge and a memory-foam mattress to sleep on. He strode over to the glass and pressed his palms against it, taking the weight off his feet. He stared out at the city lights.

He smiled.

Maybe this was the life for him.

He'd cheated death, and fought for his life, and overcome the odds for the millionth time...

... and now he could recover optimally.

He went to the fridge and pulled out two plastic containers filled with pre-prepared food. He ate chicken and braised beef and smoked salmon and avocado and spinach and salad. No dressing. Nothing unhealthy. He washed it down with thirty ounces of water and stumbled over to the Eames chair by the window. He sat down, put his feet up, and sunk into a deep meditative trance, visualising his cells healing themselves, repairing his body, preparing for the fight to come.

Because there would be a fight to come.

Without question.

There always was.

And he continued sitting there without making a sound, unaware that on the other side of the soundproof wall his closest friend was battling for dear life.

30

King absorbed most of the punches across his forearms and wrists, but the guy hit like a truck. He had considerable technique, and a muscular athletic frame to boot, so there was a certain savageness to his strikes. He wasn't blowing all his energy in the first few seconds, unloading everything in wild looping haymakers. Instead he was dropping fists like pistons, trying his best to split the guard, but King was equally as talented at defending.

King caught a mouthful of knuckles as the guy drilled a punch straight between his forearms, ricocheting off his front row of teeth. He grunted in unrest, and realised he'd need to try something drastic to escape the position or risk getting beat to death where he lay.

He couldn't roll onto his stomach, because the guy was practiced in jiu-jitsu — King could tell from the way his adversary utilised leverage. The guy would reach down and slip an arm around King's throat and choke him out in less than a minute.

But in a flash, King realised that was his only option.

There was nothing else.

He had to accept the choke, and hope to salvage the situation as his enemy's arms were busy choking him unconscious.

It was possibly the most terrifying experience of his life.

With a racing heart he rolled onto his stomach, and the guy adjusted to straddle his lower back. Then it was a simple matter of slicing the arm around King's throat and pulling tight.

King felt the crushing pressure of the forearm against his trachea.

And the devastating squeeze that followed.

He gasped and opened his mouth wide and clawed for air, but he knew it was useless. Not only couldn't he breathe, but the damage being inflicted with each passing second was obscene. His face turned red, and his eyes felt like they were set to pop out of his head, and the muscles in his neck screamed for relief, and his windpipe begged and pleaded for mercy.

Amidst all that, King clambered to his feet, wearing a two hundred pound backpack that was simultaneously choking the life out of him.

Ten seconds.

He gave himself that long before it all went dark.

Claustrophobia reared its head — he couldn't shake off the grip, and they both knew that whatever happened now would lead to the end of the fight. Either King would go to sleep, or he'd manage to pry the hostile off his back, whereupon the guy's arms would be so fatigued from squeezing that he would be helpless to defend himself.

King stumbled a few steps, testing the weight of the guy on his back, and he realised he could handle it. Anyone else would have slumped to their knees, but King had unnatural strength forged from a lifetime of power-lifting.

So he thundered out of the hallway, into the open-plan living area, and spotted a spiderweb of cracks spreading in all directions across the floor-to-ceiling glass.

The bullet I fired through the peephole, he realised.

It had gone through the first guy's shoulder, and before it lost momentum it had embedded itself in the reinforced glass window.

The pane hadn't cracked, but it was close to it.

King remembered a vital, crucial detail.

It came to him in a flash, even though he was losing oxygen and brain cells and consciousness all at once.

And he took off at a mad sprint.

Straight for the glass.

He ran, crossing the empty space.

The crushing pressure around his throat got tighter. Because the hostile on his back could see what he was about to do, but he couldn't let go, because then he'd almost certainly die. The guy must have thought his enemy had turned suicidal, so he was using every morsel of animalistic strength in his body to choke King unconscious before he reached the window.

Unfortunately for both of them, King had willpower that belied what most considered humanly possible.

Even with his vision going dark and his limbs going weak, he kept running.

He slowed, of course.

But he still had enough momentum.

He threw himself into the window pane, twisting in mid-air so they hit the glass side-on instead of impacting face-first. The glass gave out, and it was a horrifying sensory experience. King had limited consciousness left, but he felt overwhelming terror all the same.

What if it's not there anymore? he thought.

Then you die.

There was a *bang* as the glass shattered, then the even worse sensation of falling, and his stomach fell into his feet, and he started to plummet hundreds of feet to the sidewalk far, far below—

But something broke their fall.

31

S later heard the concussive thud, so faint and imperceptible that he thought it must have been his imagination again.

Then he opened his eyes and looked out the window, and saw glass fragments spiralling down to the ground, and saw two bodies plummeting.

Then crashing into *something* outside his field of view.

One of them was Jason King.

'What the f—'

He leapt to his feet, and pressed his face to the glass.

There was a service elevator hovering at the top of a shaft erected on the exterior of the building. Its roof was square, and littered with remnants of a shattered window pane, and there were two bodies sprawled out across the surface, both only inches from a fatal fall on either side.

Slater had seen the elevator resting there a couple of dozen times before, but watching the brief period of freefall had sent his stomach into his throat all the same. He'd been convinced King's recklessness had caught up with him, and that the man had leapt to his death. Briefly, his world had come crashing down around him.

Now he didn't spend any time watching what would unfold. That wouldn't help anyone. He realised that King had been in his apartment the whole time, and that Victor had lied to him, and that there had been a fight to the death playing out next door, and he turned and sprinted for the hallway.

He snatched up one of the HK417 rifles on the way, and checked it was ready to fire. He quickly slotted a couple of spare magazines into his pockets, then lifted the stock to his shoulder and threw the front door open.

He came face-to-face with reinforcements.

There were four of them, clustered together in a tight group — horrendous tactics for a close-range shootout. But they must have figured there was little point spreading out when their main focus was getting into King's apartment as quickly as possible. Which meant their initial plan had already fallen apart.

You're a tough motherfucker, King, Slater thought.

They hadn't been anticipating any sort of resistance from Slater's apartment, so when he unloaded an entire clip of ammo into their bodies, they were helpless to fight back. They hadn't been in position to adjust their aim on the fly, so they went down in a heap as he riddled them with bullets.

He leapt over their twitching corpses and ran flat-out for King's door.

On the way, he ejected the empty magazine using the release lever and chambered a fresh one. Then he pushed down on the handle and shouldered the door inwards, figuring the only thing left to do was to stand on the precipice of the shattered window frame and put a bullet in the head of King's enemy — if the hostile hadn't already been taken care of.

So when the door struck a large object halfway along its trajectory and rebounded into Slater's face, he jolted in surprise.

There was a grunt, and Slater realised he'd hit someone across the upper back when he'd thrust the door open.

More reinforcements.

A party that had already made it to the apartment, as King had leapt out the window with his current enemy.

There's too much happening at once.

Slater's Heckler & Koch rifle was now pinned awkwardly between his chest and the edge of the door, and when he dropped another shoulder into the door it didn't budge. Now the twenty inch barrel was a disservice, and he wished for something sub-compact, like an MP5. But he had to work with what he had, so he smashed the same shoulder again and again into the door until it finally caved inward, nearly tearing off its hinges despite the expensive materials.

The hostile blocking the door stumbled backward — another big guy in a balaclava, decked out in combat gear, with an M4A1 carbine in his hands.

They were only inches apart, now that Slater had forced his way into the apartment.

It was a fight to the death in a space the size of a phone booth.

The guy tried to bring the barrel around to aim at Slater, but Slater saw it coming from a mile away. He reached out and wrapped a hand around the bulk of the gun and wrenched it forward, throwing the guy off-balance. When he stumbled forward a step, Slater headbutted him on the bridge of his nose — an impact that a balaclava did little to absorb. The guy's nose cracked and Slater twisted into a spinning back elbow that struck him in the jaw, breaking more delicate bones in his face.

He stumbled back a step, and Slater found the space to raise his HK417 and put a single round through the guy's forehead.

He exhaled, shaken by the close-range brawl.

Then he remembered the reason he'd come into the apartment in the first place.

He sprinted for the open window frame, ignoring the feeling of vertigo in his stomach screaming at him to stop.

The wind howled in as he ran across the penthouse.

32

King and the enemy absorbed the impact equally. They both hit the top of the elevator on their sides, and they both lashed their heads against the metal, and they both rolled off each other with twin groans, crippled by dizzying waves of pain.

King figured he was a little worse for wear, considering he'd been perhaps a second away from blacking out. As soon as the arm came away from his throat, air rushed in, but the risk he'd taken to get the hostile off him had damaged him. He could already feel his throat swelling, and his jaw aching, and the muscles in his neck spasming as he lay on his back inches away from a precipitous drop.

If he were more lucid, his palms might have turned sweaty — being so close to plummeting to his death and all. But right now he could barely see his hand in front of his face, let alone his surroundings. He lay on his back and breathed cold air and felt the wind against his frame, and tried his best to recover.

Thankfully the guy in the balaclava was similarly incapacitated, semi-conscious from the brutal landing.

King blinked.

Sight returned.

The floating specks consuming his vision started to recede.

He gulped back a wave of pain and rolled onto his knees. *Now* he experienced the shocking vertigo. They were so high up, and there was nothing to prevent either of them toppling off the edge. No railing, no barrier.

The hostile clambered to his feet. Through the slit in the balaclava King saw his eyes were glassy, which probably put them on a level playing field.

For all King knew, his own injuries were fatal. Stress chemicals were coursing through him, masking how hurt he truly was, and there would be no way to know for sure until after the fight was over.

Better get on with it, he thought.

Woozy with fatigue and agony, he lunged forward and grabbed the guy by the neck. Hands reached up and locked onto his wrist, but he shoved the guy back all the same. One of the hostile's feet slipped off the edge, and King powered forward, desperate to finish the fight.

But he overcommitted.

The hostile deliberately went down on his other leg, getting closer to the metal surface to prevent himself falling. He went prone, and King lost the grip on his throat and almost tumbled head-over-heels off the edge. His stomach pulsed with pure fear, and he reached for the metal with palms slick with sweat. He found purchase and went down to a prone position too, heartbeat pounding in his ears.

He was inches from the endless drop.

Then the guy in the balaclava rolled over and kicked out, and smashed the heel of his boot into King's chest.

King skidded half a foot along the surface...

...but there was no more surface.

He caught a dizzying, heart-pounding view of the street hundreds of feet below at the same time as he snatched hold of the guy's boot and used it to drag himself violently back in the other direction, literal milliseconds before he would have toppled and fell.

Drenched in sweat, he gasped for breath as he rolled out of the way of another kick. This one glanced off his face, nearly shattering his nose into a dozen pieces. He used the momentum to spring to his feet, and the surface of the elevator pitched and swayed underneath him. He realised it was a figment of his imagination, but it drained him of energy all the same. He wanted nothing more than to get down on his stomach and make sure he didn't go over the edge, but he had to fight for his life instead.

Then he found his opportunity.

He was already on his feet, but the guy in the balaclava had the same idea. So the hostile was on his knees, about to follow suit, but King was in perfect position for a—

He threw a kick, ignoring the fear of balancing on one leg atop a rickety service elevator with the wind coming in strong. He used his shin like a baseball bat, and bounced it off the side of the guy's head, hard enough to kill a civilian.

But this guy was a trained killer in full survival mode.

He nearly went down in an unconscious heap, but something kept him upright, and all of a sudden he reached out with both hands and caught King's ankle.

Oh, fuck, King thought.

He tried to wrench his leg out of the man's grip, but the guy held on with vice-like strength. King hopped up and down on his other leg, off-balance, so close to the edge, so close to—

The guy stood up, still holding King's leg, and pushed his ankle toward the sky.

Making him do the splits in mid-air, throwing him all the way off-balance, sending him tipping back away from the—

Fuck it.

King committed to the fall, because he had no other choice. He executed almost an entire revolution as he tumbled backwards, and with two sweaty palms he clamped down on the edge of the elevator roof. His legs went over, spearing into thin air, and he found himself suspended by his hands. His heart pounded away in his throat, and he wasted no time hauling himself up over the lip.

But the guy in the balaclava was waiting.

The man stomped down viciously on King's left hand, almost breaking the fingers, and King's palm came away from the cool metal, already red and swollen.

Dangling from four fingers, he strained every muscle in his left arm and gripped through sweat and dirt. He was slipping, falling, and his heart was in his throat, and his stomach was in his chest, and the guy in the balaclava loomed over him and raised the same boot and brought it down and—

A bullet exited the guy's throat from behind.

King felt the warm spray of blood on his face.

Then there was a brief pause, followed quickly by displaced air washing over him. He flinched and bowed his head, thinking the final blow was still on its way, but the corpse pitched forward and toppled over him into thin air.

It plummeted hundreds of feet to earth with its dead limbs flailing.

King reached up and put his other hand on the edge as his grip was about to slip. He levered himself up, floating through a dream-like state, utterly spent from the exertion. His fingers hurt, his wrists hurt, his face hurt, his stomach hurt — everything ached deeply. When he managed to clamber over the lip and sprawled out on his back on the cool surface, he looked up to find Will Slater standing in the hole a couple of floors above the service elevator, looking out.

There was a HK417 in his hand.

King smiled through a mouthful of blood.

But his relief at being alive turned to mounting frustration.

Over the wind, he yelled, 'Took you long enough to show up.'

'The apartments are soundproof, remember?'

'Great.'

He closed his eyes and listened to the wind and wondered what the future held.

33

S later dangled the makeshift rope out the window, fashioned together from most of King's spare bedding. They were mostly bedsheets tied end to end, but they were sturdy enough to hold. He gripped the side of the window frame tight as he perched precariously on the edge of the building.

It was a long way down.

The end of the rope touched the roof of the service elevator, and King gripped it with two hands. He tried to haul himself up using his own strength, but he only made it a foot off the metal surface before tumbling back to his knees. He looked up, sighed, and shook his head.

Slater yelled, 'Hold onto it.'

King nodded, and gripped the bedsheet with white knuckles.

Slater snatched two handfuls of the material and started to haul it up manually. King was heavy, which made the effort difficult, but manageable. He could lift two hundred and twenty pounds with ease in the gym, but he'd never done it whilst trying to simultaneously balance on the edge of a precipitous drop. One moment of overcompensation and he'd topple forward, sending both of them plummeting to their deaths.

He pulled, and pulled, and pulled, and as soon as King was back inside the penthouse they both collapsed in mutual exhaustion.

Eventually, lying on their backs staring up at the ceiling grew old. Slater mustered enough energy to sit up, and he trained his rifle on the front door for a few beats, making sure there wasn't another wave of reinforcements on the way. But this was a civilian building after all, and to get up here they'd needed to bribe Victor — not to mention the rest of the staff — which meant they would be forced to scatter after they realised they'd failed.

With his gaze still trained on the door, Slater said, 'Looks like we need to go to ground again.'

King ran a dirty hand across his bloody face, wincing as he did so. 'Shame. I was getting used to a carefree life.'

'Wasn't exactly carefree.'

'Was about as close to it as we were ever going to get. Should have known it was too good to be true.'

'You think we'll be hunted again?'

'We killed over a dozen people tonight in one of the busiest cities in America. We'll be on CCTV somewhere. We don't have a choice. It's game over. Back to being ghosts.'

Slater sighed. 'What do you need from this place?'

King sat up, too, and he looked around. 'Nothing.'

'Not a thing?'

'Besides the essentials. Phone, wallet, false passport. That'll do it.'

'I'm the same.'

'Then what are we waiting for? I'd rather not get caught up here with this many bodies.'

Slater exhaled a long breath, and got to his feet. The uneasy truce they'd carved with the secret world was now gone forever. Back when he worked for Black Force, he'd been sent to hunt down and neutralise King in Corsica, a small island off the coast of France. All because King was causing too much trouble in his retirement.

Now the same principle would apply to them.

'We should talk to someone,' King said as they clambered to their feet.

Slater said, 'Who?'

'Someone in the government who worked with Williams. Someone who will understand.'

Slater shrugged, dejected, nihilistic. 'What the hell are we going to tell them? Sooner or later they're going to treat us like murderers. You think they're going to believe that—'

'Williams told me it was the Chinese,' King interrupted.

'What?'

'I tried to pull him out of the wreck, but they shot him. That was all he managed to say. He looked me in the eyes and said it.'

'The Chinese?'

King nodded.

'That could mean anything.'

King said, 'I know.'

Slater clenched his teeth. 'Why couldn't he have told us this shit straight away?'

'Because it was complicated,' King said. 'You could see it on his face. I'd wager he only knew half of it. Less than half. He'd stumbled across something, but he couldn't convey it accurately. That's why he brought his friend along.'

'That Turner guy,' Slater said. 'You think that was really his aide?'

'It was *someone*. Someone manipulative enough to

convince Williams he was needed. Who knows who he really was? We're strangers to that world. "Aide" could refer to a million things.'

'But it confirms the half-sentence he managed to get out before everything went to hell.'

'What'd he say? Something about destabilising the economy?'

'"An active operation within the U.S. government to destabilise our economy." Then he said something about two events being planned in the next few weeks. There was something else that he meant to say, but the crash cut him off.'

King said, 'Doesn't sound good.'

'Not one bit.'

A sharp *bang* came from the hallway, and they both twisted in an instant to meet the potential threat. But it was the wind blowing the door closed. Slater breathed out and looked at King.

'We need to go,' he said. 'We can discuss this later.'

King looked all around. 'I'm going to miss this place.'

'Are you, though?'

King shrugged. 'Not really. Trying to be sentimental, I guess. Figured it was worth changing things up for once.'

Despite everything, Slater managed a wry smile. 'You're never going to be the sentimental type. I don't know much, but I know that.'

King said, 'I could say the same for you.'

'Then who cares if we have to leave?'

'What's thirty million dollars worth of real estate anyway?' King grumbled.

Slater placed a hand on his shoulder and gently shoved him toward the door. King got the message. Slater figured he was still grappling with his injuries — they'd both taken several consecutive knocks to the head, and that could throw anyone off their baseline. They both strode for the door, and on the way out King snatched a few meagre possessions off the countertop — his phone, a passport, and an expensive leather wallet.

Slater said, 'I need those things, too. I'll meet you at the elevator.'

'The parking lot,' King said.

'Okay,' Slater said. 'I'll be five minutes.'

'It's going to take you that long?'

'There's someone I need to pay a visit to. I don't appreciate thin-skinned snakes.'

King nodded. 'Throw in a little something special from me, too.'

'I'd be happy to oblige,' Slater said, and made for his own penthouse.

34

The elevator was empty, and quiet.

Slater stood with his hands clasped behind his back, trying to detach himself from the barbaric skirmish. He was returning to civilisation, and he couldn't remain a savage. King was elsewhere in the building, heading for the lower levels, but after collecting the necessities Slater had made straight for the general elevator.

There was someone he needed to see in the lobby.

He wiped a few specks of dried blood off the top of his head, and scrutinised his appearance in the gilt edged mirrors. He looked okay, all things considered. He felt like shit, but that was manageable, too. He figured the hordes of mercenaries that had been sent to dispatch him felt worse.

Or, rather, felt nothing at all.

The silver doors whispered open and Slater came out of the elevator like a freight train. He didn't run — he strode with purpose, containing the black fury in his chest. He rounded the corner and there was Victor, his fat ass still planted in the same shitty swivel chair. Slater walked straight behind the reception desk and was looming over the concierge before Victor had even raised his head.

Victor looked up, his complexion pale and sweaty, and almost fainted.

Slater grabbed him by the back of the neck and smashed his face into the desk.

It left a red imprint on the wood where his nose impacted.

Victor recoiled back in his seat, bleeding freely from both nostrils.

Slater stood there, silently watching.

Victor screamed.

Slater reached out and clamped a hand down over his mouth.

'How much did they pay you?' he said.

He took his hand away.

Victor said, 'Nothing, man. Nothing. They threatened my kids.'

Slater nodded solemnly, then turned on his heel, as if to walk away.

He heard Victor audibly sigh.

He spun around violently and punched the concierge in the mouth.

Blood sprayed.

Slater said, 'It's almost like you forgot we were friends.'

Victor moaned and held his head in his hands.

Slater said, 'You don't have children, do you, Victor?'

The man went even paler still.

Slater said, 'Next time you sell me out to the highest bidder, make sure you've got a decent cover story in case it doesn't work.'

'Please, man... I thought they would win. I didn't want to get hurt.'

'Pathetic,' Slater snarled.

Then he said nothing further.

He stood there and waited for Victor to open his mouth.

Victor raised both hands and pleaded, 'Look, I don't have kids, Will, and I'm sorry for lying, but you have to understand that—'

Slater crouched down so he was inches from Victor's face and said, 'Think about what you did. You gambled on the risk that a team of highly trained killers would get the better of little old King and I. You came up short. You know what we paid for when we bought in this building? We paid for the guarantee that the staff wouldn't be slimy little weasels. You following what I'm saying?'

Victor started to sob.

'I'm going to leave you alive,' Slater said. 'Against my better judgment. But I want you to think long and hard about what you did. Then I want you to do better.'

'I promise,' Victor gasped, his brain probably flooding with indescribable relief. 'I promise, sir. I'm sorry that I underestimated you.'

'Here's a reminder,' Slater said.

He reached out, snatched Victor's hand in a vice-like grip, and bent three of his fingers back, one by one.

Victor moaned.

'You think this is harsh?' Slater said.

'Yes,' Victor moaned.

He realised his idiocy all at once.

'You know what's harsher?' Slater said.

'I know — I know. I am so sorry.'

'Harsher is a bullet in my head, and in the head of my friend.'

'I know.'

Slater said, 'It's not a mercy that I'm leaving you alive.'

Victor paused, furrowing his brow.

Slater said, 'How many men did you send up there?'

'I think seven in total. There was the first three, then four new guys ran in, so I sent them straight up. I was scared, man.'

'We left them up there. You're not cleaning up seven bodies on your own, are you?'

Victor gulped. 'I don't know how I could.'

'You're going to have to explain to your bosses how they got up there in the first place.'

Victor bowed his head.

Slater said, 'King and I are going to go ahead and disappear off the face of the planet, which is what we're best at. You won't be able to pin this on us. It's up to you to justify what happened.'

When Victor lifted his gaze to meet Slater, there were tears in his eyes.

'I thought you were a good guy, man.'

'This isn't a Hollywood movie,' Slater said. 'I'm not noble to a fault. If someone betrays me, it pisses me off.'

Victor said nothing.

Slater said, 'Good luck.'

Then he turned and walked out of the lobby. He got in the private elevator and punched the button for the exclusive garage.

The doors whispered closed.

35

King gently lowered the mysterious black box to the rear seats of his Mercedes coupé.

He couldn't leave it behind, after all.

Then he placed two HK417 rifles and almost a dozen spare magazines beside it, and slammed the door closed.

Altogether, there was enough illegal firepower and unknown tech in the car to implicate him as an international terrorist. But he didn't think about that. He got in the driver's seat, fired up the engine and swung the car around to line up with the doors to the private elevator.

Then he sat in silence in the deserted lot, stewing over what had happened. He considered hypotheticals. He thought about what he could have done differently. He grew restless over the injuries he'd sustained.

Eventually the thoughts turned oppressive, so he employed the mindfulness meditation technique Slater had taught him en route to New Zealand all those months ago. As usual, it worked like a charm. He focused on the breath, and he cleared everything else from his mind, then... there was nothing. Just a deep trance-like state, and his surroundings blurred as he filtered the external world out.

He jolted out of his meditation when Slater threw the passenger door open and ducked into the coupé.

Slater said, 'Victor got the message.'

'Did you kill him?'

Slater shook his head, chewing his bottom lip. 'He's an ordinary guy. He was threatened. Survival instinct kicked in. Us or him.'

'What'd you do?'

'Roughed him up a bit. He deserved that, at least.'

'You're a better man than me.'

King threw the Mercedes into gear.

They drove in silence to the exit. King wound down the window and fished his keycard from his pocket, but he hesitated before placing it against the panel.

'What are the odds Victor's cut our cards off?' he said.

Slater said, 'Not a chance.'

'You seem confident.'

'I broke him.'

'Did you?' King said, raising an eyebrow. 'I'm thinking it'd be fairly straightforward to call the cops as soon as you left.'

'You're angry that I didn't do things your way,' Slater said. 'You're angry I have a conscience.'

'I've got a conscience,' King grumbled.

'Scan the card.'

King rested the keycard against the digital display, and it lit up a brilliant green.

The boom gate swung upward in front of them.

'See?' Slater said.

King tossed the keycard out the window with a flick of the wrist. 'Won't be needing that again.'

As they rose to street level, Slater twisted in his seat to give the building a final glance.

He said, 'Damn shame.'

King slowed down as the Mercedes' nose dipped into the laneway, facing the opposite wall.

'Left or right?' he said.

Slater said, 'Doesn't matter. Any direction that gets us out of the city limits as fast as possible. We need to lay low for a while. The middle of nowhere sounds appealing right about now.'

'A while?' King said. 'I think you're underestimating what sort of fallout this will have.'

'Trust me, I'm not. It's going to be bad.'

King went right.

He sliced the coupé onto a four-lane road leading out of the Upper East Side. There was still some traffic, but they'd been preoccupied for a couple of hours upstairs, and it was now close to two in the morning.

Neither of them expected to sit bumper-to-bumper for long.

The hunch proved correct. They went south-west and made for the Lincoln Tunnel, and there was no resistance to be found. They whispered into the tunnel and the overhead lights flashed by.

Under the soft artificial glow, Slater said, 'Are you hurt?'

King didn't respond for a beat.

He was thinking.

Then he said, 'I think so.'

'How bad?'

'We'll find out when we get a couple of beds for the night. Until then I don't want to talk about it.'

'I can drive.'

'No,' King said with authority, and Slater understood.

Slater said, 'Are you concussed?'

'I might be. If I'm not driving, I might fall asleep. And that's something I can't afford to do right now.'

If you fall asleep in the throes of a concussion, it can lead to irreversible brain damage. This concept had been hammered into Slater for his entire career, and he wasn't about to forget it.

Nor was King.

King said, 'What about you?'

'I'm fine.'

'No you're not.'

'In comparison, I'm okay.'

'We're both roughed up. There's no point denying it.'

Slater said, 'I think we need a couple of nights off.'

'I've got the mother of all headaches.'

'Me too.'

'So we find a motel. We use false names. We rest up. We get to work figuring out what Williams was on about, and whether his conspiracies have any merit.'

Slater raised an eyebrow and looked over wordlessly.

King said, 'What?'

'You think his conspiracies don't have merit?'

'Correlation isn't causation.'

'I know. But what are the odds?'

'Slim.'

They let the silence unfold, and followed the Lincoln Tunnel all the way up to I-95. King turned his attention to making sure they weren't being tailed, and out of the corner of his eye he noticed Slater's head droop.

He woke him back up and said, 'Are you concussed?'

'I don't think so.'

Slater dropped back into a slumber.

King followed I-95 north and merged onto I-80, spearing

west, heading deeper into the mainland. Eventually Slater opened his eyes, took stock of his surroundings, and said, 'Pennsylvania?'

King said, 'I plan to find the most desolate motel in the state. Got a problem with that?'

'Not in the slightest.'

Slater closed his eyes again.

King focused on the road for close to an hour.

Then shit hit the fan.

36

S later stirred as soon as King said, 'Will.'

He understood that tone.

He was aware of the danger it implied.

Because for something to concern Jason King, it had to be damn serious.

Slater twisted in his seat and rubbed a hand against his puffy face. He flashed a glance out the rear window.

There was a car on their tail.

But they were making it unbelievably obvious. There was no attempt to be covert — their pursuers must have figured King and Slater were wise enough to spot any tail eventually.

The pair of headlights was uncomfortably close, literally tailgating them, and they weren't even on I-80 anymore. King had pulled off, taking a dark decrepit exit, and now he ran a red light at a giant empty intersection and went down a rural road, pushing the Mercedes up past eighty miles an hour.

The car stayed right behind them.

Slater reached back and hefted one of the HK417s off the rear seats.

He said, 'Don't bother running for much longer. They're not going to leave us alone. Best we get this over and done with.'

King said, 'Wait a minute.'

Then he found what he was looking for — the vast empty parking lot to a closed shopping mall, almost the size of a football field. He spun the wheel and raced in. There were streetlights dotted intermittently through the parking lot. The spheres of light radiating from the bulbs fell sharply away, leaving gaps of darkness between the lights. King pulled the Mercedes to a halt between two of the lights, whisper-quiet, and Slater was out of the car before it even stopped moving.

He ran flat out with the HK417's stock pressed into his shoulder under cover of darkness.

The car tailing them made the same turn into the parking lot.

Their headlights illuminated Slater right in front of them, and they slammed on the brakes.

There wasn't time to exchange gunfire.

Slater rounded to the driver's door, wrenched it open, and hauled the driver out, simply pulling the guy over the top of his seatbelt. If not for the empty palms and the terrified expression on the man's face, Slater would have shot him where he sat. Instead he dumped the guy down on the asphalt on his back and pressed a boot down on his throat.

Then he aimed the rifle through the interior at the passenger.

There were only the two of them in the car.

The passenger was a woman, sitting bolt upright, with her slim shoulders tucked back and her chin held high. She was blonde and had a smooth pale face. Her blue eyes bore into Slater, scrutinising and analysing him even as he aimed a rifle at her head. Her expression was severe.

She said, 'You're not going to shoot me.'

He said, 'Pleased to meet you, too.'

'Put the gun down.'

'Who's this guy?' he said, pressing his foot down harder on the throat of the man underneath him.

'My driver,' the woman said.

'I can see that.'

'He's not armed.'

'Of course he's not. He'd be dead if he was armed.'

'Are you trying to impress me?'

'I'm trying to work out what you want from me.'

'Not just you. Your friend, too.'

Slater said, 'I'm going to search you, one by one. I'll be quick, and I won't be handsy. I'm not looking for a lawsuit at the end of this.'

Despite the tense circumstances, she managed a smile. 'Don't let the charm disarm you. Many men have underestimated me in the past.'

Slater said, 'I was about to say the same about my own rugged good looks.'

Then he hauled the driver to his feet and conducted a quick frisk search. Satisfied, he shoved the guy away. Then he trained the gun back on the woman and said, 'Out.'

She pulled the door handle and slid gracefully out of the passenger seat. Slater rounded the hood and looked her over once. She was wearing a tight skirt that left nothing to the imagination, and he could tell right away she wasn't carrying a piece.

He said, 'Okay. You're good.'

He swept the rear seats, popped the trunk, and found nothing of alarm.

He lowered the gun.

Jason King materialised from the darkness.

'Didn't see you there,' the woman noted with nonchalance.

Clearly he'd been expecting to startle her.

He stood in the shadows, barely illuminated, and scrutinised the pair.

Slater said, 'They're all good.'

King said, 'They're following us. They're not all good.'

The woman said, 'Drop the tough-guy bullshit, please. And you don't need to run, by the way. Wherever you were planning on staying, it's probably a whole lot more comfortable back in New York. No-one is coming for you. The government doesn't care.'

'And what makes you so confident about that?' Slater said, clutching the rifle a little tighter.

She turned her intoxicating gaze to him and said, 'Why, because I'm the government, darling.'

37

They all stood there in a square, with each of them taking a predetermined corner.

Regarding each other warily.

King didn't know what to think.

Finally, the woman said, 'In the car, please, Foley.'

The driver slunk back to the vehicle, got in the driver's seat, and gently closed both doors.

Now they were a triangle, and the woman sauntered right up to the pair of them, throwing her hair over one shoulder. Up close, King could see her better. She was in her late thirties, but could have easily passed as younger. She was confident and physically fit and in no hurry to explain herself. The calmness she exuded was somewhat reassuring, but he'd been duped by charm before. He wasn't about to open up in the slightest.

She said, 'I'm Violetta.'

'I'm—' King started.

She said, 'I know. Jason King. Will Slater. Great. Introductions over.'

'You work for the government?' Slater said.

'In a roundabout way.'

'What's that mean?' King said.

'You know damn well what that means. It means I can't give you a business card, and you can't look me up in the system, but all that does is confirm that I'm at the right pay grade to have the right conversations. Are you both following along?'

'We follow,' Slater said.

'Doesn't mean we believe you,' King said.

She said, 'Cut the bullshit. You are both hot property right now in the secret world. The train of order has well and truly derailed. Have you seen the news?'

'We don't need to check the news,' King said. 'We were there.'

'You were at one isolated event. There's been five in total. All of them carried out simultaneously.'

'Executions?'

Violetta nodded.

'Who?' Slater said.

'Depends who you ask. If you ask the news, the victims were wealthy private citizens with no connection whatso-ever to the government. Russell Williams was killed in a violent shootout in Lower Manhattan, and the other four were executed in their homes in Washington D.C. It's a shocking coincidence, but a coincidence all the same. Just an unfortunate crime spree.'

'And if we ask you?'

'They were five men who'd united to usher in a new era of ethics to the secret world. This was an endeavour that was largely kickstarted by Mr. Slater's quest to interfere with every damn program he didn't like the look of.'

'I did it once,' Slater said.

King said, 'You think it's his fault you and your people

were so shit at keeping the Lynx program under wraps?'

A look flashed in her eyes, but it seemed playful enough. She stared at King, and tapped him once on the chest, and said, 'I like you.'

He said nothing.

Slater said, 'So this is supposed to reassure us?'

She raised an eyebrow. 'Of what?'

'Five people get killed across the country by hired guns. They're the ones trying to rein in the government's more reckless ideas, and now you — the government — come to us asking for our help. And you're expecting us to believe that you didn't have something to do with it?'

'If we had something to do with it, you'd both be dead,' she said. 'And I don't exaggerate that point in the slightest.'

King said, 'You haven't tried yet.'

She almost laughed. 'Sounds like if there's anything that needs reining in, it's your own egos.'

'I'm sure you heard about what we did tonight,' Slater said.

She shot him a withering look. 'Killed a dozen mercenaries? Congratulations. We have endless soldiers capable of that — of course, that's all hush-hush. You think just because Black Force died we got rid of the principles that started it? There's still anomalies out there. Warriors with reaction speeds you couldn't dream of. But you two are something special, which is why we left you alive, and which is why we didn't retaliate when you stuck your nose where it didn't belong. Five of the top dogs listened to you, and tried to change the way the secret world operates.'

'Then why are they dead?'

'We don't know,' Violetta said. 'But there's some serious shit going down and I don't trust a soul right now. Which is why I'm turning to the pair of you. Because you're on the outside, and I think you've established your moral superiority. So you're going to help me get to the bottom of this.'

'Why?' King said.

Slater nodded. 'I'd prefer to get to the bottom of a bottle, if you don't mind. Helps me sleep better.'

She said, 'For a million reasons.'

'List some,' King said.

She said, 'First, you both care about your country. You're not going to stand back and watch it fall to pieces, which I fear is exactly what's going to happen in the next few weeks if you don't help me *immediately.*'

They stood there in silence.

She said, 'Secondly, there are grieving families here in New York, and over in Washington. Kids who watched their fathers get slaughtered in their own homes. Wives who got the news from the authorities. And that was just five men. Five good men ... but only five. It's about to get a whole lot worse. I think the good eggs in the secret world were executed so there's no-one with a level head to turn to when the country starts imploding.'

Neither of them spoke.

She said, 'And lastly, I'll kill you both if you even think about disobeying me. You don't understand the resources I have access to. Do *not* test me. We've let you get away with endless irritations up until now, but that will all change the second I lift a finger. We'll wipe you off the face of the planet and no-one will know the difference.'

No response.

She said, 'Decision?'

King looked at Slater.

Slater looked at King.

They turned back to her.

King said, 'We'd be happy to help.'

38

Like something out of a dream, they rocketed back toward the city they'd fled from.

King drove again. Slater stewed in the passenger seat. They backtracked through the same sequence of turns, and when the New York skyline loomed up from the horizon, he shifted uncomfortably in his seat.

Unrest swept through him.

He said, 'I fucking hate this.'

King said, 'That makes two of us.'

Slater turned in his seat and looked out the rear window. 'They're a reasonable distance behind us.'

'So?'

'We could make a run for it again.'

'Then what?' King said. 'She knows everything about us. She's government. And she's telling the truth. I've spent enough time in this bullshit game to understand that, and you have too. She *will* turn all her resources on us if we refuse to help.'

'Not if the country's falling apart like she insinuated.'

'Would you want to be on the run if what she was

suggesting comes true? Would you want to sit back and watch that happen?'

Slater said nothing, but the silence said everything.

King said, 'Me neither.'

Slater said, 'I doubt she has the capacity to carry out what she promised.'

They'd talked for close to fifteen minutes after the initial agreement, hashing out certain details that made both of them apprehensive to return to New York. But Violetta had made promises, and they'd tentatively agreed. Both of them doubted what she'd said would come true, but they were willing to take the risk of finding out for themselves.

King said, 'I wouldn't put it past her.'

'What if we walk back into handcuffs? That's the way I'd do it if I was the law. Send someone like her to rope us back into the city limits.'

'She was telling the truth before,' King said. 'If they wanted us out of the equation, they would have killed us in rural Pennsylvania. Why risk the justice system for a pair like us? You know what would happen if we spilled everything we have swimming around in our heads at trial?'

Slater nodded. 'Okay. Let's find out.'

They navigated to the Upper East Side in the early hours of the morning. A mad sense of déjà vu rolled over them. They went down the same laneway, and pulled up to the same metal gate, and Slater scanned his keycard on the same panel because King had thrown his out the window.

The door to the parking garage lifted.

The darkness beckoned.

They looked at each other and shrugged in unison.

What do we have to lose?

Slater nodded forward, and King drove through. There was no-one waiting for them. The garage was as desolate as when they'd left. They parked in the same space, and Slater got out and hefted the rifles out of the rear seats. King took the black box in one hand and locked the car, and they got in the private elevator and rode it back up to the penthouse level.

When the doors whispered open, the bodies in the corridor were gone.

Where a vast puddle of blood had previously stained the carpet, there was a plastic sheet draped across the floor. It was weighed down by a yellow sign reading: CAUTION: CLEANING IN PROGRESS.

The walls were spotless, and the ceiling was spotless — both had been previously flecked with blood.

Slater followed King into his apartment.

The bodies were nowhere to be seen, and the shards of glass scattered across the living area had disappeared. The penthouse reeked of industrial cleaning products. There was a temporary plastic sheet pulled tight across the jagged hole in the side of the building where the window pane had once rested. So it was quiet — the wind battered the sheet, but didn't spill through into the apartment.

King said, 'Jesus Christ. What world are we operating in?'

'One where we're above the law,' Slater said. 'You know what this reminds me of?'

King shot him a worried glance. 'Been a while since I've been employed.'

Slater shivered. 'We're not employed.'

'The government are doing us favours. We're expected to return the same goodwill. Sounds a whole lot like we're employed.'

'We'll get through this, then we'll work it out. One step at a time.'

'I've heard that before.'

'Yeah, you have. And we're still alive and kicking.'

There was a knock at the door.

They both turned to look.

King muttered, 'Maybe not for much longer.'

Slater strode to the door and opened it. Violetta was standing there, sans her driver. She had her hands crossed gracefully behind her back, and she swept past them without invitation.

'Nice place,' she said, whistling at the view.

'Don't play the fool,' King said.

She turned, raising an eyebrow. 'You think I've been here before? I mean, I told you I liked you, but I don't recall—'

King scowled and swept a hand over his surroundings. 'That's not what I meant. Was this your clean-up crew?'

'I wasn't with them,' she said. 'I don't get my hands dirty. I was chasing after you two, remember?'

'So what the hell is this?' Slater said. 'Why meet us here? Why not just—?'

She raised a hand, and he stopped talking. Not many people had that effect on him. She was confident, sure of herself, supremely calm. She stared at him with those blue eyes and said, 'It seems the pair of you don't recall the finer details of your careers.'

'Maybe we'd prefer not to remember those times,' King said.

'You remember the way it worked, though,' she said. 'You had a single point of contact, and as far as anything else in the secret world was concerned, you were kept in the dark. You didn't need to know how the leviathan operates then, and you don't need to know how it operates now. You're foot soldiers, after all.'

'No we're not,' King hissed.

She looked at him with nonchalance. 'Call yourself what you want. For all intents and purposes, you are operatives for me — and, by extension, the United States government.'

'Not permanently.'

'Of course not.'

'Okay,' Slater said, holding his palms up toward her. 'So the ground rules are established. You make all our problems go away. We help you — but only because we're genuinely concerned, too. So this works for all parties involved. So ... what now?'

She said, 'How about a drink?'

39

They sat in a makeshift triangle — King and Slater at opposite ends of the giant sofa, cradling tumblers filled with whiskey, and Violetta in the armchair, cradling an expensive glass of wine.

Slater sipped from his glass, treating it as a rudimentary painkiller.

It burned on the way down.

He relished the relief, but made a mental note not to go overboard.

Violetta said, 'I suppose I should introduce myself a little better. I know far more about the pair of you than you do about me.'

King shrugged. 'We're used to that.'

She said, 'I'm Russell Williams' successor. It's my responsibility to manage a certain wing of black operations. I've been sponging information about how to deal with operatives, how to keep a level head, and how to analyse information on the fly for the better part of ten years. I got into this world relatively young, and I'm not just a pretty face. However, I've been told that my aura can be reassuring when communicating with operatives in the field, so this is what I do for now. I'll be relaying information from the upper echelon to you both, and making decisions about what to do with you over the next few weeks. Any questions?'

Immediately, King said, 'Who were your parents?'

She cocked her head. 'I'm sorry?'

'You heard me.'

'I didn't say anything about—'

'I know,' King said, 'but the "pretty face" comment was extraneous. You threw it in there because you have something to prove. And it's not because of your looks. You got into this world young, but no-one gets into this world young unless they're black operatives with certain specific talents willing to get themselves killed in the line of fire within a year. Then their death wish and natural abilities trump the age factor. That doesn't happen with the pen pushers like you.'

Violetta said, 'You're good.'

'I'm right.'

'My father was in this business. He had connections. He believed in me and no-one else did, so they gave me the equivalent of an internship in their world. I did well. So they kept me around. I did even better. So they promoted me. That kept happening until I got to where I am today.'

King said, 'I didn't mean to offend you. I was just curious.'

'If anything offended me,' she said, 'I wouldn't be in this industry, would I?'

Slater said, 'Okay, okay. We're all best friends now. What do you have to tell us?'

'Only what you need to know,' she said. 'So, first things first—'

King interrupted, 'Williams told me it was the Chinese.'

Silence.

She said, 'Did he now?'

'He did.'

'What else did he tell you?'

'That there's an active attempt to destabilise the economy. Possibly even ruin the country forever. Now, I'm just a soldier who can react faster than the average grunt, so I guess I'm not able to picture what that would entail. Could you give us a better idea?'

Violetta chewed her lower lip, and flashed an uncomfortable glance out the window. She said, 'I wasn't supposed to get into that until a long way down the line.'

Slater sat forward, and gave her a withering stare. 'Are you the best successor to Russell Williams?'

She said, 'Excuse me?'

'You were going to withhold that from us? Do you have any common sense? You come here asking for our help, then plan to drip-feed us crumbs of information?'

King placed a hand on Slater's chest and shoved him back into the sofa. 'Cool it.'

'Don't fucking touch me. I don't need to be here. I can see you're in love with her, but—'

'*Enough!*' Violetta snapped.

Both of them shut their mouths.

She said, 'Seems like you've forgotten how it worked your whole career, Will. You were never given all the details. Only the essentials. Seeing that you both already know the juicy part of the intel, I'll give you all the details against my better judgment. But don't even think about pulling anything like that again. Understood?'

Slater stared at her, but rationality prevailed.

He nodded his approval.

Violetta said, 'We've discovered a number of traitors in our ranks over the last few weeks. They didn't intend to get caught, but we got them all the same.'

King said, 'Who?'

'Various members of our community. Men and women who were privy to very exclusive, very sensitive information about the inner workings of the government. They're the ones who run the show behind the scenes. And they know how to manipulate certain people to get what they want. So they kicked that information out to whoever was paying them to betray us—'

'The Chinese?'

'It's a real possibility.'

'Based on what?'

'That's a story for another time,' she said. 'It's long, and I don't have time to—'

'Where are you sending us?' Slater snapped.

'Sorry?'

Slater leaned forward and said, '*Where* are you sending us? Right now. This instant.'

She said, 'In the morning I'll have you—'

Slater pointed a finger in her face. 'There we go. In the morning. So you've got time to tell us a story.'

She sighed and settled back in the armchair. She maintained the same severe expression, but she regarded them with a cool respect.

She said, 'You two don't fuck around, do you?'

King said, 'Tell us a story, Violetta.'

She said, 'What do you know about *ying pai?*'

40

King furrowed his brow and said, 'I've heard that term before.'

Slater said, 'Oh, fuck.'

King looked sideways. 'You know it, then.'

Violetta said, 'They're hardline Chinese nationalists. *Ying pai* means hawks, or eagles. They're high-ranking officials in the government who want the best for China and China alone.'

'We've got our fair share of those in our own ranks, though,' Slater said. 'I don't think hardline nationalists are exclusively a Chinese thing.'

'But we're not dangerous,' Violetta said, 'because we're on top. And we've grown fat and lazy by being on top for so long.'

'Speak for yourself,' King said.

She shot him a glare. 'You know full well that the pair of you aren't representative of the whole country. If there were a thousand clones of you running America, we'd be on top forever.'

King scrunched up his nose, and Slater shook his head.

She said, 'I know, I know. You're not politicians. You're not bureaucrats. But it's the principle. You're men of focus.'

'Right.'

'And so are the *ying pai,*' she said. 'They're the ones who see their entire lives as a long-term strategy to usurp the United States at the top of the food chain. They don't care when it happens, as long as it happens. They're supremely patient, and they'll do anything to eventually establish dominance.'

'That's a bit theatrical,' Slater said. 'Let's say they simply want the better economy. Why would King and I care about that? We've never given a shit about political squabbling and bickering. If they have a bigger GDP than us, that doesn't matter to us. We're not die-hard patriots, as much as you might like to think we are. We help *people*. At an individual level.'

Violetta said, 'And if their strategy to take over stayed long-term, I wouldn't have approached you.'

'So they're getting serious,' King said. 'And they're getting serious fast.'

'Because they've sensed weakness. They've smelled blood in the water. We have every reason to believe that they're moving fast, and any effort to establish dominance fast is always going to lead to chaos.'

'War?'

'Of course not,' Violetta scoffed. 'Could you imagine another World War in this day and age? There'd be nothing left in the aftermath.'

'So something subtle, then.'

'Subtle by today's standards, in the sense that it won't be explicitly traced back to China. But it's going to be one hell of a ride to the bottom if they pull it off.'

King connected the dots, piecing together what

Williams' had told him with the information Violetta was feeding them. 'They're going to crash the economy?'

'That's step one.'

'What's step two?'

'We don't know.'

'Where are you getting your information?'

'Trust me,' she snapped. 'There's a limit to what I can say. You both *have* to believe me. I will tell you everything we know, but the process we used to get all this information is multi-faceted. I would literally be here all night explaining it.'

King relented. 'Fine.'

She said, 'We've plugged the leaks established by the traitors as best as we can, but we're reeling. We're not sure exactly what got out, and what didn't. So believe me when I tell you I don't yet know where I'll be sending you. We're scrambling to figure out exactly what's coming, but when we do, you'll be our enforcers.'

King and Slater said nothing.

She said, 'Do either of you have a problem with that?'

King said, 'How bad is it going to be if we refuse?'

'We have our own operatives,' she said. 'But ... they're not you. And you might as well take our protection, because the *ying pai* know about you.'

'They do?' Slater said.

She said, 'Who do you think ambushed you tonight?'

'An army of white men. Maybe a couple of Hispanics thrown in the mix. I didn't see any Chinese.'

'They were hired guns,' she said. 'We've already identified most of the bodies. All ex-Army vets who were wronged or slighted in some way during their time in service. They had a collective subconscious vendetta against our country, and they were helped along by enormous bribes from unknown parties.'

'You're sure of that?' King said.

'We're already looking at the accounts of the first body we identified. He was dishonourably discharged three years ago. And three days ago, an account in the Caymans wired him four hundred thousand dollars.'

'Shit,' Slater said.

'They knew about you both, and they saw the opportunity to take you and Williams out in the same blow. Three birds with one stone. When it didn't work, they sent more men to your penthouses.'

'Who's to say we're safe here, then?' King said.

'Because now you have my help,' Violetta said. 'This building's now on the highest security level imaginable. The old staff are out. If anyone comes for you, I'll know about it in a heartbeat.'

Slater said, 'Why did they kill Williams and the other four bureaucrats?'

'Because those five men were the voice of reason,' Violetta said. 'This is the preliminary phase. They're actively trying to wipe out our countrymen who pose the best chance of being able to coordinate a resistance. Then they'll go to the next phase.'

'The economy?' King said, skeptical.

She said, 'We have information on that, too. But one step at a time.'

'And what might that first step be?' Slater said. 'Sounds like this is one big clusterfuck right now as you're trying to work out what's happening. You're plugging leaks, and you're lynching traitors. What are *we* supposed to do?'

She turned to him. 'Funny you should ask. There's

something we need to do, and I think you're the perfect volunteer to oversee it.'

'And what might that be?' Slater said.

'Do you remember Ruby Nazarian?' Violetta said, and she watched Slater intensely for the flash of surprise in his eyes that she knew was coming. 'She's going to need your help.'

41

The last time Slater had seen Ruby, she'd had a knife pressed to Russell Williams' throat.

He said, 'We've got history.'

'That's putting it mildly,' she said. 'You two were romantically involved, no?'

'I wouldn't call it that.'

'You slept together.'

'Says who?'

'Her. When she debriefed us about everything that happened in the wake of the Lynx-program disaster.'

'You tracked her down?' Slater said. 'You know where she is?'

'She's safe,' Violetta insisted. 'She was hiding from us for no reason. We don't care what she does. We recognised our mistakes with the Lynx program, so we sent her on her way. But we wanted to know what happened first. That was one of the requirements.'

'"Tell us or we'll have to kill you?"' Slater said.

Violetta smiled. 'Something along those lines.'

'Where is she?'

'Tulum.'

'Mexico?'

'We gave her a payout. For the trauma we inflicted. We felt the need to compensate her.'

'You took away her whole childhood and turned her into a remorseless killer.'

Violetta cocked her head. 'I didn't do anything. Russell Williams was behind that.'

Slater said, 'So she's living large?'

'I don't think so. As far as we know, she has a spartan hut on the beach. Near one of the jungle resorts. She's living a simple existence. Trying to find her way in the world. Build some sort of normal routine.'

'And you want me to go pull her out of that?'

'You're going to have to,' Violetta said. 'If you care about her.'

'Why?'

'We think the *ying pai* are targeting anyone at the elite level of government black operations. And we just found out that one of our traitors leaked her identity and location to an unknown party. It was... requested.'

'Why?'

'You tell me,' Violetta said, flashing him a curious look. 'How good is she in combat?'

Slater remembered her slaughtering government agents in a dark basement in the North Maine Woods using only a knife. She was lethal — impossibly agile, both graceful and violent at the same time. She was one of the most effective live operatives he'd ever witnessed in the field.

He said, 'She's good. For all its questionable morals, the Lynx program did its job. She was the best graduate, and she's got one of the most complete skill sets I've ever seen. And if the *ying pai* are making their move, then they'll want her out of the equation. She can deceive anyone. She's a phenomenal actress. I couldn't believe my eyes when she rescued me in Colombia.'

'She's a seducer, isn't she?' Violetta said.

Slater sensed ... *something.* A hint of jealousy? Some suppressed competitive instinct?

He said, 'Yes, she's a seducer. She does what you're trying to do, only a hundred times better.'

The silence was poignant.

Even King raised his eyebrows.

Violetta cleared her throat.

She said, 'I'm going to pretend I didn't hear that.'

Slater said, 'It's only fair that I treat you like a government handler — which you are. That means acknowledging reality, even if it means offending you. You're here to get us do to what the government wants, and they sent *you* specifically for a reason. Why pretend otherwise?'

She shrugged. 'I'm self-aware enough to recognise my strengths.'

Slater said, 'I'll go to Tulum, even though there's probably Chinese mercenaries on the way there, and even though Ruby and I didn't exactly part ways on the best terms. But I'll only do it with the caveat that you take us seriously. If there's intel updates, we want to know. We've been in this business before. We're not amateurs.'

King said, 'What he said.'

Violetta nodded. 'Deal.'

'Why do you want to save her, anyway?' Slater said.

'If China wants her dead, then she's invaluable. If we'd protected Williams and the other four bureaucrats like we should have, then we'd be in a much better position to mount resistance. We can't let them get these victories, no matter how small they might be in the big picture.'

'That's also why you're here,' King realised. 'We're valuable, because we survived the first attack.'

'There'll be more,' Violetta said. 'It's best if you're aligned with us when they happen. You were both excommunicated, but it's important that we come together in times like these.'

Slater nodded. 'I can accept that.'

'Find Nazarian,' Violetta said. 'Bring her to the States. You have the full resources of the U.S. government at your disposal. We think it's best that you go on your own — you're both notoriously bad at working with others, and you seem to have achieved your best success all on your own. So, Slater, you go do that, and King will stay here with me.'

'And what exactly will we get up to?' King said, barely masking a smile.

She flashed him a dark look. 'You're on standby for when we find a target.'

'A target?'

'Some of the *ying pai* are in the country, and they're actively working on a ploy to destabilise the economy. That's all I can tell you. When we have a clearer picture, we'll need you to smash heads together.'

'Why?'

'We believe they've been cooperating with a firm on Wall Street.'

'Which one?'

'I can't tell you that yet. But if it's true, it's not good. Not good at all.'

'If you need heads smashed together, I'm your man. And in the meantime?'

'I'll debrief you.'

King said, 'Is that innuendo?'

Slater shot to his feet. 'I'd love to stay and watch you two flirt all day, but I figure it's about time I met an old friend. How do I get to Tulum?'

Violetta looked up at him. 'However the hell you want.'

'Okay, then,' he said. 'Fuel a jet.'

42

The apartment felt a whole lot emptier with just the two of them.

King stayed on the sofa, and Violetta stayed on the armchair. Slater had left ten minutes earlier, after a flurry of activity as he kicked himself into gear. He'd made a number of requests, and Violetta had picked up the phone and dialled.

Then she'd nodded confirmation and sent him on his way.

King said, 'Are you really getting him a jet?'

'Whatever he needs,' she said. 'I told you — we value your contribution.'

King said, 'If China violently surpasses the United States on the world stage, there's going to be a whole lot more consequences than a ruined economy. Why wouldn't we help?'

She said, 'There we go. You're getting the big picture.'

'I don't fully understand,' he said. 'You've been sparse on the details. Why are they doing this now?'

She said, 'They've sensed opportunity.'

'Who are the *ying pai*?'

'We've always had reason to believe they were a small portion of the Chinese government's inner circle. We didn't take the threat seriously. But it's all starting to come together, now that we know it's real. We're beginning to understand the grievous mistakes we've made in the past.'

'Such as?'

'We were reassured that China's booming economy would expand peacefully, and that no-one would be hurt. But we're starting to learn that this was all a front — a deception. There has always been a plan to claim their spot at the top of the hierarchy. It's a fundamental Chinese belief — that there can only be one at the top.'

King said, 'So the *ying pai* are China as a whole?'

'No. There are moderates, of course. But they're far less common than we were led to believe. It appears the hard-line nationalists are winning the influence battle, and they think the moderates are fools.'

'How did you not see this coming?' King said. 'How did a behemoth as big as our government miss this?'

'Because they were playing the long game,' Violetta said. 'And when you're at the top, like I said before, you get fat and lazy. But you also get impatient. You get short-sighted. China has been plotting this for decades. They've relied on our support and goodwill on many occasions by convincing us they were no threat.'

'So what do you know about their overarching plan?' King said. 'Crash the economy, then...?'

She chewed her lower lip again. Then she said, 'That's what scares us so much. That's what terrifies me.'

'It's got to be something big.'

'Something that will put them on top for good. They smelled blood in the water in 2008, when the financial crisis hit. But they hadn't been expecting it either, so they didn't have the courage or the tenacity to act. Our theory is that if they manufacture their own financial crisis on our soil, they can time it to perfection. They can deliver the killing blow as we're on our knees.'

'A little dramatic, don't you think?'

'Wait and see,' Violetta mumbled. 'Just wait and see.'

They lapsed into silence, mulling over what was to come. King couldn't wrap his head around the consequences. If what Violetta was telling him was true, then the scope was unfathomable.

He voiced these concerns.

'What are Slater and I going to do?' King said. 'I mean, if this is true, and the *ying pai* are responsible for most of China's decisions on the global stage, then what are two above-average operatives going to accomplish? Sure, Slater can rescue his old flame, and I can sit here and keep you company — which I'm enjoying, don't get me wrong — but what's the point? We're helpless to stop it if it's happening.'

'That's not true,' she said. 'Every major incident in history comes down to a few isolated decisions, or confrontations, or altercations. If we have you on standby, and we *have* to succeed in a single incident, then we want to have the both of you close to rely on. Otherwise, we'd be taking a chance.'

'You're taking a chance no matter what,' King said.

She looked at him, unblinking. 'Not with records like yours.'

He said, 'I'm only human.'

'You seem to be invincible.'

'Is that why you're here?'

She raised an eyebrow.

He said, 'Concerned about your own safety?'

'If I was, I never would have taken this job.'

He said, 'I'm glad you're here with me.'

She paused.

She looked at him again.

She said, 'Are you married?'

'Isn't that in the files?'

'No. It's inconsequential.'

'Doesn't sound like it's inconsequential if you're asking me.'

'Let's class this as personal time, then.'

'So I'm not on the clock?'

'Not as of this second.'

He said, 'No.'

'No?'

'I'm not married.'

'Girlfriend?'

He looked past her, out the window. He battled his emotions.

He lost.

He said, 'Let's talk about something else.'

She said, 'I'm sorry. You were flirting with me, and I thought ... look, that was inappropriate of me.'

'It's not that.'

She looked up.

He met her gaze.

He said, 'I had a girlfriend. A partner. I lost her.'

'How?'

'She was shot in the head to lure me to New Zealand on a revenge mission.'

An uncomfortable pause.

Violetta swallowed a ball of unease.

She said, 'I'm so sorry.'

'It's not your fault.'

'I know, but...'

'Are you married?' he said.

She said, 'No.'

'Boyfriend?'

'Not for a long time.'

'Any particular reason?'

'I lost him, too.'

Another uncomfortable pause.

King said, 'Your last boyfriend?'

'Yes.'

'When?'

'Nearly eight years ago.'

'What happened?'

'He was mugged. He tried to resist. They stabbed him.'

'I'm sorry, too.'

'Like you said... not your fault.'

He ran a hand through his hair and stared out the window.

Trying to find the right words.

He said, 'Does it get any easier?'

She smiled a sad smile. 'Not really.'

'Damn.'

'Did you think she was the one?'

'She *was* the one.'

'So was mine. His name was Beckham.'

'Hers was Klara.'

'This is a stressful job,' Violetta said. 'I don't get the chance for a release often.'

She let the words hang in the air.

He let them wander through his mind.

He thought hard.

She took the silence the wrong way.

She got up and covered her eyes with her hand in embarrassment.

Again she said, 'I'm so sorry.'

She strode into the hallway, out of sight, to put some space between them.

King stayed where he was.

Thinking.

Wondering.

Would she care?

Or would she want you to move on?

To find your own happiness?

He kept thinking.

He found his answer.

He got up off the sofa and followed Violetta into the hallway.

43

I t was only a four-hour flight to Tulum, and the jet was fuelled up and ready to go when Slater reached JFK International Airport, so he figured they'd touch down in the early hours of the morning — both locations were operating on the same timezone, after all.

A couple of unassuming men in dark suits were waiting on the runway to receive him, and as soon as he stepped out of the town car they wordlessly ushered him aboard.

He was the only passenger.

There was a pilot, and a co-pilot, and not much else.

He took a long look around and sat down on the plush seats and waited for takeoff.

The co-pilot sauntered out of the cockpit.

He was short but well-built, and his uniform was impeccably pressed. He sat down across from Slater and said, 'I've been given full clearance to debrief you.'

'Okay,' Slater said.

'You're on your own when we get there, for reasons I'm sure you're privy to. We've been given special permission to land at the Tulum Naval Air Base, so as soon as you pick up your cargo, bring it straight back to the jet and we'll get back in the air. The Mexican government is cooperating, but they're not officially getting involved in this, and frankly neither are we. Whatever happens, happens. Your employers want full deniability.'

'Don't worry,' Slater said. 'I'm used to that.'

'It could go swimmingly, or it could be disastrous,' the man said. 'Either way, we'll wait as long as we need to. We'll put a heart rate monitor on you so we can track whether you're alive or dead. If you blink out of existence, we'll be in the air five minutes later. Is that understood?'

'Sounds like a plan,' Slater said.

The man nodded once, and got to his feet.

Slater said, 'You're not the co-pilot, are you?'

The guy winked. 'You think they'd tell any civilian that sort of information?'

He returned to the cockpit and slammed the door closed.

Slater kicked off his shoes, put his feet up, and stretched out across the seats. He stuffed a pillow behind his neck and stared up at the ceiling, lost in thought.

The Gulfstream taxied down the runway and lifted into the sky.

He had to admit he was accustomed to this. The general lack of information would have deterred even the most strong-willed of soldiers, but Slater had been operating on limited intel his entire career.

So had King.

It stirred remnants of dark memories. Memories he'd rather never let resurface, but they came back all the same. It was the bitter reality of hyperintention — try not to think about elephants, and all you can think about are elephants. He recalled bloodshed and violence and chaos and carnage, and amidst it all, a deeper satisfaction that had driven him to keep putting his body and mind on the line for his country.

So why the hell wouldn't he do it again?

Then he thought of Ruby Nazarian, and those memories weren't much more pleasant. She'd saved him from certain death at the hands of a drug cartel in the jungles of Colombia, and for that he would be eternally grateful. If she was in danger, he'd drop everything to make sure she was okay. He and King had a similar pact, forged in bloodshed. Nothing could break it.

He wondered what he would say when he saw her. He went down that road for a spell, but quickly enough realised he was getting too engrossed in possibilities. In the end, it didn't matter. She would either accompany him back to the United States, or disappear forever.

And if she chose the former... then what?

He didn't know.

He envied King for being able to spend the night with Violetta, but not for reasons one might assume. He would be able to pick her brains on the intricacies of the Chinese plot. Was it most of the upper echelon of Chinese government behind this sabotage attempt? Or was it a smaller ragtag band of extremists?

Either way, he sensed something coming.

Something he couldn't see how he had the ability to fix.

Not on his own.

Not even with King, or Ruby.

No, this was something greater...

He closed his eyes and drifted into a dreamless sleep,

occupied by silence and stillness as opposed to nightmarish visions of the future.

He thanked his lucky stars for that relief, at least.

Four hours later, they touched down in Mexico.

44

As Violetta traced a finger down King's chest, he said, 'Was that professional of us?'

'Does it matter?' she whispered, and gently touched her lips to his cheek.

They were sprawled out on the bed, draped in twisted sheets, both naked. King's chest rose and fell with heaving breaths.

He hadn't been able to resist getting carried away. As soon as he'd placed a hand on the small of her back and she'd responded by slipping out of her skirt, he'd wanted to devour her.

She'd felt the same, it seemed.

She'd turned and lifted his shirt off and fell on him with a recklessness that belied her ordinarily stern demeanour. That professionalism had fallen away when they'd reached the bed. The business trip turned to pleasure awfully quick.

Now they both lay coated in a thin sheen of perspiration, utterly spent.

It seemed like she couldn't believe what happened.

She said, 'I want you to know ... I never ... I don't usually...'

'Don't worry,' he said. 'I understand.'

'Is it usually that good? I mean, I've been focused on my work for so long. That was...'

'No words?'

'No words.'

'Glad I feel the same, then.'

She kissed his neck, then his chest, then his stomach. 'You are incredible.'

He said, 'Why do you do this job?'

She paused halfway down his torso, and rested her head sideways across his abdomen, so she could look up at him.

She said, 'It's hard. I guess I thrive in difficult times. If I was doing anything else, I'd get bored.'

'Interesting.'

'What about you? I'm a pen pusher. What led you to become an operative?'

'I don't do it anymore,' he said. 'I got out.'

'But you did it for a decade. I read your files. If you wanted to get out earlier, you would have. Something kept you ticking between the ears. Something kept you pressing forward.'

'You said it yourself.'

'I handle stress. That's about it. I don't handle what you used to go through on a daily basis. It would drive anyone insane.'

'But it's the same principle,' King said. 'If I'm not challenging myself, I get restless. I know I have certain talents and I'd drive *myself* insane if I didn't use them.'

'So how did retirement go, then?'

He tensed up, and she felt it.

She sighed and said, 'I'm sorry. That was dumb in hindsight.'

He said, 'It was going well. Better than I deserved, at least. I was still pushing myself every day, but my life wasn't in danger anymore. It was a thousand pound weight lifted off my shoulders. And Klara ... she was happy. I was happy, I guess.'

'But...?'

'But I was getting the same nagging feelings. I couldn't help but think of the people who were dying because I was selfish enough to worry about myself, and what *I* wanted. And just as I started getting those feelings... she was murdered.'

'Sounds like you lost someone amazing.'

'She was,' King said. 'Like I said, a whole lot better than I deserved. That's why I got out for good. Because of her.'

'Well,' Violetta said, 'if you choose to stay in, I'll be here. And I'm *more* than happy to help you through any unrest you might be dealing with. I think we can mutually attend to each other's needs, wouldn't you say?'

'Sounds like it'd ruin our professional relationship.'

She kissed his chest again. 'I think you can compartmentalise. Your file said you were good at that.'

'Could we stay detached?'

'We'd have to.'

'I guess it'd be one way to relieve stress.'

'You got that right.'

'Like the secret world's version of a work-sponsored fitness membership?'

She laughed, and climbed on top of him. Her breasts seemed to defy gravity. He ran his hands over them and listened to her purr her approval.

She bent over him and kissed him hard.

He returned the favour.

Thirty minutes later, *properly* exhausted, they fell off each other again.

King smiled.

Violetta smiled back.

Then the seriousness returned, drowning out any temporary pleasure, and she said, 'I need to debrief.'

He said, 'Make yourself at home.'

She fetched her smartphone off the bedside table and padded out of the room. King propped himself up on one elbow and thought long and hard about what he was doing.

Eventually he concluded there was nothing wrong with it at all.

He was on standby, and even though it felt like he was amidst a war, this was technically downtime. It didn't matter what he did whilst waiting to receive orders. The requisite parties were scrambling to decipher what the Chinese were doing, and when it all came bubbling to the surface King would throw himself into harm's way in a heartbeat, but until then...

It took her nearly an hour to reappear. He flashed her a curious glance, but she ignored it. He nodded his understanding, more to himself than to her.

Compartmentalise.

No matter how intimate they got, it wasn't his job to sort through intelligence channels. The bureaucracy of top-secret government operations had never been his strong suit, and he'd never been involved in the messy details. They told him where to go, and when. Violating that system was sacrosanct.

She slipped into bed and said, 'Sorry. But I don't want to talk about it. Not now.'

'Any news?'

'Some. None of it good. When we need you, we'll let you know.'

King nodded.

Then he said, 'Tell me how your boyfriend really died.'

45

S he looked at him, stared deep into his soul, and said, 'What?'

'You were convincing,' he said. 'But not convincing enough. He wasn't mugged. I could see that split-second decision in your eyes where you decided to throw in a substitute story.'

She didn't say anything for a long time, and he feared he'd offended her.

Then she said, 'You *are* good.'

'You don't have to tell me if you don't want to. I wanted to leave the possibility out there. If you want to talk about it, I'm all ears.'

Silence.

He propped himself up on the other elbow and watched her stare into the distance, her eyes glazing over as she looked out the window. She wasn't admiring the view. She was lost in murky thoughts.

He knew exactly what she was going through.

He could connect to the extremes of the emotional spectrum.

He'd seen — and experienced — it all before.

Finally she muttered, '*Plata o plomo.*'

He looked at her.

His stomach twisted into a knot.

He knew what it meant.

He'd waged war against the cartels before.

He said, 'Silver or lead.'

She said, 'You understand why I don't want to tell the truth to people I've just met?'

He nodded.

He didn't say anything.

He didn't need to.

The cartels, and the circumstances surrounding their existence in Mexico, were filled with depravity and hopelessness. Any attempt to cull them had failed, and he'd personally witnessed their amoral violence up close and personal at the beginning of his career. It had forged him into the man he was today.

And he knew about *Plata o plomo,* the offering of silver (a bribe) to any righteous opposing parties. If the subject refused, they were executed. It was a lose-lose situation. Accept a place on the cartel's payroll, nullifying anything you can do to lawfully resist them in the future, tarnishing your own reputation and record…

Or die.

King said, 'Was he a journalist?'

She nodded.

There were tears in her eyes.

'I'd never had a boyfriend before Beckham came along,' she said. 'I'm a hard bitch when I need to be — which, in my career, is practically all the time. And he changed me. He was handsome, but it wasn't that — if he found something worth investigating, he went after it like a junkyard dog. He was the most passionate man I'd ever seen. And it killed him.'

'Where?'

'Guadalajara,' she said. 'He went there to research how deep the cartel ties ran in government. I told him not to. Everyone told him not to. But he was too morally pure for his own good.'

'How'd they do it?'

'They walked up to him on the street one day and pressed a briefcase full of cash into his hands. He left it right there on the sidewalk, where they gave it to him. He dusted his hands off and went back to his hotel. He was too pure. The next day, as soon as he stepped out of the lobby, they pushed him into a car and put a bag over his head. No-one did anything to help. That's ... not something you do when the cartels are involved. Not when they own the country.'

King bowed his head.

She said, 'They found his body three days later. It had been mutilated. Before death.'

'Christ.'

'That's why I haven't been dating. That's why I do this job. Because this job takes up every waking moment of my life, and that's about all that stops me from going mad.'

He said, 'It eats away at you, doesn't it? The injustice of it all.'

She smiled a sad smile. 'Well, that's why you do what you do. You said it yourself.'

He kissed her. 'Two broken people in a broken world. That's what we are.'

'And we're damn good at it.'

He said, 'When this is over ... I'd like to see you again. Outside of work.'

'Does such a thing exist?' she said.

'Well, I'm glad we're both on the same page about that, then.'

She kissed him. 'Maybe.'

'Maybe?'

'That's as good as you're going to get.'

'So we're back into work mode now? No mention of what just happened?'

She said, 'Something like that.'

They got dressed, maintaining a shared, comfortable silence. They stole the odd glance at each other, but Violetta had been telling the truth — together, they were the masters of compartmentalisation. There was no fawning over each other — that time had come and passed, and they'd found their release. Now it was back to what mattered.

As they drifted out of the bedroom, she stopped him in the doorway and got up on her tiptoes to whisper in his ear.

She said, 'I've never told anyone what happened to him. Apart from you.'

He stared down at her, understanding the importance.

She said, 'I'd like to see you again. After this. More than anything.'

He nodded.

And a faint twitch of warmth stirred in his chest. Something reactivated — a sensation he hadn't thought he'd ever be able to find again. Not after Klara died. It was still in the earliest stage imaginable, but it was there, and that was what mattered.

She pecked him on the cheek.

She floated out of the room.

He stood leaning against the doorway, composing himself.

He didn't know what he was feeling.

But he knew it was good.

Then he left the bedroom, too, passing over the imaginary threshold.

And he descended into stoicism once more.

46

Tulum
Mexico

It was a warm, clear day.

The Gulfstream touched down at the Tulum Naval Air Base, barely a mile north of the town itself. Slater stirred from his slumber and peered out the window for a beat. He saw nothing but an endless, sweeping forest thick with dark green trees, and beyond that the small stretch of civilisation before the coast. The water was turquoise blue, and there wasn't a cloud in the sky.

It was paradise.

But he knew better than to judge by first appearances.

The co-pilot — Slater continued to use that label in his mind, despite the fact that the man was clearly U.S. military intelligence — came out of the cockpit as the wheels touched the tarmac. There was a gentle shudder as the pilot started to slow the jet.

Slater sat up.

'Got anything else to share with me?' he said.

The pilot said, 'Word through intelligence channels is that the stretch of beach around Ruby Nazarian's last known location is being monitored extensively. But we don't know everything, and we can't see everything. I'm sure you are aware of the cartel activity in Mexico. Organised crime is literally *everywhere*. It's embedded so deep in society we wouldn't even know where to start unravelling. So there's endless opportunities to take advantage of their *sicarios*. They live and breathe money. Which the Chinese have a lot of. Understood?'

Slater nodded. 'I'll be careful.'

'You'd better be, because you're not officially here. I'm sure you can understand why it's politically sensitive to be here. Hence why it has to be you.'

'That's not the reason,' Slater said.

'Excuse me?'

'I'm here because I know her, and she'll probably listen to me. That's it. Don't pretend it's anything else.'

The co-pilot shrugged. 'I don't know about that.'

'Right. You only get told what's necessary?'

The guy shrugged again. 'If you two have romantic drama, that's none of my concern. Get back here as fast as you can. Because if you fuck it up, we're gone. Like we never existed in the first place. Which we don't.'

He winked at Slater.

Slater got to his feet and said, 'Are you giving me firepower?'

'There's a Sig Sauer and an M4 in the jeep.'

'What jeep?'

The co-pilot jerked his thumb out one of the circular windows. Slater peered out onto the runway, and saw an open-topped jeep painted dark brown sitting empty at the foot of the stairs.

He said, 'It's got a full tank. Do what you need to do and get back to us.'

'Care to tag along?'

Slater was met with silence.

He slapped the guy on the shoulder and said, 'Just kidding. See you on the other side.'

He descended the stairs, adjusting the heart rate monitor the co-pilot had fitted to his chest. He relished the warmth of the sun on the back of his neck, and got behind the wheel. True to the co-pilot's word there was a loaded Sig Sauer pistol and an M4A1 carbine resting side by side on the passenger seat.

Slater sat there, his gut churning with unease, but that was all part of the game.

But why is it churning?

Because of Ruby?

Or because it feels an awful lot like you're back at work again?

He threw that idea away, because it would paralyse him if he held onto it. He'd rather sort this situation out, then dwell on where his future lay. So he put the jeep into gear and took off away from the Gulfstream, heading for a collection of official-looking buildings alongside a gate in the wire perimeter of the airfield.

There were guards, and booths, and guns, and security protocol, but Slater bypassed all of them. He barely had to look twice at any of the military personnel before they connected him to the mysterious jet that had been granted clearance to land, and ushered him straight through. He nodded politely to each of them — it was a bad idea to get on the wrong side of the local grunts — and pushed through onto a potholed road surrounded by rampant vegetation.

The heat bore down on him, and he wiped sweat off his brow.

The two-lane road led him to a small collection of buildings resting to the east of Tulum. There was a shopping mall, a federal government office, a tourist information centre, a Starbucks, and a gas station. Slater carried on past them, heading for the coast, following GPS directions on the phone in his lap.

Violetta had ever so kindly provided him with Ruby's exact location.

There was little passing traffic, and Slater found nothing to be suspicious about in the small sample size he could analyse. There were overweight tourists and deeply tanned locals, and everything in between. But there were no hard faces or cold, soulless eyes. Slater found no hostility in the beach town. Everyone was pumped full of cheap alcohol and cheap food.

He made it to the road running parallel to the Tulum Sea, inland from the beach, and turned right. He drove for nearly a mile before he reached a collection of lavish villas, collectively compromising an extravagant seaside resort. He parked the jeep and tucked the Sig Sauer into his waistband. It was devilishly hot. He squirmed as the sun beat down, and lowered the carbine into the footwell. Although there was urgency in the air, he opted not to storm into the quiet beachhead with guns blazing.

Besides, there was little sign of the *sicarios* the co-pilot had warned him about.

The cartels were busy running heroin and crack cocaine across the border, and buying entire governments, and trafficking sex slaves, and training child soldiers, and making billions in the process. He doubted the Chinese *ying pai* could even offer them enough to drag them away from those particularly lucrative endeavours.

Or perhaps they could...

But he stuck to his original plan, and draped a tarpaulin sheet from the rear seats over the carbine to shield it from any prying eyes.

Then he got out, locked the jeep, and lowered his shirt over the Sig Sauer at his waist.

He passed a couple of intoxicated Americans on the way into the resort. They offered a cheery pair of "hello"s, and he returned the favour. Then he pressed through, striding down a central path cutting through the villas, and moved straight past the reception building. He acted like he belonged nowhere else in the world, and no-one confronted him.

He made it to the private stretch of beach without incident. There were traditional wooden huts spaced a comfortable distance apart along the white sand. There was bright blue water, and overhanging trees, and the sand was silky smooth under his boots.

He figured he could spend a few years here without complaining.

He walked fast, aware of how open and unprotected the beach was. There was near limitless room for hostiles to be spread out in the jungle, but he reminded himself that wasn't the cartel's style. If they truly *had* been paid to take her out, they'd come in hard and fast. They wouldn't deem stealth a necessary facet of this particular job.

They would underestimate their target, because she was a woman.

Slater almost wished he could step back and watch that altercation play out.

But he wasn't here to play games.

He kept walking, and found the hut he was looking for, and walked right up to the closed door.

His heart thrummed in his chest.

He ignored it.

He reached up to knock.

A slim hand reached around from behind, and caught his wrist, and spun him around, and pressed a blade to his throat.

Her amber eyes glowed.

Slater didn't bother going for his gun.

He half-smiled and said, 'Hey.'

47

Ruby Nazarian said, 'Did you let me do that?'

Up close, she was as alluring as he remembered. She had the brightest, most intense eyes he'd ever seen. Her hair was tied back, revealing the same tanned, angular face, and her lips hovered half an inch apart, like she could taste the violence she could dish out with the subtlest flick of her wrist.

And she was still in phenomenal shape — she was wearing a tube top and loose floral pants that accentuated her physique in all the right places.

You don't dabble in the world of black operations without being in peak physical condition.

Slater could attest to that.

He said, 'I figured it was a possibility. I wasn't paying much attention to my surroundings. I figured you'd get the jump on me one way or the other.'

She took the knife out from underneath his chin, and returned the half-smile. 'It's been a while.'

'It has.'

'How'd you find me?'

'I have contacts.'

'No you don't.'

'I didn't used to. I do now.'

She furrowed her brow. 'You're back in bed with—?'

'No,' he said, then paused. 'Well, my friend might be. Quite literally. We've been dealing with a government handler — Violetta. You heard of her?'

Ruby shook her head. 'Of course not. Lynx was a separate beast. I didn't get access to your side of the pond.'

Slater shrugged. 'Trust me — we didn't get access to much either.'

'Told where to go and what to do,' Ruby said. 'But not why.'

Slater smiled. 'Maybe we have more in common than I thought.'

She said, 'Let's cut the shit, okay? Uncle Sam sent you. If you came to get rid of me, you'd better be more prepared than that.'

'Unless I have help,' Slater said. 'Unless I'm a distraction, and there's shooters in the trees—'

He saw her stiffen, and said, 'I'm kidding. Don't slit my throat.'

'I was about to.'

'Listen — you're in danger.'

'I'll be the judge of that.'

'No, you won't. You're not the judge, and neither am I. But the real judges have determined that you're about to be public enemy number one, deep in cartel country. Which isn't good for anyone involved who cares about your wellbeing.'

She stared at him. 'Oh, I'm sure they care about my wellbeing.'

'They do. Maybe for political reasons, but they care all

the same.'

'Political?'

'The Chinese have put out a hit list. I'm on it. Jason King's on it. And now you're on it.'

'The Chinese?'

'I'll tell you all about it on the plane.'

She stared at him. 'I'm not going with you.'

'You have to.'

'You think I care about what the government wants me to do?'

'It's not about that. It's about the fact that powerful people want you wiped off the face of the earth so you don't show up in future to cause them problems. They already sent hired guns after King and I.'

'How'd that work out for them?'

'Not well.'

'So you think I need babysitting, then?'

'I told you this is cartel country.'

'I'm aware of that.'

'You think you can handle an army storming this beach?'

'I'm sure you'll be able to protect me, then,' she said, rolling her eyes.

'Neither of us can survive that. We need to go — *right now.*'

She seemed to sense the urgency in his tone. It wasn't like Slater to get spooked. But he'd been privy to a number of episodes with various Mexican cartels in the past, and he knew the depravity and brutality they were capable of. And, despite everything, he deeply cared about Ruby Nazarian. She was a fucked-up girl in a fucked-up world, but she'd come out the other side with some semblance of sanity. And that wasn't something to gloss over.

She hadn't swallowed a gun, and neither had he.

That was something powerful, given what they'd mutually been through.

He couldn't put into words how badly he wanted her to agree with him, but she seemed to sense it.

And he knew why.

That unspoken connection they shared. They'd waged war together in Colombia, and in the North Maine Woods. That trumped any need to build a deep bond over a number of years. Besides those altercations, they'd barely interacted, save for a whirlwind one-night-stand in a hotel in Colombia, but the relationship you formed in combat was deeper than any other form.

Ruby said, 'You promise to tell me everything on the way back?'

'Only what I know.'

'What are they going to do with us when we get there?'

'It's all up in the air,' Slater said. 'I know about as much as you do. But you can't stay here. Not when the narcos are open to offers from the highest bidder, and more than happy to get involved in anything for the right price.'

She said, 'If they even think about—'

'I know,' he said. 'Trust me — I know.'

Her gaze drifted over his shoulder, and she said, 'We've got company.'

He spun fast, and his heart skipped a beat, but he breathed a sigh of relief when he saw a dark-skinned man in the resort's uniform striding barefoot over the sand toward them. He was old and bald and had a thin build, and his skin was wrinkled from years of sun exposure. He sauntered right up to them, glanced at Ruby once, then kept his gaze on Slater.

He didn't blink.

It seemed like he was thinly masking fear.

He said, 'Sir, is your car outside?'

'Yes,' Slater said. 'I'm visiting my friend here. I'll be on my way shortly.'

'I understand, sir, but that's not the problem.'

'What's the problem?'

The guy gulped. 'There is someone here to see you, and I would encourage you not to keep him waiting.'

Slater cocked his head. 'Okay. Who is he?'

Then the fear turned to frustration. Something about Slater's demeanour irritated the worker. The man said, 'We would all appreciate it if you kept business like this away from our establishment. We don't want you bringing your trouble here. Keep it away from our resort, sir. We don't deserve this sort of harassment.'

Slater realised the guy wouldn't be saying another word.

The man turned on his heel and walked off.

Left alone on the beach, Slater turned to Ruby and said, 'Have I convinced you yet?'

'I'll get my gun,' she said.

'And everything you need,' Slater said. 'I'd wager you're not coming back here.'

She said, 'My gun is all I need.'

Then she stepped forward, impossibly close, and touched her delicate lips to his. She reached a hand around to grip the back of his neck and kissed him ferociously. He returned the favour.

She stepped away, and pivoted on the spot, and threw a sly glance over one shoulder.

He watched her unlock her hut and step inside, admiring the view the whole time.

As she disappeared, she called back, 'It's sure good to see you again.'

'You too,' he said.

48

S later knew exactly what he'd find waiting by the jeep.

He only had to make it to back to the naval base. That was it. It was a short drive before they'd be in the sky and out of Mexico for good. So, frankly, he didn't give a shit who he pissed off on the way there. That was the one advantage he had over the cartels. They would expect obedience, and if he knew what was good for him he would give it to them, but that had never been Slater's strong suit.

So he approached the parking lot with the type of aggression that would get you executed in a heartbeat if you spent any longer than an hour in Mexico.

There was a scion of one of the cartels waiting for them, leaning one muscular arm on the door. Slater could tell instantly he was a third or fourth generation spoiled brat with a sociopathic streak. He was in his early twenties, with a mess of dark black hair over his forehead and a body forged from hours pumping iron each day and shooting up every designer steroid under the sun. He had that unwavering confidence too — everything he wanted in life, he reached out and took.

He had the money, and the power, and the guns, and the girls.

He shouldn't even be here, not handling a situation with stakes like this, but the head honchos must have figured if the target was a lone woman, they could send one of their descendants to puff his chest out and get some experience under his belt.

But, of course, it wasn't just the scion. Slater could see the collection of SUVs — big Suburbans with tinted windows — milling around the entrance to the resort, off the beach road. The young cocky kid had been sent in to lay down the ground rules, and the rest of the *sicarios* — the real hard-hitters — were out there on the perimeter in case the targets got any ideas.

The kid watched them approach, and he flashed a grin of pearly white teeth as he openly stared at Ruby.

He called out, 'My, oh my, señorita.'

He licked his lips.

Slater pulled to a halt right in front of the kid, up close, in his personal space. The guy didn't even acknowledge him. He kept staring at Ruby, practically panting like a dog.

Slater said, 'Hey, buddy.'

The kid glanced across, disinterested. 'I'm not here for you. Fuck off.'

'But I'm here all the same,' Slater said. 'What do you want?'

'Your whore is going to come with me.'

'Why would she do that?'

'Because those are the orders that were handed down to me.'

The kid said it lackadaisically, as if it couldn't be a genuine possibility that Slater would resist. Now *that* would be something to behold. Everyone — *literally* everyone — knew the control the cartels possessed. They knew who was who. No-one would dare to resist them. If they told you what to do, you'd do it, or they'd make it so painful for you and your family that you'd wished you'd never existed in the first place.

So when Slater reached out, took the kid's arm off the door, and shoved him away from the jeep, a ripple speared through the atmosphere.

Serious, serious tension.

Luckily, Slater didn't care in the slightest.

The kid pulled out his piece instantly, making a show of it. The Glock was in his hand before Slater or Ruby could blink, and he waved it around in a way that immediately demonstrated he had no idea what he was doing.

He pointed the barrel at Slater, then Ruby.

He said, 'If one of you motherfuckers touches me again, I'll have gasoline poured down your throats. I'll track down your families and I'll tie them up and let them watch as I burn you. Is that fucking clear?'

Slater said nothing.

Ruby smiled.

The kid ran a hand through his mop of hair. He was irritated now. This hadn't gone as planned. He turned the gun on Ruby and kept it there, and said, 'Walk.'

'No,' she said.

She flashed a smile at him.

Her eyes burned bright.

She didn't move.

He reached out to grab a handful of her hair.

She kicked him so hard in the balls that Slater thought he might pass out on the spot. But he kept some level of dignity by going down on one knee, and all the colour drained from his face, and his body started to shut down on itself. Full survival mode. And what the kid should have done right then was raise the Glock and shoot her in the face, because Slater knew those were the orders. He'd wanted to take her alive for bragging rights, and probably because he'd seen a surveillance photo and figured if he was going to take anyone alive and have his way with them, it'd be Ruby Nazarian.

But he'd severely underestimated her, so now he found himself gasping for breath and plagued by indecision. He could barely concentrate on what was happening because of the agony, so he hesitated.

He still didn't shoot her — he saw some way to salvage the situation, even at his most desperate hour.

She ripped the gun out of his hands, threw it away, and instead of mixing up her attacks she kicked him in the balls again.

He threw up on the hot pavement.

Slater stepped forward and dragged him to his feet, even though he could barely stay conscious. He took the kid's head in his giant hands — like gripping a bowling ball tight — and smashed the jeep's side mirror clean off with it. There was an explosion of sound as the glass shattered, and the scion dropped to the ground, sprawling out on his stomach. He wasn't unconscious, but he was in more pain than he'd ever been in in his life. His head was cut open in five or six different places, and he'd probably ruptured both testicles.

Slater said, 'Let's go.'

'Good idea,' Ruby said.

They got in the jeep, and Slater fired up the engine and accelerated out of the parking lot, toward the convoy of Suburbans.

49

In hindsight, his next move was an act of pure genius.

As they drove toward the main road, Slater said, 'Put your hands behind your back.'

Ruby looked across. 'What?'

'Do it.'

She obliged.

'And look down.'

She looked down.

Slater artificially inflated his aggressiveness, and let pure discontent spread across his face. As if there was nowhere else he should be in the world.

The convoy of SUVs were out of sight of the parking lot — they'd maintained a respectable distance to allow the young scion to act on his own. They'd given him privacy. Slater could see the hoods sticking out from the line of trees, preventing anyone from barrelling past without their approval, but there wasn't a *sicario* in sight. The trail was narrow, and the woods pressed in, restricting their line of sight.

So they hadn't seen what had happened.

Slater drove the jeep out of the trail and stamped on the brakes in the middle of the convoy. There were six Suburbans in total, and the *sicarios* were on him in a heartbeat. There was an army of them, and they swarmed him like flies to shit.

Even *he* recognised the danger he was in.

Ruby did too.

They could have all the firepower in the world, but it wouldn't achieve anything here.

Slater screwed up his face in a look of pure frustration and said, 'You stupid fucks sent that kid to do the job?'

He was met with silence.

Guns hovered in place, but no-one shot him.

Slater didn't even pause to take a breath. He said, 'They sent me up from Chiapas this morning. I'd already taken care of it. *I'm* bringing her back. Not that little *puta* back there. Where's the fucking communication? I thought you were professionals.'

Someone went to speak, but Slater shook his head in disbelief at the sheer incompetence.

Then, without hesitating or thinking twice, he gently pressed down on the accelerator and rolled on past.

He wasn't looking to give them answers. He wasn't even looking to make them believe him. He was stirring the pot. Causing confusion. Making them pause. Making them think, *Wait — did we fuck this up? Could it be possible?*

They put it together fast. They realised that their bosses would almost certainly have told them of a third party, despite this mystery man's confidence. And their cartel wouldn't have outsourced it to an American. They would have kept it within their ranks, no matter what. But by the time the shock of being confronted had faded, and they put two and two together, Slater had driven on past.

Because he'd only been looking to get through the road-block without getting shot.

And he'd done it.

Someone cried out in protest, and he said, 'Get down,' and stamped on the accelerator.

The jeep's rear tyres kicked up dust as Ruby flattened herself down, out of the line of sight. Slater ducked too, and gunshots erupted. Chaos exploded in the serenity of the seaside resort, but they were out of harm's way when the jeep shot onto the main road and put a line of trees between itself and the gunmen.

Slater sat up, and corrected course to avoid running off the road, and crushed the pedal to the floor.

Wind howled over the open frame as the jeep picked up speed, and when he turned to check on Ruby, he saw a brilliant shine in her eyes.

She was *alive.*

She said, 'I missed this.'

'You're insane.'

'Only in the best way.'

She took the Beretta M9 out from under her tube top and tested its weight in her palm. She twisted in her seat and peered back to check whether they were being pursued.

They were.

All six Suburbans were on the move. Slater flashed a glance in the rear view mirror, and a pang of dread coursed through him. He hadn't established the lead he'd wanted. He'd be cutting it close.

He voiced these concerns.

She said, 'The cartels are scum. Pure scum. Let's kill them all.'

'Having combat IQ means recognising when you're outgunned. We can't win a war right now.'

She reached back under the tarpaulin, and came up with the M4A1 carbine.

She said, 'This might do the trick.'

But common sense prevailed. She looked back again, and hesitated at the size of the force. Six SUVs packed with testosterone-fuelled *sicarios* were a nightmare by anyone's standards — even two highly-trained black operations killers. She nodded her acceptance, and turned back to Slater.

'How far's the airfield?'

'A couple of miles, tops.'

'Best step on it then.'

He obliged.

The speedometer climbed faster and faster. Slater spotted the turn that would bring them inland, toward the naval base. He slowed and pulled the wheel to the left and veered off the beach road. The next road opened up before them...

...and Slater slammed on the brakes.

Because there was a convoy of *federales* and their official police vehicles blocking the way forward.

At first, he debated how to proceed. If they were responding to cartel activity in the area, perhaps he'd lucked out and found protection during a time of need. He could sail on past, and wait for the federal police to intercept the charging SUVs behind them.

But then Slater took one look at the rifles being raised in his direction, and he remembered he was in Mexico.

Where the authorities were in bed with organised crime.

And he realised the *federales* were about to open fire.

ut Ruby beat them to the jump.

She'd acclimatised to the power dynamic in Mexico, and knew what was coming when she saw the *federales.* They had no reason to be out here unless they'd been paid a handsome fee to dispose of a particularly troublesome tourist. So she had the carbine up and aimed at them before they'd even registered her and Slater barrelling towards them.

Their guns came up, and Slater threw himself down below the line of sight.

And gunshots blared in his ears.

This is it, he thought.

But then he realised the noise was coming from *inside* the jeep.

And he looked across to see Ruby transfixed on the blockade, the carbine raised to her shoulder, firing through the jeep's windshield. The windshield exploded from the first shot, and glass fragments rained down on Slater. He focused on keeping the vehicle moving in a straight line as Ruby picked off one, then two, then three, then four policemen. She was utterly remorseless, and Slater didn't blame her.

It's either them or us.

A couple returned fire, but she was onto them in a flash. Slater figured the tide had shifted, and he sat back up and pulled the Sig Sauer from his waistband and fired out the open windshield frame, hitting one *federale* in the neck. The guy twisted and spun away as blood sprayed from a severed artery, but his finger twitched on the trigger in his death throes. A round whipped by Slater's face, shockingly close — so close he could almost taste it. He aimed the hood of the jeep for a slim gap between two of the police vehicles parked nose to nose, and he yelled, 'Hold onto something.'

Ruby clutched the top of the passenger door with white knuckles.

The jeep smashed into the two cars in a mind-numbing display of force. Slater lashed against his seatbelt and grunted as he took the majority of the impact to his collarbone. But it didn't break, and although the jeep's hood crumpled inward it smashed the two cars away like opening a pair of giant gates, and it coughed and spluttered and carried on through.

Ruby swivelled in her seat and shot a *federale* through the open visor of his helmet on the way past.

The guy had been milliseconds away from gunning her down.

Slater exhaled a long breath and worked on building the momentum he'd lost through the impact.

And behind them, the cartel SUVs gained ground.

What little of the *federale* forces remained stumbled aside to let the convoy through. Slater watched in the rear view mirror as the SUVs formed a single line and barrelled through the gap he'd cleared, piggybacking off his own work. He grunted his disapproval and thrashed the jeep to its limits, willing it forward.

They were approaching the main road.

Beyond, the naval air base loomed.

Slater clenched his teeth and said, 'We can't go straight to the runway if they're this close.'

Ruby spun in her seat and loaded the carbine with a fresh magazine. She said, 'Slow down, and I'll give them something to make them hesitate.'

'They've got as much firepower as you do,' Slater said. 'And there's thirty of them.'

'If we make it to the jet, we'll be fine.'

'No, we won't. They'll shoot it down before it has the chance to take off.'

'Aren't the guards on your side?'

'Not if the *federales* convince them otherwise. We need to lose them first.'

'How?'

'What's nearby?'

Ruby thought hard. Then she said, 'Go left.'

'Into Tulum?'

'Yes.'

'I don't want civilian casualties. Best to minimise—'

'Go left,' she hissed. 'We'll turn off before we get to the town centre.'

'Where are you taking me?'

'There's a *cenote* close by. We can lure them into it and use it as cover if needed. We have to hope there's no tourists there.'

'A what?'

'A sinkhole. Like an underground pool.'

Slater stared at her.

She said, 'You want to make things difficult for them? That's where we go. Otherwise it's just open roads and trees.'

'Okay,' he said.

He twisted the wheel, and went left.

They raced onto a new road devoid of traffic, and a gunshot blared behind them. Then another. Then a few more. One of the rounds came close, but the rest went wide. Slater gripped the wheel with two sweaty palms and tried not to panic. Ahead he saw the urban sprawl of Tulum's town centre, and he looked at Ruby with concern.

She said, 'Here. Go right.'

'You sure about this?'

'It's a small clearing with plenty of cover and the *cenote* in the centre. That's the only way we win against this many hostiles. Surely you can see that. What other options do we have?'

Slater swallowed a ball of unease, and again he said, 'Okay.'

He went right and they barrelled north, passing a supermarket chain on the left and a hotel on the right. There were civilians about, carting groceries to their cars and ambling down the sidewalks. They probably thought the procession speeding past was nothing but a gang of hooligans — that is, until the shots rang out. The SUVs continued to gain ground, and Slater looked back to see *sicarios* hanging out the rear windows, brandishing rifles, openly firing. He heard the faint screams of pedestrians as the jeep roared past civilisation.

They were back to dense forest and foliage on either side of the road, and Slater kept thrashing the jeep until it reached top speed.

Ruby screamed, 'Here!'

He slowed down, and figured he'd put an acceptable distance between themselves and the convoy of SUVs.

They had a little breathing room.

There was a sign reading: CENOTE CALAVERA.

Slater pulled into a dusty parking lot entirely devoid of vehicles, and he took that as a plus because this sinkhole — ordinarily a tourist trap — was about to become a war zone.

'Are you sure about this?' he said.

'Yes,' Ruby said.

'Out, then.'

They piled out of the jeep and Slater made sure he had the Sig Sauer and a handful of spare magazines for the carbine on him. Ruby brandished the M4A1 in one hand, and her Glock in the other. Together they sprinted for a trail leading deep into the woods — once again, she reassured him they were on the right track. They left the jeep doors open and the engine running. The *sicarios* would know exactly where they were headed.

The question was whether they would follow, or establish a perimeter in the parking lot and turn it into a siege.

But there were multiple ways out of the forest, and Slater didn't think they'd leave it to chance.

He and Ruby vanished between the trees as the SUVs tore into the parking lot.

Cartel hitmen piled out, juiced up on adrenaline and stimulants, and raced into the jungle in pursuit.

51

The trail spiralled deeper into the foliage for perhaps a hundred feet.

They passed a toll booth, ordinarily manned by staff charging a handful of pesos to access the *cenote*. Slater managed a quick look at the information board and noticed it was only staffed between nine a.m. and four p.m. He figured it was somewhere near eight-thirty, and he gave a silent thanks that they wouldn't run into any civilians.

The ground was uneven grey rock, and in the centre was a sinkhole.

If not for the chaos of their arrival and the thirty *sicarios* hot on their heels, the view would have taken Slater's breath away. But he didn't have any breath to begin with, so he ignored the stunning turquoise water and the small wooden ladder leading down into a dark underground chamber.

Ruby said, 'This is perfect.'

Slater said, 'Is there level ground down there?'

She shook her head. 'No. We're not going down there. There's only one way into this clearing that makes any sense. We've funnelled them into a bottleneck.'

Slater glanced down. 'So the sinkhole isn't important?'

'Unless you want to die,' she said. 'The terrain is where we'll get the tactical advantage.'

Slater said, 'Okay. You know what you're doing?'

She gave him a dark look, and shifted the carbine onto her shoulder. 'What do you think?'

'I'll try to get around behind them,' Slater said. 'You take the high ground up there, past the *cenote,* and we'll squeeze them like pincers.'

She nodded. 'That puts you in the most danger.'

He said, 'I'll be okay.'

She tossed him the Glock, and he nodded gratefully. If he was up close, he didn't need to focus on accuracy. He could easily go akimbo with two handguns.

She sprinted around the lip of the giant gaping hole in the rock. The calm surface of the water, perhaps ten feet below ground, sparkled under the sunlight. Ruby took up position behind the cover of a cluster of trees, a couple of dozen feet up past the *cenote.*

Slater ducked low and hurried into the undergrowth near the mouth of the trail. His heart hammered in his chest. He flattened himself to the dirt and swept a bunch of ferns over his back.

Then he lay still as a statue.

Insects buzzed, and birds chirped, and the hot *fizz* of the jungle simmered all around him. He wiped sweat beads off his forehead and searched for Ruby up the back of the clearing. She was barely visible — she'd burrowed in deep. And, he realised, she was right. This was their best chance at catching the *sicarios* off-guard, but it would take expert marksmanship, and there was no room for hesitation.

The serenity was shattered by the sound of racing footsteps coming up the trail.

He waited for the majority of the force to slip past. He could hear their laboured breathing. Brazen insults were unleashed in Spanish as they cursed out their targets. This was supposed to have been an easy job, and now they were running through unknown territory in the heat. At some point they should have realised the prudence of retreating and regrouping, but, thankfully, the narcos were known for their hotheadedness — especially this generation.

Slater took a deep breath, and waited for the signal.

It was never going to be a long shootout. That didn't happen in open terrain like this, with an arsenal of automatic weaponry in the mix. It was always going to be fast and violent and bloody and relentlessly intense.

He was prepared.

Then an explosion of noise sounded.

Ruby unloaded a full magazine with pinpoint accuracy as the cartel thugs spread out in the mouth of the clearing.

A couple of them who had built up enough momentum cascaded right into the sinkhole. Their bodies hit the water with twin *thwack*s, and the blood ran thick in the turquoise gloom. Others spiralled away or simply fell where they stood, caught with fatal shots to the face, throat and chest.

Slater heard nearly a dozen screams rise in unison.

He shuddered.

Ruby was *scary* accurate.

But he didn't waste a second. He leapt to his feet, rearing out of the brush like a nightmarish vision. His veins were pumping and his head roared with the knowledge that if he mistimed it, that'd be it.

He'd be dead.

But he never, ever mistimed it.

He came up into the line of sight as every *sicario* still alive turned their attention to Ruby. They couldn't help focusing on the source of the gunfire, and their guns went up to resist the attack, even as they saw their comrades fall and die in their peripheral vision. They were as accustomed to violence as Slater and Ruby were. But that didn't help them, because Ruby vanished from sight as soon as she expended her clip, and their bullets *thwack*ed into the trees all around her.

Then Slater was right there in the midst of them, and he raised the Glock in one hand and the Sig Sauer in the other.

He didn't think about shooting. He'd put in thousands of hours on ranges all over the world. The weapons were an extension of his own mind-muscle connection. He simply lined up targets and intuitively pumped both triggers simultaneously, like twin macabre staccatos.

Bang-bang-bang-bang-bang-bang-bang-bang-bang-bang.

Done.

He killed ten men with ten bullets, because he was *that* close, and they were helpless to prevent the metal storm. Bodies started to drop, and as soon as they realised there was another stream of gunfire coming from the side they were too overwhelmed to do anything about it. It was the old timeless adage — they were used to being the top dogs, but they weren't used to fighting and clawing for their lives. So they wilted, and with half the force decimated, many of the remaining *sicarios* scattered instead of returning fire.

Because they weren't real *sicarios.*

They were young spoiled brats doing their best impersonations of real gangsters. They'd inherited the power and riches that their families had fought tooth and nail to acquire, and there was a huge difference between flaunting expensive weaponry and being able to use it effectively.

Slater sensed the tide shifting.

He shot another *sicario* in the throat, and another through the chest. They spun and twisted away, and as their bodies fell, a third guy leapt over their corpses without hesitation.

He had a serrated combat knife in his right hand and his pupils were so swollen that he had to be under the influence of hard drugs.

Which stripped him of his inhibition.

And killed all concept of hesitation.

Slater gulped as he brought his aim around, but his neurons had been firing hard and his inhuman, laser-like focus was starting to deplete. So he was a tad slower to line up the next target.

Suddenly the crazed *sicario* was right there in his face, swinging wildly with the knife.

Slater had no choice but to leap backwards.

He still tried to line up his aim, but there was a root behind him and he twisted his ankle hard on it. He went down head over heels, nearly knocking himself unconscious on a hard patch of forest floor. Then there were ferns and bushes and weeds in his face, and he batted them away with the Glock and came back up with the Sig Sauer but he met the same guy charging full-pelt at him. The serrated edge of the knife missed his forearm by an inch, and with the ferocity the *sicario* swung it, it probably would have taken his hand clean off.

Panicking, Slater fought for balance, and the *sicario* swung the knife a third time, now only half a foot from Slater.

He had no choice.

He catapulted back through the undergrowth again, falling wildly to his knees, and he smashed his elbow against a pointed rock and felt a sudden jarring numbness in his wrist.

He landed on his back, and looked up to see the *sicario* diving at him with bared teeth.

52

S later rolled to his left, but he hit a cluster of rocks.

There was nowhere else to go.

The *sicario* came crashing down into the undergrowth only inches beside him, and swung the knife again. Slater used every ounce of focus he had in his body to catch the guy's wrist, milliseconds before the blade plunged into his chest. But he was forced to drop his guns to do so — an uncomfortable yet necessary sacrifice.

He used both palms to control the knife hand, and with that threat neutralised he smashed his forehead into the guy's nose, shattering it.

The guy howled and twisted away, the pain likely compounded by the drugs he was on.

Slater squeezed the guy's wrist so hard that he thought he might break it, and the knife came free as the muscles in his palm spasmed. Slater kicked it away and dropped a scything elbow down on the guy's unprotected face, bouncing his skull off the rocks, putting him out cold.

Then Slater rolled over and snatched up the Sig Sauer and the Glock.

He froze. Still sprawled out on his stomach, there was enough vegetation around him to mask him from sight. So he lay deathly still, because there were footsteps all around him — coming from seemingly everywhere at once. It was hot, and his adrenaline raced, and he was uncomfortable, but he didn't dare budge. There could be half a dozen barrels trained on the space above his head. Best not to give them something to shoot at.

Then he heard the familiar *crack-crack-crack-crack* of Ruby's carbine on the other side of the clearing.

And muttered voices, all around him, cursing and turning and firing back.

Now the worst-case scenario was unfolding.

The remaining *sicarios* were spreading out, embedding themselves in the trees around the clearing. The bottleneck was no more. Slater didn't know how many were left, or how demoralised they were, or whether they were good shots.

He stayed down, and sweat dripped off his face into the dirt as he paused for contemplation.

I sleep in the storm.

He reminded himself of the old fable. Those who stayed calm at the height of hysteria, won. So he deliberately lowered his heart rate, and above all he refused to panic.

Ruby continued exchanging gunfire with...

...with how many?

Slater didn't know.

But then he heard two shouts, right nearby — only a dozen feet ahead. There were two *sicarios* communicating back and forth from the cover of a pair of trees, weighing up their next move.

Slater leapt into a crouch, switched to a double-handed grip on the Glock, and fired once, then twice.

Two bodies keeled over, sporting twin holes in their backs.

Then a round whipped past Slater.

So, so close.

He ducked back down, and warm crimson droplets sprayed off the side of his head into the dirt, mixing with the sweat. Startled by their appearance, he touched a hand to his ear, and pain flared in the lobe.

The bullet had passed straight through it.

The wound started pouring blood, and he stayed down with his head spinning and reeling. He didn't know where the shot had come from — he hadn't been paying attention. He couldn't focus on everything at once. He hadn't even felt the impact. All he could do was hope the follow-up shots didn't come close to—

The best-case scenario unfolded.

The young *sicario* who'd shot him — thinking Slater had been incapacitated by the bullet — came right up to him and looped an arm around his throat and picked him up out of the undergrowth and pressed the barrel of his sidearm to the side of his head.

Taking him hostage.

An uneasy stalemate unfolded, and finally Slater could get a sense of how the battlefield was laid out.

He thanked his lucky stars that the guy hadn't simply shot him through the top of the head.

Which is what he should have done immediately.

But the kid was young and dumb and pumped up with adrenaline and relishing the thrill of the fight. Was there anything more emasculating than wounding your enemy and taking them alive? As far as the *sicario* was concerned, nothing had yet been found that rivalled it. Slater knew exactly what the kid was going through — unadulterated excitement. He could hear his laboured breathing, then the kid shouted, 'Got him! Got the fucker!'

Slater saw three men turn around, spaced out in the brush.

Only three.

The kid with the gun to his head roared, 'Hey, bitch! Come out from where you're hiding. I've got a gun to your boyfriend's head.'

Silence.

No response.

Slater thought, *Good, Ruby.*

Make them wait.

Make it tense.

Make them jumpy.

The *sicario* yelled, 'Do it now, bitch! I'll count to three.'

He squeezed the gun harder into Slater's temple, drawing blood. The crimson stuff kept flowing out of his ear, and his legs grew weak. But he held his consciousness, because it was the only thing he could control, and he'd be damned if he was going to give up.

'One!' the kid yelled.

He bent down and whispered in Slater's ear, 'I'm going to shoot you now. Just to fuck with her.'

Which wasn't ideal.

But Slater didn't react.

Not yet.

Then Ruby stepped out from behind the tree.

53

She was halfway up the staggered rocky hill, and she had her palms out, indicating she was unarmed. Slater noticed she'd shifted her tube top down a few inches to reveal her cleavage, and lowered her pants too, revealing the smooth tanned V-line that framed her hips. There was perspiration on her hard stomach.

She was pouting, and there were crocodile tears in her eyes.

Slater smiled.

He couldn't help himself.

It was a brilliant ploy.

Then he made the smile vanish, because there was still work to be done.

She wailed, 'I'm sorry. Please don't hurt him.'

Slater felt the palpable excitement building in the young *sicario*. The man was astonished, and he had every reason to be. Ruby was gorgeous. He would be wondering what he could do with her if he took her alive. He could taste the prospect of it on the tip of his tongue. Every part of him wanted to torture Slater in front of her then have his way with her for days on end.

The other three were no doubt having similar thoughts. Slater could *feel* the machismo in the air. The camaraderie. The brotherhood. These four were the survivors. They were the ones who'd battled through adversity and flourished where their co-workers didn't. They were the ones who would receive the rewards.

They were kings of the jungle.

So they weren't on their A-game. Not even close. They'd watched almost twenty of their friends and colleagues die in bloody fashion. This was a gruesome game, and their fantasies ran wild with the possibilities of how they could take it out on the two prisoners.

And Ruby was feeding into that by over-sexualising herself.

It was brilliant.

One of the three men in front of Slater brandished his gun and said, 'Over here, *puta.*'

He was practically salivating.

Ruby stepped forward slowly. She drew it out, elongating the time it took to cross the clearing, taking her sweet time.

The guy couldn't stand it. He wanted his hands on her now.

He was the biggest of the four — a few inches taller than Slater, with dense muscle packed on his frame in slabs. He'd pose a problem in a fistfight through sheer size alone. In competitive mixed martial arts, he'd be several weight classes above Slater, and he probably outweighed Ruby by a hundred and fifty pounds.

Slater shivered at the thought of what he could do to her if she was tied up.

But she wasn't tied up.

Not yet.

And that was where the variables lay.

The big guy stormed out of the woods and strode right up to her, intercepting her halfway across the clearing. They stood facing each other, right next to the *cenote*. The gaping hole hovered there, the blue water sparkling.

The big guy reached out and snatched her by the throat.

After all, she was a slim girl, and he figured he didn't need to hold her at gunpoint.

Big mistake.

With veins protruding from her forehead, Ruby glanced around the guy's giant frame and made eye contact with Slater.

The fake tears dissipated.

Her expression shifted from terror to focus.

The same acting transformation he'd seen when he'd first met her in Colombia.

Brilliant in its deception.

Slater reached up with both hands and simply ripped the gun out of the *sicario*'s fingers, breaking most of them in the process. Before the kid could even howl, Slater threw his skull back like a bowling ball and broke the kid's nose on the back of his head, knocking a couple of teeth loose.

Then he spun round and planted the 9mm pistol against the kid's forehead and pulled the trigger.

He pivoted again, and shot one of the guys in the undergrowth through the back of his head. When the second man turned with wide eyes to react to what was unfolding, Slater shot him too.

The bodies dropped, and Slater looked past them to see Ruby lying on her back on the rock, with her legs wrapped around the big guy's knee and her hands around his ankle.

A rudimentary leg lock, but awfully effective at nullifying larger opponents.

Of course, the guy could have bent down and thundered a giant fist into her unprotected face and probably broken every bone in it, but he didn't do that, because he was too busy keeping his balance. And that proved unsuccessful, because of the leverage and the way Ruby was torquing his ankle joint, so in an effort to keep her from shattering his foot he pitched sideways and toppled over.

Straight into the *cenote*.

She followed him in, and the pair vanished from sight, tumbling into the water.

Slater broke into a sprint for the sinkhole.

54

He didn't hesitate.

He didn't consider his own safety.

He leapt in feet-first, clutching the 9mm tight in case he lost his grip during the freefall. But it was a short plunge, and he broke through the surface with an almighty splash. He hovered underwater, getting his bearings, and the silence rattled him. Compared to the carnage above the surface, it was eerily quiet. Then his eyes adjusted to the gloom and he jolted in surprise at the sight of the gargantuan cave system sprawling out below him. The *cenote* was the start of an elaborate underwater maze, and crippling claustrophobia seized him. Then he remembered he wasn't dead yet, and that his body wouldn't sink into the caves forever.

He kicked upward and broke the surface.

Water ran off his head, mixing with the blood, stinging his ear.

He blinked once and looked around.

Ruby was in front of him.

Facing him.

Treading water.

There was blood all over her. Over her face, in her hair, forming crimson rings around her glowing eyes.

He said, 'Are you okay?'

She said, 'It's not my blood.'

She held up her knife, lifting it above the surface. She winked at him.

He said, 'Where's the body?'

'Look down.'

He plunged back under the water and saw the *sicario's* gargantuan frame plummeting into the depths. A trail of crimson clouds followed him down, erupting from a long jagged cut in his throat as he sank. He was already dead.

Slater shook his head in disbelief, and came back up to the surface. She'd washed off the blood by that point. It must have spurted all over her when she'd slit his throat. But she'd ducked underwater and come back up clean.

So did he.

He didn't even wait. He grabbed her, and pulled her close in the turquoise water, and kissed her with the sort of rabid energy that came from surviving something you shouldn't have survived. She had the same passion, and it burned hot between them as they treaded water and locked lips and tasted each other's warmth.

Between tongues, she muttered, 'We did it.'

'Yeah, we did.'

'Right here?' she said.

'Why not?'

He pulled away and treaded in a half-circle, looking for a suitable resting place. They opted for the ladder, swimming over to it and climbing up a couple of rungs, just above the surface. They could manage. They were athletic, and powerful, and in the shapes of their lives. He picked her up and placed her one rung above, and she pulled the tube top down and he peeled the wet shirt over his head and they pressed their warm bodies together and kissed harder. She trailed her tongue down his chest, and he gently lowered a finger to her nipple and caressed it. She looped her fingers around his pants and tugged them downward.

Naked and sun-drenched and *alive,* he adjusted his position on the ladder and slipped himself inside her, and she wrapped both arms around his neck and caressed him and moaned with reckless abandon. It wasn't about the sex. It was the indescribable connection, the shared trauma and the shared bloodshed and the shared *everything* — they were one and the same and only they could understand what it was like to kill and kill and kill and try to keep your soul intact in the process.

They were drawn to each other in a way neither of them could describe, and she moaned in his ear, 'Why did we ever part ways?'

He said, 'I have no idea,' and kept thrusting, and she moaned again and their surroundings fell away.

They reached a crescendo and climaxed in unison, something Slater usually had to time right, something that ordinarily took serious willpower and determination, but it was like their bodies were synced.

They fell on each other, spent, sweating, shaking, gasping for breath.

She whispered in his ear, 'We're in the middle of a serious crime scene. Better get our pants on.'

He scoffed and shook his head and wondered how on earth he'd ended up with this life, with this reality, with this world.

He wouldn't trade it for anything.

He said, 'Good call.'

They got dressed and clambered to the top of the *cenote* and stumbled back to the jeep, leaving nearly thirty bodies in their wake.

55

New York City

'Again!' the trainer yelled.

In the living area of his penthouse, King thundered a side kick into the leather kickboxing pad held at waist height. It struck with a concussive *boom,* and the high-pitched *slap* of skin against leather echoed off the walls and the high ceiling. Sweat sprayed, but they'd put towels down in preparation.

King's trainer was Rory Barker, a former K-1 kickboxing champion with one of the most accomplished resumes on the planet. Now in his fifties, he'd agreed to discreet one-on-one sessions with King for a handsome fee in exchange for radio silence on who he was training, and how good his client was — effectively an NDA. And it was important that King established those boundaries in the beginning, because as soon as Rory had taken him through his first session, he'd stepped back in awe at the power King was able to generate.

The man had said, 'Who are you? Where have you fought?'

King had said, 'Everywhere.'

'Which organisations?'

'None of them.'

'How...?'

'Now you understand the need for secrecy.'

'You'd have the UFC belt within three years if you went public. You'd be a superstar.'

'Then it's a shame I can never go public.'

'You got a criminal record or something?'

'Let's call it that.'

'You're not government, are you?'

'Of course not.'

'Did you used to be?'

King had said, 'Rory, I'm not paying you to talk. I'm paying you to train me.'

And he'd paid handsomely, so Rory Barker hadn't probed further. He'd just done his job, honing King's fast-twitch muscle fibres, and somehow made him an even *better* fighter. The kickboxing work, coupled with the gruelling fitness regime, wrapped up in the decade-plus of experience he had with dishing out violence — it had all come together during his time living in New York.

He was the best version of himself right now, and that was saying something.

Now King fired off twenty consecutive kicks into the pads with each shin, and when Rory finally nodded his approval after glancing at the clock, King collapsed in a sweaty heap on the towels.

'Not bad,' Rory said. 'Ninety minutes at ninety percent output. I think we could even crank that up a few notches next time.'

'I'd probably throw up halfway through.'

'Since when has that ever stopped you?'

'Touché.'

Rory collected his kickboxing pads and tucked them into a faded gym bag, which he slung over one shoulder. He said, 'Same time tomorrow?'

'I'll let you know, brother. There's a lot on my plate right now.'

Rory stared down at him, reading between the lines. 'You working again?'

King had never officially explained his past, but odd details always slipped out over time.

Rory was piecing it together.

King said, 'Maybe. I don't know what it is yet.'

'Make sure you stay out of trouble. I'd hate to see all your talent go to waste.'

King panted for breath and wiped his face with both palms. He watched the ceiling through swimming vision, experiencing momentary light-headedness, but that passed.

A byproduct of thrashing his body to its limit.

He said, 'You really want me to go pro, don't you?'

'You'd be the biggest combat sports athlete on the planet.'

'You've figured out what I used to do for a living, right?'

'I have an idea.'

'Think about how little time it'd take me to get assassinated on a street corner if I showed up in the public arena with cameras in my face every time I stepped outside.'

'Right. Understood.'

'Best to keep the rest of my life discreet, Rory.'

'You made enemies?'

'A few.'

'Tell me about it one day over a beer.'

King stared up at the man. He trusted him. Combat sports formed a deep, unbreakable bond. Even if it was just live drilling. 'Maybe.'

Rory pointed a finger. 'I'll hold you to that.'

Then he left.

No goodbyes.

Rory Barker was a hard, cold man, but that's what made him such a gem. When he offered a compliment, he genuinely meant it. He was as far from fake as you could get.

King admired that in a world of false praise and interchangeable personalities.

He lay on his back and waited to catch his breath. He was thoroughly spent, but he had a cocktail that would see to that. He clambered to his feet, went to the fridge, and took out a half-gallon jug of blue liquid. If anyone asked, it was harmless electrolytes, but what he'd mixed into the water had cost him well north of five hundred dollars.

It was the best stuff money could buy.

It was a poorly kept secret that every faction of special forces in nearly every military in the world relied on performance-enhancing drugs to sustain their soldiers. When you trained to your limits each day, your body broke down at an unparalleled rate. If King and Slater didn't replenish with performance enhancers, they'd never be able to recover from the gruelling self-punishment that compromised their daily routine.

The misconception that steroids only gave you larger muscles was a foolish belief — in truth, it was all about recovery. King replenished his shattered system each and every day with microdoses of designer steroids, engineered in labs by men and women a thousand times smarter than he was.

The cutting edge.

The next step in human performance.

It was safer than ever, and he wasn't about to pretend it didn't happen.

Superhumans didn't exist. To do superhuman things, you needed something extra. Something more.

But at the same time, he and Slater had never abused them. They took trace amounts, barely detectable in the bloodstream, and they improved the concoction with each passing year. Black Force had done it for them when they were employed, but now that they were out on their own they were forced to do the heavy lifting themselves.

It was Slater's realm of expertise.

He was the mad scientist giving the orders.

King took what he was given.

And he'd never been in better shape.

He drained the entire half-gallon, and returned the empty jug to the fridge. He let it digest, feeling the cool liquid snaking its way down his throat. There were no other sensations. Microdoses didn't give you molten energy running through your veins. There was nothing like that.

But he'd wake up the next morning ready to go again, and that was all that mattered.

There was a knock at the door, and he sauntered into the hallway bare-chested. He had no qualms about answering it. Violetta hadn't been lying about the ramped-up security. The building was now a virtual fortress, guarded by every possible form of government protection. A civilian couldn't see what was in place if they were looking right at it, but that was the whole point. They were there in the shadows, watching around the clock, keeping tabs on the two men living on the top floor.

He opened the door, and she was standing there.

She said, 'Big developments.'

'Am I needed?'

'You are.'

He sighed and bent over, putting his hands on his knees. 'You could have told me before I expended all my energy.'

'Too bad. Eat or drink something. Refuel.'

'I did.'

'Then you're good to go. Get dressed.'

'You going to brief me?'

'I can do it while you're getting dressed.'

'Anything we should do before I get dressed?'

She stared at him, her expression muted. 'I'm serious, Jason. This is bad.'

'Okay. Let me shower.'

He let her in and made for the bathroom.

56

As he pulled on a pair of khakis and a compression shirt in the walk-in closet, she lingered in the doorway and said, 'What do you know about high-frequency trading?'

He looked at her briefly. 'Nothing.'

'There's a few firms on Wall Street taking part in it. It exists in that soulless moral grey zone that comes with any form of capitalism. They don't contribute to anything, they don't help society — in short, they skim money off the top of the market and pretend it's not happening.'

'That sure sounds like Wall Street.'

'These guys are particularly nasty, though. Basically, they sink hundreds of millions of dollars into building technology that lets them execute trades faster than the rest of the market. Think of their fibre cables as straighter than the rest of the country's. If they do that, they can make billions by fucking around with the share prices in the milliseconds that it takes to execute a trade. Their computers are set up to take advantage of that.'

'I think I follow.'

It means that they have to get it right, though, or they can screw with the whole market. Because high-frequency trades are responsible for more than half the volume of all U.S. equity trades. And if they get these trades wrong — remember, they're happening in milliseconds — they can fuck everything up. There's something known as a flash crash. It's happened before. For a couple of minutes, the whole market can plummet, then instantly rebound. The last one happened in 2010. It wiped over a trillion dollars off the market. Then everything was back to normal within minutes.'

'Doesn't sound good that they're able to do that.'

'It's not. It means they could do it maliciously, with enough prior planning.'

Then King froze. 'Oh, shit. Is that where you're headed with this?'

'There's a high-frequency trading firm with their head-quarters right here on Wall Street. They're called Geosphere. Their existence is one giant secret. They're out there, but no-one knows how big they really are. They pay the big banks and the exchanges enormous sums of money to pretend they're not using their platforms. They operate in something called dark pools. It's corruption at the highest level, but it's technically legal, so that's what happens.'

'What's this big development you're talking about?'

'Three high-ranking employees of Geosphere — we think they're responsible for most of the groundwork that built the firm — have gone missing.'

'Fuck.'

Violetta nodded. 'That sums it up.'

'This is the *ying pai*'s plan? Cause another flash crash, or something worse?'

'Something much worse,' Violetta said. 'Look — no-one

really understands how the stock market works, besides the people who built the systems it operates on. And they're the no-names, the ones hiding in plain sight. Firms like Geosphere work closely with them, so they can do their high-frequency trading in those systems without anyone knowing any better. They could get away with murder.'

'And the Chinese could exploit that, if they knew about it. They could exploit our greed.'

'Exactly.'

'You think they're truly missing?' King said.

'What do you mean?'

'I wouldn't take that chance if I were the Chinese. They won't be able to perform complex tasks like that under duress. They'd fuck it up by being scared for their lives.'

'You're suggesting...?'

'This is Wall Street,' King said. 'And the Chinese have an endless stream of money.'

'You think they were bought? Their wives reported them missing. All three of them have kids. Families. You think they're that soulless?'

'This is Wall Street,' King said again.

Violetta furrowed her brow. 'I mean ... it's possible.'

'If they were bought, it's infinitely worse. Because it means they've been planning this for weeks, if not months, or even years. You said it yourself — the *ying pai,* above all else, are supremely patient.'

'Christ.'

'Any news on where they disappeared to?'

'No — they're ghosts. We've got the whole city's CCTV cameras looking for them. No-one's seen a thing.'

'Where's the last place they were spotted?'

'They left their offices at the end of the work day yesterday. None of them made it home. Usually that's not long enough to report a missing persons case, but it was all three of them at once. It was marked as suspicious, and we found out about it straight away, because we were scouring for exactly that type of problem.'

King rubbed his brow.

And then a harrowing thought struck him.

Guns.

And black boxes.

57

He went to the bedroom and came back out carrying the mysterious black box by the handle. He put it down in front of Violetta, and she studied it.

She said, 'Is that a CPU?'

'I don't know.'

'How'd you get it?'

'Before you showed up, Slater and I stumbled across a bunch of street thugs smuggling unmarked crates off the Hudson River. We figured we'd take matters into our own hands, and we relieved them of their precious cargo.'

'I could have you arrested for that.'

'Cut the shit.'

'No — I'm serious. If this shaky relationship between our government and the pair of you is going to work, then you have to let us gather the intelligence, and let yourselves carry out the orders. Is that understood?'

'I think you're missing the part where we did that for a decade each,' King said. 'As far as we were concerned, we were on the government's shit list. This "shaky relationship" is a fairly new development. When we did this, we considered ourselves on our own.'

'So that's what this is?' Violetta said. 'I think I get it now.'

'What?'

'The penthouses, side by side. The location — right in the heart of the city. You're a couple of vigilantes. An army of two. Waging war against organised crime.'

'This little project was our first attempt at it. We weren't sure if we were going to continue.'

'Did it work?'

'Yes.'

'So you ended up with that?' she said, pointing to the black box.

'There was more than one. And there were HK417s, and miniature claymores, and handguns.'

'Sounds like someone was arming themselves to the teeth.'

'I agree.'

'Did you find out who?'

'No. But the Whelans were the ones in charge of delivering the goods.'

'Who?'

'They're an Irish organised crime family. Remnants of the old-school mafia.'

'So they'd know where it was headed?'

'Yes.'

'And you want to track them down and make them talk?'

'Yes.'

'And you're looking for my approval to do it?'

'Yes. Like you said, you gather the intelligence, and I carry out the orders.'

'Sounds like you're gathering the intelligence right now. What does this have to do with Geosphere?'

'I think it might be connected.'

She stared down at the box. 'Some sort of foreign tech?'

'If they're trying to crash the market, they'd need some serious resources to get it done.'

'Okay,' she said, chewing her bottom lip. 'Maybe. Maybe it's a coincidence.'

'You have contacts in New York, I assume?' he said.

'Of course.'

King picked up the box, and handed it over. She took it.

'Give this to them,' he said. 'Get them to pull it apart. Find out what it is. It's above my pay grade, that's for sure.'

'Okay. But I don't want you hanging around doing nothing in the meantime. Do you know which Whelan specifically to go after?'

'No — but Slater will.'

'Why's that?'

'They've got ... a history. At least that's what I'm told.'

'Do I want to know details?'

'Probably not.'

'Then keep it to yourself. But find out. Give me a name, and I'll track him down and send you in. Discreetly, of course.'

King pulled out his phone, and Violetta pulled out hers — no doubt to contact her people in the city to arrange delivery of the mysterious black box. King dialled Slater, and noted the time as he lifted the phone to his ear.

Nine a.m.

Either everything had gone to hell, or Slater had collected Ruby and was back on the plane.

It rang, and rang, and rang.

On, and on, and on.

Just before it went to voicemail, it was answered.

Slater said, 'Hey.'

He sounded out of breath.

'You okay?' King said.

'If only you knew the morning I've had…'

'But you're still breathing.'

'Yeah.'

'Do you have Ruby?'

'Yeah. She's with me.'

'Have you had the chance to reacquaint yourselves with each other?'

'Briefly.'

'Congratulations.'

'What'd you and Violetta get up to?'

'This and that.'

'Congratulations to you, too, then. Aren't we a pair of romantics?'

'I need a favour.'

'I figured, or you wouldn't have called.'

'Give me the name of the Whelan who would know *exactly* where Gianni was taking that truck.'

A pause.

A long pause.

Then Slater said, 'That'd be Tommy.'

'Real name Thomas?'

'I wouldn't have a clue. He was the head of the family when I went to war with them. But maybe times have changed. Maybe the crown has been passed on. I can't be sure.'

'Thanks — that should be enough.'

'What are you going to do?'

'Find out where those black boxes were going. Follow the trail.'

'You think it's connected?'

'It'd be a coincidence if it wasn't. That much firepower

shows up on the streets for a private delivery. A few days later, three Wall Street power players go missing.'

'I didn't hear about that.'

'No-one heard about it. It happened last night. To the public, they're nobodies. But Violetta promises me they're the technological wizards the Chinese would need to pull off something drastic.'

'Will I be coming back to the same country?'

'If I can do something about it, you will be.'

'But if not?'

'Leave it with me. Just get back here.'

'Should you wait until I get there to execute a raid? We'd be better off working together.'

'How far away are you?'

'We just took off. Four hours to JFK.'

'I think I need to move now.'

Silence.

But an understanding silence.

After all, they'd been operating on their own for as long as they could remember. Solo missions were hardwired into their DNA.

Slater said, 'Be careful.'

'Always.'

'Don't do anything I wouldn't do.'

'You're not exactly the best example to model myself after.'

King heard a low chuckle.

'I'll be there soon,' Slater said. 'Make sure you're in one piece when I get there.'

'Will do.'

King ended the call, and turned to Violetta, who was getting off her own phone.

He said, 'Slater's alive. Sounds like he went through the ringer, but he has Ruby and they're on the way back.'

'So the cartels *did* come for her?'

'I don't know if it was the cartels.'

'Perhaps it wasn't. If it was *sicario*s, then Slater wouldn't be around to answer the phone.'

King almost smirked. 'Then you don't know Will Slater.'

She said, 'My team is picking up the box in fifteen minutes. They'll have a rudimentary analysis of it within the hour. Trust me — they know what they're doing.'

'They're tech guys?'

'They're everything. Jacks of all trades. It's a highly competitive industry.'

'I assume the pay is still handsome?'

'We have to attract the best.'

King said, 'I have a name for you. Work your magic. Find him for me.'

'Shoot.'

'Tommy Whelan.'

58

An hour later, King sat in the window of a café across the street from Tommy Whelan's building and sipped at a steaming espresso.

He was dressed in civilian clothes, but he wouldn't be for long. Violetta had kicked her request to the right intelligence sources, who revealed that ever since a violent incident at a multi-million dollar townhouse once owned by the Whelans on the Upper East Side, they'd been keeping tabs on the family's whereabouts. They'd never be able to pin anything on the Whelans — the family were meticulous criminals, after all.

But it was useful to know where they were at all times.

So it turned out Tommy Whelan was still on the Upper East Side, but he'd downgraded from an eight-figure status symbol to a seven-figure luxury apartment in a residential building.

Which was useful to him for a number of reasons.

There was collateral in the form of his civilian neighbours, so his enemies wouldn't raid the place in broad daylight like Slater seemingly had done to their townhouse the year before. The building also had impressive security in its own right, fronted by the extortionate body corporate fees and the general opulence of New York luxury residential dwellings. And, finally, Tommy could establish his own security system on top of that, doubling up on the protection.

King saw Whelan's goons now. They weren't hard to spot. They lounged around the base of the building, chain-smoking cigarettes and ambling along the sidewalks in their long winter coats. As if they were doing their best impression of real wise guys — but that was the point. They were there to stand out. They were there to say, *Hey, if you want to fuck with Tommy, you have to go through us.*

Which was entirely possible, if a trained combatant could jump them simultaneously, but at the end of the day it would result in a shootout in the Upper East Side, right there on the street. The cops would swarm the place within a minute.

So King knew he had to be discreet.

He found his opportunity fast. One of the security goons was shorter than the rest — five-eight, maybe, which mattered in an industry like this. The beefy redhead had compensated for it by packing on muscle in the gym, but it was clearly not enough. And, as King expected, the fact that he was stuck with his height in the intimidation business meant he was always having to go overboard on the aggressive demeanour. He had to play the part of the jumpy, twitchy, reckless one — the small guy who could go off at any moment. It kept him on a level playing field with the big, calm, confident street thugs. It added something new to the mix.

Napoleon complex: an exhibit.

What it meant was that the guy was permanently on guard. For the small man in an aggressive world, weakness cannot be tolerated. He smoked his cigarettes a little faster, he looked around a little more, and he eyeballed any passerby that dared to hold their gaze for longer than a second.

King noted all of this, then stepped out of the coffee shop and weaved through traffic.

In his head, he planned out an exact sequence of events.

He memorised them once.

Game face.

He stepped up onto the sidewalk like a businessman with places to be — he was dressed in a collared shirt, a cashmere sweater and dress slacks to fit the part. But smart clothing couldn't hide his massive frame, so he decided to embrace it. He kept his shoulders back, but he added a certain level of uncertainty to his gait. He was a confident man in the boardroom, and he clearly took care of himself, but did he have the *real* tough-guy streak?

When he walked past Whelan's building, he steered himself toward the shorter guy and intercepted him on the sidewalk.

He stared straight ahead, pretended the guy didn't exist, and slammed his shoulder into the man on the way past, literally smashing him out of the way.

Another way to trigger a shorter man — simply over-power them and pretend you didn't mean it.

King wheeled on the spot and scrunched up his face with clear irritation and said, 'Watch where you're walking, dickhead.'

Without even waiting for a response, he hustled down the next laneway, maintaining long strides.

He heard the short guy's rapid footsteps as he ran to catch up.

Looking for a fight.

Outraged at being manhandled.

King smirked.

Perfect.

59

The guy came running into the alleyway at breakneck speed, his face red, a vein protruding from the side of his temple. He had his fists balled and a black rage in his eyes.

If King was an ordinary civilian, he might have shit himself right there on the spot.

Because there was a world of difference between an angry thug and a soft-bodied office worker.

But then there was another world of difference between Jason King and an angry thug.

He checked once for witnesses — there was foot traffic passing by the other end of the alley, but they were looking ahead, and everyone was in a hurry. That was something King had recognised over time. Everyone passing by was a node of self-judgment. People aren't concerned about others — they're concerned about themselves. Nine times out of ten, if they happened to see two angry men fighting in an alleyway, they'd carry on walking.

Not their concern.

So King planted his feet and loosened his hips and when

the small guy ran into the mouth of the laneway he twisted into a side kick, taking advantage of the size difference. If they'd weighed the same, he wouldn't have risked taking one leg off the ground and potentially compromising his balance. Not in a street fight — not with this much testosterone in the air. But there *was* a size difference, and it was substantial, so he treated the small guy like one of Rory Barker's leather kickboxing pads and hit him so hard in the ribcage that the man bounced off the nearby concrete wall like he weighed nothing at all.

King figured he'd broken several of the guy's ribs, so he didn't even bother with a follow-up shot.

He stood patiently as the man curled up in the foetal position and moaned, and waited for the help to come.

Which it did, only a few seconds later.

One of the other bodyguards came barrelling into view — he was big, and his coat was oversized to compensate for his giant frame. He was probably an inch taller than King, and a few pounds heavier, maybe. There was a lot of risk at play. A single well-placed punch from either party would lead to their opponent sprawled out on a dirty laneway floor with the sounds of the city echoing in their ears.

So it was a good thing that King punched the guy square in the jaw first. He cocked his fist like a loaded gun and whipped it straight through the guy's raised arms and torqued his chin to the left and added all his weight to the punch as soon as he realised it had landed.

The guy's head rotated ninety degrees, then whipped back into place. Like yanking a lamp out of the power socket. His brain dimmed, and went to sleep, and he crashed to earth, landing on top of his buddy. The short guy groaned again and heaved the unconscious body off him, despite his ribs protesting every step of the way.

Because, of course, a little pain was better than the humiliation of lying underneath his co-worker.

King wasted no time. He stripped the larger man of his coat and threw it on over his sweater. It was Armani — impeccable quality. The guy was also wearing a Brixton fiddler cap, like something out of a bad British gangster film, so King put that on as well.

Then he turned and hustled back out of the laneway.

He kept his head down, and weaved through foot traffic, and kept his aching right hand in his coat pocket. He was lucky he hadn't shattered his knuckles punching the guy in the jaw. Bones — especially those in your hands — were brittle and delicate, no matter how tough you were. King much preferred the elbow, but the range hadn't been right.

He made it to the revolving doors leading into the building in less than fifteen seconds.

And ran straight into the third guard.

The guy put a hand on King's chest and said, 'Bro, what was that?'

When King looked up and revealed his face the man froze in place.

'Wait, you're not—'

King said, 'Buddy, you're fucked. There's a 9mm in my pocket pointing right at you.'

The guy gulped and went pale and didn't move a muscle.

'How about you take the rest of the day off?' King said. 'Let me do what I need to do. How's that sound?'

'They'll kill me.'

'*I'll* kill you.'

The guy nodded, already sweating from the temples, and shrugged. 'Guess I could come up with an excuse.'

'Attaboy.'

And just like that, one of Whelan's most important foot soldiers — tasked with protecting the boss himself — turned and walked off down the street, recognising it wasn't the right day to be a hero. It was simple human nature. Catch anyone off-guard, and you lead the negotiation. It didn't take long for King to convince someone they were better off not trying at all.

He walked into the lobby and approached the concierge without hesitation. There was a line of residents waiting for service, but King shoved right past all of them like he owned the place and rested his giant forearms on the shiny marble. He leaned right across and stared a thin young woman dead in the eyes.

He made himself look like a hard, cold bastard.

He was good at that.

'I'm told he needs to speak with me,' he said.

She took one look at his Brixton cap and long coat and knew immediately who he worked for. That was always going to be the case. Men like Tommy Whelan relied on bribes, intimidation, coercion. It was clearly a poorly-kept secret that he had his own security hanging around. He probably paid building management a tidy sum to let him do his thing.

And they'd passed it down to the staff.

The woman said, 'Um ... do you want me to ring ahead?'

King relaxed a little, and rolled his eyes, as if to say, *You know how it is.*

He said, 'Trust me. He knows I'm coming.'

Like he was about to be disciplined.

Which put them, subconsciously, in the same boat.

Fearful of the man upstairs.

She gave a little smile and said, 'Sure. First elevator on

the left. Hit the floor number and you won't need a keycard. I'll program it now.'

Without skipping a beat he said, 'What's the floor number?'

If he'd hesitated, it would have been even more obvious.

She looked at him.

He shrugged sheepishly and said, 'I'm new on the job.'

'Nine.'

'And the room number?'

She said, 'Seriously?'

He smiled and said, 'I'm as unhappy about it as you are.'

'904.'

'Thanks. Have a great day.'

He hadn't objectified her, or called her *doll,* or *sweetheart,* or *sugar.* Which was probably an anomaly for the men who hung around this building wearing Brixton caps and overcoats. So she took the strange development in stride and nodded with a pleasant smile and waved him through.

He put his game face back on and headed for the elevators.

60

He got out on the ninth floor and made a beeline for Whelan's door.

He passed 901, then 902, then 903...

He smacked a fist three consecutive times into the black wood.

He yelled, 'Boss, it's urgent!'

He stepped off to the side so Whelan couldn't see him if he looked through the peephole, and waited with his hands down by his sides, his fingers twitching, like a gunslinger ready to draw.

The sound of a lock turning floated out into the corridor, and the handle turned and—

King smashed the heel of his boot into the centre of the door so hard he almost took the whole thing off its hinges. Then he ran straight inside without getting a proper look at the damage he'd inflicted. He muscled Whelan inside, checked he didn't have any weapons in his hands, then threw him to the floor.

He turned and slammed the door closed and took a deep breath.

He was in.

Tommy Whelan lay gasping for breath on the cool marble. There was a chunk of skin missing underneath his chin where the door had lashed against his neck, and he was grasping his chest like all the breath had been squeezed from his lungs.

King said, 'You'll live.'

He waited for the theatrics to dissipate, and when Whelan finally sat up there was a look of confusion on his pale face. He was an old man, well past seventy, wearing a grey wool suit. He had long grey hair billowing back off his forehead, tucked behind his ears. There was no humanity in his eyes. He was a ruthless old tyrant by all accounts, and King couldn't care less what state he was in at the end of all this.

King dragged him to his feet, patted him down for any hidden blades or firearms, then manhandled him into the living area.

It was a similar setup to his own penthouse. A sweeping view of Central Park, a high ceiling, and an open-plan living area with the kitchen, dining, and living combined into one.

Seems like the whole Upper East Side recruited the same architect, King thought.

He dumped Whelan down on the sofa, and loomed over him.

'Do you have a panic button?' King said.

'What?' the old man grumbled.

'A panic button. To alert your goons if you're in trouble.'

'Yeah. It's right here in my pocket.'

'Press it.'

'What?'

'Press it. Call for help.'

Whelan sat still.

King let the silence drag out. He crouched down so he was inches away from Whelan. He said, 'There's no catch. I'm serious. Press it. But when your men get here and I fuck them up, there'll be no-one left to call for help. Then what are you going to do? If I were you I'd leave it alone, because if you exhaust your final lifeline you might go mad with stress. If it doesn't work, I can stay up here for as long as I like. But if you give me the time of day, and give me what I want, then I'll be on my way.'

Whelan said, 'What do you want?'

'Me and my friend aren't happy with you.'

'Who's your friend?'

'I think you know him.'

Whelan sat silent, oblivious. He was probably more focused on not having a heart attack than the mental acuity required to wrack his brain for what King might mean.

King said, 'You ever met anyone that reminded you of me?'

Blood dripped from Whelan's chin into his lap, staining the wool.

The man said, 'Once.'

'How'd that work out for you?'

'Not well.'

'I'm the same deal.'

'I'll say it again — what do you need?'

'You're a businessman, yes? You have a vested interest in doing what's best in the long-term?'

'Of course.'

'Then you're going to tell me exactly where that truck-load of crates was going. The ones that came off the Hudson.'

'I—'

'If the next thing that comes out of your mouth isn't

what I want to hear, I'll go find your sidearm and shove it up your ass.'

Silence.

'You think I'm lying?'

'No,' Whelan said. 'I think you're telling the truth.'

'So where were the crates headed?'

'East Harlem.'

'Where precisely?'

'There's a trio of abandoned townhouses that got halfway through construction before the developer went tits up. They haven't knocked them down yet, and they're a fuckin' haven for squatters. I was told to drop the truck there.'

'By who?'

'They kept themselves anonymous.'

'Tommy...'

'I'm telling the truth. I care more about my own life than protecting my clients. If I knew more about them, I'd fuckin' tell you.'

'They're important enough to stay anonymous, and yet you outsourced the job to a half-rate thug like Gianni?'

'He wasn't half-rate,' Whelan said. 'You and your friend are fuckin' killers. Cold hard killers. You could make a lot of cash in a business like this.'

'We do fine for ourselves.'

'Piggybacking off the hard work of people like me?'

King almost laughed. But instead of taking the whole situation in jest, he got angry. He shoved Whelan back into the couch and pressed a palm against his throat and tightened his grip. Whelan gasped and wheezed and coughed and spluttered. King said, 'Give me the address.'

'O—okay,' Whelan wheezed.

King let go, and the old man bent over and vomited on the floor.

King went over to the kitchen, fished a notepad and pen out of the drawers, and came back to the sofa.

He dropped the notepad, followed by the pen, on Whelan's head.

Whelan scrawled an address in cursive on the lined paper, and King scrutinised it.

As promised, it was in East Harlem.

King crouched down. 'If this is the wrong location, I'll come back here and skin you alive.'

'Please,' Whelan said, coughing blood. 'You have to believe me. If there's nothing there ... I don't know — shit, man, it was just the place I was told to deliver the goods. I have no allegiance to the people who hired me. I don't care what happens to them.'

'How did you communicate with them?'

'Burner phones.'

'You still got the numbers?'

'Yeah, but what good will that do?'

King sighed. 'You're right. Well, I'm going to chase this up. In the meantime, you'll probably quadruple your security here, or move to another location. It won't matter. I'll find you — I promise you that.'

'I know you will.'

'And I'll bring Slater with me.'

'Okay.'

'And we'll make your life a living hell.'

'I know.'

King looked down at the notepad and said, 'You want to change that address to the right one?'

'It is right. I swear.'

'Okay, Tommy. Don't make me come back.'

'I wouldn't dream of it.'

King left him there in a puddle of his own puke, and walked into the entranceway.

He placed a hand on the door handle and froze.

He heard something.

On the other side of the door.

The slightest twitch of movement.

The door flew open, and a body cascaded out into the communal corridor.

It was an old man.

So the shooter hesitated.

Holy shit, the guy was probably thinking, *that's the boss.*

King followed Tommy Whelan out, hustling after the old mob boss, who he'd thrown double-handed out the door. It masked the clean shot the thug was looking for, and King only needed a second to capitalise. He hurled Whelan out of the way again, and came face-to-face with the fourth bodyguard — the one he'd initially missed. This guy was also dressed in a grey overcoat and a Brixton cap, and he had a 9mm in his hand, and he was searching for an opportunity to get a shot off.

He didn't find one.

Because King was right there in his face, and he used the sudden explosion of activity to his advantage and shouldered the guy into the wall. And when King slammed a shoulder into someone, it half-crippled them, so when the guy bounced off the plaster and came right back in the other direction he was in no state to get off a decent shot.

And at that point King was ready to *pounce.*

So he did.

He had his own gun in an appendix holster under his sweater, easily accessible, but he didn't want to fire an unsuppressed shot in a residential complex — and truthfully he didn't need to. He grabbed the guy's head and crushed it between two hands and pinned it in place, then thundered an elbow into the side of his temple. He used the guy's sudden lack of equilibrium to wrestle the 9mm out of his hand and throw it across the corridor, disarming him instantly.

Then he punched him in the stomach, folding him over, which led straight to a knee to the forehead, which twisted his neck at an unnatural angle and planted him on the floor, dazed and confused. King then stepped back, lined up his aim, and booted the guy in the face.

Lights out.

King went straight across the corridor and collected the 9mm, then used it to pistol-whip Whelan on the bridge of his nose. The old man went to howl, but King clamped a hand down over his mouth and threw him back into his own apartment.

King loomed over him.

'Okay,' Whelan said. 'Okay, okay...'

'Okay what?'

'I'll give you the right address.'

King seethed with rage. 'You clearly don't understand how serious I am about needing to fix this.'

'I don't know what I was doing, man,' Whelan said. 'I needed to move some cargo. They wouldn't even tell me what it was. They just wanted local experts to handle it when it came off the Hudson.'

'You sure did a good job of that.'

'No thanks to you.'

'Write down the correct address.'

Whelan complied. Maybe because King hadn't hit him again. He was bleeding from the nose and underneath the chin, and he knew how bad King could make him hurt. So he crab-crawled over to the notepad that King had dropped in the hallway, and scribbled a new address underneath. A drop of blood ran off the tip of his nose and splashed the paper.

King picked up the notepad, then took the Glock out of his appendix holster and pointed it at the old man's face. 'Thanks, Tommy.'

The face turned ghost-white.

'I'm not lying this time!' Whelan said. 'I gave you what you needed!'

'I know that.'

'Then what the fuck is this?'

'Do you think I'm some sort of moral hero?' King said.

'I thought that's exactly what you were,' Whelan said. 'You and your friend. Vigilantes protecting the city, or whatever you're fuckin' calling it.'

'You ruin thousands of lives with what you call "unions." You extort small businesses and workers for all the spare pennies they have, and you call it protection. You run guns through the city. You arm whoever needs arming. You bring heroin and crack up from Mexico and break it down into the cheapest, most toxic shit you can feasibly get away with, then you lace it with fentanyl and sell it to the poor and the homeless and the addicted so they can OD in peace. And then, to make sure you keep your business interests in all these areas viable, you pay off cops and government workers and federal agents so you can gun down whoever you need to gun down to stay on top. You're probably responsible for twenty percent of the murders in New York City.'

Whelan sat there in silence.

King said, 'You really think I'd know all that and leave you alive to carry on getting away with it?'

'I think that—'

But King didn't care what Whelan thought.

He shot him through the forehead, as he'd done to hundreds in the past.

And he didn't feel bad about it.

Despite his stature as one of the toughest, meanest, most ruthless sons-of-bitches on the East Coast, Tommy Whelan died like the rest of them.

Quickly.

King tucked the Glock into its holster, and put the bloody notepad in his coat pocket, and left the scene immediately.

62

True to Whelan's description, there were three townhouses.

King hovered on the other side of the road, deep in the shadows of a trash-ridden alley, and scrutinised their design.

They were luxury developments, four storeys each, all modern glass and steel and brick in a haphazard amalgamation of something that was these days considered "stylish." King figured they would have gone for many millions each if they'd been completed. But they were surrounded by the old ochre residential complexes native to East Harlem, and their modernity didn't gel with the rest of the street. Not to mention the fact that they were crushed up against each other due to a lack of available land. There was no room between each building — not even a claustrophobic side passage.

And they were definitely half-finished.

Most of the exteriors had been completed, but King could see through the windows, and the interior of each building was nothing but an empty shell. There were exposed beams and tufts of insulation hanging from the ceilings. The perimeter fence — wire, see-through — ran around the entire four-building complex, and construction tape hung in loose tattered threads. But what stopped scavengers from ransacking the valuable materials was the security system still in place around the entire thing. There were CCTV cameras and visible alarms above the doors and giant warning signs plastered everywhere.

King knew it was all a front. If the developers had gone bankrupt, they weren't checking the tapes. The cameras probably weren't even on. But it deterred looters, so they stayed up as the developers scrambled to come up with a solution to their financial woes.

Until then, it *would* prove effective as a temporary, discreet meeting place.

Or something worse...

King remembered the claymores, and the guns, and the black boxes.

Like someone was gearing up to defend a fortress.

Is this where it's all happening?

A nondescript group of rundown buildings in East Harlem?

Is this where they'll bring the U.S. economy to its knees?

He'd spent close to an hour scouting the surrounding streets, looking for potential vantage points to set up a sniper, but he'd come away confident. And, frankly, he wasn't prepared to waste another second. He knew the beatings he'd dished out would catch up to him eventually through muscle fatigue and exhaustion. Besides, he was still hurting from the brawl the night before in his penthouse. Everything ached, but he was used to that. At the end of this, he'd sleep for two days straight, then get to work healing up with the same ferocity that he approached everything else with.

For now, he would fight.

So he was about to step out of the shadows and cross the street when his phone buzzed in his pocket.

He pulled it out.

Violetta.

He answered.

'Got an update for me?' he said.

'Plenty. Where are you?'

There was urgency in her tone. She was stressed.

He said, 'Out the front of the location Tommy Whelan gave me. I was about to move in. It's probably nothing, though. If I had to guess, this was the collection point for—'

'I don't think so,' she snapped. 'Are you in East Harlem?'

'Yes. How did you—'

'You need to move in, *right now.*'

'Why? If you've got information, I need it.'

'Will Kettler was spotted in East Harlem on one of the CCTV feeds about an hour ago.'

'Who the hell is Will Kettler?'

'The founder of Geosphere.'

'Oh.'

'Right... and we found out what the black box was.'

King held his breath.

She said, 'It's really bad, Jason. It's some sort of encryption device, and it's of a quality we've never seen before in civilian hands. We think it's Russian technology, so it makes sense that it's being used by the Chinese. With that much processing power, they could have done whatever the hell they wanted with the market from the safety of their own homes, and no-one would have known who started it, or when.'

'So they were planning to do it in secrecy,' King said. 'Doesn't that explain why they left their families?'

'Why?'

'Because if they had to follow through with this despite the lack of encryption, then running away to a tropical island with brand new identities would be preferable to having their families slaughtered alongside them for disobedience.'

'Or staying here, and getting found out.'

'Precisely.'

'I don't like this,' Violetta said. 'It feels like they're ten steps ahead.'

'They didn't get the tech they needed. Or the guns. Or the claymores. That's what they were using as a backup plan, so on the off-chance they were found out they could slaughter anyone that came across them until their Chinese contacts could whisk them out of the country.'

'You think that would have worked?'

'I think they did exactly what three idiotic Wall Street power players would do in a situation like this.'

'So get in there and find out.'

'Call me if you need me.'

'Be safe. I've got a feeling this is the beginning.'

'Let's hope not.'

King ended the call and slid the phone back into his pocket. He'd shed the overcoat and the cap, and was wearing the same cashmere sweater and dress slacks, and now he picked up a couple of supplies off the alley floor he'd secured on his preliminary sweep.

Namely, a Bluetooth earpiece and a clipboard, and a badge he'd had custom-printed at a small shop in East Harlem. It read, MICHAEL.

He made sure the Glock in his appendix holster wasn't showing underneath the sweater, then adjusted his shirt collar and whistled a tune under his breath as he sauntered out of the laneway.

There was no activity in the windows, or he would have waited. Save for a state-of-the-art hidden security system the occupants had installed on their own, there were no eyes on him. He crossed the busy street, approached the fence, and arched his eyebrows in surprise — a performance for anyone who might be watching. Then he shook his head, as if flabbergasted that this hadn't been included in the job description. He set his clipboard down, placed both hands on the iron bars separating two sections of the fence, and heaved them apart.

Then he wiped his brow for exaggerated effect — exactly like an office worker unaccustomed to the difficulties of manual labour — and walked right up to the middle townhouse.

Taking a wild speculative guess.

He rapped on the door over and over again, and at the top of his lungs shouted, 'Excuse me! Hello! Is anyone in there? You are politely being asked to leave! Excuse me! I have been informed by the council that there are uninvited visitors dwelling in this residence. I must assure you that this building is still the property of J.C. Randwick Developments and you must—'

The door flew open in his face, and a gun barrel came out of the darkness and skewered into his forehead.

A low voice said, 'Get inside right now, you piece of shit.'

63

oly shit, I got it right.

King turned on the waterworks, generating crocodile tears out of thin air. He'd had a pistol shoved in his face before. He couldn't remember a year that had passed since he was eighteen years old where that hadn't been a regular occurrence. So his heart rate barely rose as the cold metal touched his skin, but that wasn't how a real estate agent would react.

So he bawled his eyes out.

A hand reached out over the threshold and snatched his collar and dragged him inside.

He stumbled in through the door, and it slammed shut behind him immediately.

He couldn't see much through his tears, but that was necessary for the role. If they frisk-searched him, it'd be over. They'd find the Glock, and that would be that. He could sense serious friction all around him — there was movement everywhere.

But he sure as hell wasn't getting anywhere by kicking in

the front door and fighting an entire army at once, so deception was his best bet.

Hands were on his sweater and throwing him to the floor, and before he knew it he was spread-eagled on his back on the cool tile. When he opened his eyes and looked through the tears he saw a large cavernous space comprising most of the ground floor. The lights weren't working, because the building wasn't finished, so the shadows were long and deep and the only illumination came from the street outside. Everything was cast in muted shades of blue.

There were eight silhouettes standing over him.

He couldn't let his act slip. The next few seconds were paramount — they'd dictate how the rest of the altercation played out. Someone stomped down on his stomach, and he exaggerated his reaction. He moaned and curled into a ball and coughed and gasped, and silently thanked his lucky stars that the boot had come down a few inches away from his appendix holster.

If they discovered the Glock, then there'd be a problem.

One of the figures said, 'A fucking developer? Really? I thought you said there'd be no problems.'

'I paid them off,' a voice moaned.

The guy sounded genuinely distressed.

As if he was realising what had to happen.

One of the Geosphere guys, King noted.

Another said, 'We don't need to kill him, do we?'

'You thin-skinned bitch,' a gruff voice said. 'All this computer shit you're doing — you know how many people you're about to kill with that?'

'Yeah, but...'

'But you want to be detached from it, don't you?'

'I mean—'

'You don't want to see the consequences of your actions, you spineless fuck.'

'You want to get paid? Then stop throwing around insults. You work for us.'

'You hired us to do what's needed to protect you. Now we're doing it.'

'Fine.'

King let his disguise slip momentarily, so he could look around the room. As he suspected, four of the eight were gruff ex-military types, precisely the type of guns-for-hire that had ambushed him in his penthouse. They were easy to recruit, usually desperate for work, and had the past training to be put to good use. But they weren't wielding HK417s, and they didn't have M-1 Minimore claymores set up around the townhouses, and they didn't have their special black boxes.

King had stripped that from them, as he'd strip everything from them...

One of the gruff ex-military types said, 'If you don't want to watch, then don't watch.'

A soft, eerie voice — a new voice — said, 'I will take them away.'

King fought to see through the tears that were entirely necessary to his performance.

He saw a small Asian man with ramrod straight posture and eyes like thunder, watching him like a hawk.

King's breath caught in his throat.

Is this...?

The Asian man gestured for the Geosphere crew to follow him. They were all white and nervous and fidgety and uncomfortable, with dark bags under their eyes, indicating long-term lack of sleep.

Wall Street, King thought.

The suits shuffled out of the room with trepidation, some of them glancing back at King on their way out. He thought a couple of them might have felt genuine concern for him.

Don't feel sorry for me, he thought. *Feel sorry for your friends that I'm about to kill.*

He took his gaze away from them, and in his peripheral vision saw the Asian man shuffle out of the room too. Like he was coddling his clients. Babysitting them. Making sure it was all okay. And no wonder. The success of his operation relied on three men who'd abandoned their families to see the job through. Sure, they were brilliant, and sure, they were morally bankrupt, but there was a shred of humanity still left in them.

Not so much for the four men that stood over him. King knew their types. They'd been permanently scarred and traumatised by their stints overseas, as so many had, and their goodwill had been beaten and battered and shot out of them. And they'd returned home to a country that was indifferent to their future, and that led to places like this.

One of the big thugs snatched a handful of King's hair and yanked him up to his knees.

It hurt like hell.

King showed it on his face.

The big man slapped him on the cheek, hard enough to redden the skin instantly, and King felt the left side of his face go numb.

Now, the seeds of genuine panic stirred.

This guy was strong.

The big bearded man scratched the scar on his left cheek with grimy fingernails and said, 'Go get the silencer.'

'Just fuckin' beat him to death,' a second man said.

The bearded guy looked up, grinning. 'You think?'

King went stone-faced.

One of them noticed.

The other three didn't.

The guy up the back who realised what was happening stiffened up. He started to open his mouth, but King cut him off.

King said, 'You really shouldn't have told me that.'

There wasn't a shred of fear in his voice.

The bearded guy looked down. 'What the fuck you sayin', boy?'

But all of them could sense the atmosphere had changed.

'You can't fire an unsuppressed round,' King said. 'Not when you're still trying to keep this place a secret. That's a shame, isn't it? Means those guns in your hands are useless.'

Then he leapt to his feet and used the top of his skull as a battering ram to break the bearded guy's jaw on the way up.

64

T he bearded guy stumbled back, blind with pain, but King didn't worry about putting him down on the floor.

The guy was out of the fight from a logistical standpoint.

His jaw was broken, and that crippled you no matter how tough you were.

King darted past him and launched into a scything front kick, slamming the Gore-Tex heel of his boot home against the chest wall of the second closest thug. He was a big beefy slab of muscle and fat, like the first guy, but King cracked his sternum all the same. He stumbled back against the wall, wheezing for breath, turning pale and grasping his chest.

King used the momentum to pivot into a spinning backward elbow that struck home against the nose and mouth of the third guy. He'd been aiming for the forehead, where he had the best chance of knocking him unconscious with a single strike, but the third man had stepped into it, barreling toward the fight instead of shying away from it. That was why he was paid the big bucks, but it was also why he went down screaming, instead of unconscious.

King sprinted at the fourth guy and sidestepped a wild haymaker — as he expected, as soon as the man realised it was one-on-one, he panicked and threw everything he had into a single punch with the hope of ending the fight quickly. But King had seen a thousand identical punches in his lifetime, and he threw his head off the centre line, and it missed. Then he was free to unleash four consecutive punches into the guy's face, using the same right hand to *pop-pop-pop-pop.*

The guy fell to the floor in a miserable bleeding heap and King ripped the Glock out of his appendix holster.

The Asian man stepped into the doorway, with his hand on his belt, searching for his own weapon.

Responding immediately to the crisis.

King had the Glock pointed between his eyes before he could blink.

King said, 'Take your hand off your belt.'

The guy kept it there, his eyes drilling into King, making rapid calculations.

King said, 'When that hand moves, it had better be moving away from your weapon. If you go even an inch towards it, I'll blow your brains out.'

The hand didn't move.

King said, 'Don't tempt me.'

The man didn't react — his face remained passive, blank, unflinching. But he took his hand off his belt, and held it toward King, fingers splayed.

He did the same with his other hand.

King breathed a sigh.

He said, 'Take me to where your silencer is.'

The man stared at him.

King said, '*Now.*'

'We do not have one,' the man said in his low, whispering voice.

Like a monk breaking a ten-year vow of silence.

King said, 'I heard these boys ask for it. Or would you rather I discharged my weapon without it?'

The small man accepted defeat, and gave a curt nod.

'This way,' he said.

King didn't enjoy the more brutal aspects of the job, but sometimes they were necessary. The simple truth was that although he'd beat down the four guns-for-hire, their wounds were in no way permanent. They were bleeding, and cradling broken noses and jaws, but in the time it took King to find a silencer they could easily clamber to their feet and access hidden caches of weapons in the townhouse. So King stomped down on each of their heads in turn, taking no pleasure from it, but carrying it out all the same.

When he finished, they were all swimming in unconsciousness.

They'd be awake within a minute or so — this wasn't the movies, and staying out cold for anything more than five minutes usually led to permanent brain damage — but they'd wake up dazed and confused.

They'd be useless for the better part of an hour.

The Asian man watched with perverse amusement. When King was finished, he smiled and said, 'I know who you are.'

'Do you?'

'We tried to kill you. It didn't work. I should have recognised you when you knocked on the door. This is my fault.'

'You're goddamn right it is. What's your name?'

'Jian.'

Where are your friends?'

'My friends?'

'Take me to them.'

King strode forward and grabbed a handful of Jian's collar and shoved him out of the hallway. His heart was thrumming hard in his chest at the myriad possibilities, but when they moved to the next room and found the three Geosphere workers cowering in the corner, King wasn't surprised.

This wasn't their world, after all.

King said, 'The silencer.'

They were in a hollowed-out kitchen with the skeletons of upmarket cabinetry dotting the walls. There was a kitchen island in the centre of the room — a giant slab of marble covered in a protective wrap. It was the most expensive instalment in the building, and perhaps the only finished piece inside. The same muted lighting coated this room — the sparse illumination fell in sheets of light and dark blue.

It lengthened the shadows.

It added to the fear the Geosphere trio were feeling.

King figured he'd help them along in their terror.

He said, 'All three of you get over here.'

He jabbed the Glock in their direction, as if he were about to use it.

They practically ran to him.

He said, 'Lie down on the floor and put your hands behind your backs.'

They complied.

At the same time, Jian went over to the dusty countertop beside the kitchen island and picked up a Gemtech GM-9 suppressor.

'Toss it over here,' King said.

Jian complied.

But the tension was palpable in the air.

The guy was tensed up like a coiled spring, searching for the slightest chink in King's armour, and King would be damned if he was about to give it to him. But he knew Jian would capitalise on it if he found it, so he said, 'Come here.'

Jian seemed to realise he was about to be incapacitated.

He took three steps toward King and lunged.

King hesitated.

Because he was contemplating trying to shoot the guy through the leg so he could get answers, but by the time he went to adjust his aim it was too late, and Jian was too close, so he jerked his aim back up to the centre mass but then *that* was too late also...

The classic mistake of indecision.

King was only human.

He couldn't keep tabs on eight hostiles at once without massacring them to compensate.

Which was what he should have done in the first place.

Jian crashed into him with surprising dexterity and they both went toppling to the floor.

65

C haos reigned.

King used the size advantage to hurl Jian off him, and he lined up a shot with the Glock but the guy spun and smashed a fist down on top of the pistol, crushing it into the floor. King fired anyway and the bullet roared in the empty room and the three Geosphere workers flinched and dropped to the floor in sheer shock.

The bullet missed, and Jian vaulted off the floor and kicked out and caught King in the chest, but he rolled with it and used the momentum to dissipate most of the impact. It winded him all the same, but he didn't feel it. He used the gap to spring to his feet but Jian kept crushing pressure on the Glock, and it came free from his grip. He kicked out at it, making sure Jian couldn't get his hands on it either, and the pistol skittered away across the tiles.

Jian hit him hard in the stomach, nearly doubling him over, and *that* hurt. King hadn't been hit like that in some time. He didn't go down to his knees, but Jian sensed weakness and surged forward. When he came into range, King hit him in the jaw with an uppercut that staggered him on the spot. But he still managed a final punch in semi-consciousness, and it slammed home — knuckles to flesh — against King's ribcage.

And his liver shut down.

Fuck, King thought.

It was all he could manage.

All the pain caught up to him. His body shut down involuntarily, his liver burning like hot molten fire, and he sat down with his back against the kitchen island and tried his best to mask how badly he was hurt.

Because he realised, if he could wait it out, he'd win.

The three Geosphere workers were on the other side of the room, cowering away from the fight. It made sense — they were watching two trained murderers do their best to kill each other, to tear each other limb from limb, and if you weren't accustomed to violence it was visceral to behold. They were in commercial fitness shape, but that wouldn't cut it in an arena like this. The stakes were impossibly high.

But if they knew any better, they'd pile in right now.

Because Jian went to step in and finish King off, but when he put his foot down his ankle wobbled and gave out. And he looked down in disbelief at his legs as they refused to respond. Jian realised he was far more hurt than he realised — often, getting rocked by a punch didn't reveal itself until your legs simply collapsed on you.

That happened now, and Jian stumbled and lurched and fell to the floor.

Like two drunk bar-room brawlers, they sat on their rears and heaved for breath and tried to get their bearings.

The first one to their feet would win.

King recognised this, and went to lever himself up on one foot, trying to grip the lip of the bench above his head for support. But a sickening wave of nausea gripped him, and his liver screamed in protest, and he folded over at the waist and did his best not to let the pain show on his face.

But he couldn't help himself.

He winced, and suppressed a moan.

Jian sat still, composing himself.

The room went quiet.

And slowly, one by one, the Geosphere crew started to realise they should interfere.

Understanding spread across each of their faces. They flashed nervous glances at one another. Then the first guy — in his early fifties with tanned wrinkled skin from too many vacations in the Caribbean — stepped forward. He seemed hesitant to move, still terrified to get involved. But there was a certain detachment in his eyes — he was doing his best to be ruthless, amoral. He already did it at work everyday. What difference did it make if he had to stomp down on someone's head a few times and finish it?

He advanced toward King.

King let out a guttural groan, figuring if they knew he was hurt there was no point masking it.

That seemed to encourage the Geosphere worker. The tanned wrinkles creased into a lurid smile. And at that point King realised there was little separating a corporate sociopath from a violent sociopath, save for habits. This man would willingly kill to save his own skin. It was all the same principle. He simply hadn't done it before.

But he was about to.

The man got a surge of confidence and came forward and raised his bespoke dress shoe into the air and brought it down.

King couldn't get out of the way in time. All the combat experience and physical conditioning in the world meant nothing when you got hit in the liver. His blood vessels were dilating, his heart rate decreasing, his blood pressure dropping. Total shutdown. Game over.

So King tried to move his head, but it didn't work.

The shoe crashed down on his temple.

Crack.

Darkness.

But then he came back as fast as he'd gone out.

He blinked hard and saw stars exploding in his vision, popping and bursting and slithering around. He saw double. But he wasn't out.

The Geosphere worker clenched his teeth, and veins popped out the side of his neck. He was supercharged with adrenaline. Maybe he'd never thrown a punch or a kick with venom in his life. But he could do it again.

So he did.

He raised his foot, and tensed his core, and brought his leg down.

Straight toward King's unprotected face.

66

But the guy missed.

Because the crippling pain in King's mid-section receded by a hair, and a hair was all he needed. He catapulted out of the way and the dress shoe sailed on past his face. He harnessed the magical power of momentum and was on his feet in a split second. The colour drained from the Geosphere worker's face, and King slashed a sideways elbow into his temple, stunning him.

The guy fell across the surface of the kitchen island, stunned but not out.

King didn't care.

He walked straight past the guy, and straight past Jian, and picked up the Glock.

He didn't care about the silencer anymore.

He shot the Geosphere worker through the back of the neck, killing him instantly, then pistol-whipped Jian, keeping him semi-conscious. The other two workers were cowering in the corner, so King went back into the hallway to check on the four mercenaries he'd put down, but not out.

And they certainly weren't out.

Two of them were on their feet, with guns in their hands, and the other two were scrabbling for the weapons they'd dropped.

King shot them once each in the head.

Tap-tap-tap-tap.

He exhaled, put the gun back in his holster, and returned to the kitchen with a primitive calmness he hadn't experienced in a long time.

He had control.

The two remaining Geosphere workers were standing there, horrified at how it had all played out, and Jian was on the floor, equally stunned.

King caught his breath and said, 'It really didn't need to go like that.'

No-one responded.

King turned to the Geosphere guys and said, 'Lucky you didn't back your buddy up.'

'We were about to,' one of them said.

The other elbowed him in the ribs.

King smirked. 'If you did, he'd probably still be alive, and I'd be dead.'

They stood there, forlorn, looking at the floor.

King said, 'Let me get this straight. You couldn't get your hands on those encryption devices, so—'

Jian came up with a gun in his hand.

King pivoted, lined up, aimed, and fired.

The bullet caught Jian square in the temple and threw his head back, spraying gore from the exit wound over the unfinished cabinetry.

His body slumped to the floor.

One of the Geosphere workers let out a low moan.

King scrutinised them.

They were both younger than the other guy, probably in their late twenties, with pale complexions and thinning hair. They could have been mistaken for identical twins. King figured out the dynamic. They were programmers — the tech gurus. The other guy was the exec who'd given the entire illicit operation the green light. All three of them had been forced to flee.

King said, 'Help me put this together, and both of you might live.'

'Y-you were on the right track,' one of them stammered.

The smell of death lingered in the air.

King said, 'You were supposed to go through with this anonymously?'

Two nods.

'Using all that hardware that was on the way in those crates?'

Two more nods.

'What was it going to do?'

A pause.

The more confident of the pair said, 'You ... wouldn't understand.'

'Dumb it down for me then.'

'It would have re-routed all of it offshore. We would have made all the trades vanish at surface level. If anyone dug deeper it would have looked like it came from overseas. It was to mask the fact that we were using our firm's infrastructure to carry out the trades. But even that level of investigation would come far too late.'

'How close were you to pulling it off?'

Silence.

Terrifying silence.

King said, 'Don't tell me.'

The guy shrugged. 'Do you want us to lie to you?'

'No.'

'Then we'll tell you the truth.'

'Okay.'

'Will you kill us for it?'

'I don't know.'

'We already did it,' the second guy said. 'Thirty minutes before you showed up, we executed it.'

'Executed what?'

No-one spoke.

King's ears were ringing from all the gunshots in the enclosed space.

But outside, he heard faint sirens.

He didn't know if it meant anything.

His phone rang in his pocket, and he fished it out.

It was Violetta.

He looked up at the Geosphere workers, and said, 'What the fuck did you do?'

Neither responded.

They hadn't expected to answer for their sins.

King answered the call. 'What is it?'

'You're too late.'

67

Her voice was bleak, soulless, defeated.

He said, 'I know.'

'Jesus Christ, King. This is bad.'

'What happened?'

'The Dow Jones Industrial Average just fell twenty percent. This is worse than the GFC. That much market value has never been wiped off instantly. It's only going to get worse.'

'Where did it go?'

'I don't think there's a reasonable answer for that.'

'What are the consequences?'

'I... I don't know. It's going to be bad. It's going to be really, really bad.'

'I'll call you back.'

King hung up with his guts twisted into a knot.

The Geosphere workers stood there, shuffling from foot to foot, restless and horrified.

King said, 'I assume I'm an idiot for even suggesting this, but you can't reverse it, can you?'

Slowly, they shook their heads.

'How did you do it?' King said.

'We used the leverage of our entire firm. We overloaded the markets with trades, using capital the Chinese funnelled to us. And our algorithms did the rest.'

'How is this even possible?'

One of the guys shrugged. 'We're in deep with the banks and the stock exchanges. And I mean *deep*. We're down in the bottom of the system, in the foundations. We always figured we could pull off something like this, because we realised no-one fully understands how the market works. So we got scared because of the sheer potential of it all. That faded, and then we were approached by him.'

He jabbed a thumb in Jian's direction.

'Who is he?' King said.

'He's the right-hand-man for … you know who. He represented the nationalists. There's more of them than you think.'

'Why did you do this?'

The first guy said, 'We thought we could get away with it.'

The second guy said, 'If we didn't do it, they would have approached one of the other HFT firms. And they threatened our families.'

King had heard it all before. 'What was the plan? After this was all over?'

'Get paid into numbered accounts in the Caymans. Doesn't matter if we crash the economy if we have more money than we know what to do with.'

'But when those crates didn't show up…?'

'We lost our lifeline. Now, when we executed it, they'd know it was us. They'd find out, eventually. They'd trace it back to the source, no matter how hard we tried to cover it up. So we had to disappear, because we couldn't back out.

We had to flee. It was the hardest decision of our lives, but at least this way our families are alive.'

'I feel terrible for you,' King said.

The sarcasm hung in the air.

The first guy said, 'What happens now?'

'I killed your contact in the Chinese government,' King said. 'So you have no-one to turn to now. You said it yourself. They'll track you down eventually. I assume you have endless server rooms upstairs?'

Two nods.

'And fibre cables under the grounds?'

The first guy said, 'No. We communicated directly with our HQ in New Jersey to execute the trades.'

'That sounds like a lot of work.'

'It took months to set it up discreetly.'

'Do you think you'll be able to rip it all out in time?'

'Not a chance. And besides, it wouldn't matter. They'll find the virtual paper trail. They probably already have.'

'What was the plan after this?'

'Get smuggled out of the country. Spend our millions somewhere else. India, maybe. They'd never find us there.'

'But they'd know it was you.'

'We were going to have to do our best to purge our old lives, and pretend it never happened.'

'And now you'll have to face the consequences.'

The second guy, who'd been mostly silent, blurted out, 'Can you kill me?'

King stared at him. 'You don't have the balls to do it yourself?'

'No,' the guy admitted.

King thought about it. He wanted to. Nothing would make him happier — not because of the killing itself, but because he could close the chapter on this godforsaken townhouse forever. It was the seed of pure evil, and now millions of hard-working Americans were going to pay the price for it, and these two sociopaths in front of him were so detached from the consequences of their actions that they were practically delusional.

Or maybe they did know, and didn't care.

Which made it worse.

King said, 'I'd rather you both rot in jail for the rest of your lives. So you can live with the fact that your families will know what you did. Your kids will know. When they grow up, they'll understand that their fathers were monsters. And they'll never be able to escape from your shadow. That's what you're going to have to think about for the rest of your days.'

They were both crying when he finished.

He put the Glock back in his appendix holster, and said, 'There's guns by the front door if you really want to end it. Next to the bodies of the men you paid to protect you. But I'd wager neither of you have the guts to do it, so enjoy your lives in prison.'

There was no colour in their faces.

King didn't need to kill them.

They looked dead already.

He turned around and walked straight out of the room.

A many-months-long, multi-layered operation to destabilise the United States economy, implemented by three of the best and brightest high-frequency traders in the country, executed with the press of a button.

And King had been thirty minutes too late to prevent it.

He stepped over the bodies of the mercenaries, and cursed how easily money corrupted. They'd known full well what their employers were doing. They hadn't cared.

They'd been getting rich in the process.

King made sure his Glock was concealed before he stepped back outside. There were tiny flecks of blood all over his sweater, but they looked like a pattern.

He left the scene of the slaughter, and sleepwalked like a zombie back onto the sidewalk.

There were pedestrians everywhere, brows furrowed, hunched over their phones, refreshing news sites, murmuring to each other.

It was beginning.

With hopelessness crushing him, pressing him into the ground, weighing on his shoulders, King headed for the Upper East Side.

Then a voice stopped him in his tracks.

'Hey!' it cried.

He turned, and saw one of the Geosphere guys standing in the doorway, looking like he'd seen a ghost.

King didn't say a word.

The guy called out, 'There's something we need to tell you.'

68

Will Slater and Ruby Nazarian stepped back into King's penthouse.

They'd been sent straight up by the new concierge — a fresh face brought in by Violetta as part of her all-inclusive security package. The guy looked like Special Forces, and Slater treated him with deserved respect. He and Ruby were whisked up in the private elevator and they spent the time standing apart, staring absent-mindedly at their reflections in the doors, too shocked to speak.

As soon as they'd touched down at JFK, they'd been brought up to speed on what was rapidly unfolding across the country.

They walked in, and Violetta was there, hunched over one of the bar stools in the centre of the giant space, staring up at the wall-mounted TV, practically traumatised.

Not so much from what was happening now.

But from what was to come.

Slater said, 'What the hell is going on?'

She barely registered his arrival. She glanced sideways,

and saw him, and saw Ruby, and nodded curtly to each of them. She said, 'Are you Ruby Nazarian?'

Ruby said, 'Yes.'

'Pleasure to meet you.'

'Likewise.'

There was nothing genuine in the exchange. It was simple pleasantries — necessary introductions.

Everyone turned straight back to the television.

The market was collapsing, and it wasn't a flash crash. There was no recovery yet, and Slater knew there wouldn't be one. Not for a long time. There would be layoffs in droves — an incomprehensible number. Unemployment would skyrocket. The homeless population would soar. Infrastructure would strain to accommodate all the new soup kitchens and shelters.

It would be a disaster in the long term.

And because the country had been through a smaller financial crisis before, in 2008, everyone seemed to know what was coming.

News anchors were glum. They were reporting half-heartedly, as shocked as the rest of the nation. It was world-wide news. Speculation ran rampant, with pundit after pundit dialling in to lend their opinion on why it had happened. Perhaps the truth would come out eventually. Not for a while, though. Not while panic flowed through the population's veins.

And it would flow for the foreseeable future.

Slater exhaled, and bent over and put his hands on his knees.

Ruby rested a palm on his shoulder.

He said to Violetta, 'How the hell do we recover from this?'

'There's nothing we can do,' she said. 'Not immediately. Our greed got the better of us.'

'Surely someone understands what happened. Aren't your people working on it?'

She looked at him blankly.

He said, 'Sorry. I'm sure you're doing everything you can.'

'This is so much bigger than us,' Violetta said.

'So we failed?' Ruby said.

Violetta nodded.

Ruby said, 'Why did you save me?'

Violetta said, 'There was a substantial threat made against your life. And I've already been briefed on what happened in Tulum. The pair of you left dozens of bodies. Isn't that proof enough...?'

'No,' Ruby snapped. 'I mean — why was I a priority?'

'Because you're one of the best operatives to come out of—'

'That's all bureaucratic bullshit,' Ruby said. 'Maybe if Will had been here, he and King could have got the job done faster. Then this wouldn't have happened at all.'

'How late was King?' Slater said.

'Thirty minutes. We're getting a spoonful of reports through our intelligence channels. The shitstorm was executed twenty-four minutes before he entered the townhouse.'

Slater said, 'I could have cut that down. If I'd been here.'

'You don't know that,' Violetta said.

'You shouldn't have prioritised me,' Ruby said. 'I could have handled it myself in Tulum. I didn't need a babysitter.'

Violetta stared at them, but she didn't argue. She said, 'We've all made mistakes.'

'Neither of us could have handled that on our own,'

Slater said to Ruby. 'Not you. Not me. We came out of this alive.'

Ruby said, 'You think that matters compared to what's unfolding across the country right now?'

Slater shrugged.

He wasn't sure what any of this meant anymore.

He wasn't sure what mattered.

'So what happens now?' he said. 'The *ying pai* swoop in? They take advantage of our weakness and avenge all this time they've spent underneath us? They become number one?'

'Looks that way,' Violetta said. 'Unless...'

'Unless what?'

She chewed her lower lip. 'We're thinking there's more to it than this. They said there was more than one event...'

Slater stepped forward and hit a desk lamp off the table next to the sofa. It crashed to the floor, echoing through the penthouse. Violetta took a step back, concern spreading across her face.

Slater said, 'I'm sick of this shit.'

'What?' Violetta said.

'I know this is the way it's always been done, but if your operatives are going to be effective, they can't be kept at arm's length. You always say "we." But we only ever see *you*. You have the entire United States government behind you. Who are we talking to in their ranks? That's right — no-one. We're kept in the dark, and orders come down through you. Ever think myself, or King, or Ruby, might be integral to figuring this shit out in advance?'

Violetta came back with a vengeance. Initially, Slater's outburst had caught her off-guard, but now she descended into icy stoicism.

She said, 'If you have a problem with the way we operate, take it up with someone else. I don't have time for this shit either. I don't need you throwing a tantrum like a spoiled brat. We've got entire teams of psychologists and tacticians who've figured out the best way to approach this. It's a streamlined channel, and it allows us to convey accurate information as fast as we can to the operatives. If you and King and Ruby are in the mix, sitting in on meetings and intelligence briefings, it'll do nothing but muddy the waters.'

'And how's that working out for you so far?'

'Incredibly well,' Violetta said. 'We can't win them all, Slater.'

He lifted his gaze to the television headlines. The media frenzy was in full effect. Doomsday predictions were racing in by the second.

This time, they may be right.

Slater stumbled over to the sofa and sat down and exhaled.

Above all else, he hated to lose.

Then Jason King came in through the front door, and stepped into the room, and it all got *so* much worse.

69

King paused for a beat to take in the scene.

He saw Slater, and he saw Violetta, and he saw a new face with glowing amber eyes and deeply tanned skin and long flowing hair. She was beautiful, but he could see the killer in her. He could see the venom in her eyes, brimming below the surface, ready to unleash at the drop of a hat.

He liked that.

He said, 'Are you Ruby?'

'Yes. You're Jason King?'

'In the flesh.'

'Glad to finally meet you. Heard a lot about you.'

'Likewise.'

There was a poignant silence.

King said to them all, 'I'm so sorry.'

'It's not your fault,' Violetta said.

'It is. If I was faster, if I—'

'I got complacent,' Violetta said. 'I trusted your "one-man-army" shtick above everything else. I should have deployed all the resources I had available. I had everything relying on you, and that's not your fault — that's a tactical error. It will never happen again.'

Despite her apologetic tone, her words cut deep.

Because at the end of the day, all they said was, *You failed. I shouldn't have trusted you.*

You fucked it all up.

King said, 'What's on the news?'

'Nothing good.'

'I can imagine.'

'Did you walk back here?'

'Sure did.'

'What's on the street?'

'Nothing good.'

Violetta nodded. 'Are people panicking?'

'Yes,' King said. 'They've seen this before. But this is 2008 on steroids.'

'I don't understand,' Slater said, skewering a pair of fingers into his eyeballs in frustration. 'How can there be no way to reverse this? It was artificially created by a band of rogue high-frequency traders, right? Can't that be traced back to the source? Can't it be expunged from the records, so to speak?'

Violetta shook her head. 'That's not how the market works. The cat's out of the bag now. Even if we work out exactly what they did, it'll be indecipherable. It'll be swept up in the billions of trades happening every single day. There's no way to stuff it back in.'

'So — what?' Slater said. 'We wait for the economy to recover, and in the meantime target anything from the Chinese hardliners that could be seen as an aggressive hostile takeover?'

'It looks that way...' Violetta said.

'There's something that needs our urgent attention,'

King said.

All three of them turned to look at him.

He sighed and scratched the back of his neck.

'What is it?' Violetta said.

'There were two Geosphere workers alive at the end,' King said. 'I let them—'

'I know,' Violetta said. 'We already have them in custody — we had the townhouse under surveillance within minutes of you leaving, and we watched them try to sneak out. If we can't win, we can at least make them regret everything they've ever done. They'll be shamed for eternity for what they did, and the entire nation will hate them. We'll shout everything they did from the rooftops. We'll—'

'It doesn't fucking matter,' King snarled.

Violetta froze. 'What?'

'They wanted to do anything they could to atone for their sins,' King said. 'Some sort of last-minute salvation. So they tried to make things right. Before I left, they called me back. And they told me everything they knew about the second event.'

'Oh, Christ,' Violetta said. 'Tell me right now.'

'They don't know specific details. But you can find those out if I tell you where to look, right?'

'Yes, yes, of course,' she said, desperate to get any and all information she could.

King said, 'The next step is to artificially create a mass tragedy event. That'll put the nail in the coffin, so to speak.'

Violetta said, 'What?'

Slater said, 'Fuck.'

Ruby said, 'Oh, no.'

King said, 'China's spent years and years generating unrest towards the U.S. internationally, right? They're spending billions and billions of dollars in Africa and other developing parts of the world, providing them with aid where they need it and creating an anti-U.S. movement by spreading their ideologies.'

Slater and Ruby turned to Violetta, who nodded.

Violetta said, 'We've been keeping tabs on that for a long time. We should have moved to resist it earlier. We didn't. We thought it was harmless.'

King said, 'They're going to leverage that. All they need now is to create a serious, horrific incident on our soil. Something that paints us in a shocking light, and shows them as victims. The rest of the world will hate us for it, and if you combine that with our crippled economy, it's going to lead to a PR disaster. We'll be the laughing stock of the world. Our demise will be easily accepted.'

Violetta said, 'Go on.'

King took a deep breath, and said, 'The San Francisco Chinese New Year Festival and Parade. They're going to slaughter their own people on U.S. soil, and they're going to dress it up as a racist attack from our backwards countrymen.'

Silence.

King said, 'That's what all the weapons were for in those crates Slater and I stole. They weren't to defend the town-house. I always knew there was too much firepower in there for a few sociopathic mercenaries wanting to protect a half-finished building in East Harlem. The black boxes were for East Harlem. The guns and claymores were for San Francisco.'

Violetta sunk into the couch, and put her head in her hands, and said, 'Oh my God.'

Slater stared blankly.

Even Ruby lost the playful spark in her eyes.

There wasn't a sound in the penthouse, save for the ticking of a clock hanging on the wall.

Slater said quietly, 'When's the festival start?'

'Two days,' King said.

No-one spoke.

Then Violetta said, 'We'd better get to work.'

70

San Francisco
California

family of four stepped out of the lobby of the Hyatt Regency San Francisco into a clear, sunny day.

They were a dysfunctional family, and the circumstances that had brought them together couldn't be easily explained. But they never tried to explain them. They carried on with their lives, and strengthened the bond they all shared, and focused on human connection rather than the fact that one of them wasn't biologically related.

She was still a young girl, having just celebrated her eleventh birthday, but she'd had more life experiences than the other three members of her family put together.

Her name was Shien.

She tried not to think about her past often. It always bogged her down in misery — she'd come out the other side alive, but she'd seen things that no eleven-year-old should ever have seen. So she tried to expunge those memories, and instead live in the present.

Which, right now, was all too easy. They were only in town for a week or so, but they were treating it like the vacation they deserved. Then they would all be back on the road, travelling from sight to sight. Shien had an education — her de facto mother homeschooled her — and that was all she could ask for.

Her parents weren't made of money, but they had enough to live comfortably for as long as they needed. And that was all she could ask. For the first time in her life, she had a stable reality. They'd been living on the road for a little over a year, ever since a man named Will Slater had rescued her from hell twice, and almost sacrificed his life several times in the process. She would be eternally grateful for what he'd done for her.

So would her new parents.

Frank and Anastasia Nazarian.

They'd been through hell, too.

They made an odd group — Frank, Anastasia, their biological daughter Abigail, and Shien.

But it worked.

Now, Shien was uncharacteristically silent as they strolled through the pristine suburbs. The sun was out, the trees were green, and the sidewalks were quiet and calm.

Frank noticed her forlornness, and put a hand on her shoulder. She looked up at him, and he gently guided her away from Anastasia and Abigail, who went on ahead.

So they could talk in private.

'What is it?' he said.

She shrugged. 'Thinking about Will.'

'Nothing wrong with that, after what he did for you. What he did for us all.'

'Do you think about him?'

'Not often. I've tried to move past it. So we can create our own lives, y'know?'

She nodded. 'What about Ruby?'

He didn't respond, and when she looked up there were the foundations of tears in his eyes. He was staring into the distance.

She said, 'Frank?'

Finally, he said, 'Ruby chose her own path. She's doing what she thinks is right by keeping away from us. All we can do is respect that.'

Shien nodded. 'But you still think about her?'

'Of course. Every day.'

'Will said that she had a good heart.'

'I'm sure she does.'

'They did terrible things to her in the Lynx program,' Shien said. 'They had only just started doing them to me when Will rescued me. And she came out the other side a good person. I don't know if I would have been a good person by the end of it. So ... I don't know what I'm trying to say, Frank ... I guess Ruby is stronger than me. So you should be proud of her.'

Frank tousled her hair. 'Don't be stupid, kid. You're the strongest little girl I've met.'

'I'm getting old now,' Shien said. 'You can't keep calling me little.'

It was true. She was in the midst of a growth spurt — she'd always been undersized, tiny and frail, but now she was catching up to everyone else her age. Maybe now that the constant stress of her turbulent past life had receded, it was no longer stunting her growth. Now she could focus on having a normal future.

'When does the parade start?' she said, trying to change the subject.

'In a couple of days,' Frank said. 'Don't worry — we'll be there.'

Shien tried her best to mask her excitement. Before Will Slater, most of her life had been spent in Macau, in the care of two biological parents that equally wanted nothing to do with her. Her father had been a Chinese triad gangster, and her mother had been an American groupie from Texas who'd married a far older man for the money.

So Shien was half-Chinese, and she hoped that the festival would remind her of her childhood. That's why they were there in the first place — she'd seen an advertisement for the festival and parade in the newspaper, and expressed interest in seeing it. She didn't ask for much. It hadn't taken long for Frank and Anastasia to oblige her.

Even though her early years had been far from perfect, she didn't want them to fade from her memory forever.

So she quickened her pace to catch up to her de facto mother and sister, and in a rare occurrence the worry faded from her mind.

She hoped the celebrations would be as amazing as she envisioned.

71

At two p.m. the day after King had revealed the plan for the *ying pai*'s second event, he and Slater were grappling on combat mats in King's penthouse gymnasium.

They were drenched in sweat, wearing their traditional *gi* to adhere to the customs of Brazilian jiu-jitsu. They rolled in a state of flow, keeping their minds sharp, staying focused on each precise movement, figuring out how to get into the right position to submit each other.

It kept their minds off dark feelings of uncertainty, which had been plaguing them almost non-stop since Violetta had set to work gathering intelligence behind-the-scenes on the festival in San Francisco.

After an hour of intense physical exertion, a timer rang in the corner.

They broke apart and lay on their backs to gather their breath. Their chests rose and fell in unison, and as they lay there recovering, Ruby stepped down off the treadmill. She'd jogged at a ten percent incline for two hours, and she was sweating just as hard.

All the wounds they'd sustained over the course of the last few days had proved superficial after an assessment by a government-employed doctor, who'd visited the penthouse late the night before. They'd been patched up and given pain relief medication, which they'd both refused to take. Today, they were supposed to be resting in anticipation of a whirlwind of chaos tomorrow.

But all three of them were terrible at sitting around doing nothing.

If their bones weren't broken, and their muscles weren't torn from the bone, all they wanted to do was get straight back to work.

Habits, and neural conditioning, and mental pathways.

All that good stuff.

All they knew was work, and exertion, and improvement.

It had paved the way to where they were now.

They weren't about to let it go in a hurry.

Dressed in tiny athletic shorts and another tube top, Ruby bent over to catch her breath and tucked wet strands of hair behind her ears.

She looked down at Slater. 'Have either of you heard anything?'

'Not a word,' King answered.

He didn't sound too happy about it.

Because he wasn't.

Violetta had disappeared the previous morning, shrinking back into the shadows of the covert world. It was understandable, of course — King had pointed her in the right direction, and now all the resources in the government's arsenal had to be mobilised within twenty-four hours.

Slater and King and Ruby were cannon fodder in the

grand scheme of things, so they were kept in the dark until concrete orders were passed down the pipeline.

None of them were thrilled about it, but at the same time, they understood.

They moved out into the kitchen and started preparing post-workout meals. They were functioning effectively as a trio — they'd only been together twenty-four hours, but aside from Slater and Ruby peeling off late the night before to sleep in Slater's apartment, they'd spent nearly every waking moment together.

Because they were cut from the same cloth.

Slater looked up at the clock on the wall and said, 'It can't be much longer, can it?'

'I assume not,' King said.

'It's a five hour flight, and we'll need to be in San Francisco by tomorrow morning at the latest.'

'So we'll fly overnight. We'll take another jet.'

'I don't like this,' Slater said. 'I can't be kept in the dark much longer. It'll drive me crazy.'

Ruby said, 'What happens if this works?'

They both turned to look at her.

'Huh?' Slater said.

'Let's say we pull it off,' she said. 'We foil the plot, we nullify their plans, and the *ying pai* shrink away into obscurity. Then what?'

'For the country, or for us?' Slater said.

But he knew the answer, deep down.

He knew how much uncertainty there was between the three of them.

'As far as I can tell, all of us are in a state of limbo right now,' she said. 'You two don't know what the hell you're doing. Your vigilante business didn't go the way you wanted it to. Now you're back in bed with the government.

You're both saying it's just this one job, but who are you kidding?'

King said, 'Where are *you* going after this?'

'I was enjoying life on the beach,' she said.

Slater said, 'You can't go back to Tulum.'

'I didn't know you were making decisions for me now,' she said.

He looked at her. 'Are you insane?'

'Why?'

'You're not seriously entertaining going back there, are you?'

'Why wouldn't I?'

'Because—'

She held up a hand. 'I get it. You care about me. You don't want me to do anything stupid. It's coming from a place of genuine concern. And of course I'm not going back to Tulum. But you're not going to be the one to decide for me.'

'I know that,' Slater said.

'Good. I'll do whatever the hell I want.'

'You might not have a choice,' King said.

She raised an eyebrow.

He swept his hand around the penthouse. 'Here we are. The government's three best operatives. The top three on the Chinese hit list, but that's not the point. The point is — Uncle Sam wanted this. They wouldn't have turned to us unless they had ulterior motives. They would have fed us to the sharks when the hired guns came after us. They wouldn't be supporting us now unless there was a damn good reason for the investment.'

'To save their own skin,' Slater said. 'They need us to get the job done.'

'Maybe. Or maybe there's more to it than that.'

'We can make our own decisions,' Ruby said. 'When this all ends, we can choose what we want to do.'

'Can we?' King said. 'Or have they been letting us run wild this whole time? I mean, if they really wanted us to work for them again ... we'd be forced to.'

'I'm not doing it,' Ruby said.

'Me neither,' Slater said.

King said, 'I told you — we might not have a choice.'

The door thundered open.

They all twisted on the spot, and all three of them instinctively reached for their belts. But they weren't armed, and they regretted their mutual lack of preparation...

But they spotted the flowing blonde hair in unison, and a half-second later identified Violetta as the intruder.

She pulled to a halt, breathless, and she said, 'Wheels up in an hour. I'll brief you all on the way to California.'

n the comfort of the same Gulfstream Slater had taken to Tulum, they arranged themselves in a small circle around one of the polished wooden tables jutting out from the side of the fuselage.

The jet lifted off the tarmac, and Slater knew the pit of tension in his stomach wasn't a byproduct of the takeoff.

It was the mystery of what they would encounter in San Francisco.

Violetta had kept her mouth shut all the way to the airport — she wanted to brief them together, and make sure none of them missed any important details. It had resulted in a tense but silent car ride to the airport, and when they'd finally piled out of the Suburban onto the runway, they'd practically run for the plane.

Now, Violetta said, 'The body of the Chinese hardliner we recovered in the East Harlem townhouse proved invaluable. King, I can't thank you enough. You might have just saved the country from a brutal decline.'

'Not yet,' King said. 'We haven't done shit yet.'

She nodded. 'But it's a start. The man—'

'He told me his name was Jian.'

'We know that. We identified him.'

'Was it true what the Geosphere crew said? Was he in the inner circle around the Chinese president?'

Violetta nodded gravely. 'He's the equivalent of the head honcho in the Chinese secret world. Just as we have our own crews operating behind-the-scenes, they do too. We've been slowly amassing a portfolio of all the top dogs we could identify, and Jian was one of them. Frankly, none of us ever expected to encounter him or any of his cronies in mainland America.'

'And yet, here he is.'

'He had a phone on him. We cracked it.'

Slater interjected. 'That sounds awfully convenient.'

King nodded.

At the forefront of their thoughts was their last operation in New Zealand, where they'd been lured to the South Island by an intricate web of lies spun to look like a legitimate paper trail. Together they'd cracked a phone encrypted with military-grade technology, and it had led them right into the jaws of death.

Because that's what their enemy had wanted all along.

Violetta shook her head. 'We have surveillance on the ground in San Francisco. Our intel is legitimate.'

'What's the intel?'

'Jian's phone revealed the attack on the festival has been in the works for months. They're using three separate locations to amass their forces, equip them properly, and give them the necessary strategies for the big day.'

Slater cut in with, 'Christ — are we too late?'

'No. But you'll need to move tomorrow morning, when they're most vulnerable.'

King said, 'Why not tonight? Why not as soon as we

land? If you have boots on the ground doing surveillance, then why haven't you moved in already?'

'Because it's a unique situation with unique parameters. Decisions were made at the top of the food chain and passed down. We need the three of you.'

'We're going to need more information than that if you want our help,' Ruby said.

Violetta stared at her. 'You don't need anything more than what we decide to give you. All three of you are technically working for the government again, and if you refuse orders you'll be considered active participants who contributed to this attack by refusing to prevent it. So shut the fuck up and listen.'

Ruby bristled, but King and Slater sat silent.

They'd heard it all before.

'There are three locations that we've zeroed in on,' Violetta said. 'All three are packed with armed hostiles, recruited by Chinese hardliners over the last few weeks, if not months. They're a diverse bunch — we've got cartel *sicario*s brought up over the border from Sinaloa and Tijuana and armed in California, then there's your standard disillusioned ex-military vets who will do anything for a dollar, and finally there's something that's really worrying me — what appears to be a collection of the most unstable ex-soldiers they could find milling around an abandoned warehouse in Dogpatch.'

'How can you be so sure of all this through surveillance photos?' King said.

'Most of them aren't hiding, because they don't think they're going to get caught. Frankly, if we didn't find Jian's phone, we never would have located them. California is enormous, and they're covering their tracks unbelievably well — we think the *ying pai* have been advising them for a long time. But we're running background checks on each face we capture, and we're slowly starting to piece it together. So you'll know what you're walking into.'

'To an extent,' Slater said. 'This whole thing sounds unpredictable as hell.'

'It is,' Violetta admitted. 'But the pieces are falling into place. The warehouse in Dogpatch scares me the most. Every time we've photographed someone coming in and out, their background check rings alarm bells all through our system. Most of them have a history of mental illness — schizophrenia has been cropping up a lot. On top of that, we've spotted a couple of well-known Middle Eastern jihadists with ties to Islamic State. We think the Chinese have piggybacked off their hatred of the West and hired a couple of their experts for help with...'

She trailed off.

King said, 'Help with what?'

But he knew where it was headed.

'We think it's a makeshift bomb factory,' Violetta said.

Slater said, 'Oh, shit.'

Violetta said, 'King, that's where you're headed.'

'Just me?'

'I told you there's three locations.'

'So one of us goes to each one?' King said, flabbergasted.

'No backup?' Slater said.

'Are you insane?' Ruby said, still irritated by the earlier comments. 'Who gave you the job of handler? You should be managing a McDonald's.'

You could cut the tension in the air with a knife.

Violetta held up her hands. 'I told you to wait until I can give you all the details. If you must know, this is *exactly* the type of incident that would have been delegated to Black

Force in the past. But Black Force no longer exists, so it comes down to the three of you.'

'There'd better be a damn good reason for this,' King said.

Slater said, 'Or when we get to California we get off this plane and get a commercial flight straight back to New York.'

Ruby said, 'Does it sound like we're full of shit?'

Violetta turned hot under the collar. Flustered and reeling on the back foot, she finally snapped.

'Listen, you morons,' she snarled. 'There's close to fifty hostiles involved in this, and they're spread out between Dogpatch, the Rancho Corral de Tierra wildlands, and an outlaw motorcycle clubhouse on the outskirts of San Fran. They're all armed with automatic weapons and highly emotional, and they'll slaughter anyone and everyone they can get their hands on if they're confronted or provoked. If we do this the old-fashioned way and send in the Army, there'll be blood on the streets as soon as they realise they're sprung. Jian had instructions on his phone to relay to the hired guns, and that's what they spelled out: "If you get busted, start gunning down anyone in the vicinity. Cause chaos. Don't go down without a fight." But if you three go in posing as ordinary civilians, then strike them right in the heart before they even realise what's happening, then maybe we can prevent a series of massacres. Does that sound like a feasible plan, or do the three of you want to live with the fact that you could have saved innocent lives ... but didn't?'

King said nothing.
Slater said nothing.
Ruby said nothing.

The jet engines rumbled on either side of the fuselage, filling the silence with a monotonous hum.

Finally King said, 'We'll stay.'

Violetta nodded, wiping a bead of sweat off her brow. She was pale and clammy.

King said, 'Do you think we're crazy?'

'I thought you'd all be a little more understanding.'

'To you, we're your best option,' Slater said. 'But that also makes us cannon fodder. You're not thinking of human beings. You're thinking of tactics. These are our lives at stake, and we're not about to walk blindfolded into a slaughter if you think it's the only Hail Mary that's likely to work.'

Violetta thought it over.

She nodded her understanding.

Slater said, 'Doesn't seem like we have a choice, does it?'

Ruby shook her head.

King said, 'More details.'

Violetta hunched forward and laid it all out for them.

Everything they knew.

And everything they didn't.

When she was finished, each of the three operatives went through their nervous tics.

King rubbed the back of his neck with a calloused palm.

Slater hunched over and stared at the floor.

Ruby sat back in her seat and closed her eyes.

The gravity of what they had to do rattled them.

But, one by one, they stopped mulling over it, and looked Violetta in the eyes.

'Well?' she said.

They all nodded simultaneously.

73

It was a cool and crisp evening when the Gulfstream touched down at San Francisco International Airport.

There was no fanfare. No official military welcome. No red carpet.

Just the calm quiet of an empty runway as they stepped down onto the tarmac and slung their small carry-on bags over their shoulders. They stood there in a tight cluster, staring out at the sweeping concrete running all the way to the civilian terminals in the distance. That wasn't where they were headed. They'd been granted approval by those at the top to land and disperse in secrecy.

So they waited at the bottom of the stairs and admired the setting sun as they waited for a black Suburban to collect them.

They'd talked about operational details and the minutiae of what was to come for the entire five-hour flight. Now there was nothing left to do but wait, and dwell.

Violetta said, 'I want to make this as stress-free as possible. So if any new information comes in, I'll only tell you what's necessary. I don't want a thousand thoughts in your heads tomorrow morning. I want you to focus on what you need to do. Got it?'

'Got it,' King said.

'Your gear will be brought over from Parks Reserve Forces Training Area throughout the night,' she said. 'But you're not to worry about that. All three of you need sleep. I don't want you running on empty when the sun comes up again.'

In turn, they each nodded.

She said, 'You understand why it has to be tomorrow morning, right?'

She'd already explained why, but she clearly wanted to be sure they'd got the message.

As if reading off a transcript, King said, 'They'll be gearing up. It'll be the calm before the storm. If they're expecting anything, it'll be tonight, so they'll have guards keeping watch and guns loaded.'

'And?'

'And there hasn't been time to mobilise backup forces yet — they're all on the way from neighbouring military bases. They have to take their time because there's no telling whether the Chinese are monitoring the movements of our Armed Forces, so it has to be discreet. That means that if we do it tonight, and it doesn't work, there's nothing to stop the hired guns scattering into the dark and coming out of hiding tomorrow morning to massacre anyone they can get their hands on. If we can get enough soldiers here for the morning, they'll be able to lay down a rudimentary cordon in case our efforts fail.'

'You won't fail,' Violetta said. 'The three of you never have.'

'We've failed plenty.'

'But you're here to tell the tale.'

Slater peered at the setting sun with a lump in his throat. He said, 'There's a first time for everything.'

She said, 'I wouldn't be asking you to do this if I didn't have full faith in your abilities.'

'That doesn't make it any more likely that we'll succeed,' Slater said.

'No, but it's some consolation, at least.'

King said, 'I think we've covered most of it. Where to now?'

'A civilian motel in Ingleside.'

They all stared at her.

She said, 'Were you expecting a military base?'

'Maybe something ... a little more serious.'

'I don't want to risk it,' she said. 'If there's even the slightest chance they're monitoring our official movements, then we need to do everything as unofficially as possible.'

'That's the way it's always been,' Ruby said, and shrugged. 'Nothing new.'

'I guess that's true,' Slater said.

Violetta turned to King and said, 'How are you feeling?'

There was genuine concern in her eyes.

King shrugged and said, 'I'm alright. Just another day at the office.'

'You don't mean that,' Slater said.

King glanced over. 'You okay?'

'If we fuck this up,' Slater said, 'and we live to see the end result ... do you know what that'll do to us? Psychologically, I mean.'

'Would you rather we don't try to interfere at all?'

'Of course not. I'm just saying ... sometimes there's jobs where I'd rather die in the process than live to see the results of my failure. This is one of those times.'

King and Ruby stayed silent.

Slater said, 'That's what scares me. That's a hundred times worse than death.'

Violetta said, 'You won't fail.'

'We can't,' King said. 'Let's be honest here. Can you imagine we do?'

'The cordon will be there to intercept them,' she said, but she said it quietly.

Like she didn't believe it would work.

'There's fifty trained hostiles with automatic weapons,' King said. 'Most of them outsourced from the cartels — real killers, through and through. You think if the military moves to funnel them into a bottleneck it's going to work? I mean, of course it'll be effective, but a hundred percent guarantee? A few outliers will slip through the cracks. And that's all it takes. There's a lot of rounds to be fired into crowds nearly three hundred thousand strong.'

'I know,' Violetta said. 'Of course I know.'

A gust of wind rippled across the tarmac, and they all braced against it.

Slater turned to Ruby and said, 'You barely said a word the whole flight.'

Ruby flashed him a devilish look. 'I was taking in information. I'm not a big talker before a job.'

'You're okay with this?'

'Okay with what.'

'Going through with it.'

'Do I have a choice?'

'Let's say you did.'

'Then I'd do it,' she said. 'I was raised to be emotionless, and I had my childhood stripped from me, but I still care.'

'I'm not saying you don't.'

'It's not just a job,' she said. 'This is serious shit.'

Violetta said, 'Glad we're all on the same page, then. Here's our ride.'

None of them had noticed the Suburban pull up behind them. It coasted to a stop and the engine idled. Together they stepped away from the Gulfstream and piled into the vehicle. The driver was an unimpressive pudgy guy in his fifties who looked in no way military. He didn't even look government. But that was the point.

Violetta got in the passenger seat, and the SUV took off.

The tinted windows slid up, and they were all enclosed in silence.

They stewed with uncertainty for the entire drive.

74

Hours later, after several calls to high-ranking military officers and countless reassurances that they would get the job done, Slater and Ruby slipped away from King and Violetta and made for their motel room.

It was a soulless place with plasterboard walls and dirty carpet flooring, but they didn't need luxury.

Ruby closed the door behind them, looked around, and said, 'It's not the same as your place in New York, is it?'

Slater shrugged. 'There's not a whole lot of difference to me. I'm not in it for the money. Never have been.'

'Then why live there?'

'If I have the means to, then why not? But I couldn't care less. A bed is a bed.'

She furrowed her brow, then said, 'You know — I sort of understand.'

'Of course you do,' he said. 'We're cut from the same cloth.'

'You train like we train and devote your life to a single cause, and everything else is ... inconsequential.'

He said, 'We're creatures of habit. And we've been conditioned our whole lives to focus on the physical, which transforms our bodies and minds. Everything else falls away.'

He sat down on the bed. Ruby drifted across the room in the weak glow of the bedside lamp, and draped a leg over his thigh. She sat down facing him, taking his chin in her delicate hands.

She said, 'You okay?'

'I just ... don't know what I'm doing here.'

'You're with me.'

'Which I hate. Because it feels like I'm back at work, and I never got close to anyone when I was working.'

In the muted yellow glow of the motel room, her eyes seemed even more amber than usual. She rested her forehead against his and looked at him, judging him, assessing him.

'Is that what this is?' she said. 'Are we getting close?'

He touched his lips to hers. 'I'm starting to think we are.'

'Is that wise?'

'For you or for me?'

'You said we're both cut from the same cloth. So I guess it's just as bad for both of us.'

'Does it have to be bad?'

'One of us is likely to get killed tomorrow.'

'I know that.'

'Which will make it all the harder to move on if we're having this conversation now.'

'Would you prefer not to have it?' Slater said. 'Then if one of us goes to the grave, the other one wonders forever what it might have been?'

'So what is this, then?'

'I don't know. You tell me.'

Ruby smiled. 'I was thinking about you in Tulum.'

Slater nodded, and kissed her.

He smirked.

'What?' she said.

'You know, in another timeline this is the sort of thing that'd terrifies me. A seductive ex-assassin says she was thinking about you. They make movies about this shit. Is this the part where I end up with my throat cut, hanging from power lines?'

She smirked, too. 'Is that what I am to you?'

'Far from it.'

'That's a testament to the world of black operations if I've ever heard it.'

He nodded. 'Guess we're both as fucked up as each other, aren't we?'

'Wouldn't have it any other way.'

'Is it because we have a conscience?' he said. 'Is that what it is? In this fucked-up world, with this fucked-up job, giving us these fucked-up memories. Is that what gnaws at us? The fact that we think we're decent people doing honest work, when we're in the business of killing.'

'It's never clean,' she said. 'It's never black and white. But, yes, I think that's what it is. We think we're noble doing this work. Because we kill the scum of the earth. But if anyone saw us doing what we do best — anyone who was looking at it objectively — well, they'd think we were monsters, wouldn't they?'

'Is that why I've been thinking about you, then?' Slater said. 'Ever since I walked away in Maine. I remember thinking — was that the best chance I'd ever get at finding someone who understood?'

'I felt the same.'

'Is this smart?'

'What?'

'Doing what we do, and talking about this stuff?'

'Does it matter?'

She gently bit his lip and pushed him back on the bed, and with smooth, practiced movements they went through the motions. Their feverish excitement in Tulum had been the result of spending months apart, coupled with the raw aftermath of surviving a violent fight against all odds, but now they'd had the chance to reacquaint themselves with each other it was *so* much better.

They slowed down, and stripped naked, and it stretched out for nearly an hour, slow and passionate. Slater held the back of her neck as she gyrated on top of him, and when the natural rhythm started to lift he matched it accordingly. They climaxed together, again, and with a great shuddering gasp she collapsed on top of him, planting soft kisses on the base of his neck.

It was getting late.

He said, 'Are you thinking about tomorrow?'

'I try not to think about jobs,' she said. 'What happens, happens. If I worry about it now, it wastes time I might not get back.'

He said, 'You know, I never thought I'd meet anyone who understands.'

She said, 'Not like you. I don't understand like you. I'm too young. You've been in this game too long.'

'You've had enough life experiences for a hundred people.'

'Then you've had enough for a thousand.'

'You shouldn't stick with me,' he said. 'I'm ... bad for those around me, usually.'

'So am I.'

He smiled. He wasn't about to protest. 'Then it's a match made in heaven.'

'Or hell.'

She rolled off him and turned out the light, and despite the fact they were going to war tomorrow, they both plunged into deep and dreamless sleep.

Like clockwork.

Just another day.

75

In the neighbouring motel room, King lay under the covers with Violetta's head on his chest.

And despite his storied history with violent devastation, something about the next day felt different.

And she could tell.

She tilted her face toward him and said, 'Your heart's pounding.'

'I know.'

'What's wrong?'

'What do you think?'

'You'll get through this. You always do.'

'You haven't been around in the past. You don't see me at the end of each operation.'

'Traumatised?'

'Less emotionally, more physically.'

'You get beaten to hell?'

'It's in the job description.'

'You can do this. You've got all the information you need.'

'Let's go over it one more time. Just to be sure.'

'Of course,' she said.

She opened her mouth to say something more, but promptly shut it.

'What?' he said.

'After this, I need to leave.'

'You do?'

'I can get away with pulling another all-nighter. I won't have slept for seventy-two hours. But that's what we're all going through right now. This is a massive intelligence gathering operation. We've never had to move this fast to unpack such a coordinated attack before.'

'Then I can do the same,' King said.

'*No,*' she hissed. 'I'm not the one walking into hell tomorrow. If I crash, and fall asleep standing up, it doesn't matter. I'll be in an office, or in the back of a car. You can't afford that.'

He nodded.

She said, 'What do you want to recap?'

'Let me see if I'm getting this right. There's the warehouse in Dogpatch — that's my business. There's the wildlands near Rancho Corral de Tierra where the cartel hitmen are camped out in vans, posing as hikers — that's Slater's business. And then there's the MC clubhouse downtown that's been paid a fortune to partner up with ex-military guns-for-hire — that's Ruby's business. Right?'

'Right.'

'Each location has an unconfirmed number of hostiles, but it's estimated that there's at least a dozen at each.'

'Yes.'

'As far as your intelligence is concerned, those are the three hotspots. However, there might be rogue solo outfits. But the Army can sweep those up when they roll in.'

'Correct.'

'Are you honestly telling me the three of us are your best bet?'

She looked him dead in the eyes. 'Yes.'

'I don't want to get blamed for the fallout if it doesn't work.'

'You will,' she said. 'That's human nature. But it won't be your fault, and you'll know that, and I'll know that.'

'Love the reassurance.'

'It's the truth. You want me to sugarcoat it?'

King shook his head. 'Of course not.'

'Your track record, and those of your colleagues, are near superhuman. The executive decision was made to push ahead with this plan. We trust you.'

'That's the thing,' King said. 'I don't know if you should.'

'Why?'

'I guess it's my own issues I need to work through. But I don't feel like I deserve this. It's all been sprung on me ... on us. I still feel like I'm reacting to external circumstances, instead of going on the offence myself.'

'Sleep on it,' she said. 'You'll be up at the crack of dawn tomorrow. You can get yourself in the right mindset then.'

'Okay.'

'Until then...'

She slipped out of bed and crossed the room naked, her lithe frame glowing in the weak light. She stepped into her skirt and buttoned her shirt back up and slipped her blazer over her shoulders. Then she slunk back over to King and kissed him on the forehead.

'You're stronger than you think,' she said.

'I hope so.'

'I'll call if we get any new updates.'

'Okay.'

'Sleep well.'

She drifted to the door, and as soon as she laid a palm on the handle, King said, 'I think I know what it is.'

She turned and looked at him.

He said, 'We have no idea who the enemy is. It could be a group of outliers. It could be the whole of China. It's all shrouded in secrecy, and who's to say it stops here?'

She stared.

He said, 'Who's to say it will ever end?'

Silence.

He said, 'What if this is just the beginning? What if it goes on forever, until we're forced to crumble? How many will die?'

You could hear a pin drop.

'I mean, if we're going to be honest, what's the point?'

She said, 'Because we don't know. You said it yourself. We have no idea.'

He nodded.

She said, 'What the hell else are we going to do? Roll over and give up?'

'Never.'

'Then it's self-explanatory, isn't it?'

He nodded again.

She said, 'You're going to crush them tomorrow. The hawkish marshals and generals have been planning this for months, but you're going to rip out the throats of anyone they've paid to shoot up a festival. They're going to go back and regroup and realise they're in way over their heads. The Chinese rely on deception and manipulation and espionage. That's how they destroyed our economy — because they came at it from every angle, and they planned it for months, and they planted the seeds early and rode them through to the inevitable conclusion. They're doing the same here, but that's where we have an opportunity to crush them. You know why? Because they have everything banking on this. They've been plotting the right time to strike for years, and they've elected this their opportunity. What will they do when it doesn't pay off? They'll crumble.'

King looked up at her, and smiled.

'You'd make a fine motivational speaker.'

'Damn right I would.'

She left him there.

King rolled over in bed and turned the light out, but a kaleidoscope of potentialities played across the darkness of his vision. He saw himself failing — mortally wounded in the fight, left bleeding out on the pavement to watch the massacre take place.

And, of course, it wouldn't end there.

That would simply be the catalyst for the greater demise of the United States. The ordinary folk would have it the worst, of course. Those at the top of the food chain would be insulated by a cushy layer of savings, but if the financial crisis deepened and China overtook them as the global powerhouse — economically, militarily, and politically — then they would never regain the status they used to have.

It was still salvageable, though. The market crashing was disastrous, but without the *momentum* of more disaster, it would recover eventually. China weren't *that* close. But if Chinese New Year celebrants were massacred in the streets of San Francisco, the reputation of the United States would be tarnished on a global scale, possibly forever. King couldn't imagine a situation where it would be reversible anytime soon.

And we're used to our place at the top, King thought.

People aren't ready for drastic change.

There would be bloodshed. Riots in the streets. Looting.

You name it.

He closed his eyes, and dreamt of anarchy on the streets.

When he opened them again, it was four in the morning, and his phone was buzzing.

Go time.

76

They met out the front of the motel in the pre-dawn darkness.

Five silhouettes, materialising out of the gloom.

Jason King.

Will Slater.

Ruby Nazarian.

Violetta.

And a fifth individual — a wizened grey-haired man with a chin like granite and hard, cold eyes. King stared at him for a long time, and the silence drew out. Suddenly he recognised the look. He hadn't been able to place it because of the civilian clothing — the black windbreaker, the dark khakis, and the Gore-Tex boots. He was used to seeing their type in full military getup.

He was a general.

King said, 'Sir.'

The man smiled. 'You recognise me?'

'I think we've met before.'

'I know we have. That was years ago, though. Back when you were unofficially employed.'

Slater said, 'I'm out of the loop.'

'This man's a four-star general,' King murmured.

Slater said, 'Oh, shit.'

The general didn't bat an eyelid. King knew their interactions in the past hadn't exactly been by the book. He was used to not following procedure around Black Force operatives. He certainly didn't expect courtesy at a time like this.

Ruby said, 'What's he doing here?'

Blunt.

Straight to the point.

Borderline offensive to a man of his ranking.

Like a woman raised and trained out of the official military structure.

Which was exactly what she was.

Violetta said, 'General Scachi is here to provide you with reassurances. He flew in discreetly, off all records, so he can be here if shit hits the fan. He's coordinating the forces we've managed to smuggle into the Bay.'

'How many?' King said.

Scachi said, 'We have nearly fifty soldiers on standby, but I assume Ms. LaFleur has enlightened you as to why I'm hesitant to send them into the three locations on simultaneous raids.'

King thought, *LaFleur.*

Violetta LaFleur.

It rolled off the tongue well.

He liked it.

Then he said, 'We understand. There's too many hostiles to batter the doors down and go in guns blazing. It'll turn into a war, which will quickly spill out onto the streets. Something along those lines?'

'Precisely. And, as much as I respect my men and have faith in their abilities, they're not bred like the three of you. Half of them are grunts. We need stone-cold killers for a job like this.'

King saw Slater visibly twitch out of the corner of his eye.

'We won't take that as an insult,' Slater said.

Scachi stared at him. 'You certainly shouldn't.'

'My friend here doesn't like being seen as an assassin,' Ruby said.

'That's exactly what you are,' Scachi said. 'Anyone in the mood for a debate about that?'

They all kept their mouths firmly shut.

Scachi said, 'Let me rephrase, in case I hurt anyone's feelings. The three of you have been trained your entire careers as solo operatives. You've been taught to present yourself as unassuming civilians until it's time to get the job done, which is precisely what we need right now. My men look like Army from a mile away. So, as far as I can tell, our best bet is to send you in individually with concealed weapons and let you raise hell. Is that clear?'

'Crystal,' King said.

'That's what we do best,' Slater said.

Ruby stayed silent, her eyes piercing through the darkness.

Scachi said, 'Best of luck. If it all goes to hell, we'll be waiting in cordons. But there's no guarantee they won't get through. I couldn't think of a place that's more of a fucking nightmare to lay bottlenecks in than San Francisco. Believe me.'

'We believe you,' King said.

'What do you know about who's behind this?' Slater said.

Scachi stared at him. 'That shouldn't be on your mind right now.'

'But it is,' Slater said. 'I like to know who I'm bringing the fight to.'

'You're bringing the fight to real bad motherfuckers from the Mexican cartels, and to a certain faction of our ex-soldiers, most of whom were dishonourably discharged and willing to enact human suffering on a colossal scale for a few extra bucks in the bank. That's who you're bringing the fight to.'

'But who's paying them specifically? Who are these hardliners?'

Violetta said, 'We're narrowing in on that.'

'Does that mean—?'

Scachi stepped forward, right in Slater's face. 'Son, you are damn good with a weapon, and damn good with your fists. But right now you need to leave the planning to us. In four hours time this festival is going to begin, and there'll be early birds on the streets well before that. Do you understand how important this morning is to the future of our nation?'

Slater stepped in too, so they were even closer.

His face was inches away from the general's.

'I understand perfectly,' Slater said. 'You know why? Because I've been doing this shit my whole life. I bet you look real good in that military getup with the colours on your breast pocket, but how do you look with blood on your hands? You ever had blood on your hands like the three of us have?'

Scachi stood there, unable to respond, in disbelief that an operative would not only talk back to him but insult his legitimacy.

Slater said, 'Is this the part where you discipline me?

Make me do push-ups? Run a few miles? I don't think it's going to work in this case. Because as soon as I do this job for you, I'm gone. No matter how badly you need me. Because I'm sick of getting left in the dark. If this little relationship is going to move forward, between you and your government and King and myself, then shit's going to have to change. I want to know what I'm walking into. I want to know who I'm fighting.'

Scachi bristled with pent-up frustration.

Then King said, 'I'm with him.'

Ruby said, 'I was never not with him.'

'Look,' Violetta said. 'You want the truth?'

All three of them continued their tense stand-off with Scachi.

Violetta snapped her fingers. 'Look at me — right now. He's the general. I'm the intelligence analyst. I'm the one who tells you what you can and can't know. And understand this — as soon as we finish piecing this together, you'll know. But we don't have the whole picture yet. We don't know how bad it's going to be. Right now, we'd rather not speculate. Is that too much to ask?'

Slater paused for thought, then nodded.

'We're not cogs in a machine,' he said. 'Remember that.'

'We always have,' Violetta said.

Scachi managed to compose himself. 'Best of luck, soldiers.'

King said, 'Thank you, sir.'

Slater and Ruby said nothing at all.

General Scachi nodded once to Violetta, said, 'I'll be in touch regarding logistics,' and melted back into the shadows.

King watched his silhouette cross the street and get into a plain nondescript sedan. He fired it up and drove away.

Violetta said, 'That went well.'

Slater said, 'I don't take shit from anyone.'

'I can see that.'

Violetta took a deep breath, looked at them all once each, and said, 'Let's get down to business, then, shall we?'

77

King sat behind the wheel of a rented Toyota hatchback as the sky lightened from black to dark blue.

He weaved through the streets of downtown San Francisco, passing through the suburbs of Balboa Park, Excelsior, and College Hill, respectively. He passed suburban cul-de-sacs and quiet leafy residential apartment complexes. The sidewalks were neat and orderly, and the trees on each street were carefully manicured and tended to by the local council.

All was quiet at five in the morning.

King had pored over the intel Violetta had shown him the night before, and come away with a barebones plan of attack. Most of it would rely on improvisation, though — something he was extraordinarily adept at. It had formed the foundation of his entire black operations career. What most would call rash recklessness, he called coming up with the best solution. He'd been doing it for as long as he could remember. It was the advantage of his genetic predisposition.

Being able to react faster than anyone he came up against had its perks.

There was a loaded Glock 17 strapped to an appendix holster at the front of his waistband, and spare magazines inserted into small storage slots on his belt. He wore a U.S. Armour Enforcer 6000 bulletproof vest — one of the thinnest and lightest on the market — underneath a thick brown sweater to disguise its inevitable bulk. There was a Ka-Bar combat knife resting in a sheath connected to the other side of the appendix holster.

And that was it.

He drifted into Dogpatch as the sky brightened, and his heart beat steady against his chest wall. Not fast — hard. He could feel the pressure in his throat, in his chest, in his shoulders. What would ordinarily be mistaken for a heart attack, he recognised as stress chemicals releasing into his system, honing his acuity, leaving him in fight or flight mode.

And he'd never chosen flight in his life.

He had all the information he needed. The target was a warehouse by the waterfront, left dormant for nearly a year as the owner searched for new tenants to lease to. Interest had been sparse, and the property hadn't even been on the market for the last couple of months. It was three storeys of industrial space, and there was a fifteen foot gap on each side of the target building separating it from its neighbours, which were equally giant warehouses in turn. That left all sorts of room for twisting metal fire escape stairs up each side of the building.

There were ten ways in and out through the fire stairs, and cramped claustrophobic alleyways all around it, and endless roller doors on the ground floor to accelerate a bulletproof vehicle out of if they were sprung.

So King understood why it had to be him.

If the Army went in all guns blazing, many of the targets would escape.

And when most of them had been radicalised, *that* was an issue.

He figured he'd take advantage of the fire stairs to enter the premises. From there, it'd be a dark, decrepit close-quarters skirmish.

His specialty.

He parked several hundred feet from the address, in the heart of a grim industrial estate perhaps four streets over. There was a semi-trailer parked out on the street, and he coasted to a halt behind it. He shut off the headlights and the interior light when he killed the engine, and was left sitting quietly in the pale dawn light.

He bowed his head to the wheel, and felt the cool touch of leather on his forehead.

He breathed in, and out.

Here we go.

An unknown number of hostiles.

All highly motivated.

All armed to the teeth.

Some with a history of psychotic mental illness.

All of them wanted nothing more than to cause maximum carnage at the morning's festivities. Perhaps they'd even get a handsome bonus if the kill count was triple digits. It made King sick to his stomach, and he used that as fuel. He visualised kids torn limb from limb, babies blown from their mother's arms by bullets, parents killed in front of their children, innocents massacred at random.

Defenceless.

Unable to resist.

King got out of the car with his breath steaming in the cold morning air, and hot anger flooding his veins.

This was how he worked best.

But he kept it contained. He wiped his face of any emotion, went to the back seats of the Toyota and took out the faded hard hat and tattered high-visibility vest. He let his features droop, coating them in fatigue and exhaustion. He let his face grow slack. He invented the persona of a tradesman worn down by daily manual labour at the docks, and he embodied that role.

In his ear, a small concealed earpiece squawked to life.

Violetta said, 'Go.'

He set off in the direction of the warehouse.

78

S later had his own rented sedan, worth no more than ten grand optimistically, and he used it to coast further downtown — out of San Francisco's city limits and toward coastal western San Mateo County.

His task was straightforward. He wasn't up against the volatility that King and Ruby would have to deal with — his issue was the sheer number of hostiles. Violetta had shown him surveillance photos that had captured an overwhelming influx of camper vans around the trailheads leading down to the Rancho Corral de Tierra wildlands. The government wouldn't have thought anything of it, except for the fact that facial recognition technology had scored two hits on a couple of Mexicans in one of the vans. They'd been leaving their vehicle as the surveillance car rolled past, and it had confirmed they were José Luis and Miguel Ángel — the Gómez brothers.

Slater knew all too well about the reputation of the Gómez brothers, and, frankly, he was shocked they'd show their face over the border.

They were two of the Sinaloa cartel's best *sicarios*, but

they weren't exclusive. They were independent contractors who sold their services to the highest bidder. Together they were unofficially linked to close to a thousand deaths in Mexico, leaving a trail of disembowelled, decapitated, defiled bodies in their wake. They killed men, women and children with equal detachment.

And every piece of intel the United States government had collected on them showed that they ate, drank and breathed money.

So it was no wonder the Chinese hardliners had got their hands on them.

The Gómez brothers would mobilise all their underlings in a heartbeat to slaughter Americans in droves if it meant a few extra pesos in the bank.

Slater drove into the woods. The trees swallowed him up, masking the sunrise from view. He was left speeding through the muted shadows in search of the trailheads Violetta had pinpointed on a map the previous evening. She'd fed the coordinates to his smartphone, and that's what he was going off.

He could already feel the anger swelling in his chest.

In that regard, he and King were cut from the same cloth. Well, truth be told, they *were* the same cloth, but what linked them inextricably was their mutual hatred for anyone who put money over human decency. And it was a common theme in most of their enemies — the unending fight for profits. It was the clearest sign of a sociopath, and it was a trait shared by nearly everyone they came up against.

The Gómez brothers were simply the most clear-cut example of that principle.

He couldn't wait to get his hands on them.

The road rose into the hills, and Slater kept both hands on the wheel. He was equipped with the same arsenal as

King — Glock, Ka-Bar, lightweight bulletproof vest, and spare magazines. But he was dressed from head to toe in hiking apparel — a North Face windbreaker, black hiking pants and Scarpa boots. He'd shoved a woollen beanie over his bald scalp to complete the outfit.

At first glance, he was a big, muscular exercise freak, ready to hit the trails for a long day of hiking.

And he could act the part when required.

He wasn't as talented as Ruby, but he'd manage.

His GPS shrieked at him to turn right, and he steeled himself for what was to come.

This would be the first obstacle — a wide gravel parking lot cut into the roadside woods, which led to a pair of smaller unpaved tracks that were traversable by vehicle. Those two trails in turn led to a couple of lesser known clearings overlooking the Rancho Corral de Tierra wildlands. It was perfect cover before the trees fell away, replaced by scrub and barren plains.

Perfect cover for the cartel to stockpile their *sicario*s in camper vans.

It was estimated that there were twenty or thirty hitmen from Sinaloa, Tijuana, Juárez and Guadalajara spread out across the vans.

It was a damn good disguise. If a random sweep of San Mateo County hadn't turned up with the Gómez brothers caught in the act, the encampment never would have been found.

Which posed the question — *are there more that we've missed?*

Slater tuned that out. There was no use worrying about it — it would only drag him down into nihilism. What if he fought his heart out to neutralise this encampment, and hundreds were massacred in the streets all the same?

But Violetta had been confident.

'We've never conducted a surveillance operation of this magnitude,' she'd said. 'The amount of resources we were able to mobilise in a single day has been staggering. We're confident it's just the three locations.'

It better be, Slater thought. *You don't have a fourth operative here in San Francisco. Scachi's boys would have to handle it.*

He rounded a crest in the trail, and the gravel lot opened out in front of him, surrounded by thick clusters of trees. Pilarcitos Creek lay a mile or so to the north, but there was no sign of it. The trees boxed them in, dense and oppressive.

Ahead there were some camper vans — two large RVs that probably cost a few hundred thousand dollars apiece. They were beat-down and faded and the paint was chipping, but Slater took one look at the vans and realised their age had been artificially manufactured. The Gómez brothers had probably picked them up brand-new on the way, so they were able to fit six or seven men in each. They'd beaten the shit out of their exteriors to make them look unimpressive. An expensive operation, but the cartel had money to blow, especially if they were making obscene sums from the Chinese hardliners.

Slater pulled his sedan into the parking lot, and stopped alongside the twin behemoths.

He couldn't see inside the RVs.

The windows were tinted to the maximum.

But he knew he was being watched.

In his ear, Slater heard Violetta say, 'Go.'

Plastering disinterest over his face, he got out and stretched his arms and legs. He spun in a slow half-circle, savouring the scenery.

Then he waltzed right over to the closest RV and knocked sharply on the door.

79

R uby swept her hair back over one shoulder and did her best to wobble in her oversized Balenciaga shoes.

She was dressed in nearly five grand worth of designer clothes. Gucci over-the-shoulder purse, Off-White black fleece lounge pants, Dolce & Gabbana leather jacket, and a sequinned tube top. She had her lipstick smeared to one side and patchy mascara under her eyes.

She stood out.

And that was the intention.

The tube top exposed her supple midriff and pushed her breasts up so they were firm and perky. She made sure the leather jacket was practically dangling off her shoulders, revealing her body. There was a combat knife in the oversized lounge pants and a Glock strapped to her thigh — the zips on either side of the pants gave easy access to either of the weapons.

She was your typical trust fund brat who spent her days posting her high-roller lifestyle on Facebook and Instagram for the world to see.

But she'd made sure she looked *gorgeous* in the process.

Because the plan had to go off without a hitch.

The makeup had taken an hour to get right, and Violetta had taken no chances, carting in a Hollywood makeup artist who happened to be vacationing in San Fran for the festival. She'd signed a hundred NDAs and spent the time accentuating Ruby's amber eyes, highlighting her supple lips, and at the same time adding the impression that she'd spent all night at a club and was stumbling home in the early hours of the morning.

She was in downtown San Francisco, far outside the city centre, trawling through one of the last remaining rough patches in the gentrified city limits. She sauntered to the end of the street and saw the clubhouse halfway down, lying dormant in the dawn light.

A sign above the porch read: JUNKYARD DOGS MC.

Appealing, she thought.

She lingered on the street corner until she saw activity in front of the clubhouse. The front doors opened and a grizzled fifty-something guy with a grey beard and thin receding hair swept back off his forehead stumbled out. He had a gut the size of a keg, and he wouldn't do much harm in a firefight. But he was one of the hardline gangsters in the Junkyard Dogs who'd agreed to house the hired guns for the entirety of their time in California.

He knew exactly what they were doing here.

He was scum in human form.

Ruby set off instantly, making a beeline for the sidewalk in front of the clubhouse. When she reached it, she stumbled past, flashing her trademark devilish grin at the biker.

He returned the smile, exposing yellowing gums.

Momentarily distracted from the tension of the morning.

Because everyone in that clubhouse knew what was at stake that day.

He needed some sort of distraction from it.

'Big night, honey?' the guy said, leering.

Ruby could pick up on a million subtleties in the inflection of his voice. He floated the question out there in a playful manner, never expecting to receive a serious response. His mind was elsewhere — this was the big day, after all — and he'd probably been turned down catcalling a thousand times in the past. It had become something half-hearted now, something he didn't expect to receive anything from, except for a dark look and a quickened pace.

But when she wanted to, Ruby could play a bad girl.

She could play anything.

The Lynx program had taught her that.

She flashed something tantalising in her eyes. As if she was contemplating ... this. She said, 'Very big.'

'Ain't got no man takin' you home?'

She shook her head. 'Lost my friends.'

'I could be your friend.'

She smiled at him. 'Maybe next time, big boy.'

He liked that.

He said, 'Why next time?'

She kept walking, but she slowed her pace. She reached out and touched a finger to the nearest fence pole and used it to playfully twist into a pirouette. Then she ran a hand down her stomach, smoothing her abs.

'I don't know you,' she said. 'Stranger danger, y'know?'

'I'm a nice guy.'

'Are you?'

'My name's Phil. What's yours?'

'I'm Natasha.'

'Natasha... I like that.'

'I'm fucking wired,' she said. 'I don't want to go to bed. I want to stay out. I want to party.'

'Party with me, maybe.'

Still said in jest. Like he didn't believe it would work.

Ruby said, 'I've been warned off guys like you.'

'I don't bite, honey.'

She looked at him, shedding all niceties. She said, 'What if I like guys that bite?'

He smiled, exposing the same yellow maw, and the dynamic changed. There was a sudden look in his eyes. A switch had flipped in his brain — something primal rising up, something that hadn't been activated in a long time. Because he wasn't exactly the most appealing package on the dating scene, but now there was some small part of his brain going, *Wait — could you pull this off? Is she serious?*

She realised she'd have to put in some work to make him less suspicious.

Because never in a million years would someone like her go willingly with someone like him.

So she said, 'You're lucky I'm horny. Had a real big guy with me at the club. Then I lost him. He would have made me *so* happy.'

She rolled her eyes and turned away. She started off down the sidewalk again.

He shouted, 'Hey!'

She looked back.

Then she kept walking.

He came down off the porch and moved through the overgrown weeds in the unkempt lawn and pulled up right in front of her.

She reached out and ran a finger down his leather vest, and slurred, 'Yurr cyoot.'

'What was that, honey?'

'I said you're cute.'

'Ain't get called that often.'

'Well, I'm telling you it now.'

'Why you telling me it?'

'Because I'm horny,' she said. 'I told you that. Bet you got something big for me down there. Maybe I'm tempted.'

'You should be tempted.'

'You'd have to convince me.'

'What do I gotta do?'

'Tell me what you're packin'.'

'Something big, honey. You said it yourself.'

'You promise?'

'Let me show you.'

She took another step forward and said, 'You really got something special down there, I'll give you the ride of your life.'

She stepped back and pouted and looked at him through unfocused eyes.

Tempting him.

Enticing him.

Sending the blood rushing down there.

Because when that happened, all bets were off the table. Men did unbelievably idiotic things if they were promised the ultimate reward.

Most things in life are done for sex, Ruby thought.

She'd killed her fair share of corrupt businessmen back when she was employed using similar tactics.

He looked back at the clubhouse, and she could see a million thoughts running through his head. It would be a violation of the privacy the guests had demanded. It would be stupid. Moronic. Unfathomable. If he had any common sense, he'd shoo her away.

Because either right now, or within the hour, a force of

hired ex-Army mercenaries who hated their country and everything it stood for would be gearing up to massacre civilians for a few extra digits in the bank. And if there were witnesses to that who hadn't been paid off, then they'd need to be neutralised. But the biker would also be coming up with every excuse his primitive brain could muster.

I've got my own room in the clubhouse. Maybe no-one's up yet. I could sneak her in, and sneak her out. When else am I gonna get this fuckin' opportunity again? When do these trust fund Instagram models even look at me? Am I about to give up this ultimate fantasy?

He wasn't.

He said, 'Why don't you come in and I'll show you, honey? I'll take care of ya. I'll rock your world.'

Ruby forced herself to smile.

'I'd like that,' she said. 'I'm already wet. I need you inside me.'

That tipped him over the edge.

He took her by the hand and led her toward the clubhouse.

80

King knew he was being watched.

He could sense it.

He stepped into the street, with the bay on one side, barely visible through the warehouses lining the waterfront, and another industrial zone on the other. There was little activity this early in the morning. Shifts wouldn't start for another hour or so. But he spotted a handful of drab, dreary labourers shuffling down the sidewalks, some slinging duffel bags over their shoulders, some carrying equipment and tools.

Heading to punch the clock.

King mirrored their movements, and he could do a damn good job at that when the situation demanded it. Even though he'd never worked at a normal occupation in his life, he injected as much existential dread into his posture, minimising his bulk and slouching toward the concrete as it flowed past under his feet.

He noticed the target warehouse in his peripheral vision. It was tall, dark and rusting, looming up against the backdrop of the dawn. He saw metal stairways twisting down the sides of the building like cages, and iron girders running across the exterior, and large smudged windows. He kept walking, staring straight ahead, not paying the building any attention. It didn't exactly stand out — there were a dozen like it on the street.

Then, as he came directly under the ground level awning, he turned straight into the narrow alleyway between the building and its neighbour. He did it in one smooth motion, making sure not to draw the eye. No jerky movements, no sudden change of direction, just a slick slicing sidestep.

Then he was under the shadow of the fire stairs.

He climbed them immediately, keeping a close eye on what lay above. The walkways, like a series of cages sprawling into the heavens, were deserted. There wasn't a soul in sight.

Instantly he saw the sanity of using solo operatives. He hadn't been able to grasp the necessity before, but now it was clear. The bomb team were no doubt watching the street like hawks. Any attempt from Army grunts to infiltrate the warehouse wouldn't have lasted very long, unless they were coming in on their own like King had. But then they'd be operating alone, and they weren't prepared for that the way he'd been conditioned all his life.

It would be the same with Slater, and the same with Ruby.

Espionage. Deception. The silent slash of the blade.

He slid the Ka-Bar out of his belt, and the Glock out of his appendix holster, and started up the first steep flight of stairs. There was no use keeping the weapons concealed. He was on the side of the building, and if anyone saw him, they'd understand he wasn't a lost tradesman.

They'd know immediately.

So this was the most dangerous stretch of the operation. Before the first strike. The fate of the country hung in the balance, and that pressure simmered his brain like it was on a hot plate. The dull throbbing of adrenaline and stress and fear started behind his eyeballs, and gripped his temples, and ran cold down the back of his neck.

He was totally alert, firing on all cylinders, ready to react at the drop of a hat. Sheer focus settled over him, and he took it all in stride, because he'd felt it before.

Never like this, but the underlying sensation wasn't foreign.

He reached the first floor, and crouched low on the grated metal floor of the walkway, and listened hard through a thin wooden door for any signs of life. He couldn't hear a peep. Moving quiet as a mouse, he reached out and touched the door with a single gloved finger. There was no handle, and maybe, just maybe...

It swung inward, a few inches.

He breathed out.

A way in.

Perhaps this was all possible after all.

He gripped the Glock tighter, ready to burst up off the walkway and *explode* through the door, unleashing all the energy building up in his core. He figured he could kill a dozen men with the first clip if he picked his shots correctly, which he knew he'd manage to do. He had a brain unlike most on this planet, and if he could—

The door swung open in his face.

King stood up, fast, and aimed the gun, but he didn't fire.

Because the figure standing in the doorway wasn't holding a gun.

He was thin and small and pale with hollow cheekbones

and a shaved head and gaunt eyes. There was no life in them. It had been conditioned out of him. King had seen the same look in prisoners of war. Immediately he knew the guy was one of the mentally ill Violetta had referenced from security footage, discharged from the military, probably held here against his will and brainwashed by the Chinese or the cartel or other disillusioned vets to carry out a suicide mission.

Because he was wearing a vest packed with plastic explosive.

And he was holding a detonator.

And his thumb was tight on it.

He looked King in the eyes, and panic rippled through him, and he twitched imperceptibly, as if he were about to let go right then and blow them all to hell because of the sheer shock.

King hissed, '*No.*'

The guy kept staring at him.

Neither of them blinked.

They were inches apart.

King thought his heart might burst in his chest. He'd never felt it pound like this before. Sweat came off his brow, and leached out of his temples, and stained the vest he was wearing under his shirt.

They stood there in a mortal stalemate.

King said, 'Wait.'

The guy didn't say a word.

He was sweating too.

It was cold.

Wind rippled against the fire stairs, and rattled the walkway.

King said, 'Let me talk. Please, fuck, just let me talk.'

The guy might as well have been a Greek statue.

There was nothing left in his eyes.

King thought, *That's it.*

That's all she wrote.

My life ends here.

Then the guy said through dry, chapped lips, 'Talk.'

81

The RV door slammed open, and Slater came face to face with Miguel Ángel Gómez.

He recognised the repulsive cartel *sicario* from the surveillance photos, but he didn't let it show. He spread the familiar warm smile onto his face that fellow nature lovers shared, and said, 'How ya doin'?'

And he did a good job at it.

Because Gómez didn't suspect a goddamn thing.

He was short and squat but built like a bull, with a thick neck and giant hands and tree trunks for legs. He looked like he could tear someone limb from limb.

Then again, so did Slater. And Slater was doing his best to disprove that preconception.

Gómez stared.

Impassively.

Disinterestedly.

Slater said, 'You got a toilet, brother?'

Gómez said, 'No.'

'Please, man,' Slater said, feigning genuine pain. 'There ain't nowhere around here to go.'

'Piss on a tree.'

'Man, I gotta shit, y'know?'

Slater cracked a broad smile, like it was the funniest thing in the world.

Gómez didn't.

The bull-like man said, 'I said no.'

'Why you gotta be so rude, man? You hiking these trails? What are ya doin' here?'

Gómez was about to slam the door in the stranger's face, but Slater saw that momentary pause of concern in his eyes. As if he were thinking, *What if this looks suspicious? How are hikers supposed to act?*

He didn't want to get busted in the final hours before it was all about to kick off.

So he switched from total aggression to searching for a lame excuse.

The man said, 'Yes, I hike these trails. But no toilet.'

'No toilet?' Slater said. 'C'mon, man, you ain't gotta be like that. This is a big RV, brother. You got a toilet back there for sure.'

'It's broken.'

Slater sighed and bowed his head.

He started to cry.

Gómez had no goddamn idea what to do. He stood there with his hands by his sides and an expression of total confusion on his face.

Slater mumbled through blubbering tears, 'I just ... I just been drivin' around out here for a long time, brother. I'm hurting. I'm in pain. I need a—'

He stepped up onto the first step in mid-sentence.

Gómez almost didn't notice — he was transfixed by the range of emotions he was witnessing.

Slater took another step up into the RV.

Now he was out of sight of the second RV. He knew they'd all be watching him through the tinted windows, searching for any sign of suspicion. But now, in their eyes, Slater had been welcomed aboard, so Gómez obviously was in control of the situation. Maybe Gómez would kill the hiker. Maybe not.

Whatever — it wasn't their concern anymore.

But as Slater made it onto the second step, Gómez snarled and shook his head, refusing to let the stranger any further into the RV. He reached out and planted a hand onto Slater's chest and shoved him hard. Because if this was an ordinary civilian coming aboard, he certainly couldn't be allowed to see the arsenal of automatic weaponry spread across the tables and chairs and beds.

Slater caught the railing with his palm and held tight, and Gómez shoved him again, but he didn't budge.

Bedlam erupted.

Gómez turned at the top of the steps to shout something to his comrades — probably to the effect of *'Help me get this crazy motherfucker off the bus before I blow a hole in his chest!'*

But he didn't even get one word into that sentence, because Slater shot out a hand and grabbed the back of his neck and used all his weight and the assistance of gravity to drop his face into the top of the railing. Gómez's nose struck the metal banister on its rounded tip and he cried out in pain as blood erupted from his nostrils and his nose cracked.

Slater activated.

He hurled Gómez aside and shouldered past the thick Mexican, and ended up facing off in a tight claustrophobic space with four angry dark-featured *sicarios*. They were the cream of the crop — far from the youthful amateurs he'd encountered in Tulum. They ranged from early thirties to late forties and sported lean wiry muscle. The sort of physique you got from farm work, or, perhaps, regularly beating people to death.

Hard motherfuckers, through and through.

And they reacted instantly.

Because they were born and bred in war. They were uncivilised men, and uncivilised men were always the most dangerous.

The closest man to Slater instinctively reached for the rifle on the table in front of him, but then pulled back, because he remembered he'd been cleaning it. It was lying disassembled, in pieces. The hesitation cost him. Slater kicked him hard in the chest, sending him careening back into two of his colleagues, pinning them all against the small countertop.

Slater went for his Glock, but then he remembered the second RV.

He swore under his breath.

It was too close. They'd hear the gunshots, and it'd be over. They'd fire up the engine and peel out of there, never to be seen again until they materialised in the centre of San Francisco with guns loaded.

So instead he pulled his Ka-Bar out and sprinted across the tiny space, meeting the fourth guy head-on. That *sicario* had been going for his sidearm, and he even managed to get it free from its holster. But then Slater was on him, and he slammed into him so hard that the gun ended up crushed between their bodies, and Slater used the opportunity to slide the knife into his ribcage and twist upward, piercing his heart with a grotesque muted *crunch*.

He pulled the knife out and spun and slashed the throat

of the guy he'd kicked in the chest. Blood sprayed as arteries were severed.

It's a brutal world, he thought.

That guy went down and the other two weren't close enough to weapons to snatch them up. Slater caught one of them in the stomach and practically disembowelled him. He tried to pull the knife out but it was lodged on something.

So Slater let it go and leapt onto the fourth guy with all his weight, crushing him against the countertop, maybe breaking a rib. He thundered an uppercut into the guy's mid-section then head-butted him hard, forehead to forehead. They both reeled from the impact, but Slater was accustomed to getting smacked in the head. He recovered in a couple of seconds, and worked the knife free from the third man and inserted it into the fourth guy's throat.

Then he saw Gómez dashing for the open door, his nose streaming blood.

Slater leapt across the RV, clearing an entire partition in the process, and spear-tackled Gómez into the wall, spilling them both across the steps. He knocked his head on the way down and landed awkwardly on one shoulder, nearly dislocating it. But he righted himself at the last second and spilled across the steps in an awkward tangle of limbs.

Gómez came down on top of him.

The guy was short and square, so he practically tumbled off Slater like a bowling ball, heading straight for the entrance again.

In the claustrophobic tightness of the stairwell Slater reached out and looped his arm around Gómez's throat and locked it tight. The *sicario* wheezed for breath, but Slater yanked him back on top of him and looped his legs around the guy's stomach, so Gómez was wearing him as a backpack.

Then Slater squeezed and held on for dear life.

Gómez went red, and gasped for breath.

They slid down a step.

Now they were inches from tumbling out through the open door, which would send them both sprawling out onto the gravel. And the *sicario*s in the other RV would still be watching, and they'd see, and they'd radio out the call to scatter, and that would be that.

Slater squeezed tighter.

He felt his forearm burning out, lactic acid flooding the muscle, killing its power.

And Gómez's thick neck was still protecting him.

He was nearly out, but not quite.

Slater strained and squeezed and wrenched and screwed up his face in exertion.

Gómez kicked out with both legs, flailing them in thin air.

One foot darted over the threshold.

If they were watching, they would have seen it.

With his heart in his mouth Slater kept squeezing, and finally Gómez went limp.

Slater held on for another full minute until he was sure the guy was dead.

He let go of the corpse, and wriggled out from underneath it, and dragged it back up the steps.

His lungs burned, his chest heaved, and he couldn't feel his right arm because of the lactic acid build-up.

But he'd done it.

He'd cleared the first RV.

A few more vehicles to go, he thought.

He bent over at the waist and sucked in air, contemplating how close he'd come to failure.

But now it didn't matter how much noise he made.

He drew the Glock from its holster, rested his finger an inch off the trigger, and composed himself.

Now.

He leapt down the steps and sprinted for the second RV.

82

Ruby gave a small ditzy laugh as Phil led her through the knee-high grass.

She purred, 'Oh, you're bad...'

'Am I?' he said. 'Want to know a secret?'

'Sure.'

'I shouldn't be doing this.'

'Why's that?'

'There's some important people in there. They don't want visitors.'

She tiptoed forward and touched her lips to the side of his neck, grazing his grey stubble. 'I thought you didn't give a fuck about anyone else.'

'I don't.'

'Then let's go. I don't have all day.'

He grinned and lumbered up the steps, still holding her by the hand. She followed willingly. It was honestly pathetic how effortlessly she'd convinced him to betray the request of a collection of serious stone-cold killers, but that was the power of an ill-timed erection.

He opened the door and pulled her into a communal

area that reeked of old beer and weed and tobacco. There were tattered couches scattered across the room, and an ancient television in the corner, and a faded pool table in the centre of the room lit by pendant lights covered in the Budweiser logo.

It was obvious the mercs hired by the Chinese weren't using the clubhouse because of its amenities. She figured the Junkyard Dogs were the only organisation in San Francisco so far to the right that they were willing to buy into murderous ideologies. Not that the mercs possessed those ideologies. They were contract workers through and through, doing everything for the money, but they could probably justify the massacre to the Junkyard Dogs under some thinly veiled anti-immigration shtick.

There were guns and knives and chunks of plastic explosive all over the place.

Rifles, pistols, a few shotguns, even an RPG.

Jesus Christ, Ruby thought. *It's going to be a slaughter.*

She felt sick to her stomach.

There was a single guy in the communal area — the rest were in their rooms. He was cleaning an automatic weapon, but he looked up from it to see Phil leading a ditzy young socialite by the hand. He was probably late twenties, but built like a powerhouse, with long black hair and a surprisingly handsome face. He had a chiselled jawline and slate grey eyes and olive skin.

Sociopaths come in all shapes and sizes, Ruby thought.

The guy's eyes went wide and he hissed, 'What the *fuck* do you think you're doing?!'

Phil waved a hand dismissively, but he looked nervous. 'Relax, brother. She hasn't seen anything. Have you, honey?'

Ruby giggled and rolled her eyes and looked at the opposite wall to prove her point. 'I ain't seen shit.'

He liked that.

He pulled her toward one of the corridors on the opposite side of the room.

He said, 'Trust me, it's all good.'

He ushered Ruby into a dark hallway with stained carpet and hung back for long enough to whisper, 'She's coked out of her mind. She won't remember this in a few hours. Give me a spell.'

Ruby heard every word.

And she heard the guy respond, 'Might have to kill her.'

'We'll work that out later. Let me get my rocks off first.'

'Alright.'

She took a couple of steps down the hallway before he entered, so there were no doubts as to whether she was out of earshot. She didn't want him making a lunge for her. She needed the upper hand from the jump.

Wired, pulsating with nervous energy, honed in on micro-reactions and micro-expressions, Ruby turned and walked backward down the corridor when Phil followed her.

She kept her eyes on him, watching for any sign of sudden aggression. But there was nothing there behind the milky unfocused pupils, and she could immediately tell there were a thousand thoughts running through his head that had nothing to do with situational awareness — thoughts like, *What if I don't impress her? What if I finish early? What if I ruin my one chance to fuck a supermodel?*

She almost smiled at his vulnerability.

Phil led her to a tiny bedroom with no windows and a musty odour. The air was stale — with no ventilation, the biker's dirty laundry and general untidiness had been left to fester. The single mattress in the corner of the room had no bed frame, and the sheets were stained yellow from sweating in his sleep.

Ruby nearly gagged, and briefly doubted everything.

Does he think I'd be stupid enough to come here?

Is he *the one roping me along?*

But she'd forgotten the most fundamental law of human nature.

Men often think with their privates, and that makes them stupid.

She sauntered into the room and twisted at the waist, looking back, flashing him the universal *fuck-me* eyes. He practically ran inside and shut the door behind him.

Immediately reached down to his belt and unbuckled the catch and...

The Ka-Bar was in her hand in an instant and she slashed his throat with a slick horizontal swing. She clamped her other hand tight over his mouth as his arteries erupted and gently lowered his bleeding, shaking, dying body to the mattress.

She watched his eyes glaze over, and felt nothing at all.

Wiped the blade on his leather vest, and danced over to the door.

Quietly opened it and slipped out into the corridor.

83

K ing battled down the urge to react with desperate aggression.

It wasn't going to work.

His default mode was fundamentally useless here.

The guy was sweating and shaking and there was nothing binding his finger to the detonator. No tape holding it in place. No fail-safes. Which meant he was a live operative. There was no turning back. He'd pressed down on it, and they'd sent him out into the field. He'd no doubt been ordered to head straight for the earliest festivities and let go in as crowded a location as he could find. And now King could see he was wearing a jacket at least three sizes too big, with the sleeves rolled way up and the buttons undone. When he adjusted those, he'd look like any other junkie roaming the streets in clothes that didn't fit — not, by any stretch of the imagination, a suicide bomber.

King floated a glance past the man, inside the warehouse. His view was stunted, but he saw an interior metal walkway running around the perimeter of a cavernous central space. There was no sign of anyone else. This guy had pressed down on the detonator on the first floor, and made straight for the fire stairs. Maybe to breathe. Maybe to comprehend the gravity of what he'd done.

King knew, deep in his soul, that every word he uttered would be the difference between life and death.

Between victory and failure.

On a national scale.

Sweat ran down his face but he didn't dare reach up and wipe it.

He kept his voice low and calm, and he said, 'You don't want to do this, do you?'

The guy gave him a blank stare.

As if looking right through him.

King said, 'You regret pushing down on that thing. You regret listening to everything they told you. You regret believing them.'

Silence.

King said, 'You're angry at the country. Angry at the world. But you're not insane. You hear me? They might have told you you're crazy and that there's no hope and that you might as well go out with a bang and take as many of these motherfuckers with you along the way, but you don't believe that deep down, do you? You thought you did but now you're realising you don't.'

The guy — no, not a guy; a kid, because he couldn't have been more than twenty-five — didn't say a word. Didn't give any sort of emotional reaction besides a twitch of the eyelids. He stared at King — not looking him in the eyes, vacantly gazing — with a look of utter nihilism. He'd given up all hope.

But he hadn't let go of the detonator.

King said, 'How much do you hate them?'

'Who?'

'The people you're going to kill.'

'Fuck them.'

'Why?'

'You think any of this matters? What's it matter what I do?'

'I don't think you're weak.'

'What?'

King said, 'I don't think you're as soft as they think you are.'

'You fuckin' think that I'm—?'

'No,' King said. 'They do. Not me. I think war or trauma has fucked with your head like it's fucked with mine — like it's fucked with all of ours. You go overseas and you fight against people you don't know or understand and it ruins you. You dream. You wake up sweating. I know what it's like, brother. You hear voices. Maybe they're powerful voices. But you know what those guys downstairs did to you? They put you in a place like this with a dozen other guys that feel the exact same way, and they made an echo chamber out of it. Because if everyone hears the voices, then they must be there, right?'

The guy brought the detonator up in front of his face and looked hard at it.

King's heart rate spiked.

But he kept his voice controlled, at all costs.

He said, 'Look at it. You don't want to be here.'

'Keep talking,' the guy said, still sweating, still shaking, still locked in a staring contest with the small inanimate object that could, through second- and third-order consequences, change the fate of the developed world.

King said, 'They took advantage of you because they think you're weak, and they think you'll cave to what they tell you to do. And I'm not going to sit here and say life's a

fucking fantasy and that you'll get that vest off and everything will be fine, because those voices never go away and
they only get worse and if you want the truth life's going to
be hell from now on. But you're a warrior and warriors don't
take the easy way out. I'm not letting you off the hook. You
let me help you and you can do whatever the fuck you want
with your life. You want to jump off a bridge, then do it. But
you'd be doing it with honour, and you'd be taking responsibility, even though your head's falling apart like all of our
heads fall apart.'

Dead quiet.

King said, 'Don't be weak. Be strong. Fight that battle
between your ears and win. Winning's all we do, brother.'

The guy was pouring sweat now. There was perspiration
running down his face, and King realised some of it was
tears. His eyes were bloodshot and etched with deep,
visceral pain. The sort of pain you couldn't fathom. The
pain of a crippling, devastating, soul-sucking mental illness.
Probably exacerbated by post-traumatic stress.

But deep in there, somewhere hidden, somewhere
untapped, he was still in there.

The man he used to be.

He looked at King with crippling existential pain, but he
fought through it, and he said, 'Okay. Get this fucking thing
off me, man.'

King exhaled.

84

Slater came in like a freight train.

His natural athleticism aided him as he made it to the second RV in a couple of seconds flat. He was a charging bull, swollen with momentum, and he crashed into the flimsy door so hard that the whole thing snapped off one of its hinges and dangled loosely inward.

Then he was past it and up the same short flight of steps and inside before any of the occupants realised what the hell was happening.

One of them was reasonably close to a few Heckler & Koch sidearms on a table so Slater shot him in the face first, then turned and pumped two rounds into the chest of the guy standing next to him.

So all at once there was the *crash* of the door crumbling and the ear-piercing roar of unsuppressed gunshots in an enclosed space and the warm *smack* of blood spraying against furniture and the meaty *thunk-thunk* of two corpses hitting the floor. Not to mention the flash of the muzzle flare to disorientate, and the presence of sudden brutal violence. If the three remaining *sicarios* had been ordinary civilians they might have had panic attacks, but even though they were soulless killers who raped and murdered men, women, and children, they still had the same biological and physiological reactions to sudden shock.

They flinched.

A couple of them cowered away from the gunshots, protecting their heads with their forearms, as if that would do anything at all. Slater shot one of them in the back of the skull and dotted three rounds across the upper back of the next guy, because he was further away and it was harder to guarantee a headshot.

So the process repeated with those two, accompanied by all the same horrific sounds and sights.

Which made the fifth guy freeze like a deer in headlights in the middle of the room, surrounded by his dead colleagues.

He put his hands up, and said, 'Surrender. I surrender.'

Slater stared at all the guns in the RV. There was some serious firepower here — the same deal as the first vehicle. Rifles, pistols, shotguns, and combat knives as a last resort.

He said, 'What if everyone at the festival surrendered? What would you have done then?'

The guy didn't respond.

Then, after some thought, he said, 'You wouldn't kill an unarmed man. Have some honour, *esé*. That's how we do it in Mexico.'

'No it's not.'

Slater pumped the trigger.

Only once.

That was all he needed.

He ejected the magazine and chambered a fresh one, and swept the RV meticulously for any fail-safes, like explosives set to detonate on a timer, or tripwires. He didn't expect to find anything, and he didn't. Then he went over to the fifth guy and pulled his corpse off the floor to preserve his clothes. He didn't want them coated in the blood that was spreading from the other four bodies.

He needed the garments for later.

He went to the door and pushed it shut.

85

R uby shed the oversized puffer jacket and took off the cumbersome Balenciaga shoes.

Then she padded barefoot into the hallway, quiet as a mouse. She would do it quietly. All of it.

She braced herself for the violence to come — none of it would be pretty, none of it would make her feel good, but all of it was necessary.

And she'd done this before. The Lynx program, despite its morally bankrupt foundations, had shaped her into the monster the world needed. She'd infiltrated dozens of discreet meetings between sex traffickers and paedophiles and corrupt international businessmen and dictators and warlords. They all shared a common theme. They had money, and they relished power. Even if they went the other way, it was always good business to have pretty girls on the boats to impress clients.

So she was the woman for the job.

She padded to the end of the hallway and held the Ka-Bar in a reverse grip and knocked on the wooden archway leading to the communal area. Just a light rapping, but it echoed in the quietness of the clubhouse. She heard the soft sounds of the mercenary preparing his weapons go silent. Then there was total quietness — but Ruby Nazarian saw quietness as an advantage rather than a hindrance.

She pressed herself up against a slight alcove in the wall and waited for the guy to materialise in front of her.

He did.

She saw his strong jawline and long flowing hair and piercing eyes and almost shivered at how little he looked like a killer. She'd be drawn to his charm if she passed him on the street, and here he was about to gun down civilians en masse.

Then again, everyone she'd killed felt the same about her.

But she only killed when it meant something.

When a soulless psychopath needed his ticket punched.

Ruby punched this guy's ticket with one jabbing downward motion. She always marvelled at how effortlessly a blade could slice through skin. It almost felt like cheating. She stabbed him through the side of the throat and clamped the same hand over his mouth, silencing him with an expert's precision. Not a shred of muted air escaped out the side of his lips.

She propped him up, using all the strength in her arms, and he valiantly remained standing for a few beats as his life sapped away. She used that time to encourage him down the corridor, taking a series of short weak steps to Phil's bedroom.

She shoved him through the door, and he sprawled out on his stomach next to the biker and finished dying.

She quietly pulled the door shut, sealing them in, and plotted her next move.

There were sounds of faint commotion all around her,

and with her hearing still intact she could zone into them.

She focused on a collective murmuring coming from the end of this hallway, deeper into the building. There was a closed door set into the far wall, and she went toward it.

She stopped right in front of it and pressed her ear to the chipped wood.

Thought about pulling out the Glock, but there could be twenty men in the building, and she figured the odds weren't in her favour.

Yet.

She heard low voices — maybe four separate ones. They were all speaking fast as hell, cutting each other off with mutual intensity.

'Should I do another one?'

'Why the fuck not?'

'Dunno about that, Joey.'

'It'll help us get through the day.'

'You havin' doubts?'

'Nah.'

'Better not be.'

'The fuck you gonna do about it?'

'Chill.'

'Can't chill. I'm three lines deep, man. You're going for a fourth.'

'I can handle it. Done it before.'

'We need that many? You really think?'

'Makes you feel like a god. Best results come from this shit. We ain't fightin' anybody. We just killin'.'

'We'll stop at a few, right? We ain't massacring.'

Silence.

But it was a coked-up silence.

So it only lasted a few seconds.

Then one guy said, 'Did the fuckin' instructions say to

stop at a few?'

'Let's do what we gotta do and get outta there.'

'You *are* having doubts.'

'Not doubts. Just ... we don't need to go overboard.'

'When'd you have a change of heart?'

'Joey, I told you I'll do what I gotta do. I'll gun down a few kids in front of you if you need me to fuckin' prove it to you. But if we hang around too long emptying clip after clip, we'll get caught. And you know how bad that'll look.'

Another voice said, 'Relax, man. Do another line.'

'Okay. All at once?'

'Fuck it, why not? We're outta here in an hour.'

There was the sound of credit cards tapping against a table, over and over and over again, then four or five snorts in unison.

Ruby took all this in, and applied ruthless analysis, and figured out how to play it.

Sometimes it took courage.

She knocked.

There was a pause, and she tensed up in anticipation, but she put the Ka-Bar behind her back. Then someone crossed the room and threw the door open.

He was a grizzled merc, with red skin starched by a cocktail of testosterone and HGH, and a thick beard flecked with grey and short close-cropped hair. He was wearing a denim shirt that was tight on his corded musculature, and there were veins running up and down his forearms like road maps. And his eyes were crazed — four lines of cocaine would do that to you. Especially if it was the good shit, which Ruby guessed it was, given their co-workers for this particular job were from the Sinaloa cartel.

They'd probably been gifted a whole brick for the companionship.

The second the door opened Ruby battered her eyelids and gave a warm smile and said, 'Hey, honey.'

The merc stiffened. 'Who the fuck are you?'

But he didn't immediately go for a weapon. In her peripheral vision, she noticed there was an empty holster at his waist. So if he wanted to arm himself he'd need to go back into the room.

Ruby said, 'Phil hired me. You boys need a good time before the big day, after all.'

He relaxed a little, because it initially made sense, but the more he thought about it the less it added up. She didn't give him time to think it through, though — she breezed past him and ran a hand along his barrel chest.

Without the jacket, she was in her tube top and lounge pants. Her midriff was on display, and her breasts were pushed up, and her eyes were as tantalising as ever.

She turned and and saw four sweaty mercs hunched over a table with lines of white powder in front of them and rolled-up hundred dollar bills between their fingers. The guy at the door must have been the most conditioned to railing lines, because the other four almost drooled when they saw her.

They'd heard what she'd said, after all.

And in their current state, that was their idea of heaven.

'Hey, boys,' she said with a smile.

The red merc by the door figured it out first. He said, 'Where *is* Phil?'

He was onto her.

Ruby didn't care.

She was through the door.

She turned and swung an uppercut with the knife and plunged the blade up through the underside of his chin and into his skull.

K ing said, 'Don't move a muscle, okay?'

'Okay,' the shaking bomber said.

'Now step out here, brother. Out on this walkway. Trust me, I'm going to help you.'

The guy came out over the threshold. Out of sight if anyone inside was watching.

King said, 'I'm going to open your jacket and take a look at the vest.'

'Okay.'

King inched forward and delicately placed his fingers like pincers on either side of the jacket. Then he lifted them apart. He kept a keen eye on the sweaty finger the guy had planted on the detonator, depressing the trigger. One slight twitch, or a tiny slip, and they'd both get mopped up in buckets.

It was plastic explosive, arranged in neat cylinders, packaged and taped to the guy's chest and stomach. It was a harrowing amount — enough to kill at least fifty people in crowded conditions. And there were a dozen others in this building.

Unless...

King gulped back fear.

Unless this guy wasn't the first.

Keeping his voice low, King said, 'How many others are there?'

'Twelve. Not including me.'

'What are they like?'

'Worse than me.'

'All of them?'

A slight nod. 'I was the only one giving this second thoughts. But ... you know how it goes. Suddenly everyone's moving and there's no time to say, "Hey, maybe not?" then they had the vest on me and they were telling me, "Go get revenge on everyone who messed you up," and I believed them but now I don't and I—'

He trailed off and broke down in tears.

'What's your name?' King said.

'Cody.'

'Cody, I'm Jason.'

'Hey, Jason.'

'You're going to help me, Cody. Because I'm going to fuck them all up for what they did to you. But I need you do to everything I say for the next few minutes.'

'I'll do my best, man. Move fast. I ... go in and out of lucidity. My brain's all fucked. That's how I ended up here in the first place. I'm inconsistent. Right now I'm good. Help me, man.'

King stared at him. 'You're a brave kid. How old are you?'

'Twenty-six.'

'Christ.'

'Help me, please.'

Still sweating, heart rate still through the roof, King bent down and scrutinised the vest. It was a professional job, but they'd been rushing to get everyone outfitted in time for the parade, so duct tape had been used liberally. He breathed a momentary sigh of relief and reached for a patch that wasn't attached to any of the wires.

He said, 'Stay real still, Cody.'

'I'm still.'

King reached out and tore off a small patch of tape, his fingers and wrists and forearms straining to exert the effort necessary.

He was down on his knees, working the tape free, when Cody started to freak out.

'Y-you're not with the government, are you?'

'Breathe, Cody.'

'Nah, man, fuckin' tell me. Because the government covers up so much shit, man. They're globalists hungry for power. They've got a breakaway civilisation and they're hoarding all the best scientists and creating their own fuckin' utopia, and if you're part of that you'd better tell me because I'll let go of this trigger if you are, I swear to God, I'll—'

I'm inconsistent, King remembered him saying. *Right now I'm good.*

Well, not anymore.

King said, 'I'm not with the government.'

'Who are you?'

'A friend, trying to help.'

'Oh, that's good.'

King stood up, aware of his every movement, how precious each moment was. He glanced at Cody face-to-face and saw the anguish behind the kid's eyes. The bomber was battling his demons, fighting for control.

King said, 'I'm going to place this piece of tape between your finger and the detonator. We're going to have to do this *slowly.* Even the slightest error could ruin it for both of us. You understand?'

Cody nodded.

King said, 'Okay.'

He gently brought the tape down with both fingers. Cody's thumb was on the detonator, slick with sweat, and his whole hand shook.

King said, 'Lift the corner of your thumb, Cody. *Gently.'*

Cody's thumb tilted sideways.

A little too far.

King's heart stopped.

But nothing happened.

The thumb was half on, half off the button.

The button stayed down.

King moved the tape a few millimetres onto the edge of the button — the new surface that had been exposed. Then he stuck the edges to the side of the detonator, creating a cocoon around the button.

He said, 'Keep your thumb right there, Cody.'

He didn't know whether the tape was creating enough pressure to keep the button down on its own. He bent down and worked another piece of tape free from the vest. He transferred that to the detonator, too, sticking it down hard on top of the first piece, doubling up on the support.

Then he said, 'Let go, Cody.'

He was terrified of what might happen, but there was no other way to test it, and he didn't have time to waste.

If he was going to succeed at this, he had to—

Halfway through the train of thought, Cody let go.

Nothing happened.

The detonator hovered there between his shaking fingers, the button depressed, the tape quivering.

King breathed out and held up an open palm,

instructing him to stay exactly where he was. Then he skirted around behind the guy and stripped the jacket off him, allowing him to scrutinise the back of the vest. Sure enough, as he suspected, there were plastic cable ties locking the contraption together, preventing Cody from removing it if he had second thoughts.

Ensuring he died inside the vest, wherever it happened to go off.

Too much collateral to let them escape if they got deterred.

King said, 'Stay still, Cody.'

But the man wasn't going anywhere.

King wiped his palms on his pants, then slid the Ka-Bar knife out of its sheath. He held it tight, and took a deep breath. His heart thudded. His limbs turned cold.

But he snaked the tip of the blade through the mass of exposed wires, precariously avoiding an explosive death, and nicked each cable tie with a slight downward jerk.

He extracted the blade.

Narrowly missing a red wire.

Then he re-sheathed the knife and took his sweet time extracting Cody from the vest. He made no sudden movements, no jerky actions, and before he knew it he was clutching the vest in one hand and the taped-up detonator in the other, and Cody spun away from the plastic explosive like the vest had turned white-hot. He collapsed against the exterior wall of the warehouse and ran his hands along the metal grille underfoot, pale and wide-eyed.

King said, 'You said there were a dozen more like you?'

'Yes. And you won't change their minds. They've been well and truly radicalised. It's been going on for months.'

King bowed his head.

87

José Luis Gómez swallowed a couple of Dexedrine tablets and sat with his leg twitching as he waited for the stimulants to kick in.

He was in a small camper van, sitting in murky darkness. There were curtains pulled tight across all the windows, with only slivers of natural light allowed to spill through. He was hunched over a small flat tabletop.

He was with two other men. Men he'd grown up with in the shanty towns. Men he trusted with his life. Men like him, who'd do practically anything for a dollar, because money was everything when you broke down what made society tick. Money made existence a little less miserable — or, at least, that's what Gómez had found. It was the difference between spending every waking moment at work making less than minimum wage so you had the privilege of stumbling home exhausted in the dark, and drinking Dom Pérignon at a nightclub with two high-priced call girls going down on you in the VIP booth.

That was what money could do.

So he'd gladly live in shit conditions for a few days and

spray a few clips into a crowd if it meant adding to his growing investments that funded the narco lifestyle.

Sure, it was a risk.

But everything was a risk, and when you came from where he came from, you were open to a little risk.

Ordinarily the Sinaloa cartel didn't prostitute itself out to the highest bidder, but the offer had come down the pipeline, and it had been irresistible.

Irresistible, even, to the narcos with billions.

So the Gómez brothers got the go-ahead. They were off to California with a couple dozen of their best men in tow. They'd met up briefly, and discreetly, with a horde of ex-U.S. military mercenaries that had been hired for the same job, and even more briefly with a couple of sketchy-looking Middle Eastern men who hadn't said much, but their silence had said everything. Gómez had known immediately who they were and what they were here for.

And it had sent shivers down his spine.

Because that was a world even he didn't fuck with.

Too barbaric, too savage.

There were a couple of bare single mattresses spread across the inside of the camper van, stained yellow in patches from the night sweats. It was hot out here, and they'd been ordered not to show their faces under any circumstances, so that led to a whole lot of sitting around doing nothing — mostly getting high, playing cards, and pulling the curtains back to get a glimpse of nature every once in a while.

They were parked in one of the clearings near the trails at the top of the Rancho Corral de Tierra wildlands. Hikers that flocked to San Francisco always seemed to pass over these trails, which was exactly why the Sinaloa cartel had selected them.

They'd been told to lay low here until they were given the go-ahead, and they were set to receive that in less than an hour.

So they were all jumpy, which was helped along by the Dexedrine tablets, and Gómez was even considering doing a line of coke he had in a small baggie when he noticed a shadow pass over the curtains, right by the door.

He tensed up and snatched a small .22 off the floor.

There was a knock at the door, and it rippled through the van.

Gómez's two companions stiffened, too. They went for their guns, but Gómez inched one of the curtains aside and caught a glimpse of the figure standing there. He had his back turned, but he was dressed in familiar garb, with the same woollen balaclava they were about to don.

Gómez breathed out. 'Don't worry. It's one of us.'

His two friends nodded and lowered their weapons.

Gómez undid the latch and swung the door outward. 'Time to move?'

'No,' Will Slater said, and killed them with a tight trio of headshots.

88

S later knew he'd killed the other Gómez brother the second he pulled the trigger.

He'd found a silenced Heckler & Koch USP .45 Tactical pistol in the second RV, and now he used it to kill José Luis Gómez, followed swiftly by his two colleagues. Of course, there's nothing truly *silent* about a silencer, but it shifted the horrific *bang* of a regular gunshot into a compressed, guttural *punch.*

Which, from a distance, was indistinguishable from a car backfiring.

And there was only one other camper van in this clearing, which led him to believe that the real fight rested in the final clearing, so he was keen to clear this place out as quickly as possible.

He double-checked that everyone in the camper van were corpses. One of Gómez's thugs twitched — probably an involuntary death spasm — but Slater didn't have time to wait around and make sure. He put another bullet into the guy, then swung the door closed and left them there to rot.

Then he sprinted for the second camper van.

And his luck ran out.

The front windshield shattered as gunfire erupted from within.

Unsuppressed, fully automatic gunfire, deafening in its intensity, accompanied by muzzle flashes.

Slater dropped and rolled into the nearest ditch, which put him below the wheels of the camper van. He put it at a couple of dozen feet away — close enough to cause problems for both of them — but what terrified him was the sudden explosion of noise. They weren't that far from the other clearing.

So those narcos would hear.

Lead ripped over the top of his head, thudding into the gravel, and Slater became keenly aware of the newfound urgency. He had to sort this out *right now,* or risk the other *sicarios* escaping. They could take any number of roads down the mountain, so Scachi's cordon wouldn't work. That was the soulless beauty of their plan. If your goal was to massacre as many civilians as possible, there was almost no way to prevent you from doing that if you were armed to the teeth and scattered across a bustling city. You only needed minutes to accomplish your task.

Slater raised his head a few inches to get a sliver of a view, and a round whisked past his head to reward him for his endeavours. He pressed himself back down into the gravel stomach-first, and reached into his back pocket for something else he'd picked up in the RV.

Something he hadn't been willing to use unless shit hit the fan.

Which it had.

So he reached his arm up blindly and fired three shots in through the windshield frame as suppressive fire, then ripped the pin out of the olive M84 stun grenade and got to his knees. He hurled it like a fastball at the open maw, and watched with satisfaction as it struck home.

It went off with ferocity, and the flash half-blinded Slater when he didn't turn away in time. His ears rang from the concussive blast, but he still had enough wits about him to stumble out of the ditch, throw the camper van door open, and shoot all four men inside dead. They were in no position to mount any sort of resistance — they'd been totally blinded and deafened by the blast. He took his time, saving ammunition, and put one round into each of their heads.

He found a MAR compact carbine variant of the Galil rifle resting on the van floor, and snatched it up.

Then he slotted the silenced USP back into his belt, because there was no use going with suppression anymore. The stealth aspect was over. Everyone in the vicinity would have heard the firefight, and now there was nothing to do but charge forward.

He had minutes — no, seconds — before all the narcos in the other clearing scattered.

So he ran flat out, feet pumping over the gravel.

'Shit,' he snarled under his breath. 'Shit, shit, shit, shit.'

This wasn't how he'd wanted it to play out.

He thought he'd had it sorted.

He double-tapped his earpiece as he ran and between laboured breaths shouted, 'I might be compromised here. I'm running into a war zone.'

Violetta said, 'They know you're coming?'

'Couldn't stay silent the whole time.'

'Get this done, Will. You *need* to get this done. There's no other option.'

'Tell Scachi to mobilise whatever he's got into the hills. In case I don't get them all.'

'I can't.'

'Why?'

'Ruby called him in first.'

'Is she okay?'

'I don't know. But she's outnumbered, and it's all going to hell.'

'And King?'

'Radio silence.'

Slater gulped and double-tapped again, ending the connection.

And with the breath rasping in his throat, he ran for his life into the trees.

89

The guy named Phil collapsed with most of his lifeblood coming out the underside of his chin.

Ruby pulled the knife free and spun, but she hadn't counted on the cocaine elevating the rest of the mercs' reaction speed. They were already charging at her like wild crazed bulls — a mistake she knew they hadn't made consciously.

Because at surface level she was still a thin woman, and even though they didn't have guns within easy reach they were all north of two hundred pounds and hardened military vets, who got up early and worked out hard and did the difficult tasks that no-one else wanted to do. They were men's men — alpha males who took no shit and got what they wanted from life by simply going after it and refusing to give a shit about who they hurt along the way.

So they figured, *Yeah, I could take her.*

I could rip her apart for what she did to Phil.

And I'm about to do just that.

Maybe due to the cocaine, maybe not.

But it certainly helped.

And she *did* feel true fear. Because there was merit to their plan. There was eight hundred plus pounds of them, and a hundred and thirty pounds of her, and the room was small and tight and cramped and there was little room to manoeuvre out of harm's way.

She was already backed up against a desk, and she couldn't juke to the side because all four of them were barrelling toward her in a line, as if each of them wanted to be the first to get their hands on her, and she *knew* it had to be the cocaine. Because simple logistics meant that one of them was going to get sliced open, but it seemed none of them cared who that was going to be.

She thought, *Is that all this is going to be? Kill one of them, and let the rest beat me to death with their bare hands?*

The primal part of her brain thought that, but then she overrode it.

Because she remembered who she was.

She locked onto her target with laser precision — the exposed throat of the closest mercenary — and jabbed the Ka-Bar into the soft flesh. The skin broke and arteries were severed and blood sprayed. He fell forward immediately, his body shutting down on him, and she sidestepped him and he crashed into the desk and it caved in with an almighty *boom.*

Blood flowed over the papers and onto the carpet but Ruby ignored them, recognising she was going to have to take a couple of bumps and bruises if she wanted to get out of this alive. She was out of position when the second guy reached her half a second later and he dropped his shoulder into her and sent her careening back into the wall.

She let her limbs go weak, and bounced off the plaster like a rag doll, denting the wall in the process, but she made it look far worse than it was. She still smacked her head against the hard surface and saw stars and a few black spots in her vision and felt the searing discomfort in her central nervous system, but she was by no means down for the count.

But the second guy thought she was, and he reached for her with outstretched arms, probably to pull her down to the ground and subdue her there so he could have his way with her.

What he should have done was throw a punch into her chin, using the considerable size advantage to smash her unconscious.

Instead she slashed four of his fingers off in one go, and he screamed and she slid the whole blade into his stomach and wrenched it out, and he collapsed too.

The third guy muscled his dying friend out of the way, sending him spilling to the floor, recognising how important it was that he didn't hesitate. So he came in fast, and Ruby wasn't prepared, and he wrapped his beefy arms around her in a crushing bear hug, nearly breaking her ribs in the process.

He started to squeeze.

At that point the fourth guy barrelled in and swung a massive haymaker right at Ruby's unprotected face, which would have destroyed her if it connected. She was possibly the most dangerous female on the planet, but that did little to help defy the laws of physics. If an angry two-hundred pound ball of muscle hit her in the nose with a giant wind-up punch, she'd be dead or unconscious on impact.

But it didn't connect, because she turned her wrist inward and sliced the Ka-Bar blade along the wrist of the guy holding her, who howled as his skin peeled apart and blood ran down over his fingers. Which loosened his grip, allowing her to shoot downward into a half-squat, and the fourth guy's punch came over her head and hit the third guy square in the chest, probably cracking his sternum, definitely freezing him up.

He loosened his grip even more, so she spun around and took advantage of it by cutting his throat.

Then she turned back and intercepted another giant looping haymaker punch with her knife blade.

The guy ended up punching the knife.

It was a horrific result.

Ruby didn't concentrate on how badly she'd mangled the guy's hand — she never focused on anything that didn't matter in the heat of combat. Instead she stepped forward and wrapped a hand around the back of his neck and punctured his ribcage once, twice, three times, driving the knife upward into his heart with each stabbing motion.

He was dead before he hit the floor.

She wiped the blade on one of their corpses, stepped over the bodies, and left the room.

There'd been grunts.

There'd been shouts.

There'd been screams.

She heard movement all through the clubhouse — frantic energy being released as mercenaries rocketed out of bed and snatched up their weapons.

She stood at the end of the corridor, covered in blood, panting with exertion, and swore under her breath.

She touched her earpiece and said, 'Violetta.'

'What?'

'Tell Scachi to try the cordon. I think some of them are going to escape.'

'How many have you killed?'

'Not enough.'

'If we do this, we'll be understaffed for King and Slater. We won't be able to help them.'

Ruby hesitated, but the commotion was increasing — there was sounds of banging and jumping and footsteps from seemingly everywhere at once.

'I need it,' she said. 'There's more here than I thought.'

'Christ — okay.'

The line went dead.

Ruby was alone, surrounded by mercenaries.

Alone in a hostile world.

90

K ing stood still as a statue with the vest and detonator clutched between his fingers.

He said, 'Cody, listen to me. Are you one hundred percent certain there's no hope of helping them?'

Cody stared at him skeptically. 'You think you're going to repeat that performance another twelve times?'

King said, 'Fuck.'

Cody said, 'Take a look, man. They're down there.'

King froze. 'What?'

Cody gestured through the door he'd come from. 'You can see them. Step inside, but be quiet about it. They're all down on the ground floor.'

'Why are you up here, then?'

'I needed space. They didn't care, once they had the vest on me. They knew it wasn't going anywhere. Even if I could find a knife, I couldn't reach the cable ties.'

King imagined what would have happened had he arrived a few minutes later — he let the gravity of it sink in.

He said, 'Wait here.'

He crept forward over the threshold, and that was all it

took. He could see right down through the interior metal walkway, through the grille flooring, to the bottom of the warehouse. This section of the building was arranged like a hollowed-out arena, with room for all sorts of multi-storey machinery. Right now it was a gargantuan cavern, entirely empty, with the walkways on each floor arranged like viewing platforms in a colosseum.

King looked straight down, and saw a vision of hell.

There were twelve men in various states of distress, most of them similar in appearance to Cody, sitting bolt upright on portable camping chairs arranged in the centre of the concrete wasteland. They were all sweating and shaking, but they weren't protesting. Basic human instinct was kicking in, but psychosis was overriding it. They were all wearing vests with plastic explosive strapped to the front, and two Middle-Eastern men were conducting last-minute checks, hunched over the vests, moving from man to man and whispering muted reassurances in their ears. Around this macabre display, four or five mercenary types patrolled the ground floor, rifles in their hands, searching for any hint of a threat.

None of them looked up.

The whole place, despite its size, had the stench of fear and desperation.

King backed out onto the fire stairs, and said, 'Why'd they let you go first?'

'I'm the most lucid,' Cody said. 'They thought if I was around the others, I'd have too much time to second guess myself, and they didn't want me convincing them to change their minds. Which is a dumb idea, because I know the others won't.'

'Cody,' King said, and the pale man stared at him.

'Yes?'

'I need to ask you something again.'

'Okay.'

'I need you to take it very, very seriously.'

'Of course.'

'Are you sure they're beyond saving?'

'Yes.'

'Okay.'

King hardened his heart.

You can't protect everyone.

War is made of impossible choices. King had been determined, no matter what, to neutralise the active hostiles — the mercenaries, the ISIS guns-for-hire — and subdue the suicide bombers as best he could. Because they weren't suicide bombers — they were psychotically ill, and they'd been preyed upon and taken advantage of. Then again, he guessed that was the case for most bombers. Everyone is the same after radicalisation.

And, in any case, they already had the vests on.

The situation was irredeemable.

So King had a decision to make.

And he made it quickly.

Because what other choice did he have?

He sized up the gap between the fire stairs and the neighbouring warehouse. There was an old grimy window one floor below, across the alleyway. It looked set to shatter at the slightest provocation. He lined up the angles, but they weren't favourable. It didn't matter. This was the only way. In seconds, the bombers would be on their feet, and who knows how long it'd take them to scatter out of all the exits?

Then they'd be en route to the festival.

King said, 'Cody.'

'Yeah?'

'Brace yourself.'

He stepped back into the shadows of the warehouse's upper levels, and with two fingers he gently peeled a layer of tape off the detonator. Now the button was half-exposed, and the slightest disturbance might break the rest of the tape free and set off the explosives.

King let a cloud of focus descend over him.

He muttered, 'I'm sorry.'

He threw the vest, and the detonator, over the railing.

Then he sprinted back outside and bent down and heaved Cody off the walkway like he weighed nothing, and he hurled the man over one shoulder and put one foot on the low railing and pushed off it, and he was airborne, with nothing but a plummeting drop to the concrete below but he cleared the width of the alleyway and crashed down through the glass window of the neighbouring building, which cut him to pieces, but he kept falling and they landed on a metal flight of stairs somewhere inside the darkened interior, and he let go of Cody and they fell and bounced and spun down the staircase until...

Thirteen suicide vests detonated in the building next door.

91

S later had the Galil at shoulder height as he burst
into the clearing's outer limits.

And his stomach fell.

It was bedlam. There were three camper vans — all in motion — and another RV, the same size as the first two.

He stayed low, underneath some scrub, and tapped his earpiece again. 'Violetta.'

'What?'

'This is bad.'

'We don't have the resources, Will. Seems that King just blew up half of Dogpatch. It's chaos.'

'Holy shit. Is he alive?'

'We don't know.'

'Got to go.'

He noticed the three vans were turning in half-circles, powering for the trail leading out of the clearing, back onto the main road. Thankfully, that rested only a few dozen feet to Slater's right — their trajectory lined up with where he lay.

He stood up and shot out the tyres of the first van.

It veered off-track and shuddered to a halt, cutting off the path of the other two. One of the other vans powered around it, and a Mexican *sicario* with an AK-47 leant out the passenger window.

Slater shot him in the chest, then shot each of that van's tyres in turn.

It ground to a halt in the gravel.

The third van roared toward the trail, and Slater shot at the tyres and missed. Everything went to hell — the vehicle kept speeding and Slater saw glimpses of five or six men through the windows and he knew, if he let it get through, there'd be blood on the streets. Because their closeness to death would invigorate them, flood their brain with stress chemicals before they'd even started shooting, so they'd charge toward the festival — or any civilians they could get their hands on — with rabid intensity.

So Slater emptied the entire magazine at the van.

A couple of rounds grazed the front tyres and they both popped, and the speed at which the van was travelling made it plunge forward on its nose, grinding to a standstill in the earth.

Sicarios piled out of all three vans at once, spilling out the doors with automatic weapons in their hands, and at the same time the RV pulled up from behind and more men piled out of that, too. Thankfully the vans had formed a rudimentary cordon around the mouth of the trail, preventing the RV from skirting around. So Slater had funnelled them into a bottleneck, but that was the least of his concerns as close to fifteen men emptied out of the vehicles.

He crouched lower in the brush and realised the Galil was dry.

Pulse racing, he reloaded, using a spare magazine he'd

slotted into his belt. But he was intensely aware that this was his second-last clip, and if he expended these two he'd be wielding a sidearm in an open gunfight with a dozen cartel *sicarios*.

He didn't like his chances.

He fired, and fired, and fired — picking his targets based on a predetermined threat list. He killed three of the closest men who'd spilled out of the first van — they all had Kalashnikovs in their hands, and they had the highest likelihood of spraying bullets into the scrub and gunning him down in the initial barrage.

They dropped and spun and pirouetted, and Slater turned to fire on the others and—

Bang.

Thwack.

Bang.

Thwack.

He took two bullets to the chest.

Both smashed into him with ferocity, knocking him off his feet. The Kevlar stopped them in their tracks but the blunt force trauma resonated through his core, rattling him deeply. He figured he'd cracked his sternum, or a couple of ribs, as he sat up in the woods and white-hot pain creased through him. He grunted and snarled and quashed it down, but there was little he could do. It was overriding his system, threatening to neutralise him on the spot.

But he battled his way back to his feet and hefted the Galil back onto his shoulder and killed the two men who'd shot him with twin headshots.

The pain was making him alert, and the alertness gave him clarity. Maybe it was a second wind before he collapsed for good, but he'd be damned if he wasn't going to take advantage of it.

So he fired, again and again and again, picking targets off like they were cardboard cutouts. The insanity blurred together into a never-ending stream of bloody consciousness, and he continued popping targets in the face, neck and chest until the Galil ran dry once more.

With a pang of sudden understanding, he realised there were only two *sicarios* left. Out of the entire force sent over the border — the best hitmen of the multi-billion dollar Sinaloa cartel — Slater had decimated all but two of them. He couldn't comprehend it. Sure, it came down to a simple equation — talent, plus genetic reflexes, plus a decade of experience, plus the advantage of cover, plus the element of surprise, plus the capacity to remain deadly calm in conflict, equalled an unparalleled killing machine.

But it surprised him all the same.

He lowered himself into cover, reached down to extract the final magazine from his belt...

And a hail of bullets smacked through the brush into him.

It was a perfectly placed volley, a display of marksmanship so precise that it had to have been a fluke. But luck was impartial in a firefight. It fell to whoever ended up with it, often by chance, and it didn't discriminate. Now it meant that three or four rounds passed over Slater's head and on either side of his shoulders, missing his brain, keeping him alive ... but three rounds hit him in the chest again, one after the other — *thwack-thwack-thwack.*

They destroyed his insides.

He felt his bones break.

He felt his insides bleed.

He collapsed to the forest floor for the final time.

And the two remaining *sicarios* advanced on their crippled enemy.

92

R uby pulled her Glock, because stealth was no longer a factor.

And lucky she did, because two mercenaries stormed into the corridor — atypical guns-for-hire, with big bushy beards and big muscles and big guns in their hands. Ruby shot one in the forehead and the other in the throat, but she was rattled, and she knew the unease would compound if she allowed it to. Her heart would beat faster and her blood would run colder and her head would pound with hypertension.

She took a deep breath.

Then she ran flat out down the corridor, understanding she'd be trapped in a bottleneck if she stayed put. She sprinted past Phil's room and leapfrogged the two dead mercenaries and chanced a look into the communal area of the clubhouse.

A hail of bullets assaulted her.

She threw herself back in the blink of an eye, capital-ising on reflexes honed over years of combat, and nearly lost her footing in the process. Shredded wood splintered off the door frame and lashed her face and chest and arms, but she turned her head away to preserve her eyes.

She stumbled, righted herself, and took a knee inside the entranceway.

She raised the gun to shoulder height.

The mercenary with the rifle came charging in, probably thinking he'd hit her in the barrage, but he hadn't come close. She figured there was some sort of gender bias there — *this little bitch isn't any type of threat* — but he paid for his hubris with a 9mm round planted squarely between his eyes. His head snapped back on his shoulders and he dropped the gun — an M4A1 carbine — and splayed to the floor under the archway.

Ruby snatched it up and swept the room and found no resistance. Bullets came through the front windows and dotted the communal area at random. One whisked past her — so close she could feel it — and she fell back out of necessity.

From outside?

There must have been multiple ways out of the club-house, which meant some of the mercenaries were already on the front lawn, which meant they had access to vehicles, which meant...

Ruby touched her earpiece as she heard someone outside roar, 'Scatter! The job needs doing! Let's get it done!'

She swore and hissed, 'Violetta.'

'What's up?'

'Where's Scachi?'

'En route.'

'How close?'

'They're trying to approach from multiple directions but the logistics are a nightmare. There's so many streets they can flee down. Do you know which direction they're headed?'

'No. I'm inside.'

'Have they found vehicles?'

'I'm not sure if—'

'Find out!' Violetta barked. 'We need license plates if you can get them.'

'Alright.'

'Hurry.'

She could hear the panic leaching through Violetta's tone. She wondered how King and Slater were faring, but there was no time to think about—

A closed door only a couple of feet to her right was hurled open from the inside and a thick muscular body crash-tackled her into the opposite wall, smashing the breath from her lungs, nearly immobilising her. She dropped the gun as a fist smashed her face and she realised one of the mercs had been lying in wait, preparing for an opportunity to charge. He'd been sitting there in his bedroom, unarmed, and now he'd pounced.

She took another punch to the jaw, and saw stars, and realised the mercs outside were getting away.

She panicked.

93

S later couldn't breathe, couldn't see, couldn't think.

He clutched his chest, but that didn't help. Then he saw silhouettes advancing toward him through the woods and patted the dirt around him feebly, searching for his weapon. It had ended up somewhere nearby when he'd dropped it, but if it was out of reach, it might as well have been a hundred miles away.

It was futile to try moving.

Of course it had all gone to hell. What was the government thinking, entrusting the demolition of a mercenary force spread throughout San Francisco and its outer limits to a trio of solo operatives?

Regret flooded him.

He pictured the twin *sicarios* murdering him here in the wildlands, then peeling off to commandeer a civilian vehicle. That was all it would take. They could drive right up to the outskirts of the parade in total anonymity and park mere feet from the crowds. Then they would only have to get out, point, aim, and fire. There'd be bedlam, which would give them the opportunity to reload and empty fresh magazines, so they could probably kill fifty people by the time everyone scattered, even if there were armed police right there. It would take them mere seconds.

The wonders of modern weaponry, Slater thought.

That hypothetical scenario played out in his head, and synchronised with one of the *sicarios* stomping through the brush right by his head, looming over him with a sneer.

He drew a sidearm and aimed the barrel down at Slater's exposed head.

A Mexican-style execution.

Up close and personal.

Poetic revenge for all his dead comrades.

But, Slater thought, *you don't play those fucking games with me. You shoot me from a distance.*

So he shot a hand out and grabbed the *sicario's* ankle and yanked it towards him and rolled into the guy at the same time, and the gun went off but the bullet smashed into the dirt inches away from Slater's skull, which deafened him, but he ended up alive. And from there the momentum shifted as the guy tumbled off-balance and sat down on his rear on the forest floor, landing on his coccyx, which stunned him for the half-second it took for Slater to grab hold of his wrist and angle it upward and shove the barrel under the guy's chin and crush his palm down on the guy's trigger finger.

So the gun went off in his face and his brains came out the top of his head and Slater wrestled the USP .45 off him and sat up and traded a single bullet with the last *sicario,* like a classic Western.

The *sicario's* bullet hit Slater at the top of his Kevlar vest, embedding half in, half out, crumpling him where he sat, tipping him over the edge, knocking him unconscious from the sheer dull force. His brain, overloaded with pain, simply gave up and retreated to murky darkness to recuperate. He sprawled out in the undergrowth, and a bystander would have assumed he'd dropped dead.

Slater's bullet hit the *sicario* in the mouth.

It ripped through the back of his skull and came out the other side in a grisly exit wound.

The clearing went quiet.

94

Ruby turned the panic into motivation.

Something clicked inside her, and the reality that maybe hundreds would die if she didn't get through this hit her like another punch from a two hundred pound man, and it changed the dynamic in an instant. She slipped the next punch, even though she couldn't feel her nose or her jaw, and the guy's fist crashed into the plasterboard behind her head, caving a hole in it.

He grimaced, and hesitated because he wasn't used to having the tables turned on him by a slim woman, so when she delivered an uppercut elbow into the bridge of his nose and broke it so hard his eyes started to water, he froze up.

Like, *Is this happening?*

It most definitely was happening, because Ruby followed it up by lurching out of his grasp, utilising the power of leverage and angles to slide right out of his grip. Then she had space, and she ended up right on top of the Glock, so she picked it up and shot him in the head before he had the chance to realise that he'd lost.

Then the chaos faded, replaced by horrid silence.

Because silence only meant one thing.

Ruby ran for the front door.

She kicked it open and took cover in the entranceway, even though it left her vulnerable to return fire — right now, that was the least of her concerns. She saw the giant garage next to the clubhouse with its roller doors open. Vehicles spilled forth — pick-up trucks, ordinary sedans, even a couple of unassuming hatchbacks. True to their word, the mercs were scattering. There was no sign of Scachi's cordon — no Army humvees flooding the street, no resistance whatsoever.

'Where the fuck is he?' Ruby snarled under her breath.

The first of the vehicles reached the road. It bounced and jolted across the sidewalk and came down on the asphalt. Then it was free of the driveway's constraints. The driveway was narrow and congested and only allowed two cars to drive side by side, so there was a rudimentary bottleneck.

Ruby eyed a handful of mercs in each of the pick-up trucks' rear trays, all armed to the teeth, and the hatchbacks were full, and the sedans had three or four men apiece.

There were at least twenty hostiles that she'd missed.

She raised her Glock to fire at them, but she knew she'd get killed as soon as they decided to return fire.

She was signing her own death warrant.

But if she took a couple of these bastards out of existence, then that was good enough for her.

Her finger tightened around the trigger.

Then a civilian truck — a big Ford Raptor — surged into view on the street. It came in at an angle and instead of slowing down to avoid a collision, it sped up. Its bull bar demolished the front of the first mercenary vehicle — an old pick-up truck designed to blend in. The pick-up spun and groaned and Ruby saw the occupants thrown around the inside like dolls tossed by a giant child.

They hadn't been wearing seatbelts, obviously.

Before anyone could comprehend what was happening, the passenger window of the Raptor rolled down and someone hurled flash grenades like fastballs at the convoy clogged up in the driveway. Some skittered under cars, some went through open windows, some landed on hoods. They went off in a roaring cacophony, and Ruby had the good sense to dive back into the clubhouse so she didn't get blinded and deafened by the destruction.

When she stuck her head back out, she half-expected to see a couple of Scachi's best and brightest grunts pouring out of the Raptor, dressed in their military fatigues, guns blazing.

What she didn't expect was a half-dead Jason King, bleeding from multiple cuts, his face blackened by dirt and dust and soot, leap out of the truck and charge like a demon at the neutralised vehicles.

95

S later didn't know how long he'd been out.

He cracked one eyelid open, then the other.

Everything hurt.

His life was pain, his world was pain.

He was on his back, in the undergrowth, surrounded by bodies.

He heard sirens in the distance.

They might as well have been coming from another planet.

He didn't know if he'd make it.

He didn't know how King was doing, or Ruby. Whether they'd succeeded or not. Whether, as he lay there, helpless and useless, innocent men, women and children were being massacred by automatic weapons on the streets of San Francisco.

There was no way to tell any of that.

So he lay there, hurting and throbbing, and when he realised unconsciousness wouldn't come and rescue him again, he used all his effort to roll onto his side. He stared the corpse of the last *sicario* in the eyes, and realised it had taken some time for the man to die. Because there was a smartphone in his hand, clutched between cold bloody fingers, and the screen was on. He'd half-dialled a number before succumbing to his fatal wounds.

Slater reached out and plied the phone from the man's death grip with shaking fingers.

He didn't know why.

He figured, if he couldn't move, at least he could check what he might have prevented.

Might was the crucial word.

He scrolled aimlessly, barely lucid, unsure what he was trying to do. The language was set to Spanish, and he only had a rudimentary grasp of the language.

So he opened the camera roll.

And he found a sinister photo album.

They were surveillance photos, taken live from the parade, timestamped to show they'd been taken only half an hour earlier and sent through for the *sicario*'s viewing pleasure. Like a macabre layout of the battleground. Showing the scores of pedestrians in position to be slaughtered.

Some were taken from CCTV cameras, and Slater wondered how deep the corruption ran.

Some were taken at street level.

He swiped, and swiped, and swiped, and stared at endless photos of happy, smiling families under a cloudless sky. They were oblivious to what could have happened.

To what might still happen.

Slater swiped again...

...and his heart stopped in his chest.

He nearly passed out.

He hunched over the screen, and zoomed in, aware that he was dripping blood over the smartphone.

But he had to know for sure.

And as he zoomed, his terror grew, until it almost over-whelmed him.

In the crowd, he saw the face of a child he'd sacrificed everything to protect. A child he'd considered his own, and treated as such. Shien had been through the worst a kid could imagine, and then some. She deserved the whole world, and everything in it, and he'd learned most of what he knew about mental resilience in later life from her. She was an eleven-year-old kid, but she was the best person he'd ever met, and he'd sacrifice himself a thousand times over to make sure she was okay. She was the family he'd never be able to have. She was the shred of humanity he'd held onto when his own life devolved into chaos again and again. She was the reason he couldn't stay in one place, because if he did he'd end up settling down with someone, and he didn't have the stomach to have a family that would be put in danger by the nature of his existence.

She'd taught him that, inadvertently, over the last couple of years. He hadn't seen her in a long time, but that was the way it had to be.

Sometimes, you had to let go of the things that mattered most, so they could be allowed to grow.

And now here she was, standing in a crowd in down-town San Francisco with a smile on her face.

If there was even the slightest chance...

The pain overwhelmed Slater and he passed out, and his last wish before he slipped into a turbulent unconscious-ness was that, above all else, she would be safe.

96

Ruby took a step forward.

She wobbled and fell.

When she righted herself, she was still on the front porch, but her vision was all over the place, and her temples throbbed and pulsated and hurt like hell. She realised the concussive blasts of the flash grenades had been too close for comfort. She'd put a wall between herself and the detonations, but the sheer volume of the noise had thrown her equilibrium off and deafened her. It was like moving through an old-school silent film — she saw King firing, she saw the muzzle flashes, she saw him sprinting and punching and kicking and brawling, but she heard none of it. And there were missing frames — he jolted from one place to the next, moving too fast for her disrupted vision to handle. Like freeze frames, inching forward.

She tried to aim the Glock but she could barely lift it to shoulder height.

She vomited on the porch, letting it splatter between her feet.

She straightened up, and wiped her mouth, and fought the urge to pass out.

It all opened up before her, in beautiful simplicity. Through the carnage, she saw everything moving like chess pieces on a board. King was in the driveway, fighting his heart out, cutting down mercenaries left and right who couldn't see, couldn't hear, couldn't breathe, couldn't even stand up. But he was maximally preoccupied with that endeavour, and to the side of the convoy, Ruby spotted one of the pick-up trucks fire up its engine. She peered through the tinted window and made out a merc in the driver's seat with a balaclava over his face, his eyes shielded by sunglasses. He seemed disoriented, but he wasn't out for the count. There was a guy in the passenger's seat, and three more in the back of the cabin.

They all had weapons.

Rifles, sidearms, even a shotgun.

But they didn't use them on King, or Ruby.

Instead the driver floored the accelerator and the truck twisted out of the vehicular wasteland and sliced through a gap at the front of the driveway. Paint chipped off the chassis as it forced its way past the Raptor. Then it was out on the street, free of the logjam.

King didn't notice.

He was locked in a rabid brawl with three blind mercenaries, smashing fists into faces, kneeing them in the head, scrabbling for his own weapon.

Ruby saw it all.

It was straightforward.

It was clear.

It was inevitable.

She started running before she was stable, but it didn't matter. She somehow stayed on her feet and focused in on the idle Raptor, chugging throatily as it rested nose-first in the demolished pick-up truck. She leapt over the hood of the pick-up, skirted around to the driver's side, got in, threw the car into reverse, and stamped on the accelerator.

With an almighty groan the Raptor peeled out into the street.

Ruby spotted the pick-up loaded with juiced-up mercenaries in her rear view mirror.

She spun the Raptor in a tight arc, held on for dear life, and surged forward.

She knew what was at stake.

She wouldn't fail.

She couldn't.

Then the worst-case scenario unfolded.

One of those awful, ill-timed coincidences that nature seemed oblivious to.

No-one was favoured in the heat of combat — bad luck fell to either party in equal measure, regardless of innocence — and she learned that the hard way.

She noticed her door was hanging open, and as the Raptor accelerated, she reached over to snatch the handle out of thin air and heard a dull, muted clattering noise at her waist.

A perfectly innocuous gesture.

She looked down, and watched the Glock slide off the seat by her hip and disappear out the open door.

Fuck.

97

Turn around to retrieve it, and she'd lose the pickup forever. She had no chance of finding the vehicle with a twenty-second delay. The streets were narrow, and the corners were tight, and suburbia would swallow it into its gaping jaws and spit it out unharmed at the outskirts of the parade.

Because wherever the hell General Scachi was, he wasn't making any effort to get involved.

Ruby had her suspicions.

She swore and pulled the door closed and accelerated. Then she tapped her earpiece and said, 'Violetta.'

'Yes?'

'Where the fuck is Scachi?'

'I'm trying to get in touch with him.'

'What?'

'He's not responding.'

'Of course he isn't.'

'I'll keep trying—'

'Tell me something,' Ruby said. 'Do you have any reason to believe he wouldn't be susceptible to bribes?'

'He's a General in the—'

'That's not an answer.'

Silence.

Then, 'No, nothing concrete.'

Ruby said, 'Start thinking along those lines.'

'Where are you going?'

'You can see me?'

'We're tracking the earpiece.'

Ruby swerved through an intersection in pursuit of the pick-up truck, narrowly avoiding a collision with a semi-trailer. The truck horn blared, startling her, and she corrected course in time to shoot between the rest of the traffic. Cars swerved, more horns shrieked, and the pick-up raced away from her, gaining ground as she had to slow to navigate through the chaos.

But she kept her hands on the wheel and said, 'Get anything you can to intercept me right now. I'm on the tail of one pick-up truck. It got away.'

'Are there any others?'

'King's dealing with them.'

'King?!'

'He's alive. He must have handled his business in Dogpatch, because he came straight to the clubhouse.'

'Where is he now?'

'Still there.'

'Okay — so it's just the one truck?'

'There's five of them in it, and they've all got rifles. They could kill fifty people before I get my hands on them.'

'Okay, okay... we're tracking you. We'll do what we can. Christ, you're moving fast.'

'If I crash, it's all over.'

'I have to go. I need to coordinate this.'

'Go.'

Ruby surged forward, urging the Raptor faster, risking death at every sharp turn. There was no consideration for the rules of the road — the pick-up she was chasing barrelled through intersection after intersection, missing oncoming traffic by a hair's breadth each time. They roared through Bernal Heights, then the Mission District, and Ruby knew exactly where they were headed.

Market Street.

Where the festivities began, early in the morning.

The pick-up charged through another intersection and Ruby clenched her teeth and followed. She saw a civilian sedan racing in from the left-hand side in her peripheral vision, but she'd already racked up nearly a dozen near-misses in the row, which gave her some semblance of confidence, so she—

Smash.

The sedan crunched into the Raptor's rear tray and threw the whole truck off-course. The Ford was a big beast and Ruby barely felt the impact amidst the adrenaline, but the tyres screeched on the asphalt and the whole thing threatened to career onto the sidewalk and wrap itself around a tree.

She fought for control.

She got it.

But it put her even further behind, and now the reality was *truly* drilling in.

You don't have a gun.

She had her knife, slotted neatly into the holster at her waist, but that wouldn't cut it against five armed mercenaries, probably stimulated to the eyeballs, almost certainly sporting a collective half-century of experience under their belts. These weren't idiots — they were trained killers, and they'd get rid of her in a heartbeat if she let them.

They entered the grid of roads leading into Market Street, and reached the edges of the crowd they'd been preparing for months to slaughter, and the nightmare became reality.

98

R uby threw caution to the wind.

She didn't care whether she lived or died.

They'd entered a bustling stretch of central San Francisco with gridlocked traffic. A couple of lanes had been cordoned off to pave the way through the crowded city centre to the Chinese New Year Festival. Long shadows fell across the scenery, elongated by the rising sun drenching the single-storey buildings. There were cafés and souvenir shops and grocery stores, all open for business, all thriving because of the uptick in pedestrians.

And there were hundreds of pedestrians, moving in swarms down the predetermined pathways, all happy and smiling and jovial, because there was joy in the air that morning. Later that evening there would be the parade, featuring dragons and dancers and performers on stilts and endless firecrackers, and it would be a spectacle to behold. For now they could gorge on traditional cuisine and enjoy the cool crisp morning air and hold their loved ones close.

They were collectively carefree, if only for a few days.

Then the beat-up pick-up truck screeched to a halt. Its doors popped open, and sweaty livid men in balaclavas piled out, wielding death in their hands. The sun glinted off the automatic rifles, and in unison the five mercenaries raised the barrels toward the crowds and took aim.

A couple of bystanders screamed.

They knew this wasn't a drill.

Given the national climate of fear, they knew what they were witnessing before the first shot had even been fired.

Then Ruby struck the back of their vehicle with the Raptor's hood.

The airbag detonated in her face and masked all sight and sound, and the impact rattled her bones, and she nearly lost consciousness as the dull *thwack* nearly crippled her, but she found a way to override her basic motor functions and throw the door open and leap out of the truck before the Raptor had even come to a standstill.

Her chest hurt, her head hurt, her bones hurt, her muscles hurt.

Everything hurt, and her vision wavered.

But, still, she persevered.

The pick-up rested at least a dozen feet from its original location, smashed forward by the concussive impact. Two guys were on the ground, either dead or crippled — they hadn't been able to get out of the way of the open doors in time, which had smacked them like fly swatters.

The other three were standing.

And angry.

One of them had his rifle halfway raised toward Ruby's face. Luckily, he was mere feet away. She leapt at him — despite not being able to see straight — and somehow tackled him successfully. She would never win a strength battle with a two hundred pound man, but she didn't need to. As soon as she was within arm's reach she slashed hard with the blade and ripped his forearm open from elbow to wrist, crippling his ability to pull the trigger.

She didn't even think about delivering the killing blow — there wasn't enough time.

She needed *every* gun pointed away from the crowds *that instant.*

But there wasn't enough that one person could do against three.

She was never going to protect them all.

She shoved the first guy aside as he dropped the rifle, his arm torn to shreds, and she sprinted at the second man. But he wasn't focused on her. He was focused on the crowds. Half had decided to flee, but half stood transfixed, watching the scene unfold like they were the live audience of a macabre theatre production.

They'd be the first to fall.

And they did.

Ruby pushed herself faster but she couldn't defy the laws of physics, and she watched in slack-jawed horror as the second man pointed his carbine rifle at a horde of innocent bystanders and pulled the trigger.

Rat-a-tat-tat.

The sound of hell.

It was hard to see the impacts from a distance, but Ruby figured she saw two or three people collapse under the gunfire. Then everything truly went to shit, and the bystanders all fled like rabid dogs, running in every direction at once, and the second gunman kept firing until—

Ruby seized him from behind and wrenched the blade across his throat and he fell, stone dead.

She felt sick to her core.

The third guy wasn't interested in killing more civilians. He was focused on Ruby.

And he was nihilistic, recognising he was the last survivor, and that made him terribly angry. He aimed low and shot her through the thigh.

She felt the bullet pass through, and in that instant there was no way to tell whether it had nicked an artery or not — she'd find out when she bled out in five minutes, if she made it that far.

No, in that instant, she felt nothing.

Which enabled her to lunge feebly at the guy, but she missed with her half-hearted knife swing.

He battered her hand away and struck her in the face, sending her toppling to the asphalt.

She was bleeding everywhere.

Amidst the screaming crowds, the guy knelt down and pressed the barrel to her throat, nearly crushing her wind-pipe with it, and he looked her in the eyes and paused for a single second to gloat over his victory.

To savour what little he'd accomplished.

She closed her eyes.

And felt the pressure alleviate as the barrel came away from her neck.

She opened them again and saw a man had peeled himself away from the panicking crowds and bullrushed the lone gunman, and tackled the guy off Ruby, and now they were brawling wildly against the side of the pick-up truck.

And the mystery man won.

He smashed a fist into the gunman's face and the guy went limp.

He wrestled the gun off the gunman and shot him in the head.

Then he turned, panting, to check if she was okay.

Her heart stopped in her chest.
She hadn't seen him in a long, long time.
But she knew the face.
She'd recognise it anywhere.
Through bloody lips she said, 'Dad?'

99

I t had been years since she'd seen Frank Nazarian.

Over a decade, in fact.

It felt, still, like more than that.

Like a lifetime ago. Like a separate universe. Like a remnant of a fantasy world that couldn't possibly be reality, because reality was bloody and violent and cruel, and a middle-class family in Brooklyn couldn't possibly have stayed together amidst all that carnage.

But, she reminded herself, she'd initiated that downward spiral. She'd been the one to run away from home at ten years of age, and, yes, she might have intended to go back after a day of pouting, but as fate would have it her dad's old military buddy Russell Williams had picked her up and put her straight in the Lynx program before she knew any better. Then her old family was just that — an *old* family, a memory she could detach from. And she'd detached from it well — with the help of psychological conditioning, of course — and it had taken Slater's fateful arrival in her life a little over a year ago to break her out of the way she'd been neurologically wired and slowly start to realise that she'd been brainwashed.

But she hadn't been able to go back and show her face to her father or mother or sister after that.

There was too much shame.

Too much guilt.

Too much horror at what she'd become.

She knew they'd probably understand, but although she was strong in some aspects, she was terrifyingly weak in others. She hadn't been able to do it. She knew Slater had met them, and she knew they'd asked about her, and wanted to see her, but by that point they were little more than faint memories and she preferred to keep them at an idealistic distance so they didn't have to see the truth of what their precious daughter had become.

Frank said, 'Oh my God,' and ran over to her.

He pressed his palms down on her leg, trying to stem the bleeding.

She lay on her back, staring up at him.

She didn't know what to say.

Frank said, 'It is you, isn't it?'

'It's me.'

'I thought I was seeing things.'

'Y-you've still got your old reflexes.'

Frank had served.

That's how he'd met Russell Williams.

He said, 'That stuff never dies.'

Then he looked around, and for the first time they seemed to notice their turbulent surroundings. There were bodies everywhere — mostly gunmen, thankfully — and sirens in the distance and people were still screaming and shouting and wailing and running.

But all that seemed inconsequential, because Ruby was

looking at her dad, and she wanted nothing more than to stand up and hug him. Hold him tight — never let go. Underneath the hardened exterior, she was still the same scared kid. No-one ever lost that part of themselves.

Then she noticed something unique. Amidst the mass panic, amidst the hysteria and the craziness and the palpable terror in the air, there was a child standing still as a statue as everyone around her lost their minds. She was small, with straight jet black hair falling over her forehead, and a confused look on her face. But she wasn't scared.

Because she'd been taught, albeit briefly, how to control her emotions.

Ruby knew her from the Lynx program.

And from what Slater had done to rescue her.

She said, 'Hi, Shien.'

The child stepped forward.

And said, 'Hi.'

Frank rested a hand on the little girl's shoulder.

'It's okay,' he said. 'They're all dead.'

'I know.'

'You're bleeding, Ruby,' he said.

He didn't seem to be paying attention to the words floating out of his mouth. They were cool and detached, and he couldn't take his eyes off her. He couldn't believe it. There was no protocol for such an unlikely, complicated situation. Such an odd twist of fate.

She lay on her back, panting. Then she said, 'Hard to find the right words, isn't it?'

He nodded.

Tears in his eyes.

Because what could you possibly say?

What neat package of syllables could make up for what had torn their family apart?

It was no-one's fault, besides Russell Williams and his misguided intentions. But how did you heal the bridge after such irreparable damage?

You didn't.

Ruby knew that. She looked at Shien and she saw everything she hadn't been. A small, kind, compassionate, caring soul who'd experienced the worst that life had to offer. A pure spirit in a catastrophic world. A vestige of hope. She'd seen the Lynx program and its horrors, and she'd seen the child sex slavery scene in Macau, and she'd been ripped from her own family and Slater had given her a de facto foster home and she hadn't complained a single step of the way.

That night Ruby had spent with Slater in New York ... he'd told her everything.

He'd told her how special the little girl was.

And, Ruby realised, she'd filled the void left in the Nazarian family after her disappearance.

They could now raise the daughter they'd never had.

And that was when it happened.

Shien got an odd look on her face, and she looked past Ruby, over her shoulder, and Ruby already knew what she was looking at. That's where the two mercenaries had been struck by the doors (either dead or unconscious, as she'd recalled at the time), and it seemed one of them had lost the "unconscious" label.

Ruby rolled onto her stomach — every movement hurt — and she saw the guy standing there on wobbly legs with blood in his beard and both cheeks torn up from where he'd hit the asphalt face-first. But he was awake, and he had a Glock in his hand, and an empty holster at his belt.

Ruby put it together.

Frank and Shien were frozen behind her, and it all clicked, and she knew what she had to do.

She scrambled to her feet and sprinted directly at the guy.

There was no way he was going to miss from that distance.

He shot her five times before she reached him — three bullets smashed into her chest, and the other two went through her stomach. But momentum was on her side, and she collapsed into him with enough force to knock them both off their feet, and as chance would have it the Glock spilled from the mercenary's hands when his head lashed against the ground.

She picked it up, and emptied its contents into his head.

Then she collapsed.

100

Darkness swelled at the edges of her vision.

She didn't have long.

Not long at all.

She couldn't feel her hands, or her feet. She was cold. So, so cold. She somehow managed to roll onto her back, but her circle of vision grew smaller with each passing second. She coughed blood, but she couldn't taste it.

She thought she saw Frank, watching in horror. She understood. He wouldn't be able to process this in real time. A chance encounter with his long-lost daughter, and now ... this.

But Shien could process it.

Ruby watched the little girl walk over and take her hand. Shien crouched over her, and sobbed, even though she was fighting to put on a brave face.

Ruby said, 'It's okay.'

She sobbed harder.

Ruby said, 'Be good to them.'

'I will.'

'They deserve you. Not me.'

'That's not true.'

'It's true. It's not pretty. But the truth never is.'

'I'm sorry,' Shien said.

'For what?'

'That you got wrapped up in this world.'

Ruby smiled through a mouthful of blood. 'Don't be sorry. I met you. You met them.'

'It should be you here.'

'But it's not. That's life.'

Shien bowed her head.

Ruby said, 'Don't worry. I'm happy. I did good with this life.'

Shien found the composure to keep her tears at bay, and she looked Ruby in the eyes and said, 'I'll make your parents proud. For you.'

Ruby Nazarian died with a smile on her face.

101

Three days later...

Will Slater came out of the induced coma the same way he did everything.

Stoically.

He simply opened his eyes, and blinked as he scrutinised his surroundings.

He nodded with satisfaction when he realised he was in a hospital bed. He wasn't getting shot at. He wasn't in a war zone.

Nothing else mattered.

So he lay patiently, covered in medical apparatus, and waited for lucidity to return. It wasn't a public hospital — it was probably a military installation somewhere in California.

Doctors and nurses came in and out of the room, but they were floating on clouds. He was in a dream world, drifting merrily through blissful obliviousness. He figured he was on a cocktail of drugs, up to his eyeballs in pain medication, and he certainly didn't mind.

He lay there for what could have been hours, and waited for sanity to return. There was a nurse with him for the majority of the time, making sure the drugs brought him back to reality without incident. She took a tube out of his throat, and checked his vitals.

He tentatively sat up in bed and croaked, 'Where am I?'

'You're safe,' the nurse muttered. 'And you're stable. There's someone that needs to speak with you.'

She walked out, and Violetta stepped into the room a minute later.

Violetta was a hollow shell of her former self, with deep bags under her eyes and pale, clammy skin.

Sleep deprivation would do that to you.

Slater said, 'You look worse than me.'

She managed a half-smile.

Silent, she crossed to the chair by the bed and sat down.

She put her head in her hands.

'Everything okay?' Slater said.

'I guess.'

'Tell me everything.'

She sighed. 'I don't know where to begin...'

'From the start. I remember ... the woods. And not much else.'

'You were half-dead when EMTs got to you. You had cracked ribs, a broken sternum, and serious internal bleeding and inflammation. You've been in a coma for three days.'

'But I got them all, right?'

She nodded. 'You got them all. Not a single cartel hitman made it out of those woods. It's indescribable what you've done for your country, and you'll be rewarded with a Medal—'

'I don't care,' Slater said.

Straight to the point.

He said, 'Let's cut the official shit. Tell me about the fall-out, okay?'

Violetta looked at him.

She was gaunt.

She said, 'Ruby didn't make it.'

Straight to the point, too.

He thanked his lucky stars he was still numbed by the pain relief.

It allowed him to keep his composure.

Inwardly, he collapsed.

But out loud, he said, 'I'm sorry to hear that.'

'I can give you some time.'

'No,' he snapped. 'Tell me the rest.'

She didn't say anything.

He said, 'What?'

She said, 'Are you sure, Will?'

'Yes.'

'Do you understand what I told you?'

'Yes.'

'I think you need some time.'

'For what?' he said, and now there were tears in his eyes. 'To think about how fucked up my life is? To consider the fact that no-one I get close to stays alive? Is that what you want me to think about? Trust me — that's been the case for years. A decade, even. Ever since I got involved in this mad world. So what's one more to add to the pile? I mean, really? Why did I expect anything would ever work out?'

Now she was crying.

She said, 'I'm sorry.'

'Not your fault.'

'It's the life we chose,' she said.

Slater's gears stopped turning and he froze up in mortal horror as he thought, *Why is Violetta so distraught?*

Then he thought of the hypotheticals.

Under his breath, he whispered, 'No.'

She lifted her gaze to meet him. 'What?'

'Is King...?'

'King's alive. Hurt — hurt real bad — but alive.'

Slater exhaled.

He didn't know how he'd be able to survive if it had been the alternative.

He said, 'What about the festival? Did anyone slip through the cracks? Did we lose?'

Violetta said, 'There were three casualties. One gunman managed to fire into the crowd, but Ruby stopped him before it got any worse. We got unbelievably lucky.'

'You call that lucky?'

'Yes,' she said, unblinking. 'I do.'

He sank into the bed, and the numbness receded, and he felt all the pain of loss, of anguish, of despair. He remembered those glowing amber eyes, and he knew he'd never see anything like them again, and he closed his own eyes to compose himself and stared into the abyss.

But if you do that for long enough, as Nietzsche says, the abyss will stare back into you.

So he fought valiantly to open his eyes and found Violetta watching him with a keen eye.

She said, 'You didn't fail, Will. Did you see how many gunmen there were in total? All of them armed with weapons. Thirteen suicide bombers. There would have been hundreds dead at the very minimum.'

Slater exhaled.

Finally he said, 'What's the news saying?'

'The same thing the media says every time there's a mass

shooting. We're suppressing as much information as we can. As far as the public knows, there was only one real gunman, and he had his cronies with him to incite fear. We're down-playing it as much as we can, and it's working. I hate to say it, but right now everyone's more focused on the economy.'

'What happened there?'

'It's still a disaster. But we've been through a financial crisis before. We'll get through another one — and, hey, maybe we'll fix the errors in the system that allowed this to happen in the first place. Maybe it was the wake-up call we needed.'

'So there's no need for damage control?' Slater said. 'The Chinese hardliners don't have a narrative to feed to the rest of the world?'

'No,' she said. 'You stopped that. You, and Jason, and Ruby.'

'But they'll keep trying.'

'Unlikely,' she said.

'You don't know that.'

'Fifteen members of the Chinese president's inner circle have disappeared over the last twenty-four hours.'

Slater felt his jaw go slack.

He said, 'You're not serious.'

She said, 'They failed. They had their chance and they blew it. This proves what we suspected all along — the government hardliners weren't the only prevailing ideology floating about. Some of them were moderates, perhaps including the president himself, and this ploy for a hostile takeover was a test. Everything we've heard about China's plan to overtake the U.S. as the economic, technological and military powerhouse of the world has been focused on the long-term. There's always been whispers, but they're more "survival-of-the-fittest" in nature. If China overtakes us in fifty years, so be it. But they'll do it the correct way. This was obscene, and the disappearing officials reflect that they've acknowledged their failure.'

'Because the timing had to be right,' Slater said.

'Exactly. It was a stunning deception, and a stunning plan, but it had to go off without a hitch. The economic failure had to lead straight into the worst mass shooting in United States history, with racially charged intentions. What little shooting occurred happened on the outskirts of the festival, and the three victims were Caucasian. Not exactly the gut punch of a news headline they were going for.'

'It's still awful.'

'I know. Unforgivable. Thankfully, it seems China is cleaning up its mess for now. If it came out in the public eye, I have no doubt they would have strung the hardliners up from the rafters. Labelled them traitors, too. But it didn't come out, so they're doing it quietly.'

Slater struggled to comprehend the scope of the conspiracy. He said, 'Was there anything else?'

'We arrested General Scachi yesterday on suspicion of treason.'

Slater eyed her. 'Why?'

'We traced his financial records to an account in Panama. There were ... a number of suspicious deposits.'

'Of course there were.'

'He did an impressive job of convincing us he never received word to move in. But we confiscated his communication equipment before he could protest, and tested it. It worked fine.'

'He deliberately hung back?'

'Money can sway any of us.'

'Only if you're a piece of shit.'

Violetta nodded.

Slater said, 'So what happens now?'

'Now, as best as we can, we keep a close eye on what's happening in the Chinese president's inner circle. And we pray the hardliners were a brief but violent spark in history.'

'You don't think it's going to happen again?'

'Not for a long time. That plot took months, if not years, of preparation, and it didn't kickstart the snowball effect they were looking for. So they're imploding. For now, we're safe.'

Slater couldn't believe it. He said, 'So that's it?'

'That's it.'

'Where to from here?'

'We don't need to talk about that right now,' Violetta said. 'You need to recover. You and King both.'

'How is he?'

'He's good. He's resting up.'

'You spending much time with him?'

She said, 'I'm too busy,' but her eyes revealed the truth.

Slater said, 'You don't think this will complicate things?'

'You and Ruby seemed to manage okay.'

He didn't respond.

She winced. 'Sorry. Poor timing.'

'You said she stopped the last truck all on her own?'

'Yes. If you want the truth, the three of you pulled off the most impressive feat in combat history. It's a goddamn shame she isn't here to understand how deeply important she was to the future of our nation.'

'I think she knew.'

'I know she did.'

Slater went quiet.

Violetta said, 'Bad things happen to good people.'

'I know,' Slater said. 'Trust me, I know.'

'There's going to be a funeral service at an undisclosed

location. Probably a week or so from now. It'll be a small crowd. Certain parties have been granted ... special access.'

Slater froze.

The memory came back to him, striking him like a gut punch.

The photo of...

It couldn't be possible. Violetta said there'd been three victims. If, by some cruel twist of fate, it happened that Shien had been one of them...

Slater blinked back tears.

Violetta said, 'What is it?'

'Is she safe?' he said.

'What are you talking about?'

'You know,' he said. 'You know perfectly well. One of the victims. Was it—?'

'Shien?' Violetta said. 'No.'

Life was still worth living.

She said, 'Shien was there, with Frank Nazarian, when the shooters showed up. Ruby...'

Then she trailed off, wracked by her own emotion.

Slater said, 'What?'

Violetta lifted her gaze to meet his, and her eyes were damp. 'Ruby died protecting her.'

Slater didn't respond.

He stewed silently.

It was poetic, after all.

Violetta said, 'You'll see Shien at the funeral. You can talk to her about it then, if you want.'

Slater hesitated. 'I don't know about that.'

'What do you mean?'

'We made a pact.'

'Will...'

'I bring nothing but ruin to people's lives,' he said.

'That's why I've never been able to stay in one place for too long. I'm a leech. I can help people, but then I need to go, immediately, or things will get worse and worse. I'm a magnet for this shit. That's why Shien was in San Francisco — I'm sure of it. It wasn't coincidence. To anyone hoping for a normal existence, I'm a cancer.'

'No, you're not. You're incredibly good at fixing problems that anyone else would shy away from, so you barrel head-first into danger. That doesn't make you a cancer. That makes you a cure.'

'I can't go.'

'Think about it.'

'I promised her I'd stay away from her.'

Violetta got up. She put a hand on Slater's shoulder.

She said, 'She wants to see you.'

Then she walked out.

102

One week later...

They lowered the coffin into the grave.

True to Violetta's word, Ruby's funeral was a modest affair, and the small gathering had formed around an unobtrusive war grave in Calverton National Cemetery on Long Island. There was Frank and Abigail Nazarian, and their daughter Anastasia, and Shien, and Violetta, and a handful of military officials, and up the back stood a big broad-shouldered man with a couple of fresh scars on his face.

Jason King adjusted his tie and clasped his hands together behind his back.

He stayed quiet.

He wasn't the centre of attention, and he didn't need to be. He'd barely known Ruby Nazarian, but the impression she'd left on him during their brief period of acquaintance would stay with him for the rest of his life. He remained a stoic statue up the back of the procession as Frank stood over the coffin with his head bowed.

'I didn't know you,' the man said. 'But ... what you did for us. I'll never forget it. Thank you, my daughter. Thank you.'

He made to say more, but he couldn't.

He stepped back, and cried silently into his wife's shoulder.

Shien stepped forward, and said, 'Thank you. For everything.'

She stepped back.

She didn't cry.

She didn't waiver.

There were none of the official procedures for military funerals. There were no soldiers or marines or sailors or airmen. There was no flag draped over the coffin. Because Ruby Nazarian didn't exist — she'd never officially worked for the government in any capacity. She'd been a black-ops killer in a dark, secret world, much like King. Their achievements went unrecognised in the public eye, because if their efforts were revealed, the shadowy reality of the secret world would need to be revealed in turn.

King instinctively glanced to his left, but there was no-one there.

He didn't blame Will Slater for staying away.

He understood the principle.

They attracted violence, he and Slater both. It allowed them to contribute to the world in a way they'd never anticipated in their youth, but it ruined the balance in their lives and in the lives of those around them in equal measure. Because they were never far from a fight, never far from a war.

Never far from death.

The service ended without fanfare, as an unknown military official read a statement regarding what Ruby had contributed to her country. It was suitably vague, suitably unclear.

As everything in their lives had to be.

Then the small procession dispersed.

Violetta walked up to King and whispered, 'You okay?'

He nodded, and took her hand. 'Will should be here.'

'He made a pact.'

'He told me.'

'I can understand.'

'There's not many people here,' King said. 'He was important to her.'

'More than either of us thought.'

'I think they were good for each other.'

'Like us?'

King half-smiled, then grew solemn. 'You know — I never thought anyone would fill the void Klara left.'

'Don't say that.'

'Why not?'

'Because she changed you for the better. Don't paste me over her memories.'

'I never would.'

'You understand why he didn't come, right?'

'I guess.'

'Because that's what this is for him. The void. And it'll never get filled. Not the way he spoke about Ruby.'

King said, 'It'll be hard. Unimaginably hard. But that's all our lives have been. Maybe he shouldn't shy away from that.'

A hand came down on King's shoulder, softly, gently.

'Speak of the devil,' Slater said.

King didn't react.

He knew, all along, that Will Slater *never* shied away from anything.

King turned, and there he was, hunched over a walker, wearing a vest under his suit to brace his core. He was still badly, badly hurt. There'd be a long road to recovery.

But he was out of bed, and moving around.

There wasn't just physical pain in his eyes, though.

There was something deeper.

King said, 'Glad you could make it.'

'Figured some pacts are worth breaking.'

They had little left to say to each other, because King saw Shien in his peripheral vision, and he knew he had no place in this equation. He gently placed a hand on Slater's shoulder, gave the man a reassuring look, and led Violetta away through the rows of war graves.

They didn't look back.

King put an arm around her shoulder and said, 'We haven't spoken about the future.'

'In what sense?'

He paused. 'Personally and professionally, I guess.'

'Let's leave the professional talk for when Slater's finished. Personally, I think you know where I stand.'

He looked into her eyes as they walked. 'Do I?'

She said, 'I haven't met anyone since Beckham was killed in Mexico. I haven't tried. Now ... now I'm willing to try.'

'That could get complicated,' King said. 'If our professional lives keep intertwining.'

'I thought you said you were done forever.'

'That depends on what you're going to offer Slater and I.'

She paused. 'Let's not talk about that right now. Let's talk about us.'

'What's there to say?'

'Where do you want to go from here?'

'I haven't cared about anyone the way I care about you

since Klara died. You understand me. I understand you. Isn't that all there is to it?'

She smiled, despite the forlornness of the graves on either side of them. 'You're a simple man.'

'I make decisions fast, I guess.'

'I approve of this one.'

He squeezed her tight. 'We'll make it work.'

'In terms of professional—'

King held up a hand. 'Let's wait for Slater to come to peace with his past. Then we'll all talk. Together.'

103

S later felt the grass under the soles of his dress shoes as he tapped his foot nervously against the ground. Shien stood there, quiet, observant.

Frank Nazarian spotted him. They nodded to each other.

Then the man stepped back, ushering his wife and daughter aside.

He understood the personal nature of the conversation that had to take place.

He let them have their space.

Slater said, 'Hey, kid.'

Shien managed a sad smile. 'Thought we agreed never to see each other again.'

'I had to be here. I hope you understand.'

'I do.'

'How are you?'

'Should we be having this conversation?'

'What do you mean?'

'Isn't it best we keep it...'

She trailed off, searching for the word.

Then she said, 'Impersonal.'

He smiled a sad smile, too, mirroring Shien. 'Maybe that is best.'

'But I want to know how you are, too,' Shien said. 'I don't want to play this stupid game anymore.'

'I'm good, kid,' Slater said, hunching over his walker. 'All things considered, I'm good.'

'I know you were close to Ruby.'

'I was.'

'I'm sorry for your loss.'

'It happens.'

'You seem like you've already accepted it.'

'It's not about me, or how I feel. It's about her, and what she did. What she did for you.'

Shien said, 'It should have been me instead of her.'

Slater stiffened. 'Don't ever say that.'

'Why not?'

'Because those thoughts lead down a dark road. Don't do that to yourself. Ruby made her choices, and you're here to talk about it. This is what she wanted. We can't disrespect that.'

'But I'm a normal kid,' Shien said. 'She was a warrior.'

'And that's what warriors do. They put themselves in harm's way for people they think are important.'

Shien half-smiled. 'That's what you did for me.'

'Yes.'

'I still can't thank you enough for that.'

'You don't have to.'

'You're here to pay your respects,' Shien said. 'Then what? Will I be seeing you around?'

Slater said, 'How's life been?'

'It's been good. It feels ... normal. I've never felt like that before.'

'You like Frank and Anastasia?'

'Yes.'

'You like your sister, Abigail?'

'Yes. I feel like I was supposed to be here all along.'

'Then you won't be seeing me around.'

'Will...'

'That's not what I'm here for. I have a purpose. It's not to savour life. It's to make sure people like you can.'

'Isn't that hard to deal with?'

'I manage.'

'I hope that's what you want. I hope you're not pressured into it.'

Slater laughed softly. 'You think anyone's ever pressured me into anything?'

She smiled. 'No. That doesn't sound like you.'

'It's what I want,' he said. 'It's what I need to do.'

'Does that mean you're going back to work?'

Slater paused.

Shien said, 'I saw the blonde girl here, at the funeral. I know she's from the government. I'm not stupid. She's going to ask you to work for her.'

'You think?'

'I know.'

'And how do you know that?'

She shrugged. 'Sometimes I can tell.'

'You're smart, you know?'

She smiled. 'I know.'

'I think you might be right, Shien.'

'Are you going to do it?'

'I'm considering it.'

'You'll get hurt again.'

'That's okay. By this point it's strange when I don't get hurt.'

She stared at him. 'Sometimes I don't understand you.'

'I don't expect you to.'

'But, I guess, I get it.'

'You'd be the smartest kid in the world if you did.'

'I guess I've been through a lot.'

'That's what we have in common,' Slater said. 'Tell me one thing.'

'Yes?'

'Are you enjoying your life?'

'I am.'

'Then I'll keep doing this again and again. That's what I live for. Hearing things like that.'

She said, 'Are you enjoying yours?'

'I am.'

'Then why would I tell you to stop?'

He smiled, and a particularly vicious gust of wind howled through the cemetery and lashed at his suit. He steeled himself against the walker. His ribs hurt.

He said, 'I'd best get going.'

'Okay.'

'Promise me you'll keep enjoying life.'

'I promise.'

'That's all that matters.'

'You take care of yourself, Will,' Shien said. 'Thank you for everything.'

'You say that too much.'

'Because I mean it.'

He shifted the walker in the grass and turned away from her. Then he looked over his shoulder and said, 'I'd do it all over again.'

He limped away.

104

They met in a cold grey gazebo at the edge of the cemetery grounds, surrounded by desolation.

It was quiet, save for the wind, and Slater sat down on one of the wooden benches and wrapped his overcoat tighter around his tender mid-section.

It would be some time before his insides healed.

Physically, and psychologically.

King sat down alongside him, but Violetta remained standing.

She crossed her arms over her chest, and managed a paranoid glance in each direction, as if worried a bystander might overhear.

But there was no-one around.

She said, 'We have a lot to talk about.'

They both nodded.

She said, 'I've been radio silent on you since San Francisco. I've given you time. But now I need an answer from each of you.'

'Regarding what?' King said.

They all knew.

Violetta said, 'As you're both fully aware, Black Force has dissolved. It was effective for a decade, but it overstayed its welcome. And, as you both know, it proved too flexible to control. There was too much capacity for discretion, and corruption bled in at the highest levels. It fell apart because of the way it was structured.'

They said nothing.

She continued. 'But it worked. Solo operatives, genetic outliers, with unparalleled reaction speeds. It was foolproof. They simply worked better in isolation, without having to rely on fellow soldiers to slow them down. But it got too big, too broad, with too many variables. It wasn't tight. It wasn't controlled. It wasn't effective.'

Silence.

She said, 'And we never thought about putting the operatives together.'

King nodded.

Slater nodded.

They knew where this was headed.

'We kept them apart,' Violetta said. 'Because if it ain't broke, don't fix it. But I think the pair of you proved what you can do in a small unit.'

'The three of us,' Slater said.

She nodded solemnly. 'The three of you.'

They both sat there, mulling over the loss.

She said, 'You would have made an incredible trio.'

Slater said, 'We have to accept reality.'

She nodded. 'Yes. We do.'

'What are you proposing now?' King said.

Violetta studied them. Their expressions, their demeanours.

She said, 'I don't think either of you are adverse to an offer.

Otherwise you would have turned and run for the hills a long time ago. Or gone to ground as soon as you stepped out of the hospital. But you're here. Listening to me. Open to discussion.'

King said, 'Our priorities have shifted.'

Slater said, 'We're not sure the vigilante lifestyle works for us.'

King said, 'And we're smart enough to understand our value.'

Violetta said, 'You're valuable. There's no denying it. You might be the best assets on offer right now. So we're going to make you a proposal.'

'We?' Slater said.

'This is coming from the highest level,' she said. 'Trust me.'

'We trust you,' King said.

Violetta said, 'Here it is. We recognise the fact that you have your external lives sorted. You don't need the official military structure. You train, you eat well, you supplement effectively, and those are your lives. So we want you to keep doing that, because the results you achieved for this last job were some of the best we've ever seen. You were outnumbered fifty-to-one and you decimated everyone in your path. So we don't want you to change a thing.'

'But?'

'But, if you want, we'd like to offer you exclusive operations whenever we deem the situation demands it. Think of yourselves as independent contractors. There'll be less oversight, less control, less rules.'

Slater stayed quiet.

King stayed quiet.

She said, 'You'll train yourselves. You'll have the full resources of the United States government at your disposal, and an unlimited budget for honing yourselves into the weapons we know you are.'

They said nothing.

'You'll be responsible for your own wellbeing,' she said. 'Your own training. You'll receive offers from us, but when the need arises for your assistance, you'll need to be there with no questions asked. Because there's an intense screening process that goes into this. We'll determine if it's the right job for the pair of you, and we'll only come to you in our darkest hour. At our time of greatest need.'

Slater half-nodded.

King stayed still as a statue.

Violetta said, 'Truth is, we need you in our back pocket. You're invaluable. We made a mistake in cutting you off the first time. We admit that.'

The wind rippled through the gazebo.

She said, 'What do you say?'

They only looked at each other for a heartbeat.

That was all it took.

They were bred for warfare.

They wouldn't have it any other way.

They turned to her, and in unison, said, 'Yes.'

MORE KING & SLATER THRILLERS COMING SOON...

Visit amazon.com/author/mattrogers23 and press **"Follow"** to be automatically notified of my future releases.

If you enjoyed the hard-hitting adventure, make sure to leave a review! Your feedback means everything to me, and encourages me to deliver more books as soon as I can.

Stay tuned.

BOOKS BY MATT ROGERS

THE JASON KING SERIES

Isolated (Book 1)

Imprisoned (Book 2)

Reloaded (Book 3)

Betrayed (Book 4)

Corrupted (Book 5)

Hunted (Book 6)

THE JASON KING FILES

Cartel (Book 1)

Warrior (Book 2)

Savages (Book 3)

THE WILL SLATER SERIES

Wolf (Book 1)

Lion (Book 2)

Bear (Book 3)

Lynx (Book 4)

Bull (Book 5)

Hawk (Book 6)

THE KING & SLATER SERIES

Weapons (Book 1)

BLACK FORCE SHORTS

The Victor (Book 1)

The Chimera (Book 2)

The Tribe (Book 3)

The Hidden (Book 4)

The Coast (Book 5)

The Storm (Book 6)

The Wicked (Book 7)

The King (Book 8)

The Joker (Book 9)

The Ruins (Book 10)

Join the Reader's Group and get a free 200-page book by Matt Rogers!

Sign up for a free copy of '**HARD IMPACT**'.

Experience King's most dangerous mission — action-packed insanity in the heart of the Amazon Rainforest.

No spam guaranteed.

Just click here.

ABOUT THE AUTHOR

Matt Rogers grew up in Melbourne, Australia as a voracious reader, relentlessly devouring thrillers and mysteries in his spare time. Now, he writes full-time. His novels are action-packed and fast-paced. Dive into the Jason King Series to get started with his collection.

Visit his website:

www.mattrogersbooks.com

Visit his Amazon page:

amazon.com/author/mattrogers23

Printed in Great Britain
by Amazon